MONKEY ON A CHAIN

M●NKEY

DOUBLEDAY

NEW YORK LONDON TORONTO

SYDNEY AUCKLAND

ON A CHAIN

HARLEN
CAMPBELL

PUBLISHED   BY   DOUBLEDAY

a division of Bantam Doubleday Dell Publishing Group, Inc.
1540 Broadway, New York, New York 10036

DOUBLEDAY and the portrayal of an anchor with a dolphin
are registered trademarks of Doubleday,
a division of Bantam Doubleday Dell Publishing Group, Inc.

BOOK   DESIGN   BY   CATHY   BRAFFET

Library of Congress Cataloging-in-Publication Data

Campbell, Harlen.
Monkey on a chain / Harlen Campbell. — 1st ed.
p.   cm.
I. Title.
PS3553.A457C58   1993
813'.54—dc20   92-37195
                                    CIP

ISBN 0-385-46905-5

Printed in the United States of America

September 1993

1   3   5   7   9   10   8   6   4   2

First Edition

THIS BOOK IS DEDICATED TO THE MEMORY OF
DR. MARION P. HARDMAN
AND WRITTEN FOR
DONNA, AMANDA, AND LISA

MONKEY ON A CHAIN

APRIL BOW

T HE ROAD TO MY HOUSE TWISTS UP THE WEST FACE of the northern end of the Sandia Mountains, doubling back on itself in a number of hairpin curves. It is a hard run. I run it every day, and as I jog, the occasional breaks in the pine and cedar forest on either side offer a comfortable hundred-mile perspective on the human race.

Even at sea level I hate jogging. At a touch under seven thousand feet, it's like running in a vacuum. I'd never do it if the twenty-three hours a day when I don't run weren't so flat and lifeless without the exercise. It keeps my carcass as lean as can be expected and helps my mirror maintain the polite fiction that I'm still a year or two on the cradle's side of forty. I hate running, but I do it. Still, I get by with the bare minimum—two and a half miles to the ridge above Placitas and then back again.

The ridge makes a good rest stop. Directly below, the village lies strung along the tail end of the pavement. A pine and juniper forest dies into grassland farther to the west. Beyond that, a golden plain falls away toward the dirty green line that marks the bosque, the cottonwood and scrub cedar forest along the Rio Grande. The dry plain is interrupted only by the thin north-south thread of Interstate 40.

Albuquerque is south, behind a shoulder of the Sandia Mountains. At night, especially when there is a high overcast, the lights of the city provide a waning moon's illumination. But in the late afternoon, when I do my running, the only hint that five hundred thousand people are playing out their lives twenty miles away is the sunlight glinting from the cars and trucks strung out along I-40.

From my resting spot, you look down at a steep angle on the white and brown stucco, the adobe, and the weathered wood of the village of Placitas. You look down at a lesser angle to the river, ten miles away. Above the river, the high desert of western New Mexico looms as if you could scratch it with a short stick.

The desert is dry. A wet year brings seven or eight inches of rain and snow. A number of low volcanoes interrupt the mesa toward the southwest. Black on brown. To the northwest lies the dark purple smudge of the Jemez mountains. Seventy miles away and snow-capped most of the year, Mt. Taylor sits on the western horizon like an ancient Navajo god.

There's a lot to look at if you like things that don't change from day to day. I stand there, waiting for my lungs to get over their excitement, and I watch nothing happening. Maybe a hawk or an eagle wheeling high overhead, a black speck against the turquoise sky. A woodpecker hammering in the forest. I can take a lot of nothing happening without getting tired of it. I get nervous when things start happening.

That Thursday a car growled somewhere below as it climbed the ridge. I only have five neighbors on my road. I know them all well enough to say howdy, and they know me well enough not to say anything more than howdy back. Only one could be called an acquaintance—Jenny Murphy, who has the place next to mine. Neither she nor any of the others was likely to be traveling at that time of day.

2

I turned reluctantly from my resting spot and began the jog back. I kept my ears open. The car was a surprise, and I didn't like it. There had been too many surprises in my past. When it was about a minute behind me, long before I could be seen, I slipped off the road and into the trees and watched it pass.

It was a red 'eighty-seven Jag with California plates and one occupant. Female, dark hair, yellow scarf against the wind, dark glasses. She was driving slowly, as though she didn't know where she was going or was uncomfortable so far from civilization.

When she was well past, I shrugged and moved back onto the road. She'd kicked up enough dust to make me run with my mouth shut. I set as steady a pace as the terrain permitted. It's hard to run uphill without slowing down, or downhill without letting gravity encourage you too much, but I had years of practice. I spent the time wondering which of my neighbors had a visitor and checking the dust in their drives.

I have the last house on the county road. When I passed Murphy's place, I was still following the Jaguar, so I had a visitor. A little prudence was called for.

Half a mile ahead, the driveway cut off to the right and then turned back south. I picked up my pace for a few minutes and then climbed into the forest on the uphill side. At that point, the house was about two hundred yards above me and maybe the same distance north. I slowed to a walk and recovered my breath, then climbed straight up the mountain, well above the house, before turning north. Eight minutes of quiet walking took me to a point from which I could see the front of the house, the driveway, and the graveled parking area. The car sat in the center of the yard, between the garage, below me on the uphill side, and the front of the house.

The girl stood by the front door, looking dejected. She pounded on the door halfheartedly and then stepped back from the house. She walked over to the kitchen window and peered in, then moved to each of the other windows on the front and repeated the process. She tried to walk around the house, but the steepness of the slope and the cactus I'd planted stopped her. She went back to her car and sat in it. After a few minutes, she rested her face against her arms on the steering wheel. Her shoulders shook gently.

I got up and moved silently back along the drive. Once out of sight, I climbed down and began jogging toward the house. I kicked a couple of rocks to make some noise, but the girl apparently wasn't listening. When I reached the yard, she hadn't moved.

I called out a friendly hello and walked over to the driver's side of the car. She was about twenty, Eurasian, pretty. Her black hair fell halfway down her back. The bangs were cut square above the slope of her eyes. She seemed a little nervous. I smiled. "Are you looking for me? I was running."

She sat up quickly, wiped her eyes, and managed a smile. "Hello. Ahh . . . you are Mr. Porter?"

She spoke with a faint accent. English wasn't her first language, but she was comfortable with it.

"What can I do for you?"

She hesitated a moment. "I don't . . . Do you know . . . ? I mean, did you know a James Bow?"

The name threw me. And the past tense. Jimbo. Good old Toker. I kept my voice noncommittal, my face open, friendly, and curious. "Why do you ask?"

"He's my father. I mean, he was. He's dead now."

That made no sense. The last time I saw Toker, sixteen years ago, there had been no child. This girl was young, but she wasn't that young. Maybe half my age. I closed in a little, just in case action was called for. "Sorry to hear it. So?"

She seemed to sag a bit, as if she'd had a lot riding on my response. "Maybe you're the wrong man. I'm sorry." She reached for the ignition.

"Maybe not." I reached through the window and took her keys. "Come into the house. Tell me about it."

I walked over and unlocked the house, leaving her to follow. My back felt exposed, but what the hell, sometimes you take a chance. If she was armed, she wasn't carrying anything under that thin silk dress. There was barely room for a bra and panties.

4

She came in as I was pouring a glass of club soda. Angry and frightened at once. She stopped just inside the door. "You took my keys."

"You came from L.A.?"

She nodded. "Give me the keys."

"That's too long a drive for nothing. Would you like something to drink?"

She licked her lips. "Water. And the keys."

I handed her a glass and motioned toward the sink, then lobbed her keys onto the dining room table and dug a cigarette from my stash. She watched me, looking surprised.

"You jog and smoke?"

"Nicotine's good for the soul."

She savored the word. "My father never spoke of a soul."

"Maybe he didn't have one."

She ignored that. Or maybe she didn't. "He was a good man. He was good to me. He gave me my car."

"How did he die?"

"You haven't said you knew him."

"I knew him."

She hesitated, licked her lips. Her lipstick was a deep red. It went well with her coloring. "He was killed. Murdered." She put a lot of emphasis on the word.

The front door was open. I gave the yard a good once-over, then locked up and led her through the living room and onto the deck that hangs off the back of the house, fifteen feet above the ground. A piece of the county road is visible from there, and you can hear any traffic. The only sound was wind in the pines and an occasional bird. The road was empty.

There is a wrought-iron patio set on the deck. I sat at the table and motioned her to a chair opposite me. She hesitated, but she sat. I considered her carefully. She was good to look at. Her hair was long and straight, brushed until it shone. Her eyes were dark brown, not quite black. The dress was some kind of print, off-white with a pale green leaf pattern. Very snug.

Very attractive. But it didn't look comfortable for a long drive and it wasn't wrinkled. I decided to clear the air.

"When I saw your father the last time, around 'seventy-four, he didn't have any kids. Where did you come from?"

"Hong Kong. He was on vacation there when he found me. That was in nineteen eighty-one."

"You don't look Chinese."

"I'm Vietnamese. Half Vietnamese, anyway. My father was an American. I was one of the boat people." She hesitated a moment. "I was in a refugee camp when Dad found me."

I had recognized the Vietnamese blood in her face, of course. But this wasn't making any sense. "You said he found you?"

She nodded. "And brought me home. He took good care of me." She looked about to cry.

"He was your father? Your real father?"

"Oh, no! My adopted father. My real father was a cowboy. Or that's what my aunt said."

A cowboy. How the hell would a Vietnamese aunt recognize a cowboy? And why an aunt? "What did your mother say?"

"That's what she told my aunt. I don't remember my mother. She was killed a long time ago. In 'seventy-one."

A lot of people were. I made a polite noise anyway. "What happened to your aunt?"

"I don't know. She put me on the boat. She said there wasn't enough money for her to come with me. A family took care of me, at least until we got into the camp. Then they sort of forgot me. Things were scary in the camp. Everyone was trying to get to America. Maybe Mr. Nguyen thought his family would have a better chance if there were fewer people on the application. But they never got out. Only I did, when Dad found me."

"And brought you to America."

She nodded. "And put me in school. Then helped me get into UCLA."

"And now he's dead."

She lowered her head and blinked.

6

"Tell me about it."

She swallowed. "I was in class when they came. The police, I mean. Mrs. Stillwell told them where I was. They took me to her. She lives right next door. She heard the explosion and ran over and found him and called the cops." She took a deep breath. "They wouldn't let me see him. I guess he was messed up pretty bad. They said it was a clayman bomb. In his office."

"A Claymore."

"What?" The interruption confused her.

"Not a clayman. A Claymore. It's an explosive device a little bigger than a paperback book," I told her. I didn't add that they can make a hell of a mess if they're used right. She knew that. After a moment, I asked, "Who did it?"

"They don't know."

"Do they know why?"

She shook her head. "It wasn't money. Nothing was taken. At least then. And he didn't have any enemies. He was just a businessman. He had a foreign car dealership in Westwood. I don't know why anyone would do this."

Of course he'd had enemies. We all do. I hoped that he had made some recently. And the dealership. He'd put his share to good use. It also explained the Jaguar the girl was driving.

"When did this happen?"

"Tuesday. Two days ago."

I whistled. I'd thought we were talking about something older, something she could have a little perspective on.

"Why are you here?"

"Mrs. Stillwell asked me to stay with her that night. The police let me in the house to get some things. I guess I was kind of numb. I didn't notice much. The door to the master bedroom was closed and I could hear some men talking in there, but everything else looked normal. Anyway, I took my toothbrush and went with Mrs. Stillwell. But later, way after midnight, when I was trying to sleep, I remembered . . . something. I went back to get it, but there was this tape on the door that said it was a crime scene, and I was afraid to break the tape. I got a flashlight from my car. I was going to climb in my window.''

"You what?"

She blushed and looked away from me. "I used to do that sometimes, when I was in high school. When I was grounded.''

I wondered if Toker had known. "Okay. So you broke in. Then what? Why did you come here?"

"But I didn't! I was going to, but when I looked in the window, everything was a mess. It looked like the house had been searched or something. Things were everywhere. All the drawers were emptied on the floor. I went around and looked in all the windows. It was the same in every room. . . ."

She paused for a few deep breaths. "His office was there, in a little sitting room off his bedroom. I even looked in there . . . where it happened . . . and it was torn up too. There was stuff thrown on the blood and on the outline of his . . . of Dad's. . . ."

She was right on the edge. I looked out over the valley while she composed herself. It took a while, but not as long as I expected. This wasn't the first bad thing that had happened in her life.

". . . anyway, I thought I might be in danger. Because it wasn't the police, you see. When I was there, they were being pretty neat. So I thought somebody else had been there, in my house, and that scared me. I got my purse from Mrs. Stillwell's and then I just got in my car and started driving. At first, I didn't know where to go. But a couple of weeks ago, Dad told me to come to you if I ever needed help. He was very serious about it. He even wrote down your name and address and put it in my purse. He told me to say something to you."

That got my attention. My eyes jerked to her face. "What did he tell you to say?"

She looked straight into my eyes and said, "You owe me."

"That's all?"

She nodded.

8

I let out a sigh. It was a mess, and the worst of it was that she'd dragged it straight to my doorstep. But of course, Toker had been right. I did owe him, in a sense. I spent a few minutes looking and listening. The trees hadn't changed a bit. The same birds were making the same noises. The breeze still whispered through the pine needles. If she'd driven straight through, she was probably untraceable.

All the trouble was in L.A. There was no choice. I had to go there. I had to find out exactly what had happened to Toker, make sure it was something recent, not something from the past.

It was hard to judge how much danger she was really in. A Claymore was good for killing, but it wasn't selective. Whoever had set it must have watched Bow and the girl long enough to know their schedules. The killer had taken out his target. If he'd wanted the girl, he could have had her. But something had drawn him back to search the place. That was the thing that didn't make sense—one of the things. The house should have been searched before the bomb was set. Maybe there hadn't been time. But there were problems with killing first and searching later. Re-entry would have been dangerous, and whatever the killer wanted might well have been found by the police during their investigation. Or moved by someone else. Of course, the killer might not be the searcher.

I looked at the girl and smiled reassuringly. "What's your name?" I asked.

"April. April Bow."

I offered her my hand. "Hello, April. Your father called me Rainbow. You can too."

She shook hands. "Does this mean I did the right thing?"

I nodded, and she began to tremble. I stood and walked around behind her, put my hands on her shoulders and squeezed gently. She stiffened, then relaxed. After a moment she rubbed her cheek against the back of my hand, wetting it.

"It's been hard on you?"

"I haven't felt so lost for a long time. Since the boat. When I left Vietnam."

"What happened then?"

"Auntie took me to the docks at night. The boat was old and small. It was very crowded. It cost her a lot to buy my passage, more than she could afford. But she did it. She said it was my only chance. Because my father was an American, you understand . . . ?"

I nodded. "Go on."

"We couldn't take much. I had a little sack, an old rice bag, with some clothes and some food. And a little doll she'd traded cigarettes for. That was all I could take. It was all I had. Auntie gave it to Mr. Nguyen to keep for me. He put it in the pile with his family's things. They were going to watch over me. Anyway, I hugged my aunt and then she left me. She stood on the dock and watched while we left. I tried to watch her, to call out goodbye and that I loved her, but it was too crowded. I couldn't see her, except for just flashes, between the people crowded by the rail. I was crying. Everyone was nervous because of the patrols and wanted me to be quiet, but I couldn't. I was only ten, and I was very afraid. Then Mr. Nguyen slapped me until I was quiet. Later, after we were past the patrols and it was time to sleep, I asked for my doll. He told me it was lost. He was still angry because I had made too much noise and the others had yelled at him, I suppose. But he said my doll was lost, and it was the only thing I had from my aunt. Later I saw his daughter playing with it. When I asked her for it, she threw it into the water. I ran to the back of the boat and watched for it, but it was gone into the darkness. I spent the rest of the night there, looking back into the dark. I was so scared. But I didn't cry anymore. Not in front of Mr. Nguyen, anyway."

She had spoken quietly, staring out over the pine forest. She noticed that my hands were still on her shoulders and shrugged them off. I walked over to the rail and stood with my back to her. "What happened then?"

"Nothing. The trip wasn't too bad. It seemed to take forever, but it couldn't have been more than two weeks." Her voice was steady again. "Mr. Nguyen gave me my things a day later. He acted indifferent to me. Not sorry that he gave away the doll. But I suppose he thought it was justified. I had to be punished, you see. To learn about keeping quiet.

10

"We were low on food toward the end, but we were just hungry. That was all. Many people in the camp had it much worse. And I didn't have to stay in the camp very long. Only six months. Some of them are still there, I bet. Mr. Nguyen. The girl who threw away my doll. Serves her right." She managed a small laugh. "Some sad story, huh? My father's dead and all I talk about is a stupid doll!"

I shrugged. "It's a story, anyway. You hungry?"

She nodded. I went into the house and started some rice. There was a small pork roast in the refrigerator. I sliced it into long strips and dumped them into a bowl with cornstarch, oil, and a dash of soy sauce, then put the wok on the fire and left it to heat. While I was chopping a head of broccoli, I heard her clear her throat behind me. When I looked over my shoulder, she was standing in the doorway watching me, her keys in her hand.

"Bring in your things," I said. "There's a spare bedroom on the left of the hall." She stared at me for a long moment, then nodded and disappeared. I stir-fried the meat and the vegetables, added some oyster sauce, and let the mixture simmer.

When I heard the shower running, I walked quietly down the hall and opened the door to her room. The bathroom door was half open and the glass shower door was steamed up. April was vaguely visible, a slender shape moving behind the mist. A small suitcase was open on the bed. I went through it quickly. It was new. Two days' worth of dirty clothes were wadded up on one side of it. The clothes on the other side still had price tags. Her dress, underwear, and sandals were on the floor by the bathroom door. Her purse wasn't visible. I took another peek into the bathroom. It was on the vanity, beneath the mirror. Some cosmetics had been taken from it and spread over the counter. I avoided taking a longer look at the body in my shower and went back to the kitchen, closing the bedroom door carefully.

Dinner was on the table when she appeared. I'd opened a bottle of chablis. She accepted a glass, but didn't do much more than sip at it. She ate the meal without commenting on it. While we ate, I questioned her about the trip.

She had driven as far as Phoenix, taken a room, and slept most of

Wednesday. She awoke in time to find a mall and a new wardrobe, then got back on the road. She made it to Albuquerque early this morning. Instead of driving straight out, she took another room, slept for a few hours, and asked the desk clerk if he knew where Placitas was and how to get here. She dithered around for a few hours, working up her nerve, I guess, and then drove to the village and asked around until she found someone who knew who Paul Porter was and where he lived. The rest I knew.

When I asked what she was doing for money, she looked surprised. If I'd had a daughter, I probably wouldn't have thought to ask. Credit cards, of course. That gave me something to worry about. Plastic leaves a trail. But it was probably all right. It's a hard trail to follow, unless you have access to the right computers. There was another problem. I asked whose name the cards were in. Of course they were in Toker's.

"You know you're probably breaking the law?" I asked.

She looked surprised.

"They aren't your credit cards. They belonged to Toker. He's dead. The card companies will consider them invalid."

"But they're all I have! They can't take them away!"

"They can and will," I told her.

"But how will I live?" She thought a moment. "And who's Toker?"

"Your father. It was his nickname when I knew him. He called me Rainbow and I called him Toker. Don't worry about living. I can take care of you for a while. Your father must have had a lawyer, and he probably left a will. You can pay me back later if you want to."

"His lawyer." She nodded. Then a thought struck her. "Do I have to go back? Right away?"

"Tomorrow morning. I'll go with you. There's the funeral, for one thing. And the police will want to know why you ran away and where you went. We have to find the lawyer and the will. We have to find out who is executor of his estate and get that settled. You'll have some explaining to do to your professors. There are other things I haven't thought of yet."

She took a deep breath. "What about the man who searched our house?"

"That's another problem. The cops probably think you did it. They will want to ask you why."

I didn't add that they might want to ask her what she knew about detonating a Claymore mine. If she hadn't called it a clayman bomb, I'd be damned curious about that myself. I asked her what she was studying at UCLA.

"Business administration," she said.

At least it wasn't theater. If she were an actress, that would be one more thing to worry about. I stretched and started heading her toward bed. There are two bedrooms in my house, both the same size. Big. Eighteen by twenty feet, with large closets and one large bathroom between them. It has a shower, Jacuzzi, regular tub, double sinks in the vanity, everything I thought might be useful when I designed the place.

It's a good floor plan for me, but as the contractor told me, stupid if you think about resale value. I told him I didn't give a damn about resale value. He told me my heirs might feel differently. I told him to build the damned place and mind his own business.

April appreciated the bedroom and bath, but looked a bit uncertain when she realized that the second door off the bath opened onto my room, and that neither of them had locks. I knew what she was thinking and waited to see if she would say anything. She didn't. My opinion of her went up. Common sense is a rare thing.

She closed the door behind her. After a few minutes the radio in her room came on. I headed into the office off my bedroom and spent a few minutes thinking. I made a call to a man in Albuquerque and got the number of a man in West Los Angeles. I fired up my computer, logged on to Compuserve, and found an account of the bombing. There was nothing of interest there, except that it had really happened. I made two reservations to Las Vegas in the name of Miller, then dug out a suitcase and packed for a week. Just in case, I dug out a fall-back identity. Harold Stephenson. I hadn't been Harold for ten years, but I'd kept him alive.

I poured myself a double scotch, grabbed another cigarette from my stash, turned out all the lights in the house, and walked out onto the deck.

The woods aren't quiet at night. Things move in them. But I was used to the woods. I was not used to the things that were stirring in my mind.

Toker. I hadn't seen him in sixteen years. I'd seen a lot of him in 'seventy-four. And of course, I'd seen him daily from June of 'seventy through July of 'seventy-one, while we were both in-country. In-country meant Saigon, mostly. What had happened there after I left? Or what had happened to him later, that led him to seek out and adopt a Vietnamese child? Did he go to Hong Kong looking for one, or was he really just on vacation, as April had said? Was there some significance to the fact that he'd picked a girl?

There had been two kinds of soldiers in Vietnam. Those who hated the locals and those who liked them. Toker was one of the first type. He called them slopes or gooks. That made April harder for me to understand. Had Toker been trying to assuage some guilt I didn't know about?

Guilt. That word sent a lot of things scurrying for cover in the recesses of my skull. I let them go. I knew all their hidey-holes if I had to track them down. With luck, they would sleep peacefully for the next few weeks.

I finished the cigarette and the scotch, then just sat on the deck for an hour and listened to the night. No one was stirring.

The radio was off in April's room when I locked up. I tapped gently at her door. There was no answer, so I opened it and slipped inside. I stood for three or four minutes, an eternity, breathing through my mouth, listening. No sound. My eyes adjusted to the darkness. Her head was a dark blotch against the white pillow case. Her clothes were spread on the foot of the bed. Her purse was on a table under the window.

I padded over and took it, made my way out of the room, and went to the kitchen. Her driver's license said April Bow. It was dated over a year ago. The plastic case looked scratched enough to be a year old. She had the right student ID as far as I could tell. All the credit cards had the right name on them. There were no weapons beyond a nail file. It took ten minutes to get my night vision back and another three to replace the purse. It was after midnight when I turned out my bedside lamp.

At seven-thirty I had breakfast going, a large omelette with vegetables

and a mild chile sauce. Toast and coffee. April answered my knock by open-
ing the door a crack and peering around it. I glanced past her. The mirror
above the dresser on the other side of the room showed her naked back,
pale, without tan lines, slender. My thin face and blond hair peered over her
shoulder through the cracked door. Her backside was very attractive. I didn't
like or trust the looks of the fellow in the mirror. I looked back into her eyes
and told her breakfast was ready.

She grumbled a bit. "So early?"

"We've got some stops to make, and our flight leaves at eleven. Eat
now. You can dress later."

She appeared in a few minutes, barefoot, wearing a pair of new jeans and
a cream-colored blouse. I gave her our schedule while she worked on the
omelette, then took a tour of the property while she cleaned up and dressed.
I wanted to be outside, far from her bedroom door. It had been too long
since I'd had a woman. And at least to part of me, she qualified. Despite her
age and looks. Or maybe because of them.

The first stop in Albuquerque was at my bank. I picked up five thousand
in cash. Then I made some arrangements with the woman who manages
certain of my properties and left her with a check for a thousand in case I
was gone longer than expected. We barely made it to the airport in time to
pick up our tickets and take the long walk to our gate.

LOS ANGELES

THE FLIGHT FROM ALBUQUERQUE TO LAS VEGAS TOOK about an hour. When April asked why we weren't flying direct, I told her I didn't want to leave a trail back to New Mexico. She nodded, then dozed throughout most of the flight. As soon as we got off the plane, she started for the nearest restroom. I told her I'd meet her in the bar, then headed for the ticket counter.

I paid cash for two seats on the four o'clock flight to LAX, using Harold and Ann Stephenson for names, and arranged for a car at the Hertz counter, again using the Stephenson name. Then I met April, led her to a different ticket counter, and bought two first-class seats on a flight the next morning to Orange County.

I gave our names as James and April Bow and paid for those tickets with fives and ones. I fumbled around with the bills as much as possible, lost track, counted the payment all over again, and argued about the number of pennies in my change. By the time I was satisfied, the clerk and the people lined up behind us were steaming, and April was pretending she wasn't with me.

I grabbed a cab and headed for the first hotel I could think of, the Flamingo. April was getting nervous. I leaned into her ear and whispered, "Play along with me. You can always start screaming later."

She relaxed a bit, and even gave me a tiny smile. The driver was watching us in the mirror. I made a kissing noise at her, then overtipped the driver by ten dollars.

Getting a room was easy. I laid two hundreds on the counter and asked for a single for the night. The clerk looked from me to April and said, "Yes, sir!" He made the bills disappear.

I signed the register as James Bow. A bellboy came over and asked about our luggage. I told him I'd carry it and could find the room myself, but he could do me a tremendous favor by locating a cold bottle of good champagne and getting it to the room as quickly as possible. I winked and told him I'd be very grateful. He handed me the keys and disappeared.

The room was like almost every other I've been in. Narrow. Bathroom by the entry. A double bed against the long wall, with a dresser and plenty of mirrors opposite. Windows behind floor-to-ceiling curtains at the end of the room, with a small table and two chairs.

Once the door closed, April walked to the table and sat, looking as though she had put up with enough nonsense. Well, she had, and she deserved an explanation. When I sat opposite her, she relaxed a bit. Maybe she'd expected me to make a move toward the bed. "We've got to talk before we get to Los Angeles, April," I said, "and we can't do it on the plane. The room buys us privacy for a few hours. For talk, nothing else."

There was a discreet knock. The champagne arrived, open and in ice. The bellboy presented it with a bill for forty-five bucks. I gave him a fifty and a twenty, told him to keep the change, and slipped the DO NOT DISTURB sign over the doorknob.

She looked at the bottle skeptically. "Why the champagne?"

"You look thirsty."

"I'm not."

"Fine." It was window dressing anyway. I upended the bottle in the bathroom sink, dirtied two glasses, and returned to the chair opposite her. It was time for some questions. "How much do you know about your father's business?" I asked.

"The dealership? Everything. I was his secretary. At least part-time. During the summers and on weekends."

"Tell me about it."

"There isn't much to tell. It was a Jaguar dealership, but we bought and sold other cars, too. Mercedes and BMWs and the ones we took in trade. We never kept the American or Japanese models, though. They went to the auction. Dad didn't like them."

"Was it a good business? Profitable?"

She nodded. "I suppose we turned between four and five hundred cars a year, counting the trade-ins. We did all right."

"Did you keep the books?"

"I saw them, of course. Mrs. Walters actually kept them. I only worked part-time, and we needed someone permanent for the books."

"But you had full access to them?"

She nodded. "Of course."

"How was the business going? At the end, I mean."

"There wasn't any change. You're asking if he was in financial trouble, aren't you? Well, he wasn't! We netted about two hundred thousand a year, before taxes. We owned the land, too, so there wasn't any rent to pay. We were doing very well."

"Was all of the income from sales?"

"Yes. All of it."

"And there was only the one set of books? He didn't keep anything off the books?"

She looked at me scornfully. "Of course not. What are you asking? I thought you were his friend!"

"I'm trying to find a reason for someone to kill him, April," I said. "Money's the oldest reason there is. Or one of the oldest."

18

"There was nothing like that. Everything was aboveboard. Very simple. 'Buy cars, sell cars,' he used to say."

"You're sure? Would you know if anything funny was going on?"

"I was studying business," she said indignantly. "Of course I would have known!" She lowered her eyes. "I . . . I was hoping that . . ."

"You wanted to take over the business," I finished for her.

She nodded.

"Did you know his lawyer?"

"Mr. Pearson. I know him."

"When did he see him last?"

"A month or so before . . . before . . ."

"Okay." I let it slide. "What about the correspondence? Did he ever type his own letters?"

"No. I did all that."

"Visitors? Did he make any calls that he was secretive about? That he didn't want you to know about?"

She cleared her throat. "No. Not to . . . No." She wasn't meeting my eyes.

"Tell me, damn it."

She blushed. "Just to women," she said.

"Talk about the women, then," I said.

She hesitated. "There weren't many . . . girlfriends. . . ."

"Women from the office? He was rich. Didn't any of them ever make a play for him?"

"No. Never. Well, maybe they tried, but he was never interested. He said . . ."

"What?"

She blushed again. "He said you don't shit where you eat."

I let that settle for a minute, then asked, "What about others."

"Well . . . maybe Mrs. Stillwell. Our neighbor. She and I were pretty good friends when I was fourteen or fifteen. She used to ask me about him. And one day she invited us for dinner. It was really nice. She'd worked hard on it. She had candles and everything. After dinner, they sent me home. I was watching a movie when he came in a couple hours later. He was kind of drunk and went right to bed. And she never asked us back again.''

I stared at her. "And you never found out what happened?"

She shook her head.

"God damn it, April, he wasn't gay! There must have been women!"

"There were. Always different women. I hardly ever saw them, though. He would just go out for the night, after I was old enough to stay alone. He never introduced me to any of them. When I was little, I thought he was ashamed of me. But then I realized it was just that they didn't matter.''

I finally saw what she was trying to say. "They were prostitutes," I said.

She nodded and glanced up at my face. "I think so.''

"No one else? Only prostitutes?"

"Yes. And always different ones.''

"Well, that makes it a little easier," I said. "I've never heard of a prostitute bombing a man. You said he was drunk that time he came home from the neighbor's. Did he drink much?"

"No. It was the only time I ever saw him drunk.''

"What about drugs? Did he use them?"

"Never. He hated them.''

"Tell me about his personal life.''

"He didn't have one.''

"He didn't belong to any clubs? Civic organizations?"

"No.''

"His family, then. What about them? Where did his parents live?"

She made a face, as though she tasted something foul. "They lived in Los Angeles. He didn't see them very often. I think he sent them money sometimes, but not often.''

"He didn't take you to see them?"

"Once. It was on my eleventh birthday, right after he brought me home. He had bought me a new dress. It was blue, I remember, and I thought I was very pretty in it, like an American girl. It was the first new dress I'd ever owned. I was so proud of it, and I really wanted them to like me. But they hated me.

"I sat in the living room, all alone, and they were screaming at each other in the kitchen. His mother was screaming, anyway. She said that she wouldn't have the little Commie gook bitch in her house. She yelled at him to get rid of me. I sat there in my new dress and listened to his mother for a long time. Then Dad came out and took me home. He never took me back." She looked at me impassively.

"Some people are like that," I said. "Was that all of his family? Just his parents?"

"There was a sister. He sent her cards on her birthday and at Christmas. I helped him remember them. I even bought the cards for him, when he was busy. But I never met her."

I made a face. "There's not much there. As a motive."

"No. There's not much there."

"What about you? How did he treat you?"

"He loved me."

"You're sure?"

"Of course. He bought me lots of nice clothes. Just last year he gave me my car. He let me have my friends over whenever I wanted. Of course he loved me."

"Did he ever hug you?"

She looked down at her hands, where her fingers twisted together on the table between us. "No. But he didn't have to hug me. I knew he loved me. I know it."

"Did he beat you?"

"Never. I told you, he loved me."

It sounded cold to me. I watched her playing with her fingers and tried to read her. If Toker hadn't hugged her or displayed much emotion of any sort, she was apparently willing to overlook it.

Of course, she had grown up Vietnamese-American in a land where any sort of mixed-race person was looked down on. She had been sent off alone by her aunt, and that must have felt like an abandonment. She'd survived the boat to Hong Kong and the British internment camp. She'd developed an American veneer, but underneath she was a survivor. She seemed to consider the food, the clothes, and the absence of blows enough. She talked about Toker as though she loved him. She wept when she spoke of his death.

Three hours later I had a better picture of Toker's life, but his life didn't seem to have much bearing on his death.

April seemed tired, or possibly depressed. She had answered my questions as well as she was able. I couldn't think of anything else to ask at the moment, and it was getting late. "We'd better go," I said.

"Can I ask a question?"

"Of course."

"Why did Dad tell me to come to you?"

I shrugged. "He said to come if you needed help. Sometimes I help people."

"You mean you're like a detective?"

"No. That takes a license. I call what I do Crisis Management." I stood, hoping she would leave it at that, but she was persistent.

"Does that mean you solve problems for people?" she asked.

"Sometimes. Sometimes I create them."

She thought about that for a few minutes, then asked, "Do you charge a lot?"

"I'm cheap. One dollar and all found."

"A dollar isn't much."

"I find a lot."

She shook her head uncertainly. "That doesn't seem right."

"Sometimes it isn't," I told her. "But when there's a clear-cut question of right and wrong, people don't need me. They call the cops. I only come into a situation when everyone is wrong. I try to help the person who is most right. Sometimes it works out. Sometimes it doesn't."

"And you decide who is most right?"

I nodded. "I decide."

"But why you?"

"Because I'm willing to live with the consequences."

She thought about it a minute, then asked if I wanted a dollar. I told her Toker had paid me a long time ago.

22

She left it at that. While she used the bathroom and reworked her makeup, I went downstairs. There was a cabby in the ranks outside the hotel who seemed smart enough to recognize an opportunity when he saw one. I sold him the Orange County tickets for ten dollars each and went back up to collect April and the bags.

The flight took an hour. I looked up Pearson's number as soon as we landed and caught the lawyer as he was leaving his office. I told him I had a question about a title, made an appointment for the next morning. Then I checked out the car I'd reserved, and found a hotel near the beach.

April almost balked when I led her into the room. It was of average size, with two double beds. But it was only one room.

"Can't I just go home?"

"Not until we've got things straightened out with the police," I said. "Maybe tomorrow night. But they're probably looking for you. Your neighbor certainly called them when you disappeared. They'll want to know where you went, and why. They may even think you had something to do with your father's death."

"But I didn't! I'll just tell them I didn't."

"You'll spend all night at the station telling them."

"But why can't I have my own room?"

"The police are looking for you. Someone else may be looking for you, too. But they'll all be looking for a woman alone. This way, you're just half of a couple. No one is going to wonder why a man checks into a hotel with a much younger woman." I gestured at the mirror, where we stood side by side. A young, pretty Oriental girl with dark eyes and a blond man about twice her age with a thin, sharp-featured face, watchful green eyes, and a tense way of holding himself. "We're so obvious that no one will even see us."

I didn't add that as long as she was in the same room with me, I could keep her off the telephone. Until I had a better idea what had led to Toker's death, I didn't want anyone to know she was back in Los Angeles. And I especially didn't want anyone to know I was here.

The possibility that the police might find her didn't seem to bother her, but the idea that someone else might be looking for her shut her up.

"Tomorrow, we'll talk to the lawyer and the police. If everything works out, you can sleep in your own bed tomorrow night. At home."

She nodded reluctantly.

While she changed for dinner, I put four thousand dollars in a hotel envelope. I wrote the last number I had for Roy on a piece of stationery and stuck it in with the money. The envelope went under the mattress at the foot of my bed. A poor hiding place, but good enough for a couple of hours.

We ate in the hotel dining room. I've cooked better and eaten worse. April was quiet during the meal, but when the waiter brought our coffee, she asked, "How did you know my father?"

"We met in Saigon during the war. He was in supply and I was attached to the Military Police."

"So you were friends?"

"In a way."

"But I never heard him talk about you, except the one time when he told me to go to you for help. I mean, it doesn't sound like you were friends. You never saw each other."

"We weren't that kind of friends."

She thought about that for a few minutes, then changed the subject. "Where you live . . . it's really out of the way. Do you really like it there?"

She seemed to mean far away from people. There was no good explanation for that. Anyway, it wasn't precisely true. I just shrugged.

"Do you always live alone?"

"Not always. Usually." I saw that she was still thinking about the sleeping arrangements. "Sometimes a woman will stay with me for a while. One closer to my age." Without really knowing why, I added, "They just never last. That's all."

"Do you ask them to leave? Or do they go on their own?"

She seemed to want to analyze me. I didn't feel like talking about my failures with a girl too young to have gambled on sex. "Maybe a little of both, April. But stop prying. I'm here to help you, that's all. If I wanted sex, it wouldn't be with a girl young enough to be my daughter.''

She finished her coffee in silence. I took her out to the car and drove to the nearest supermarket. One of the nicest things about America is that you can buy anything you need, any time you need it. April wasn't wearing a watch. I bought her a cheap one. I also picked up a flashlight, a roll of electrical tape, and a pocketknife. I made a call to a man named Pedro at the West L.A. number I'd gotten from my contact in Albuquerque.

The address he gave me was fifteen minutes away by freeway and almost an hour away by city streets. I took the streets, since it was still too early for what I had in mind. The drive took us deep into the barrio. I made April wait in the car while I went in. She acted nervous about the neighborhood. I didn't much like it myself.

Pedro was suspicious, but he must have checked my credentials. He sold me a .45 automatic and two clips of ammunition for three hundred and fifty dollars. I slipped the weapon under my sweater before getting back in the car.

It was after ten o'clock when we reached April's neighborhood. We cruised by her house once. It was large, set well back on a large lot. There was no activity around it, and no cars on the street.

I found an all-night market half a mile away and bought a pack of cigarettes and two Styrofoam cups of coffee and carried them to the car. I made sure her new watch told the same story as mine, then I asked April for her keys.

''What are you going to do?''

''I want to see the house. I want to see where Toker died and get a feel for what happened before we meet the lawyer. And I don't want anyone to know I went in. The only way is to do it tonight.''

''What if someone sees you?''

''Nobody will see me.''

''Somebody might be there.''

''There's no one around now. It should be safe.''

She looked excited. ''I want to come too.''

"No. We can't leave the car parked in front while we go in. Someone has to drive it and pick me up. You."

She looked like she wanted to object, but she didn't.

"At exactly eleven o'clock, you're going to drive around the block once. If anything looks suspicious, we'll call it off. If everything looks okay, you go around the block again. Memorize the cars on the street, what lights are on, everything. Slow down to two or three miles an hour in front of your house. I'll get out by those bushes next to the street. You drive away. At exactly eleven-twenty, you drive around the block again. Have the headlights on high beam. If everything looks exactly the same, flick the lights down to low beam and drive around the block. Slow down again when you get back to the bushes. I'll be waiting. Do you understand?"

She nodded.

"If anything has changed, don't flick your headlights to low. Drive away. Come back in ten minutes, at exactly eleven-thirty. Repeat the whole procedure. If there is still something suspicious, don't flick your lights. Drive back here and wait for me."

"Okay."

"Don't wait more than an hour. If I'm not here, go back to the hotel. I left an envelope for you there. It's under the mattress at the foot of my bed. There's some money and a man's telephone number. Pack up and find another hotel. Use the cash. No credit cards. Call the man and tell him what happened. He might be willing to help. He might not. If he isn't, you're on your own."

That bothered her. After a long pause, she nodded. I took her wrist and squeezed it gently.

"One other thing. You know people here. Probably most of them are on your side. But at least one person isn't, and he might be one of the people you know. So don't call anyone. Don't let anyone know you're in town. Unless I don't come back and you can't get any help from the number I gave you." I smiled at her. "Everything's going to be all right."

She smiled back hesitantly. "One thing. Could you get my diary?"

"Your diary?"

26

"It's what I went back for that night. It was on my bedside table. I write everything in it. I wanted to write what I felt about him. About Dad. Being dead, I mean."

"I'll try."

We traded places. I tossed the cigarettes in the glove compartment, removed the bulb from the overhead light, and gathered my stuff. Flashlight. Knife. Key. Gloves. Gun. I made sure which key worked the back door and asked her about the layout of the house and the security arrangements. Toker had not had an alarm system installed. That surprised me. You think you know someone.

There was no moon. Only a few lights were on in the houses on her block when we made the first circuit. No cars parked on the street. Nothing suspicious. The second time around the block, April slowed almost to a standstill. I opened the door, slipped out, and ducked behind the bushes. She accelerated and was gone.

It was very dark. A dog barked a block away. It took a few seconds to get to the side of the house, a few more to reach the backyard. I stood there with my eyes closed, waiting for my night vision, and counted to a hundred, listening.

There was no sound from the house or from Mrs. Stillwell's next door. I moved slowly past the pool to the back door and ripped off the police tape. The key slid in and turned noiselessly. I pushed the door open an inch and ran my fingers along the edge from top to bottom. Nothing. I slipped inside.

The interior was about as April had described it. I was in a utility room. There were clothes on the floor. Ahead was a short hall leading to the kitchen. The cabinets had all been opened. The dishes were on the floor. The refrigerator door was open. That made me nervous. The normal human thing would be to close it, but I left it open and headed for the bedrooms.

I had taped the flashlight so it threw only a tiny spot of light. I used it sparingly. Furniture had been turned upside down, cushions cut open, pictures pulled from walls, lamp bases shattered. Whoever did this was looking for something smaller than a bread box. Maybe bigger than a matchbox. The smallest hiding places hadn't been touched. There was no sign the pockets of

the clothes in the master bedroom closet had been searched, but the shelves had been emptied, suitcases opened.

Toker's office had been in a sitting room off his bedroom. It was easy to find. The wall was missing. Oh, the studs were there, but the wallboard had been blown away by shrapnel. A Claymore is beautiful in its efficiency. A small, heavy package, wider than it is high, with a slight curve along the width, it throws a wide arc of shrapnel that shreds anything in its path. Wallboard. Meat. Bone. Anything. The outline of Toker's body lay six feet back into the bedroom from what had been the door to the office. The remains of the mattress covered part of the outline and part of the dried goo under it.

I stepped between two studs into the office area. The desk had been pretty heavily damaged when the Claymore detonated. There was no drawer that hadn't been opened or up-ended. Paper was everywhere.

Any hope I had carried into the room evaporated. There was no place left to search. No time to search in. I crouched down on my heels and let the feel of the place seep into me. It wasn't good. What happened to Toker had been efficient, cold, ruthless. No one had wanted to talk to him, ask him questions, get information from him, demand money from him. The only thing his killer wanted of Toker was his death. But then he, or someone, had come back. Looking for what?

In Saigon, Toker had been a sharp, lively man. Average height, dark hair and eyes. Intelligent. His degree in business administration from UCLA had bought him a silver bar by the time he rotated in-country from Germany. He was assigned to Johnny Walker's supply unit at Long Binh. That was how we got him.

He'd had nerve and a quick laugh. I'd liked the man, despite his attitude toward the locals. He was reliable. He had to be. We trusted him enough to let him close down the operation. Of course, he knew what would happen if he violated our trust. So his reliability was, in a sense, coerced.

The last time I saw him, when I made his final delivery in 'seventy-four, he had been dealing in small parcels of land down toward San Diego. He'd smiled a lot. We'd had more than a couple of drinks and chased a couple of stewardesses out in Manhattan Beach, not really caring if we caught them. We hadn't, but the night had felt good anyway. Full of possibilities.

Now he was a crust of dried blood on the carpet and a sack of chopped meat in a cooler downtown. And the night didn't feel like it had a single good thing in it for anyone. It felt like my first night standing perimeter guard in the boonies, when every sound was ominous and every silence menacing. It felt like war.

I turned over a few pieces of paper and flashed my light on them, but they weren't anything I recognized. I stood and headed for April's room.

Maybe it was thinking back to the old days that stopped me outside her door. Something spooked me. I knelt down and stuck my head in slowly, with the flash directed along the floor. I stopped breathing.

What looked like a ray of light flashed across the doorway, three feet above the carpet, then abruptly disappeared. I took a breath, and there it was again. It took a minute to recognize it. Fishing line, pulled taut and running from a thumbtack stuck in the top of a girl's desk toward the headboard of a brass bed on the other side of the doorway. I held the flashlight next to the line and followed it. It disappeared into a tin can taped to the headboard. I felt immeasurably cold. This was about the worst thing I could have found.

It was a simple booby trap, very popular in some parts of my past. You take an ordinary fragmentation grenade, tie a line to it, and slip it into an ordinary tin can. Once the lever is inside the can, pull the pin. Tie the can somewhere convenient. Stretch the line across the path of someone you don't like and tie it.

The bad guy comes walking along. His foot catches the line and pulls it. The grenade pops out of the can and the lever flies away. The bad guy realizes something is wrong and starts to think what it could be. Then the grenade goes off and the bad guy stops thinking. Of course, bad guy can be a relative term.

But this was wrong. The line was too high. When your target is walking, his foot is the part of his body moving fastest. It is also the one part of his body he can't stop without losing his balance. The line should have been lower, no more than six inches off the floor. It didn't make sense until I remembered the target. A young woman. Never been in the jungle. Not wary of sudden death. With a target like that, the technical details wouldn't matter much. Still, the lack of craftsmanship bothered me. If you're going to do a thing, you should do it right.

The dog was still barking a block away. I crouched in the dark and tried to work up enough spit to swallow my fear. Then I took out my knife, reached into the room, and cut the line where it lay against the desk top. It fell to the floor, and I moved into the room. Very cautiously. I flashed the light around. Her room had received the same attention as the rest of the house. Clothes, paper, pillow stuffing everywhere. It seemed almost pointless to search, but then I saw the diary lying next to the bed. It had not been what the killer was after.

I scanned a page here and there and read the last few with greater care. She had written about school, her friends, her life. It seemed unimportant, at least in the current context. The last few pages were about her father. Not Toker, though. Apparently she had some idea of finding her real father. I closed it and tried to decide whether to reset the trap. No matter how I figured it, it seemed like the smart thing to do. But somebody was going to trip it if I did, and maybe not a bad guy. Feeling like a fool, I searched the floor until I found the pin, then eased the grenade slowly from the can and replaced the pin. I dropped the grenade in my pocket and left the house.

Two minutes later the car cruised past. The headlights dimmed. I dashed to the bushes by the street and took cover. Nothing moved. The damned dog finally stopped barking. It took about five seconds to get in the car when April slowed for me. I collapsed on the seat, breathing heavily. She accelerated smoothly. A few seconds later, the shakes tried to come. I fished the cigarettes out of the glove compartment and lit one. It took two matches, but that was just because of the wind from my open window. The cigarette kept the shakes away. By the time I was done with it, my breathing was back to normal. But I still felt explosive, like that damned grenade I'd brought away with me.

April kept stealing glances at me. I told her to keep her eyes on the road.

Then I repented and pulled her diary from under my sweater. When she saw
it, she said ''Ahh!'' and I saw that she was crying.

''The beach,'' I told her. ''Then the hotel.''

She took the freeway. The trip lasted three more cigarettes. When she
pulled into a parking lot, I tossed the rest of the pack. If I didn't, I'd only
smoke them, and I was way ahead of my quota already.

I left April in the car and walked out into the surf. I fished out the
grenade and pulled the pin, then heaved it as far as I could. There was a
splash in the dark, followed by a dull *whump* that built a hill of white water in
the distance. I returned to the car and April took off without a word.

As soon as we entered our room, she headed for the bathroom and
closed the door. I took the envelope from under the mattress and destroyed
the paper with Roy's name on it. Then I carried the diary to the table and
examined it more carefully. It covered less than two years, beginning in
January of 'eighty-nine. I guessed it had been a Christmas present.

She had made entries every couple of days through February, and then
they had slowed down to every few weeks for almost a year. During the past
month, she had been more conscientious, or had more to say.

The early entries were devoted to boys, girls, descriptions of parties.
Despite that, she didn't feel she had many close friends, either male or
female. She blamed the lack on her half-Vietnamese ancestry. There was a
flurry of entries about the time Toker gave her the Jaguar. She'd loved it,
even though it was three years old. And apparently it had increased her
popularity.

Five weeks ago she'd written two pages speculating on her natural father.
All she remembered about him was what her aunt told her—he was a cowboy, and very handsome. She had tested a couple of scenarios in which he
came looking for her. He would be very rich, very handsome, and love her
very much. He would take her away and she would be very happy. She made
no mention of Toker, or how he would react.

There were several entries in that vein over the following weeks. Then
she reported a conversation with her dad—Toker—about her interest in

finding her biological father. He had been upset by her questions. In fact, his reaction seemed strange. Her interest was surely natural, and it couldn't have threatened him, and yet he had exploded. He'd shouted at her, forbidden her to talk about it, and stormed out of the house. But later he came to her room and spoke more calmly. He explained how impossible it was to try to find one man among the six hundred thousand or so who had been in-country at the time she was conceived.

He was correct, of course. Even though there were only about twenty or thirty thousand in the Saigon area, chances were good that half of the men from Texas, or anywhere in the Southwest, had been nicknamed Cowboy by the other men in their units. And she had absolutely nothing else to go on.

And what if she did find him? It wasn't likely he would even remember her mother. April knew nothing at all of what her mother had been doing at the time. Her aunt had either not known or had not wanted to tell her. She could have been a bargirl, a hostess in one of the shops, a mama-san, a street girl, anything. There was no point of departure for a search, and no likelihood that finding the man would ease the girl's loneliness.

Apparently her car had broken down shortly after the confrontation over finding her natural father. It was in the shop for a couple days and no loaner was available. Her diary entries were about how hard it was to get around in Los Angeles without her car. The last few entries were about the classes she was taking and how she hoped to use the things she was learning at the dealership. I was skimming them when April appeared.

"What the hell are you doing!"

She stood by the bathroom door, eyes blazing. She stormed over and grabbed the book from my hands. "I mean it! What do you think you're doing? This is private! You have no right to read my private diary!"

I shrugged. "I thought it might give me an idea."

"It won't! There's nothing in this book but me! And it's none of your goddamn business!"

"There's your father."

"No! He's not in here! I only wrote about finding him!"

32

It took me a moment to see what she meant. Her biological father. "I meant your real father. James Bow." I spoke mildly.

"Oh." She didn't know what to say. She sat on her bed and stared at me. "I thought you meant . . ."

"I know what you thought. But you shouldn't be upset. Or ashamed. It's natural to want to know who you are, where you came from."

"I came from Vietnam. From the war. That's all."

"That's where you came from. It's not who you are, and it's nothing to be ashamed of." After a short silence, I added, "I came from Vietnam, from the war, too. And so did your father. Both your fathers."

She sniffed back her tears. "It's not the same thing. You existed before the war. All of you. You have history."

"I suppose." What she meant was obvious, but it wasn't as true as she thought. "And maybe your book isn't important, but the war might be."

She stared. "What do you mean?"

"There was another bomb. A booby trap. In your room." I explained what I'd found in her house.

She shuddered. "You could have been killed. Like Dad."

"No. He wasn't expecting anything. I was."

"Another clayman? I mean Claymore?"

"Something like it. But this wasn't a Claymore. It was a fragmentation grenade." I told her how it was set up, how it worked. She asked if it was important that it was a grenade instead of a mine.

"I think so. But I don't know why. Or how."

"What do you mean?"

"That sort of booby trap was very common in the boonies. In the jungle. As far as I know, it was invented by Charlie. But everyone used them. They were simple, easy to put together. The materials were everywhere. A tin can, a grenade, and some string was all you needed. Every grunt in the field knew how to make one."

"But there aren't any grenades here."

"There are grenades everywhere in the civilized world," I said. She had a point, but I let it pass for the moment. "The thing is, the Claymore is a military weapon. And the booby trap goes back to 'Nam, too. Maybe your father was killed by the war, by something that came out of it. I just don't see how."

"What do you mean?"

"There were two wars. There was the field, where Charlie and our guys snuck around shooting at each other, and there were the cities. Except for Tet and some bombings and random killings, the cities were fairly safe. And the men stationed there, like your father, didn't set booby traps. They were support personnel."

"But there were bombings. And a bomb killed my father."

Well, yes. Some things are hard to explain. I wasn't sure, myself, that a direct connection didn't exist. I just didn't understand it if one did exist. Toker had been a supply officer. He moved equipment and goods around, kept the PXs supplied with cigarettes, booze, toilet paper, toothpaste, condoms, and *Playboys*. Neither he nor any of the men he worked with regularly had spent any time in the jungle. Except me.

April broke the silence with a question that astounded me. She asked, very seriously, "What was Tet? Wasn't it a holiday?"

I just stared at her. There was nothing that could have emphasized the gulf between us more than that simple question. She was half Vietnamese, but she'd gone through puberty in Los Angeles, worrying about proms and a car. She was half my age and had never heard of the Tet Offensive.

I sighed, vaguely depressed. "The Tet I mean was before you were born. There was an attack. Some people were killed."

"But it didn't have anything to do with my father?"

"No. Nothing. He wasn't even in-country at the time."

"Then why mention it?"

"It was an example. Forget it."

She fingered her diary for a few minutes. I just watched her. She cleared her throat. "Do you think what happened back then has something to do with why Dad was killed?"

"I don't know. It just feels like it might. We'll know more tomorrow."
I stood and stretched. "We have to get going early. Let's get some sleep."

She nodded somberly and took her suitcase into the bathroom. I turned
on the television and scanned for a local newscast. It was way too late, and I
wound up spending half an hour with Letterman. I turned him off when she
called my name.

She had the bathroom door cracked and was hiding behind it. I was
reminded of last night, at my house, and my glimpse of her in the mirror.
"What do you want?"

"It's just that I don't have a nightgown," she said.

I found a T-shirt and tossed it to her. When she came out a minute
later, I realized it was kind of thin. Her body was still damp, and the white
shirt clung to her, outlining her shape. Her nipples were faintly visible, but
that might have been my imagination.

When I finished with the shower, I realized I hadn't planned my wardrobe any better than she. I wound up wearing shorts and a towel. She was in
her bed when I came out, with the light off and her back turned toward me.
I dropped the towel and slipped into my own bed. We lay there in the dark
for maybe half an hour. Then she said my name.

"Yeah?"

"Thank you."

"What for?"

"For coming. For helping me."

There hadn't been any choice, but I wasn't honest enough to admit it.
"You're welcome," I said.

"And Rainbow?"

"Yes?"

"At dinner . . . you said you were old enough to be my father. But
you're not so old."

"Go to sleep." I had trouble following my own advice. I was feeling
younger than I wanted to. But what the hell could you do with a kid who
didn't know what Tet was?

The tension I'd felt toward the girl was gone in the morning. She was one of those women who look good first thing, and I liked looking at her, but that was all.

Pearson's law offices were on the third floor of a glass building on one of the main drags, about half a mile from Bow's car lot. He was expecting me, and his receptionist showed me right in. I hadn't told him who I was or that April would be along. When he saw her, he spilled some of his coffee.

"April!"

She smiled shyly. "Hello, Mr. Pearson."

He fumbled with some papers, trying to regain his composure. I put April in a chair to one side and took the seat facing him. His reaction to the girl puzzled me. Since he didn't want to start the conversation, I took the initiative.

"I am an old friend of James Bow," I told him. "I understand you were his attorney."

He admitted he was.

"Did you handle his personal affairs as well as his business?"

"I did." He cleared his throat and avoided looking at April. "May I ask what this is about?"

"His death. At least insofar as it affects his daughter."

That made him even more nervous for some reason. He asked what I meant.

"He was murdered. You know that."

"I read the papers," he said. "I know he was killed."

"Murdered. In a way that threatened April. I want to know what happened, why he was killed. But first, I want to be sure it had nothing to do with April, and that she will be safe."

"I don't know why he was killed."

"You know something about his business. You may know if his death resulted from something he was doing there."

"I don't. As far as I know, his business dealings were all aboveboard. He was scrupulously honest."

"There was no unexplained income? No missing assets?"

"No."

I stared at the man for a few seconds. "Did you write his will?" I asked.

"Yes, I did."

"Was there anything unusual in it, any strange bequests?"

He wouldn't meet my eyes. "No. None. He left everything to his family."

I was getting a very bad feeling. "Do you mean the reading has already taken place?"

"Yes." He cleared his throat. "Yesterday afternoon."

"How could that be without his daughter present?"

Pearson looked directly at me for the first time. "James Bow didn't have a daughter." He looked at April. "I'm sorry," he said.

I looked at her too. She sat frozen in her chair, staring at the lawyer. "Then who is this?"

"She is a woman known as April Bow. She lived with my client. She represented herself as his daughter."

"Did he represent her as his daughter?"

"He may have."

I looked at him like a target. "May have . . . ?"

He seemed to shrink a bit. "Yes. . . . Yes, he did. As his adopted daughter."

"But she isn't." I kept my voice as flat as possible.

"No. To my knowledge, Mr. Bow never adopted anyone."

"Do you know why he told people that April was his daughter, that he had adopted her?"

"I do not."

My face felt flushed. I was angrier than I'd been in years. "God damn it!" I said, "You must know something!"

Pearson flinched. "Nothing," he said. "Nothing about his actions with respect to Miss . . . to April. . . . And nothing about his death. I'm sorry." He was speaking to the girl. She sat with her eyes wide open, her cheeks wet. "I am very truly sorry," he told her.

I controlled my breathing. Anger is an enemy. "Then what do you know? Who were his heirs?"

"I can't say that. You know I can't say that."

I stood suddenly and leaned over his desk. I grabbed his tie and pulled him toward me. His face turned purple. I hissed in his ear. "You can say. You will say. Look at me."

He rolled his eyes upward until they bulged at my face. They widened at what they saw there. "Yes." He croaked.

I let him go and he fell back into his chair. He started to reach toward the telephone, but I had the gun out and he saw it and stopped. After a moment he closed his eyes. "Put that away," he said.

"Do you know what's at stake here?" I asked.

"I think so."

"Then don't make any mistakes."

"No," he agreed. "Can you be discreet?"

"I'm a grave."

He took a deep breath. "What do you want to know?"

"Who inherited?"

"The family. His parents and his sister."

"What was the size of the estate?"

"A million two, book value. Twice that in the right market."

"Who is his personal representative?"

"His mother. I'm representing her."

"What was her reaction to the will?"

"She was satisfied."

"How was it split?"

"Half to the parents, half to the sister."

"Was April mentioned at all?"

"She was mentioned. She was specifically excluded. It wasn't like she was cut out recently. This is an old will. But it was reviewed less than two months ago."

The girl made a small noise deep in her throat, as though she had been cut inside.

"And no one else? No women? No friends?"

"No women. He had no friends." But there was something in his eyes that made me suspicious.

"There was nothing else?" I asked. "No codicil? No special bequest?"

He hesitated, then decided it wasn't worth a lie, whatever it was. "One thing. I don't know what to do about it. It wasn't even in the will."

"Tell me."

"About a month and a half ago he brought me a letter. He told me I'd know who to give it to. There is a name on it, but no address. A rather strange name."

April made another noise. She was looking at me. Pearson looked at me too. "Can you guess the name?" he asked softly.

I felt like I was back in April's bedroom, looking at the grenade. "Rainbow," I said.

The lawyer nodded slowly. "I guess it's yours." He touched a button on the phone and asked his secretary to bring the envelope from the Bow file in the safe.

When she came in, April stood abruptly and rushed out. Pearson took the envelope from the secretary's hand and put it directly in mine. I stuck it in my breast pocket and started after April. Pearson stopped me. "Mister . . . ahh, Rainbow!"

I looked at him.

"What happened here . . . the irregular aspects . . . I'm going to overlook them because of my feelings for April. About what Bow did, I mean."

"You'll overlook them because you don't want to think about the alternative," I told him coldly.

After a moment, he nodded. "Nevertheless, I do feel badly about it."

I left the secretary looking back and forth from her employer to me with bright, curious eyes.

April was not in the reception area. I found her leaning against the wall by the elevator. I pushed the button and stood silently beside her. Her cheeks were still wet and her face was very white.

When the elevator arrived, she moved woodenly into it. Then she stumbled and fell against me. She threw an arm over my shoulder so that her face was against my chest, and her knees buckled. I held her and she began to sob, but by the time the door opened, she could stand again. A man waiting for the elevator glared at me as I led April off.

When we reached the parking lot, she leaned against the car. She didn't want to get in. "I'm sorry," she said.

"Don't apologize. You have nothing to apologize for."

"I lost it. I just lost it all."

I waited for her to continue. I thought I knew what she was talking about. Her self-control. I was wrong.

"I had a father, and I lost him. And now I lost him again. And it was all because of me, because I wasn't satisfied. I had to try to find my real father. And then Dad . . . he cut me out. I hurt him."

"You were never in," I told her. "Get in the car."

She nodded. I held the door for her.

When we had been on the road for five or ten minutes, she said, "The envelope. What was it?"

It had been burning my chest. I'd been ignoring it. I pulled into the parking lot at the next strip center and took it out. The writing on the envelope was in Bow's hand, of course. I tore it open. It held a single sheet of yellow lined paper with just four sentences. I read them once, cursed, and read them again. Maybe my face was white. I didn't feel like I had an ounce of blood in me.

"Well?"

I wasn't sure it was the right thing, but I didn't know what else to do. I read the paper to her. "Squall Line was broken. The accounts were short. Take care of April. I don't know who else to trust and I can't say any more."

She stared at me. I stared out the window, watching the civilians. Men in short-sleeved shirts. Women in shorts and halter tops. Kids on skateboards. Some of them were even laughing. Civilians. I felt a thousand years old, six thousand miles removed from them.

"He said take care of April," she said slowly.

"Yes."

"Then maybe he did care. About me."

"I think he cared."

"But the rest of it. What does it mean?"

"I don't know."

She started crying again. "You do know, you lying son of a bitch. You're the only one who knows and you won't tell me." She got out of the car and walked toward the shops. I let her go and stared out the window.

You can feel old and tired, and then you think if you get any older, if a thing lasts even one more minute, you'll die. You'll die and your body will turn to dust and blow away like you were a vampire in one of those stupid movies. A mass of corruption. But time passes and you get older. And you don't die. Eventually you will die, you know that, but you don't yet. You just feel worse. And then you get hungry, or thirsty, or you get an itch. Something happens that reminds you you're alive, that it isn't time yet, and somehow you feel better and at the same time ashamed of feeling better. You take a couple of deep breaths and look around to see what has to be done. And you see someone else standing alone, maybe thinking about death.

April was under the awning, over by the shops. I pulled myself out of the car and walked over to her. "We should talk, I guess," I said.

One of the places was a bar. I led her to a table in the rear. The bartender came over and I ordered a double scotch. She ordered a Coke. We said nothing until the drinks came. I took half of mine and patted my shirt for a cigarette, then remembered I'd thrown the damned things away again. I looked back at April. She was waiting patiently.

"It looks like it goes back to Vietnam," I began. "I'd hoped that it wouldn't, that it was something recent. But it wasn't.

"I told you I knew him over there, that he was a supply officer and I was with the Military Police. Well, Toker was involved in something. Along with some other people." I took another sip of my drink. This was harder than I'd expected.

April decided to try to help. Or to hurry me up. "And you arrested them," she suggested.

I shook my head. "I was in it too."

"It was wrong?"

"It was illegal."

"The black market? You were stealing things, selling them on the black market?"

"No. We were buying things and selling them on the black market. Nothing was stolen. Everything was paid for. The accounts were always in balance. We were very careful about that. But we bought a lot of things. Liquor. Cigarettes. Gasoline. Clothes. Everything. Let me tell you how it was." I focused on the far wall.

"There were four kinds of valuables over there. The first was goods and services. We dealt in goods, not services. The other three things were money. There was Vietnamese money, called piasters or dong, that was number one. We called it pee or dong. Then there was MPC, or scrip. MPC stood for military payment certificates. The soldiers were paid in scrip. And then there was American currency. The good old green-backed dollar. We just called that green. It was illegal for soldiers to have green. All we could have was scrip or pee. But nobody gave a rat's ass about the Vietnamese money because it was almost worthless.

"Anyway, the American government was propping up the Vietnamese government by creating an artificial value for the piaster. In order to keep the economy from inflating too rapidly, the exchange rate for scrip was set at a hundred eighteen to the dollar. But scrip could buy stuff from the PX, and that made it worth between two hundred fifty and four hundred pee to the dollar for the LNs who could find soldiers to buy for them."

"So much? Three times?"

I nodded. "But even that was a gyp. Scrip was funny money. The real stuff was green, and you could get six hundred to one for a twenty-dollar bill, more for higher denominations, depending on how the last battle went or what the markets were short of. One time I watched a buddy sell a thousand green at twelve hundred to one. A week later he traded it for MPC at eighty to one when the word went out that the military was going to change the money. They did that sometimes to discourage currency specula-

42

tion. All it did was screw the poor Vietnamese one more time. Anyway, after trading the pee for scrip, he had turned one thou' into fifteen. If he'd been caught with that much, he would have been in the stockade for sure.''

April looked confused. ''What did he do?''

''He bought five thousand bottles of Courvoisier cognac. And after the currency-change excitement was over, they were worth twenty bucks apiece on the street if you were willing to take piasters. Which he was, of course, because even piasters could be used to buy some things, and goods varied in price too, depending on what you had to sell, what you were willing to buy, what currency you were holding, and what time it was.

''For instance, Vietnam is close to Thailand, and there are lots of stones in Thailand. Rubies, sapphires, emeralds, jade. Gold and silver bullion came in from India. And there was art. Ivory and porcelain and drawings from China. Some European stuff when the upper classes fell on hard times. Lots of things were available for piasters you could buy at eight hundred to one. And those things could be sold stateside, or in Japan or Hong Kong or the P.I., for a decent price. Especially if they didn't have to pass through customs.''

I gave her a quick glance. ''Military transport went all those places. And customs was rarely a problem, because so much war materiel was moving around.''

She was impassive. ''So that's what you did. What my father did.'' Her voice was stone cold.

It wasn't all we did. Some of us died, too. And they were paid cheaply. I didn't know how to explain that, but I felt I had to say something, so I said yes.

She said nothing for a long while. Then she cleared her throat. ''You used some words I didn't understand. P.I., for instance.''

''P.I. is the Philippine Islands.''

''LN.''

''Local nationals. The Vietnamese.''

''The gooks, you mean.''

''Yes.''

"Like me."

I shrugged. "Gooks. Slopes. Honkies. Niggers. Kikes. Spicks. Polacks. Gringos. There's a name for everyone."

"Names can hurt."

"They don't kill."

She looked at me as if I were from another planet. I was.

"I want you to go. Leave me alone."

"I want to help."

"I don't want your help."

"Think about it." I stood up. The bartender watched me leave, then headed toward her booth as I reached the door. He was about twenty-five. Also too young to understand.

I found a phone booth at the drugstore next door and looked up the address of James Bow, Sr., then bought a pack of cigarettes and took them to the car. When April came out an hour and a half later, she was walking very carefully. She climbed in beside me. I could smell her breath. I said nothing, just put the car in gear.

When we'd driven half an hour, she asked where we were going. I told her to see Bow's parents. She made a face. "Why?"

"I want to know how they feel about Toker's will. If there's anything for you here."

"That's up to me, isn't it?"

"Yes. When you can make the decision."

Bow's parents had a nice split-level in Westwood. His mother led me into the living room. She looked somber. Her husband sat quietly in a chair by the window, looking out. I wondered if he could see April waiting in the car. She had refused to come in.

I explained to them that I was a friend of April's. They looked unfriendly.

"What does she want?" the mother asked.

"To understand," I told them. "Your son took her home. He told her he had adopted her. He treated her like a daughter. He acted like he loved her. He let her trust him, even love him. And now this. There was apparently no adoption. He has left her nothing. He owes her. At least an explanation.''

The old man started to say something, but his wife cut him off. ''He's given her a fortune. Too much. More than she deserved.''

''Other people might not think so. A judge might think he owed her more.''

The woman glared at me. ''He gave her a car,'' she said. ''She can keep that. She won't get another dime. Tell her we said so. Not another dime.''

''He had a sister. Does she feel the same way?''

''She does.''

I looked at the husband. He nodded.

''But why? What did April do to you?''

''She's a goddamn gook,'' the husband said.

His wife silenced him with a sharp look. ''Let me tell you something, Mr. Porter,'' she said. ''Before the war, we were a close family. We were happy. Jimmy did very well in school. And then he was drafted, and he went for OCS and became a lieutenant. Then he went to Vietnam and he came back changed. The war changed him. It was fought for those people. I mean, he went over there for them. Nobody appreciated it, what he gave up. Not my neighbors, and not those people in Vietnam.''

She pursed her lips. ''It didn't bother Jimmy, what he gave up, but it bothered us. Our family. We were close before he left. Loving. When he came back, he wasn't loving anymore. And it was their fault. Those people's. He lost the ability to be close, to be loving. And it was for nothing. For a bunch of lousy . . . gooks!''

I stared at her. Her face was pinched white with her hatred. I understood what she felt, but it left me cold. ''April didn't do it,'' I said. ''She was just a little baby.''

''They should all be dead. They killed the best part of my baby.''

I looked at her husband. ''Do you feel the same way?''

He just turned his head a little farther away from me and said nothing.

There was no way I could see to move either one of them. I didn't think April would even want to try, but that was her decision. "I'll tell her what you said. She may want to talk to a lawyer. It will be up to her."

"Tell her she can keep the car he gave her. I wouldn't have it now. But she won't get another cent. Not if I have to spend every dime fighting her. I'll waste it before she'll have it."

I stood and said goodbye. The mother saw me to the door. She wouldn't look at my car. On the step, I turned and asked her when the funeral would be. She told me it had been yesterday, and I left her standing there. When we were back on the road, April asked me how it was. I told her it was unfriendly. "I'll bet," she said.

We headed back to the hotel. There was still one chore left to do. The police.

April lay down on her bed and stared at the ceiling. I took an illegal little gadget that looked like a pocket calculator from my suitcase and called the switchboard for an outside line. When I had one, I dialed a 900 number. When I had the trunk line, I interrupted the call by holding the device to the phone's mouthpiece and pressing a couple of buttons. Then I routed the call through Mexico City and back to L.A. I dialed the police department and asked for the detective handling the Bow homicide.

The police operator was reluctant to transfer me without a name, so I gave her Marlon Brando's. I really didn't give a damn if they tried to trace the call. Nobody can trace a call through Mexico City.

Eventually I was put through to a Detective Blankenship. He was polite but very circumspect. "Can I help you?"

"Maybe. I want to talk about the murder of James Bow."

"Okay. What is your name?"

"I am a friend of his daughter, April."

"Where is April? All her friends here are worried about her. Mrs. Stillwell is worried about her. Where is she?"

"She's safe. She came to me because she was afraid for her life."

"That doesn't make sense. She should have come to the police if she was afraid. We would have protected her. Where is she?"

46

"What is the nature of your interest in her?"

"We want to protect her. Where are you calling from?"

"Guess. Do you know that she was in classes all morning on the day her father was killed?"

"I am aware of that. Why did she run away?"

"Later. Do you know that she left home before her father the morning he died?"

"Yes."

"Do you think she had anything to do with his death?"

"We don't believe she set the bomb that killed him, no, but we don't understand why she ran away. She should come to the station and explain her behavior. Are you her attorney?"

"No. Do you have any other reason to believe she was connected with his death?"

Blankenship decided to try an end run. "If you aren't her attorney, I really can't talk to you about April Bow. Is she there with you? Can I talk to her?"

"Yes, she's here. No, you can't talk to her. Do you have any evidence that she was involved in the killing? Other than speculation?"

"She disappeared immediately after her father's death. Naturally we are very curious about that." He sharpened his tone. "If she is concerned about protecting herself, she can contact an attorney or the Public Defender's office. Someone will be provided to look after her interests. Someone who is an attorney."

"The night of his death, she went back to her home to get a diary. She was very upset and wanted the emotional comfort and sense of closeness to her father that the diary would give her. She found that the house had been torn apart. Did your officers do that?"

"Of course not. Torn apart, you say?"

"I say very thoroughly searched. Miss Bow naturally became very frightened. She came to me for help. Despite her natural desire to help locate her father's killer, I have advised her that going to the police at this time might be dangerous. I suspect that her father's killer is targeting her as well."

Blankenship abandoned the formal tone he had used up to that point. "Why?"

"Have you been in her house recently?"

"Not since the investigation."

"Go again. Someone set a grenade with a trip line. A booby trap. For her. I disarmed it, but the line and can are still there. Do you know what I'm talking about?"

"I was in 'Nam," he said slowly. "Damn it, who are you?"

"Just a friend. An uninvolved friend. One who doesn't want to see her stuck for a killing she couldn't have done just because she's convenient."

"Look, if she's in danger, we can protect her. Better than you."

"Maybe," I told him, "but she'd lose her freedom while you were protecting her. And I don't think you're going to find the killer."

"Why not? Do you know who did it?"

"I know who didn't do it. April Bow didn't do it. Bow was still home when she left the house. So the bomb had to be set after he left. He returned, for some reason, and the bomb went off. But April's time can all be accounted for. She was in classes until your officer notified her of the death. On top of that, she had a very good relationship with her father. She loved him. He treated her very well. She gained nothing from his death and she lost a great deal. She didn't kill him. You have no interest in her."

"I have an interest in talking to her," he said. "Who are you? Why is she afraid to talk to the police?"

"She's afraid for her life," I said.

He asked again where I was calling from.

"We just flew into Orange County," I told him and hung up.

April was still staring at the ceiling. Her eyes were full. "I did love him," she said. "I honestly did."

"Get up and pack. We've got to get moving."

She just lay there. "Where are we going?"

"Phoenix."

She didn't ask why. "You told them we are in Los Angeles."

"I told him two people named James and April Bow are in Orange

48

County." I explained about the other two tickets I'd bought in Vegas and why I'd made the scene at the airport.

"The police should assume those people were us. If they check back to Vegas, they'll find we spent last night at the Flamingo. I knew I was going into your house, April. I wanted to be able to prove you weren't in town in case they learn about the entry. Maybe they'll look harder for another suspect."

"You think ahead." She was almost whispering.

She hadn't moved from the bed. I sat beside her and took her hand. "Only stupid people act without thinking," I said softly. "What's wrong, April? Don't you feel well?"

"I'm just tired," she said. "I don't know why. I'll be okay in a few minutes. Go away."

April kept her eyes shut while I packed our bags and called Hertz about keeping the car for a couple more days. Her breathing was slow, but irregular. I didn't know what to do about her. I carried our bags down and packed the car. When there was nothing left to do, I alternately coaxed and growled until she began moving.

We were on the road by five, headed east. I stopped in San Bernardino long enough to pick up a sack of burgers, fries, and a six-pack of Coke, then pulled back onto the freeway. It was a waste of money. April wouldn't eat. She wouldn't talk. She just sat in the green glow of the instrument panel and stared into the darkness ahead. Somewhere near the Arizona border, she fell into an uneasy sleep. I turned off the radio so that it wouldn't disturb her and drove through the night in a silence broken only by the girl's occasional soft whimpers.

PHOENIX

T NIGHT, PHOENIX TELEGRAPHS ITS PRESENCE FROM
fifty miles away. As you drive across the desert of western Arizona,
the lights of the city gradually smudge the eastern horizon. You feel
like you're driving into the dawn, even when your watch says it's a
little after two in the morning.

I found a motel on the outskirts of the city and left April in the car while
I checked us in as Harold and Ann Stephenson. She didn't awaken until I
pulled our suitcases from the backseat. Then she just followed me into the
room.

The drive had tired me. I dumped the suitcases and hit the shower.
When I came out, she was asleep. It was then that I realized the room had
only one bed. It didn't matter. I just crawled in beside her, closed my eyes,
and let the world go away.

The shower woke me the next morning. I lay with my eyes closed while the world gradually came into focus. April on my doorstep. Toker dead. The booby-trapped bedroom in Los Angeles. The interview with Pearson. Toker's last message.

Bow's death and April's predicament were the clearest elements of the situation. The Claymore had orphaned her a second time, counting the death of her mother. And then the will that cut her completely from his estate left her with nowhere to go.

Her immediate needs could be taken care of. I could provide her with a whole new identity, if it came to that. A name, a degree, eventually a job. The message Toker sent with her, "You owe me," was the last IOU he would ever call in, but it was a good one. I had owed him a debt that was not fully paid by the money I'd funneled to him in 'seventy-three and 'seventy-four, a debt I didn't mind repaying to his daughter. At first glance it looked as if we could both walk away from Los Angeles, if April would abandon another chunk of her past. But she probably couldn't do that. She was showing some of the signs of depression, and she didn't seem to be grieving as I'd expected her to. She hadn't asked me about the funeral. She might not even have thought of it. What she needed was a resolution.

She wasn't alone. The letter from Toker more than implied a connection between his death and our past, 1991 Los Angeles and 1971 Saigon. And that connection could lead the killer to New Mexico, to me, and perhaps to the others. Rodgers and Coleman. If the past was stalking them, they would have to be warned. So I needed a resolution, too.

The shower died. I opened my eyes and looked around, then remembered that there had been only one bed. I wondered how April would handle meeting me this morning, if she would be embarrassed.

She handled it like a zombie. Her eyes slid over me as easily as they passed over the decorative art on the wall behind the bed. She stood in front of the mirror and toweled her hair dry mechanically. She was naked.

I got up and took the towel from her and led her back to the bed. When I pushed her down, she folded like a rag doll. I pulled the covers over her and told her to rest awhile. There was nothing to do until later in the afternoon. Maybe nothing for her then. I showered quickly. It was easy not to think of her breasts, her thin dark triangle. The memory stirred no excitement in me. The emotion I felt was pity. She was reacting like a child and I found myself responding to her as if she were a child. Women had aroused my protective instincts before, of course, but only after a sexual relationship had been established. With April . . . well, there was some sexual tension. I couldn't deny that. It had been there since I saw her in my shower the night she arrived. Before that. Her eyes, her hair, her faint accent, all were ghosts of what I had lost in Saigon. But she was only half my age, and I wasn't fool enough to hope that what was lost could be found again. Time had closed the door.

I dressed and went out to get my bearings. The motel was laid out in a rectangle, with rooms stacked two stories high along the sides and back. The area facing the street was devoted to the lobby, front desk, gift shop, offices, restaurant, and lounge. A pool and flagstone court occupied the center. The parking lot surrounded the whole complex. The entrances faced the parking lot, but each room also had a patio door and a balcony overlooking the pool. The ground-floor rooms, like ours, opened directly onto the courtyard. Fifteen or so wrought iron tables, about half with red, white, and green umbrellas that advertised Cinzano, were scattered around the court. The day was warm, the sun bright. Morning in the desert.

I left by the patio door and cut across the court toward the lobby. Two boys were splashing in the pool. The contest was apparently to see who could kick up the biggest wave. A woman and her teenaged daughter sunned themselves on two towel-draped lounge chairs. They lay facedown, in identical blue bikinis, as far from the boys as they could get. They were smart to go for the early sun. By midmorning, it would be brutal. Already their backs were dotted with perspiration. The mother looked up when I walked past them.

The coffee shop was serving the tail end of the breakfast crowd. I bought two papers from machines in the lobby, the *Times* and the *Sun,* and ordered coffee and a Denver omelette. There was nothing on Bow's killing in the L.A. paper, and I discarded it. I looked over the *Sun* more carefully while I finished my coffee, but there was nothing in it to indicate that the trouble

had come to Arizona. I flagged down the waitress and ordered another omelette with two large coffees, to go. While the order was prepared, I went to
the gift shop and bought a couple of bathing suits.

April was lying with her eyes closed when I got back to the room. Her
breathing was irregular. I put the breakfast and one of the coffees on the
table beside the bed and made her sit up. She said she wasn't hungry and
weakly tugged the sheet up over her breasts. I put the plate in front of her
and told her to eat anyway. Then I rummaged through drawers until I found
a telephone book and carried it and my coffee out to the pool area. I took a
table close to our room.

The boys were still splashing. The woman and her daughter had rolled
over and put on dark glasses. They lay with their arms beside them, palms
up, and their legs slightly spread, about twenty feet away. The similarity
between them was more pronounced from the front. I watched them for a
few minutes, thinking about April. About April and death.

Four of us had survived the operation in Saigon. Lieutenant James Bow,
nicknamed Toker, died in Los Angeles six days ago. Captain William Rodgers, nicknamed Roy, was somewhere in the El Paso area. Staff Sergeant
John Coleman, nicknamed Johnny Walker, had settled in Phoenix.

Toker had been the last of us to leave the republic, as we called the
Republic of Vietnam. He had closed the operation down in 1971 and knew
about the end of it. And left a message. Two messages, really. First, that the
books had been off. Second, that Squall Line was broken. I didn't want to
think about the second unless I had to, so the first had brought me to
Phoenix. Just as Toker had seen the end of our operation, Johnny Walker saw
the beginning.

Actually, the operation hadn't ended in 'seventy-one. Only the active
phase of it stopped then. Roy and Walker had decided at the beginning that if
they were going to do it, they would do it right. They would cover all tracks.
There would be no large sums of money to explain when their war was over.
Taxes would be paid on everything. They wanted to live the rest of their lives
as though Vietnam had never happened, as though Saigon were just another
city, a beautiful city in a land far away.

The rest of us had to agree to that before we were brought in. At first we hadn't seen exactly how it could be done, but a plan had evolved over the years, over countless bottles of whiskey and packs of cigarettes and all-night sessions at Miss Phoung's house off Tu Do Street, while artillery fire from distant firebases drummed like muted thunder. It was a complicated plan. Corporations had to be set up in Panama, the Philippines, Japan, and Mexico, as well as in the states. Money had to be transferred frequently, becoming a little more legal, a little harder to trace, each time it was moved. But the plan had worked. For twenty years, anyway.

And now Toker had implied that there had maybe been a second plan, that the accounting was off. I needed to know if Toker's post mortem accusation was true, and if it was, when the second set of books were opened. And who had benefited. If Toker's death was connected to an old treachery, the question of who had benefited was crucial. It would lead to his killer, to the resolution April needed and I wanted.

The problem was that twenty years had gone by. Actually, the problem was that they had gone by peacefully. Even supposing a hidden agenda had existed, it was buried deep in the past. Everyone had been happy for a long time. We had each taken a little over six hundred thousand home, after taxes. I had been the candyman, the delivery boy. I knew how the funds were transferred, how they had been invested. Toker hadn't needed money before his death. No one should have needed anything. And yet Toker was dead. Things were falling apart. What had happened?

I sighed and spent a couple of minutes dredging up sixteen-year-old names from my memory, then opened the phone book. Only two of the companies were still listed. I memorized their numbers and carried the book back into the room.

April had stirred her food around a bit. She may have eaten a couple of bites. She had finished her coffee and was watching a television evangelist threaten his flock with the hereafter. She looked up dully when I entered. I dug out the bikini I'd picked out, tossed it to her, and told her to get dressed.

"Why?"

"Because it's a beautiful day. Because I asked you to."

After a long pause, she sighed and told me to turn around. I turned around and watched her pad into the bathroom in the mirror. There was no spring in her step. I opened the drapes and patio door and let the sun in. She came out after a couple of minutes wearing the suit. It looked good on her. Not too tiny, but she'd be able to get some sun if she wanted. I asked if she liked it.

She flashed a faint smile and nodded. I pointed to the courtyard. She left. I carried the phone to a chair where I could watch her and dialed the first number, Peacemaker Investments, and asked to speak to Mr. Coleman. The receptionist asked me to hold a moment, and then a man picked up the line.

"Can I help you?"

"John Coleman, please."

"There's no one here by that name." His voice was smooth, deep. It wasn't Walker.

"When did he leave?"

He hesitated. "There has never been a Mr. Coleman at this number."

I was patient with him. "Peacemaker Investments was incorporated in 1972 by John Coleman and Harold Stephenson," I told him. "This is Mr. Stephenson. I'd like to speak to Mr. Coleman."

The next pause was longer. "I'm sorry, but Mr. Coleman has retired."

"Fine. What is his home number?"

"That's confidential information. I'm sorry."

"He wants to talk to me."

"I doubt that very much."

"Ask him."

"Could you tell me the nature of your business with Mr. Coleman?"

The hook was in. "It's confidential. Tell him I have to see him."

"Have to?"

"Yes. Tell him Toker is dead."

"Toker is dead." He repeated the message flatly. "He'll call you if your message interests him. What is your number?"

"I'll call back in an hour. I expect him to answer."

"Call at four. He may not be here, but I'll try to reach him and tell him about Mr. Toker."

That seemed like the best I was going to get out of the man. I thanked him and hung up.

April was sitting at the table I had used. The boys were gone. I walked out to her, scooped her into my arms, and carried her over to the edge of the pool. She screamed and beat at me with both fists, but her heart wasn't in it. I tossed her in. She came up sputtering and cursing.

"Swim," I told her.

She hung on the side of the pool and stared at me, but after a few minutes she began a slow backstroke toward the other side. I watched her for a while, then went in and put my suit on. When I returned, she was still swimming, grimly. The mother and daughter team were sitting up, watching us.

I sat on the edge of the pool, dangling my legs, and let April do another ten laps, then slid in and paced her for ten more. At first she tried to pull away from me, but I made a race of it, and we gradually synchronized our strokes. The sky was that hard turquoise blue you only see in the desert. It was getting on toward noon, and the sun was fierce.

Finally I'd had enough. I climbed out, grabbed our towels, and went to sit under one of the umbrellas. The mother and daughter had apparently lost interest when no further drama materialized. They were on their bellies again, and they'd both undone the straps on their tops. They were the same shade of golden brown. If the mother hadn't been fifteen pounds heavier and puckered just the tiniest bit where her cheeks met her legs, they would have passed for sisters.

April walked out of the shallow end of the pool and sat beside me. A waiter wandered by and I ordered two beers. When he left, I asked how she was feeling.

"Okay, I guess."

"Did you sleep well?"

She shot a quick glance at me, probably remembering that she hadn't slept alone. But she just shrugged.

56

"Okay, I guess."

The waiter wandered back with the drinks and I signed for them. They were cold, the sun was hot, the shade was pleasant, and a pretty girl sat beside me. But Toker was dead, Walker was playing hard to find, the books were off, and Squall Line had been broken. I felt okay, I guess.

"They buried him the day before yesterday," I told her.

She nodded slowly. No tears.

"How do you feel about that? Don't say okay."

"I don't know. Empty."

"His mother said you can keep the car."

"I don't know if I want it."

"He wanted you to have it."

"Did he?"

"He gave it to you."

She took a swallow of her beer and shivered.

"We have a couple of hours. Is there anything you want to do?"

"Where are we?"

I stared. She seemed serious. "Phoenix."

She closed her eyes and lay her head back in her chair. I looked at her. Her skin was faintly red above her top and on her face. Her passivity bothered me. When the waiter stuck his head out again, I ordered two club sandwiches. April groaned when they arrived, but I made her eat one and then walked her back to the room.

She sat on the foot of the bed and stared at the television. It wasn't turned on. I opened her suitcase, picked out a pair of panties, a brassiere, white slacks, a cream-colored blouse, and laid them beside her. She didn't seem to notice.

"God damn it, do I have to dress you?"

She stood and started taking off the bikini top. I grabbed some clothes and headed for the bathroom. When I came out, she was dressed. She had picked out a different blouse. I thought that was probably a good sign.

We spent a couple of hours in the nearest mall. I told her she had to buy some clothes, that I wouldn't let her leave until she'd spent two hundred dollars. She shopped apathetically at first, but toward the end she was showing a little enthusiasm. We got back to the motel by three-thirty. I made her model the dress and pants outfit she'd decided on. She acted pleased when I complimented them.

At four o'clock I called the number again. The man I'd spoken to earlier answered on the first ring.

"Mr. Stephenson?"

"I don't want to talk to you," I told him.

"Unfortunately, Mr. Coleman will not be available. He asked me to convey his regrets and to say that he remembers the last time you met with fondness, but he will not see you again." The man's voice never strayed from gentle civility. "Goodbye, Mr. Stephenson."

I hung up before he could. His politeness irritated me. Walker's caginess was beginning to irritate me. I said "Shit."

"What's wrong?" April was watching me from the bed.

"Nothing. I'm just irritated." She waited. I threw myself on the bed beside her. "Walker wants to play games. Or maybe he's scared. I don't know which."

I stared at the couple in the mirror opposite the bed for a long minute before adding, "This cat and mouse shit makes me nervous. But at least nobody is shooting at us."

She said nothing. Well, there was nothing to say. I told her I was looking at a long night and to wake me at seven. She reached for the television controller as I rolled over. I spent some time deciding how to play the few cards I held, and then I let myself drift off. I woke a few minutes before seven. April was asleep. I woke her and prodded her to dress. She wore one of the new outfits. Before we left the room, I turned on the radio and all the lights and opened the curtains over the patio door. We ate a leisurely dinner at the motel and were on the road by eight-thirty.

My last meeting with Walker, the one he remembered with such fondness, had been in a lounge near the American Airlines gates at the Phoenix airport. I was delivering some papers that would transfer ownership of a shipment of machine tools being held in bond at the port of Los Angeles.

58

The value of the cargo had been small, around fifty thousand. The twenty thousand profit he would make on the shipment represented the last payment on Walker's account, and I hadn't expected to see him again.

He had to catch a flight too, and we barely had time to meet. The transfer had gone smoothly. I had walked into the lounge, seen him standing at the bar, handed him an envelope, shaken hands quickly, and walked away. Very businesslike. But as I walked away, I'd felt as though I were floating. It had been the last payment. I had felt as if the war was finally over. Maybe he had felt the same. Maybe he actually did remember the meeting, but I doubted that he remembered it with fondness.

I parked in the long-term lot at the airport, as far away from the rest of the cars as possible. There was only one vehicle nearby, a late-model Cadillac Brougham. I left the automatic under the front seat and we walked in.

When you suspect a man might have a reason to want you dead, an airport is a good place to meet him. There are plenty of people around, none of whom have the slightest interest in your business. And if you're meeting by the gates, both you and he have to clear the metal detectors. No guns allowed, in other words.

Only ticketed passengers are allowed in the gate area, so I bought two tickets to Las Vegas, just because they were cheap, and led April down the concourse. It took a few minutes to find the right lounge. Walker was waiting at the bar. It was like the last sixteen years had disappeared.

He nodded when he saw me enter, then gave me a hard look when he realized I wasn't alone. I ignored him and led April to a table away from the crowd around the television. Once we were seated, he carried his drink over and joined us.

Johnny Walker was a black man, about my height, only twenty pounds or so lighter. In fact, he was almost too thin. But he'd always been that way. His suit was well tailored. He carried himself with a slight stoop. His hair was about half an inch long and going gray. It framed his narrow face like a halo.

"Long time no see," I told him.

He grimaced and said, "What's happening, Rainbow."

"You know the answer to that."

He looked April over carefully, then said, "I thought this was a business meeting."

"There's business and then there's business. She's business." I introduced them, told him who she was.

"Ol' Toker must have been pretty busy after I left," Walker said. "Looks like he did pretty good work, too."

April gave him a faint smile.

I told him she was adopted, one of the boat people from Hong Kong.

"I still don't like it. How much does she know?"

"Some of it."

He shook his head. "I don't like this at all," he told me.

"There's no way to keep her out of it. Toker's dead."

"So I heard."

"And there's this." I gestured vaguely at the bar, the airport. "Is there something you want to tell me?"

He gave me a long, measuring look, then pulled his chair forward and leaned over the table. He spoke quietly. "Some questions, first. Are you active in my town? You been checking up on me, maybe for old times' sake?"

I shook my head.

"Roy, then. What about Roy?"

"I haven't seen him in years. I don't know what he's up to. I'm not even sure how to find him. All I have is a fifteen-year-old phone number."

"You found me. You could find him."

"You've got family," I said. "You were kind of stuck here. Roy is different. You know that. What's all this about?"

He took a deep breath and lowered his voice again. He spoke directly to me, as though he wanted to exclude April. She sensed it and looked around the bar, pretending to ignore us, but I could tell she was listening.

"I protect myself," Walker said. "I keep my eyes and ears open, and I've got trip wires out, little signals that will let me know if someone is getting interested. Lately, a couple of them have gone off. There was a credit check when I didn't apply for credit. The outfit that ran it doesn't seem to exist. Someone has been investigating my properties, to see what I own and where it is. I don't like it. I get nervous. And now you show up, like some kind of honky ghost, talking about dead men. I don't like it at all."

"Something is happening," I said. "Some more bad news out of the republic. I don't know what it is, but I don't think it was finished when Toker got wasted." I told him how Toker died and what I'd found in April's bedroom.

He cursed.

"There's more," I said. I told him about the meeting with the lawyer. Then I told him about the letter from Toker.

He grew as pale as I'd ever seen him, a kind of dark gray, and looked nervously over his shoulder. "I don't like this at all," he said. "I feel like I'm sitting in a goddamn fish bowl here."

I suddenly felt the same way. "Look," I said, "we've got to trust each other. Like in the old days. I came here and I didn't know what you were up to. But now I think we have the same problem. And we have to talk about it, figure out how to make it go away. Can we get out of this fucking airport?"

He looked uncertain. He jerked his eyes toward the girl. "What about her?"

"She's in it too." But I knew what he was thinking. "The problem existed before she came along. It would still be here if she were gone. Besides, she's Toker's kid."

"Or somebody's," he said.

April had given up pretending. She was watching both of us carefully, warily. Walker turned to her. "Who did you say your father was? Your real father?"

"My aunt said he was a cowboy." Her lips were tight. "That's all I know."

Walker made a decision and stood abruptly. "We'll go to my place," he said. "It isn't in my name. I think it should be safe." He gave me an address and we started out. At the entrance to the lounge, he hung back and grabbed my arm, pulled me away from April and close to his lips.

"Let me give you something to think about," he hissed. "Who was the most famous cowboy of all time?"

As we walked toward the lot, I puzzled over his question. And then I saw what he meant and felt a chill in the hot Arizona night and missed a step.

He noticed. "Got it, huh?"

I nodded.

"Got what?" April asked.

"I'll tell you in the car."

We walked out of the airport in silence. I moved like a mechanical man, eyes scanning the passages ahead for congested points, knots of travelers to avoid, potential ambushes. But I had no thought for the process. One question preoccupied me. If Roy was her father, who was her mother?

Walker split off in the long-term lot and headed for the Cadillac. I noticed that we seemed to have the same sort of self-protective instincts and knew that was a problem, something an enemy could use to his advantage. I decided to try to be less predictable.

In the car, April was silent, waiting. I said nothing, and after a mile or so she cleared her throat. "Well?"

"Well, what?"

"What did Mr. Coleman tell you about me?"

"It's just a possibility," I said. "Your aunt told you your father was a cowboy."

"So?"

"The other man, the one who started the operation in Saigon, was Bill Rodgers. He was a Captain in the Military Police. He had a nickname too. We called him Roy. Roy Rodgers."

"Like the cowboy," she said.

"Yeah."

She said no more until we pulled up in front of Walker's house. She put her hand on my shoulder to hold me when I opened the car door. "Do you think Roy was my father?" she asked.

"I don't know."

"But if he is . . . ? Do you think he might be the one? You think my real father killed my . . . killed Dad?"

"I don't know that either."

Walker met us at the door. Behind him, a thin, pretty black woman, about thirty-five, looked anxious. He introduced her as his wife, Joyce. I shook hands and said her name. April tried to smile at her, but it was a total failure. Her lips didn't want to cooperate. Walker gave his wife a meaningful glance and she excused herself.

We went into the den. Walker asked if I wanted a drink. I asked him if he was still on scotch. He shook his head and rubbed his belly. "Not anymore," he said. "The doctor cut me off. Ulcers. But I keep it in the house."

I told him a Johnny Walker would be fine. April didn't want anything. She took a chair and looked impatient. Walker disappeared, came back with a glass of ice, a glass of milk, and a bottle of Black Label. He poured for me, then looked over his shoulder at the door and quickly tipped the bottle over his glass.

"Scotch and milk?" I asked him.

He smiled guiltily. "Gather ye rosebuds . . ."

I shrugged and sat. The scotch was smooth.

April broke the ice. "What makes you think this Roy Rodgers was my father? My real father?" she demanded.

"So you told her?"

"In for a penny," I said.

He sighed. "I don't know if he was or not. It might explain some things, but it would raise other questions."

"What questions?"

He wouldn't meet her eyes. He acted embarrassed. "About Toker," he said. "About why he adopted you."

I knew what he meant. That had bothered me ever since April first told her story. She looked her question at me.

"Toker was prejudiced," I told her. "He didn't like the Vietnamese."

"The gooks, you mean," she said.

"Yes."

She took her time to let it settle in, then began to tremble. "So all the time, when I was calling him Dad, he was looking at me and thinking . . ." Her cheeks were wet.

"You don't know what he was thinking," I said. "Nobody does. People change."

"That's why, then," she said softly.

Why he had never filed the papers, she meant. But I wasn't so sure.

"What was your mother's name?" I asked. She gave the answer I was afraid of.

"Phoung."

Miss Phoung, we'd called her. She had been Roy's woman, in a way. Sissy had found her and she lived with him until he bought it, then transferred her loyalty to Roy. For a while, I'd thought I was in the running. But I hadn't been. And now it was sinking in, slowly and painfully, that she was dead. The girl sitting opposite me was all that remained of her. April had sat on my deck and told me her mother was dead, killed in one of the war's smaller spasms of violence, and I'd shrugged it off. I felt a sense of shame for that. I shrugged it off, too.

Phoung had been a slight girl, very pretty, about twenty when I first met her. There was a trace of French in her ancestry, from an earlier generation of the war. When Roy left, she had inherited the house we used as our headquarters in Saigon. He had apparently left her with more than the house.

"Still doesn't mean anything," Walker said. "You know how it was then, man. Lots going on. People coming and going all the time. Only one it couldn't be, for sure, is me." He smiled at her.

April looked at me and began to blush.

"Not me," I said quietly. "I never slept with Miss Phoung."

Walker was still making a joke. "Don't be too sure," he said. "You did some powerful drinking in those days." Then he noticed April's blush. "Uh, oh."

I stood and walked away. There was a phone on a table under the window. I memorized the number automatically, then stared out at the night. "No," I told the room behind me. "I'd have remembered that. Miss Phoung was like . . . I mean, she was something I couldn't ever have. I had other women. Sometimes I brought them there, to the house. And Miss Phoung was a lady. She always treated . . . I mean, she knew how it was with me." I felt my train of thought slip completely away. It wasn't possible to explain what it had been like for me, not even to Walker. I had been too young then, and I was too old now. I blinked rapidly and rubbed my eyes.

Walker cleared his throat. "Woman's mother said it was the cowboy," he said. "She ought to know. And you sure ain't no cowboy. So, say it was Roy. What does that mean?"

I turned and walked back to them. April sat in her chair with her knees pressed closely together, her hands in her lap, her eyes cast down. I felt very tired. "I don't know. What does it mean?"

"Why would Roy kill Toker? Why would he try to kill his own daughter? It doesn't make any sense."

"Maybe he ran out of money." But even as I suggested it, I knew it was wrong. Roy would never run out of money. "Maybe he ran out of luck."

Walker was shaking his head. "He could have come to me. To you. To any of us. We were brothers."

I knew what he meant. There was no one alive I could trust the way I trusted the black man sipping a scotch and milk opposite me. And that would be true if I didn't see him for another sixteen years. We had the same mother, the war, and that made us brothers. I nodded and lifted my glass to him. I didn't mention Cain and Abel. It wouldn't have been appropriate. "Just don't forget the letter."

"Do you have it?"

"Of course." I tossed the damned thing on the table in front of his couch. He picked it up and read it aloud: "Squall Line was broken. The accounts were short. Take care of April. I don't know who else to trust and I can't say any more."

He looked at me. "It says he didn't know who to trust. I guess that means he didn't trust me."

"It doesn't sound like he was very sure of me, either."

"Okay. So something was coming down, and he didn't know where it was coming from. But if it was coming from Roy, he would have known, right?"

"He might have. We don't know. Let's take the things it says for sure." I glanced at April. "First, he was concerned about her. He wanted her taken care of. Second, it says the accounts were short. And third, it says Squall Line was broken. We'll take them in order. You want to start?"

Walker was also looking at the girl. "She is Miss Phoung's girl. I can maybe see it, a little. So we got to take care of her. Not just because Toker asked us to, but because she's part of the family. Right?"

"Right. What about the accounts?"

He looked troubled. "I just don't know what to think about that. Roy started the operation in 'sixty-six, I think. But it was small potatoes until Sissy joined him. That would have been about May of 'sixty-seven. Two months or so before I got roped in."

"Exactly how was that?"

"I was in supply. One of the enlisted men in the command got picked up for a little bit of nothing. He chambered a round and shoved his M16 in the belly of some shithead second lieutenant in a bar on Tu Do Street. Well, the louie shipped out the next day and I went down to the cop shop for a sergeant-to-sergeant talk, you know?"

I nodded.

"Anyway, we worked out a trade. I got my boy and the sergeant got a case of Martell cognac. I worked that kid to death. I thought I'd made a fairly decent soldier out of him. But he was born dumb, I guess. He put in for an intratheater transfer and wound up at Khe Sanh. I heard he got dusted. But the sergeant turned out to be Sissy. He knew I was reasonable from the booze I traded, and a week later he called me. We met at the VNAF club. There was a first lieutenant with him, a stocky white dude with brown hair and tiny little eyes."

"Roy."

He nodded. "It was pretty cute for a while, the three of us talking around it and nobody committing to anything. But finally Roy just came out with it. It was like he was making a business presentation, once he got started. When I saw what they were doing, and how it would go with my end, I was hooked. I told them I wanted to think it over, but I was already in and they could see it."

"How were the accounts handled then?"

"Same as when you came in. They were always handled the same. One of us kept the books. Roy, until he rotated out in November. Then Sissy. Of course, it didn't amount to much that early. Maybe twenty a month."

"And the records for each transaction were destroyed as soon as it closed out?"

"Sure. As soon as the funds cleared shore."

"Was there ever any question about the amounts?"

"Never. Anyone could see the books. Anytime. In fact, we were usually together when we posted, and we all agreed, every time, about when to destroy the pages."

"Where was this? At Miss Phoung's?"

"It wasn't her place then. Sissy didn't meet her until later, maybe June of 'sixty-eight. He bought the house from a colonel in the White Mice named Thieu. It was a payoff for ignoring the Thai connection."

"He bought low, sold high, and kept his eyes closed?"

Walker smiled. "Well, there was a little more to it."

April interrupted. "What are white mice?"

"The national police," Walker explained. "They wore spotless white uniforms. Very crisp, starched, clean. They'd kill anyone, do anything. Price negotiable."

"Like everything else," I said.

"That's right. Everything was negotiable. The generals were spending the weekends with their wives in Bangkok. The ARVN didn't leave camp without a payoff. The White Mice were for sale to anyone with cash, goods, or services. Air America was flying missions and drugs. Our government was making the soldiers pay for the war that was killing them. Everyone was for sale, even us." Walker's voice was bitter. "Everyone except Charlie," he added. "Maybe that's why Charlie won."

"Bullshit," I said. "Charlie won because he couldn't afford to lose. Everyone else had a cutout. The Americans went back to the land of the round-eyes. The Vietnamese politicians had their Swiss accounts and apartments in Paris. Everyone in the republic was playing a game, even Charlie. The only difference was that Charlie was playing for keeps."

"Not everyone," April said. "Not my mother. She died."

That silenced us. "You are so right," Walker admitted finally. "She was playing for keeps. We were all playing for keeps. It was like a secret that only Charlie knew, that the game was for keeps."

Miss Phoung was on my mind. She had been so alive for me, back then. Always with a smile, laughter like little silver bells. "How did she die?" I asked April.

"Someone shot her. My aunt never knew who did it. She thought it was the VC. But she told me to say it was the Americans when people asked, after the Communists came. That made it easier, a little. Saying the Americans killed my mother. But people still treated me like dirt. For a long time I hated everyone. I even hated my mother for giving me an American father. I cried a lot in those days."

April spoke softly. "But it turned out to be a good thing, having an American father. It made it easier to get on the boat. I could pretend that I was going to see him. That he would find me, somehow, and love me."

Sometimes you hate seeing how things end.

"When was she killed?" Walker asked.

"In 1971. In September."

"After I left," Walker said.

"I was gone too," I told him. "I mustered out at Oakland in July. But I didn't see her for the last six months. She disappeared a couple months after Roy took his discharge in-country. That was in November of 'seventy. Thanksgiving Day, I think."

"I never understood that," Walker said. "It was hard to get an in-country discharge. How did Roy swing it? And why?"

"He said it was to close down the Thai connection. I think he promoted some sort of job with Air America. Anyway, he got the discharge and then he disappeared. Miss Phoung disappeared too, shortly after that. I figured they were together, maybe out of the country. I got messages from him now and then, but the next time I actually saw him was in 'seventy-one. He was busy setting up the stateside end of the operation."

"That's when you became the candyman?"

"You got it. We were bouncing money from country to country like a ball around a racquetball court. We were both in and out of the country a lot in those days. Roy more than I because he still had some kind of special passport left over from Air America. There were accounts in the Caymans, Panama, Japan, Manila, and Switzerland at one time. We finally brought the last of it home through Mexico."

"And there was no question about the accounts then?" Walker asked. "The rest of us never knew. We just set up the transfer companies like he told us and funneled the commodities you delivered through them. It seemed like the totals were right, but we had no way of knowing."

"As far as I could tell, Roy never dropped a dime," I said. "The books were always open to me, and he explained everything he did, every move he made. He took two shares, for closing out the accounts, and the rest of us got one share apiece, just like we agreed in Saigon. Yours went into Peace-maker Investments and Sunpower Investment Company. Toker's went into his land and properties in L.A. Mine went into property in the Albuquerque area. Roy kept half of his in the El Paso area and washed the rest of it through Quintana Enterprises, a holding company that invested in land in northern New Mexico. He closed that down just before I made the final deliveries to you and Toker. And that was it. Of course, I don't know what happened after the final deliveries."

"Was that the last time you saw him?"

I nodded. "In late 'seventy-four. Just after I saw you. I met him in

Juarez, at the American Bar. We had a couple of drinks, and then I walked out.''

Walker picked up the bottle and poured two inches of scotch over his ice cubes. The liquid turned a milky amber. He passed the bottle to me and I gave myself a couple more inches just to keep him company. He looked troubled. "It doesn't make sense, then," he said. "Toker said the accounts were off. But where? And when?''

"There's only one place left," I said.

"Squall Line.''

I took a healthy drink. "Yeah. Squall Line.''

"What was Squall Line?'' April asked.

"You don't want to know," Walker told her. "It was just something we got roped into, a payoff. A government operation.''

"A payoff?'' She wasn't going to let it alone.

"Something we had to do to stay in business. It began in September 1968. I was working at a warehouse in Long Binh. It was hotter than hell that day. The humidity was up around ninety, and inside the warehouse you felt like you were swimming in your own sweat. We were loading a shipment for some of the exchanges up north. I had a couple of spec fours running fork lifts, putting pads on a truck for the airport, when a skinny Honky named Max Corvin showed up.

"I knew he was trouble the minute I saw him. He was in civvies, starched shirt, light blue blazer, tie, the whole nine yards. He even wore a hat, in that heat. And pure white! He was the whitest man I ever saw. Living in 'Nam, and he looked like the sun never touched him. The guy scared me even before he opened his mouth.

"I walked him into the warehouse where we could be out of sight, and he laid it on me. He knew everything we were doing, who was involved, how it worked, everything. I was sweating like a stuck pig after five minutes. And then he told me that we were going to slide. If we played ball.

"Sissy and I were the only guys in-country at that time. Roy had wrangled an assignment to the Southern Command, in Panama, ten months earlier. He was setting up receivers for the money. We were dragging about

70

sixty a month and living like kings. And this guy had us by the short hairs. We talked about everything. Wasting the dude, everything. But there was no telling how far up the line Corvin had taken the story, so we just had to sweat it out and wait for him to yank our chain. Man, those were some bad weeks!'' Walker shuddered at the memory.

April looked at me. "Where were you when this happened?"

"I was at Fort Benning. I didn't arrive in the republic until January of 'sixty-nine."

She turned back to Walker. "What did he want?"

"A piece of the action at first. Ten thousand a month. But later, he wanted errand boys. He said he was with Air America. Thinking back, I don't believe it, but I did then. He was spooky enough."

"What kind of errands?"

I cut in. The conversation was going where I didn't want her to follow. "We had to make some deliveries out of country," I told her. I turned to Walker. "This is not a good thing to talk about," I said. "Maybe there was a shortage out of Squall Line. The best way to find out is to ask Roy. The only other way is to find Corvin. And I don't know how to do that."

"There is a third way," he said.

"I don't want to go back there."

"Back where?" April asked.

"Where Sissy was killed," I said.

We sat in silence for a while. Eventually Walker said, "There is one thing we haven't talked about. What to do if it is Roy behind all this."

"We'll do what we have to do."

"And if it's Corvin? Or someone else?"

"Same-same," I said.

"I can't go with you."

I just looked at him. He wouldn't meet my eyes.

"There's Joyce," he said slowly. "She's pregnant. And I've got another kid, a boy. He's only ten." He swallowed and looked across the room, away from me. "I'll pay you, of course."

"I'll bill you," I told him, and stood to go.

When we were back in the car and on our way to the motel, April asked, "What did you mean, you'll do what you have to do?"

I studied the traffic for a long time before answering her. Finally, I said, "This has to be stopped. Even if Roy is behind it. But I don't think it is him."

"Why not?"

"Because there's no reason I can think of for the trouble to have started now. I mean, all this happened twenty years ago. That's a long time. Why would Roy have started hunting us now?" I glanced at her. "Did anything happen recently? Anything that might have changed the status quo?"

It was her turn to take a long pause. I assumed she was thinking, but when I looked at her I saw that she was crying again. "Just one thing," she said softly. "I told Dad that I wanted to find my real father."

There wasn't much to say to that. I just drove, trying to make sense of it and of what I'd learned about the girl. She was Phoung's child. That changed the way I thought about her, somehow. And then the possibility that she was Roy's changed it again. Some part of me didn't want to think about that, preferred not to know who was her father. But it had to be thought of. It seemed tied to what had happened in Los Angeles.

Suppose Roy was April's father, as now seemed likely. And suppose Toker knew how to get in touch with Roy, and told him she was looking for him. There was still no reason for Toker's death. Roy could have denied being the girl's father. There was no way she could prove it. And even if she could, so what? He couldn't be found unless he wanted to. And she would have no legal claim on him. There was no way she could hurt him. Embarrass him a bit, maybe, if he had a new wife who wouldn't like a Eurasian daughter crawling out of the woodwork. But that kind of wife was impossible to imagine, for Roy. Any kind of wife was impossible to imagine for Roy. A wife would imply a commitment to someone besides himself. More, it would imply a human need. Roy had no needs for anything that couldn't be bought.

So just the fact that April was looking for her father was no threat to Roy. He could be threatened only if his paternity were connected with something else, some other fact that suddenly made April, Toker, Johnny Walker, even me, a mortal threat to him.

Even then, the situation didn't have Roy's signature on it. He always used the minimum force necessary to achieve his ends. If there had been a threat, he would have disappeared, left it behind, or found a solution that required the minimum force. Something better than a Claymore or a grenade.

But I wondered how much of my thinking was accurate and how much was just a reluctance to believe that Roy could have suddenly begun killing his old friends.

I don't know why I parked in front of the motel instead of around the side, by the door to the room. I think it was because I was still nervous over finding that Walker and I had both decided to park in the long-term lot at the airport. My decision to be unpredictable. Whatever the reason, I did park in front, and I led April through the lobby and out into the courtyard by the pool. There, I froze.

The drapes covering our patio door were closed.

I distinctly remembered leaving them open, with the radio and all the lights on in the room. The lights were still on, but you couldn't see into the room.

I pulled April to me, squeezing her arm hard to get her attention, and whispered to her to go back to the car and wait for me. She looked frightened, nodded, and took off. I walked around the perimeter of the buildings at a normal pace, listening intently. As I passed our room, I heard nothing. I should have heard the radio. It had been turned off. If someone was waiting for us inside, the radio would have been turned off so our key could be heard in the lock. I walked to the end of the building, then cut back across the pool area, out through the lobby, and to the car. April looked up when I slid in beside her.

"What's wrong?"

"There's been somebody in the room."

"Roy?"

"I don't know who, or how many. Or if they're still there. Or if they left anything behind."

"Are we going to find out?"

"No."

"Why not?"

"You don't let an enemy pick the time and place."

"Then what are we going to do?"

I thought a minute. "Leave town," I said. I put the car in gear and drove as quickly as I could to the airport. I parked in the short-term lot and left the keys under the front seat, along with the automatic. I didn't like leaving the weapon.

We could still make the flight to Las Vegas I'd bought tickets for earlier. When the flight was announced, I called the number I'd memorized at Johnny Walker's house. He didn't sound sleepy when he picked up.

"Yes?"

"Me."

"What do you want?"

"Two things. We had visitors while we were at your place. They may have been waiting when we got back to the room. We didn't go in to find out."

He thought about that and then asked, "What else?"

"I'm leaving the car in the short-term lot." I gave him the license plate number. "It has to be returned to Los Angeles. The gun needs to be dumped. And someone has to watch the room, see who comes out."

"I told you I can't get involved."

"You can have this done. There's no danger. Just watch. See what happens. I'll take care of the rest of it."

After a moment, I heard a sigh. "Okay. Call the office number. I'll leave a message."

He hung up. Ten minutes later, we were in the air, climbing toward thirty thousand feet.

ALBUQUERQUE

I WAS GETTING SICK OF THE LAS VEGAS AIRPORT. Fortunately, we didn't have to stay long. There was a flight to Albuquerque in twenty minutes. We made it easily and flew out under two new names. I was Andrew Hofstat. She was Angela Romero.

April had said nothing on the flight to Las Vegas, and she didn't show any sign of saying more on the flight to Albuquerque. I told her that we were going to be okay. She said she wasn't worried. I knew that had to be a lie. I was worried.

"Then why the long silence?" I asked.

"All my things. The things you bought me," she said.

"We'll get more," I told her. "They were only clothes."

She said nothing for the rest of the trip. It was still hours before dawn when we arrived in Albuquerque and headed for the parking lot.

We made a cautious approach to the car. I checked the undercarriage and opened the hood before I let her approach it. There was no sign it had been disturbed. We drove straight out to Placitas and made the same cautious approach to the house. Again, there was no sign anyone had been by since we left.

I opened the door to the deck and left it open to air out the house. Then I threw together a breakfast of sorts and put April in bed. After I cleaned up the kitchen, I locked the place carefully and put myself to bed just as the sky was beginning to lighten. I fell asleep immediately and only woke once, when April crawled in beside me. She rolled her back toward me and went back to sleep. After half an hour, so did I.

The morning was half gone when I pulled myself from one of my stranger dreams. I was sharing a life raft on the open sea with a faceless child. The raft kept shrinking, or maybe it had a leak. I was afraid of drowning, and more afraid of drowning the child. I slipped into the water and woke in a sweat. April was still asleep. She slept like a kitten, limp and sprawled over the bed. A lot limper than I was, anyway.

I put on a pot of coffee and showered, then stepped outdoors for a tour around the land. There was nothing obvious to see in the parking area. I walked around the house, keeping my eyes on the ground. Someone else had taken the same tour within the past day or two. There were footprints leading from the parking area to the stairs that came down off the deck behind the house.

I ran quickly back to the front and into the bedroom. April smiled up at me and stretched. "Good morning," she said. I told her to get up and get dressed, and to do it quickly. Then I checked the door from the deck more closely than I had been able to in the dark the night before. It was scratched around the lock, but there was no indication that anyone had entered. The house was all right.

April padded into the kitchen while I was pouring coffee. I handed her a cup and surprised myself by telling her what I'd found. Normally I don't like to tell people a thing until I know what to tell them to do about it. But she was different. Or I was. I wasn't sure which.

She put her feet up on a free stool and asked, "No one's here now?"

"No. But we can't count on that for long."

"Maybe it was a prowler."

"We don't have many prowlers out here. I may be the only person on the road who bothers to lock his doors."

She nodded. "You think it was Roy," she said flatly.

"I don't know who it was. But it wasn't a friend."

"Are you scared?"

"Aren't you?" Her attitude didn't make sense.

"Not as long as you're here. You'll take care of me."

"If I can," I said grimly. "But we have to leave. The trouble followed us. Somehow."

She stared at me over her cup. "Wouldn't Roy know where you live? He wouldn't have had to follow us."

I liked that. She was thinking, maybe for the first time since she had walked back to her house and found the place torn apart. "He could have found out easily enough," I admitted.

"So where do we go now?"

"We find Roy. But first, we've got some errands to run."

"You're the errand boy," she said.

I grimaced. "Watch your tongue. And hit the shower before you make me mad."

"Are you going to watch again?"

That surprised me. She must have seen me in her room when I searched her luggage the day she arrived. "No," I told her. "I've got better things to do."

There was no way I could trust the phone, so my calls would have to wait. While April showered, I burned some of my records, packed up others, and erased a few computer files. I pulled a package from the safe under the house. I threw everything that might spoil in the refrigerator into a box and carried it to the car. I packed another suitcase, this time for an extended trip. By the time April was dressed, I was ready to go.

We locked the house and took off. I pulled into the driveway next to mine, the one with MURPHY on the mailbox. Jenny came to the door looking

surprised to see me, but she took the groceries with a smile when I told her I would be going out of town for a couple of weeks and didn't want them to spoil. I didn't have to ask the question I'd really stopped to ask. She asked me if my friends had gotten in touch with me.

"What friends?"

"They didn't leave names," she said. "They came by yesterday. Sort of short and dark."

"Mexican?" I asked.

She wasn't sure. They could have been, but the accents weren't right. She thought they might have been Filipino. They had asked how to find the house and had thanked her when she told them, then driven off down the road.

She looked at April a couple of times, but I didn't introduce them and she politely ignored her after that. I looked as puzzled as I could manage. "Well, they didn't leave a note," I said. "They'll probably get in touch with me later."

"They might come back," she said. "Can I tell them where you're going?"

I told her Los Angeles, for a short vacation. I drove off feeling sick. Filipinos.

Thirty minutes later, my records were in a safe-deposit box and we were checked into the Albuquerque Howard Johnson's. Camouflage. Blend in with the family types. We were Roy and Dale Evans. I shouldn't have done that, but I was getting sick of being run around the country. And anyway, I didn't plan on using the room for more than one night.

I made a couple of calls to Phoenix from a pay phone about a mile away. There was no answer at either Johnny Walker's number or at his Peacemaker Investments office.

I took April to the Coronado Mall, bought her two suitcases, then turned her loose in a department store with my credit card. She managed to fill the cases without much trouble, once she quit trying to duplicate the things we'd abandoned in Phoenix. She made a point of consulting me on her choice of brassieres and panties. It made me uncomfortable until I realized she was having some fun with me. Then I started voting for the skimpiest things on the rack, and she soon left me alone.

On the trip back to the motel, I pulled into a gas station and made another call to the same number that had gotten me the pistol in L.A. This time, my problem was more difficult. I had a couple of passports I could use if necessary. One of them, Harold Stephenson's, was rock solid. But April had no ID she could use, just in case the LAPD had a warrant out on her. It wasn't even clear that she was in the country legally. She needed a birth certificate, passport, driver's license, everything. Fortunately, my man regarded such difficulties as opportunities for negotiation. The price went up. The paper would be forthcoming. All I had to do was get him some recent photographs.

That was more of a problem than the negotiations had been. Taking a picture was serious business for April. We went back to the motel and spent an hour deciding which of her new clothes would look best. Then it was back to the mall for shoes that would match. I told her that her feet wouldn't be in the picture. It didn't matter.

I would have enjoyed the afternoon if Jenny hadn't said my two friends looked kind of like Filipinos. Well, I would have enjoyed it more. It wasn't so bad. By the time we found a restaurant, I was feeling almost boyish. Full of vim, vigor, youthful enthusiasm. Not myself, in other words.

Dinner was pleasant. We had a couple of steaks and a bottle of wine in Old Town. Parts of the restaurant were almost three hundred years old, according to the advertising on the menu. That impressed April. The food was good. The chile was hot. The wine was smooth. We talked about April's school. She wanted to go back as soon as possible, and I pretended that she might be able to. We didn't talk about Roy, or Toker's death, or the fact that I couldn't go home. The evening was—well, we stretched it out. We didn't want it to end.

After dinner, we drove out to the airport to use a pay phone, just in case. I called Johnny Walker. There was no answer. Just in case, I dialed Peacemaker Investments. There was no answer there either.

My mood was not so good when we returned to the motel. I was worried about Johnny Walker. April tried unsuccessfully to bring me out of it. Eventually she gave up. She sat on the bed and asked where we were going next. I told her El Paso. She said she didn't realize you needed a passport to go to Texas. I told her you didn't. She lay back against the pillows and stared at me until I gave in.

"Okay. The papers are insurance. In case we can't find Roy. Or in case something happens to me. You will be legitimate, as long as you don't attract too much attention."

"Nothing will happen!"

"Maybe Toker thought the same thing."

"He didn't have any warning!" She looked angry. "You know something is wrong. And you're . . . more careful."

"Not always. If I'd been careful, I'd never have gotten into this thing."

"What do you mean?"

"How I got involved. I was at China Beach, taking an in-country R&R, when I met Roy. I was there because I caught a piece of shrapnel in a firefight out of Chu Lai. I was stupid, rash. They gave me a medal for it and two weeks of R&R when I got out of the hospital."

"You got a medal?"

She had the same look on her face a lot of them got. There were only two looks, unless they'd been there. The one on April's face now and the older one, back when the faddish slogan was BABY KILLER. Both of them make me sick. You can't talk to either face. And even if you could, it wouldn't make any difference. You wouldn't feel any better, and they'd never understand. Ask Buddha what nirvana's like and he smiles. Ask a vet what 'Nam was like and he shrugs. You can't describe the important part of either thing. If you try, you'll just lie to people. And to yourself.

"Yeah, I got a medal. Last time I saw it was in a drawer in the kitchen, I think."

There I go, lying again. I know exactly where the damned thing is. I'll never forget where it is. But it's not like I'm proud, exactly. Half proud and half ashamed. Like a hick who buys a piece of the Golden Gate Bridge. Sure, he knows he got ripped off, but by God, he got a piece of the Golden Gate!

80

Biggest damned bridge in the world. He's a fool, but he's not a little two-bit fool. He bought a piece of the best, and if it was a rip-off, maybe that says more about the con man than it does about the poor schmuck who was dumb enough to believe in something.

April was waiting. I tried to remember where I was in the story. China Beach. One of the most beautiful beaches in the world.

"I was drinking bau-mi-baums. Beer 33. Vietnamese beer. Pretty good. And watching the surf. A lieutenant came along with a cooler, and we just sat there for a couple hours. After a while, we got to talking. He asked what I was doing, and I told him I was getting ready to go back to my unit. Just saying goodbye, sort of.

"He asked a lot of questions about what sort of unit I was with, what kind of action I had seen, that sort of thing. Anyway, the upshot of it was that he offered me a deal. He could get me a transfer to the Military Police in Saigon, under him. I knew there would be a payback, but I thought about it for a while, and then I said sure, why not."

"You were afraid to go back to your unit?"

"No."

"Then, why?"

I shrugged and lied. "I was in a hospital in the Saigon area. I got out on passes a bit, and I saw what was going on there, what the REMFs were up to. And I felt embarrassed, I guess. Like I was being played for a sucker."

"What are REMFs?"

"Rear Echelon Mother Fuckers."

She was frowning at me. "A sucker," she said. "You mean you thought you were fighting for the oil companies?"

That made me impatient. "The only people I ever met who believed Vietnam was sitting on a pool of oil," I told her, "were the peace freaks. The guys who went over there believed they were doing the right thing, helping people, saving the world, defending America, whatever. Even the officers I knew believed that."

"Then what do you mean, you felt like a sucker."

"When I got there, everything was simple," I said. "Charlie was the bad guy. He wore black pajamas and hid in the jungle and cut off the heads of old men and little babies just to make a point. We were the heroes. We wore jungle fatigues and had clearly defined free kill zones and protected the old men and babies, no matter what we had to do to them. But in Saigon, I met people who didn't believe anymore, who had quit saving the world and were trying to make a living in it. People who asked what difference the old men saw between us and Charlie.''

"You're saying there was no difference between us and them.''

"No. There was a big difference. Charlie never asked if he was doing the people any good. He knew the answer. And he was going to fight the evils of capitalism with the last drop of blood in the last child's veins.'' I looked at April sitting on the bed, and I felt very tired. "Look," I said, "all this is ancient history. It doesn't make a damn bit of difference to what's happening to you now. And it isn't going to help us find Roy. I wanted to tell you about how I got involved, but if you don't mind, I want to stop telling you now. I want to get some sleep.''

"So get in bed.''

"Are you going to stay in your own bed?''

"Of course,'' she said.

I showered quickly and turned the bathroom over to April. I called the desk for a seven-thirty wake up and crawled between my sheets. She came out wearing a towel.

I asked her why she hadn't bought any nightgowns. She said she didn't wear them. She always wore Toker's old T-shirts. They were softer. I told her I'd buy some T-shirts tomorrow. She said it wouldn't work, they had to be real old. She dropped the towel and slipped into her bed. I made a note to buy her some nightgowns and turned off the bedside lamp. I lay in the dark, trying not to think about Saigon. She was doing some thinking of her own.

"Tell me about the passport.''

"If anything goes wrong, really wrong, you take off. Get out of the state. Don't go back to California. Maybe Washington or Oregon. You can use the papers for identification for a while. You'll have some money. Get a job, start school under your new name. You'll have to let go of UCLA and the rest of it. But you'll be alive.''

"I don't have any money.''

"I'm going to leave you some.''

"You mean if you die.''

"If things don't go well.''

"But you're going to be careful?''

"Very careful.''

After that, we lay in silence for a very long time. I thought she'd gone to sleep, but then I heard her covers stirring and she slipped in beside me. She put her lips next to my ear and whispered, "Tell me about the passport.''

I cursed. "I just did.''

"No. You told me about the birth certificate and the other stuff. The passport isn't necessary for identification. Why did you get me a passport?'' She lay her head on my chest and waited.

I didn't answer her. Eventually, she said softly, "I can't help you if you won't tell me what's going on.''

"I'll tell you when it's time,'' I said. "But it isn't time yet.''

"Promise?''

I promised. We lay together, listening to the infrequent noises from the parking lot and to each other's soft breathing. My hand was on her back, high on her ribs, and I caressed it gently. I was getting sleepy. I asked if she'd answer a question. Her hair tickled a bit when she nodded.

"What happened? Yesterday, you were crying all the time. You were like a little girl. I had to do everything for you. And now you're more here. It's like you got over Toker, or quit grieving, or something.''

"Yesterday there was only me. I mean, all I had to fight for was my life, and that wasn't worth anything. Even Dad thought so, or he would have adopted me. But I'm not alone anymore. There's Johnny Walker in Phoenix and his wife. What was her name? Joyce? And there's you.''

"That brings up another question.''

She yawned. "What?''

"Why won't you stay in your own bed?''

"You're warmer."

"It isn't cold in here."

"I've been cold for the last week. What's the matter, don't you like sleeping with me?"

"It's a little hard on me."

April laughed softly. "It's more than a little hard on you," she said.

I smiled, but took her hand and pulled it away from me. "What about you?"

"It's hard on me, too."

"That's not what I meant."

"I know." She rolled away from me.

Just before I fell asleep, I said, "Don't ever say you're worthless, April. You don't know why Toker left you out of his will. I don't know. But I know it couldn't have been because you're worthless."

When the phone woke me the next morning, we were sleeping back to back, only our buttocks touching. I had to reach over April to get the phone. It was the desk with my wake-up call. I poked her and told her to get up. She grumbled, but climbed out and walked toward the bathroom. She was good to look at. I found myself smiling at my reflection in the mirror.

We had breakfast in the coffee shop and then came back to the room. I made a couple of calls and we checked out. It was good to get out from under the Roy and Dale aliases. Someday, my sense of humor was going to get me in trouble.

Our first stop was to pick up April's new identity. She waited in the car while I went in for the papers. When I came out and tossed a thin envelope on the seat, she scooped it up and opened it. A block later, she said, "What the hell is this? Who is Holly Carter?"

"You are. Get used to the name."

"But Holly? And Carter? Why didn't you let me pick who I wanted to be?"

"I didn't think it mattered. Next time, you can pick the name. I just picked one that sounded pretty."

"You think *Carter* is pretty!"

"Holly is pretty. And there are lots of Carters around. It's a good name."

She was quiet for a couple of blocks, then asked, "Did you ever know a Holly Carter?"

"I knew a girl named Holly once," I told her. "She was very beautiful."

April studied me carefully. "How well did you know her?"

"Fairly well." I kept my face expressionless. "She went to school with me, after the war."

"Did you sleep with her?"

She looked dangerous. I decided this wasn't a good time to tease her. "No," I said, "but I wanted to."

She smiled. "That's okay, then."

The next stop was the bank. I transferred twenty thousand to a joint account with Holly Carter and got April to sign the card on that account and on one of my safe-deposit boxes. I picked up another ten in hundreds. It made an awkward bundle. Finally, I got a letter of credit for fifty thousand, and we were done.

Next was my lawyer's office. I hadn't made an appointment, so we had to wait half an hour. Lewis came out to the reception area smiling. I knew that smile was going to cost me, but it couldn't be helped. I introduced April as Holly, then told her to wait for me.

It took about forty-five minutes to explain what I wanted, convince him that my reasons were really none of his business, and get some papers signed. When I stood to shake his hand again, April was covered in case things really fell apart. He followed me back out, as much to get another look at April as to say goodbye.

The final stop was a pay phone across town. I tried the numbers in Phoenix again. Walker's telephone had been disconnected. The smooth voice at Peacemaker Enterprises assured me not only that there was no one named Coleman at that number, but that he had never heard of anyone by that name. And there were no messages for anyone with an improbable name like Rainbow.

I tried not to let my concern show as I walked back to the car, but April picked up on it. She made a questioning face.

"Walker's skipped," I told her.

"He's gone?"

"Like his mama died a virgin. Like he never was."

"But why?"

"Something must have scared him. He had too many chips on the table, I guess. He's grabbed them and run."

She had nothing to say to that.

There are a number of fenced parking lots on Yale Boulevard, near the airport. The security isn't perfect, but it's better than at airport parking. I picked the lot farthest away and we took the shuttle to the airport. By one o'clock, we were Steve and Mary Davidson, waiting for our flight to El Paso.

EL PASO

ROM LIFT-OFF TO TOUCHDOWN, EL PASO IS JUST OVER forty minutes from Albuquerque. Less than an hour to cover two hundred and fifty miles of desert so forbidding that the Spaniards called parts of it the Jornada del Muerte, the Journey of Death. We landed early in the afternoon. It was not as hot as it had been in Phoenix, but the light had a sting it lacked there.

The first order of business was to establish a base of operations. I settled on the Executive Suites on the west side of town, about half a mile north of the freeway. I'd never stayed there before. It hadn't even existed the last time I was through. I registered us as Benjamin and Trudy Stepford. April didn't look like a Trudy, but I was running short of names.

It was still early in the afternoon, so I left April at the hotel, over her strong objections, and found a pay phone. I only had one link to Roy, the same number I'd written on the hotel stationery in Los Angeles before I entered Toker's house three days ago. It was a very old number. I had no confidence in it, but it was all I had. A woman answered the phone in Spanish. I fumbled my way through a conversation that led nowhere. She'd had the number for six years and she'd never heard of Señor Rodgers. It was about what I'd expected. I returned to the hotel.

April wasn't in the room. There was no note. I wandered around until I found her by the pool. She was wearing a black and orange bikini. More like a string bikini. Two teenage boys were performing on the diving board for her benefit. I bought a club soda and carried the glass over to her. The boys glared at me. "Nice threads, miss," I said. "Mind if I join you?"

She was still sulking about being left behind. She just shrugged. I sat and nursed my drink, watching the boys with friendly interest. They had been drinking and did their damnedest to splash me. I smiled at them. "Friends of yours?" I asked.

"They're okay," she said.

They must have been listening. The larger one took encouragement and walked over, followed by his buddy. "Hey, is this guy bothering you?" he asked. "Because if he is, we'll be happy to take care of him for you." He gave me a challenging look. "Real happy," he said.

I ignored him. "Your move, Trudy," I told her.

She smiled at the boy. "It's okay," she said. "He's my father."

"Oh." He looked abashed. "Sorry, sir," he told me. "We was just looking out for her."

"I could see that. Go play."

He glared again, but turned and left. His buddy tagged along behind, whispering to him. They swaggered around a bit to show me what they thought of me, then picked up their towels, tossed their beer cans in the pool, and left. I fished out the cans and dropped them in the trash.

April had closed her eyes and turned her face to the sun. I sat on the chaise by her feet and watched her. The bikini left nothing to my imagination. The top covered her breasts like two candy wrappers. She let her legs relax and they fell slightly apart. The orange triangle stretched over her mound from just above the hairline to a strip between her legs be-

88

fore it began to widen again over her cheeks and disappeared under her. A few stray tufts of hair peeked out the sides like shy children hiding behind a playground slide. Her legs flowed toward me. She had done her toenails bright red, or maybe it was a more delicate shade of pink strengthened by the sun.

She breathed deeply, as though she were asleep. She wasn't asleep, though. She was totally aware of me. She didn't want me to know it, but I did. The cloth over her nipples slid from side to side as she breathed. I didn't blame the boys for trying to chase me off. They must have felt some kind of awe when she walked out to the pool. It was their tough luck that I was too old to be chased away by the kind of silliness they had to offer.

I reached out and tugged on her big toe. She didn't pull it away from me. "Nice suit," I said. "Better than the one I got you in Phoenix."

"Are you enjoying the view?" she asked.

"The perspective is nice. Hillary must have felt like this the first time he saw Mount Everest. Or Cardeñas, the morning he discovered the Grand Canyon."

"You're obscene." She moved her legs together.

"Nuts. I'm in the presence of great beauty. There are no words to describe the view. It's a work of art. I'm speechless."

"You're full of shit." But her legs relaxed again. "You aren't looking at anything you haven't seen before."

"Some things, you see one and you've seen them all. Other things you can look at forever."

"So I'm a thing now, am I?"

"If the Mona Lisa is a thing. If the Venus de Milo is a thing. If the——"

"You're full of it," she broke in. "Do you suppose I could have my toe back?"

I released it and lightly tickled the arch of her foot. She sat up and faced me intently, one leg on either side of the chaise, her hands on her knees. Her eyes were dark brown under her black bangs, her cheeks slightly flushed.

"Why did you leave me here?" she asked. "Last night you promised I could help you."

"I promised I'd tell you about Squall Line if I had to. I didn't promise I'd let you help me find Roy."

"You have to. He's my father."

"Maybe." I meant maybe he was her father, but she took it the other way.

"If you don't let me help, I'll find him on my own," she said seriously.

"How?"

"Any way I can. If I have to, I'll put an ad in the paper."

"Right. That's how ducks locate hunters, by landing on the pond and watching for muzzle flashes."

"Then let me help you. I have to find him. I have to know if . . . if he's involved."

"We both have to know that," I told her quietly.

"So let me help." She wouldn't give it up.

"All right, you can help," I agreed, "but you have to do it my way. You're too young. You don't know how to protect yourself. You could get hurt. You have to let me protect you."

She put her right hand on my left shoulder and looked squarely into my eyes. "As long as you're just protecting me from the killer," she said. "Don't ever protect me from the truth. I've got to know it, all of it. You can see that, can't you?"

I could see it. I grimaced and said, "I hope it frees you."

"If it doesn't, nothing will."

I took her hand from my shoulder and set it back on her knee. "We'll get started in the morning."

"Why not now?"

"It's almost five. The places we need to go will be closing in a few minutes."

"Where do we need to go?"

I told her about the dead end at the phone number. "We're going to have to start in the past," I said, "and work our way forward."

"What about tonight? We can't just sit here."

"There is nothing to be done now. Tonight, we wait."

90

"I'll go crazy."

"No, you won't."

"Then you have to do something for me. Entertain me."

"How?"

She'd already figured that out. "We'll play a game. Truth or Consequences."

I knew of the game. I never played it, on principle. The consequences were always something I didn't want to do, and the truth was always something I didn't want to tell. "Grow up," I said.

"I am grown up. I'm twenty."

"You're twenty-one. Didn't you look at your driver's license?"

"I am? Twenty-one?" She sounded delighted.

"Go see," I told her. "And get dressed while you're up there. I'll meet you in the bar."

She stood and walked quickly toward the elevators. I watched her go, smiling. She was excited. If she'd been a couple of years younger, she would have run. I should have made her thirty-one. See how she liked that.

I ordered another glass of soda in the bar and passed some time looking at myself in the mirror, thinking about the day I turned twenty-one, the day before my flight out of Tan Son Nhut airport in Saigon. Only Toker and I had been left in-country. He was going to help me celebrate leaving. I hadn't told him it was my birthday.

We met at the Joy Blossom downtown. We did some business with the man who ran the place, a short thin man in his early fifties. Everyone called him Bob. He was an ex-captain in the ARVN, the Army of the Republic of Vietnam. He had a broad face, deeply lined, with high cheekbones, black eyes, thick black hair that he combed straight back, and one leg. He always smiled when he saw me and set a beer on the bar before I asked, and he always offered me my pick of the girls. I wasn't sure that he wasn't VC. Really, I hadn't given a damn. I respected him a bit, liked him a bit, and did a bit of business with him. On the other hand, I despised him, hated him, and did a bit of business with him. That was life in the republic.

I'd been in the Blossom all afternoon, listening to a Stones tape on the

Japanese stereo behind the bar and putting down some beer. My jeep was out front with one of the street kids watching it. There was a little trick: You take a grenade, wrap a rubber band tightly around the release lever, pull the pin, and drop it in one of the gas cans strapped to the back of a jeep. After a while, the gas destroys the rubber band and the grenade and gasoline do what God intended them to do. That's why I always hired a kid to watch the vehicle when I parked it downtown. That and the fact that the kids needed work.

Toker slid onto the stool next to me. "You drunk?" he asked.

"Better. I'm short."

He smiled. "How short are you?"

"I'm so short I could walk under a snake with my hat on." It was the thing to say when you were really short. It wasn't funny. It wasn't funny because the first time you heard it, you weren't short. The land of the round-eyes was three hundred and sixty-five days and a zillion miles away. And later, when you finally became a short-timer, you'd heard it so often that it wasn't a joke, more like a prayer. Give me one more day. One more day and I'm free. Sometimes the prayer worked and sometimes it didn't.

"You been here a long time," Toker said.

"Two and a half years."

He whistled.

We sat there, thinking about two and a half years. The walls were unpainted concrete, the bar was plywood, the windows were small and covered with chicken wire netting, and the lights were dim. A new girl was dancing naked on the bar, looking bored, staring out over our heads. She looked like a village girl, stocky, with broad feet, strong hands, chipped nail polish. Probably came to Saigon to escape the war. Maybe lost some family to us or them. Wanting a job and a little peace. Winnie was the name she used. I hadn't bothered to ask her story. I'd asked a lot of her sisters, in the past, and their stories didn't change much. She saw me watching her and danced over in front of me. She put a foot on either side of my beer and did a deep knee bend. I grabbed the beer just in time.

92

She showed me some teeth. "You want go back room, GI? Fuckee-suckee?"

I pushed a bill at her. "You too much woman for me," I told her. "You go dance."

She wiggled her twat in my face for a minute, trying to change my mind, then made the money disappear and danced her way back down the bar. When she was out of reach, she told me, "You fucking queer, joe. You number ten."

I laughed at her. "Come back here," I told her. I waved another dollar at her. "Tell me you love me."

She walked back and stared down at me. "You number one GI, joe. I love you too much." She snatched the paper and pranced away, giggling. "You number ten queer, joe!" she said.

Toker was shaking his head. "Fucking slopes. I don't know how you stood it. I'm out of here the first chance I get."

"You got what, another year?"

"Less. Nine months. Then I take off my little silver bar and say fuck you to the Army, the republic, anybody I want." He sucked on his bottle. "Start spending some of that sweet Green Roy's baby-sitting for me. Buy myself a piece of round-eyed tail. I don't care if she's black or white, long as her pussy's on straight."

I looked at him. "They're all on the same way," I told him. "Take a look." I gestured toward the girl on the bar.

"You know what I mean," he said. "American pussy. Nothing could be finer."

I shrugged. "What are you going to do, first thing?" he asked. "You're riding the Freedom Bird tomorrow."

"Take a break. Hook up with Roy."

He nodded. "Take good care of him. I don't want to have to come looking."

"You won't."

"I know it. If I was worried, you wouldn't be here."

I laughed at him. He was dreaming and we both knew it. "Just do your end," I told him. "Payday will come."

"Right on. I've got nine months to go. Just enough time to put baby to bed." He bought two more beers. "Here's to the Real World," he said.

I drank with him. To the Real World. But it was hard to imagine anything more real than life in the republic.

Toker left me in the Joy Blossom just before curfew. He took the keys to the jeep when I told him I was going to stick around, and promised to get it back to the motor pool. I thought about finding another bar, but I didn't have the spirit to move. My duffel bag was packed and waiting, back inside the green line, and I had already walked my papers through admin. All that was left was to show up at Tan Son Nhut before the plane left. And then see how the Real World had changed while I was gone.

Bob wandered over and leaned on the bar opposite me. "You not going back to base?" he asked.

"I'll stay here," I told him. "I'm celebrating tonight."

He nodded. "You leave tomorrow, go stateside?"

"That's a fact, jack."

"You spend your last night here, with me?"

"You mind?"

"I'm honored." He smiled at me. "You tell me something?" he asked. "Why you come here?"

"I was drafted," I told him.

He shook his head. "No. I mean, why you come here? Last day, maybe you excited to go home. Why you come here?"

He was watching me carefully. I thought about it. "I like it here," I said. "You have number one place. Number one beer. We do good business. I know you pretty good. You and me different," I told him, "but I know you."

"You long time Vietnam," he said.

"Long time."

"You like?"

I smiled at him. "Vietnam number one."

He looked over my shoulder. "Your friend don't like."

"He wants to go home."

"Maybe better he go."

"He can't."

Bob nodded. "Too bad."

"Yes. Too bad."

He noticed my bottle was empty and picked it up. "This number ten shit," he said. "You wait."

He ducked behind the bar and came up with a bottle of cognac, Martell's. "This number one shit," he said. "You drink, on Bob."

"We drink together, Bob," I said. I poured him one and we touched glasses.

"You tell me something," he said. "You army, right? You ever kill people?"

I nodded.

"Vietnamese people?"

I looked him in the face and nodded again, slowly. "You army too," I said. "You kill people? Vietnamese people?"

He met my gaze levelly. "Kill all kinds people. Even kill Chinese, one time. All kinds people. No difference." He took a sip of cognac. "Too bad," he said.

I agreed. "Too bad. Vietnam number one. Too bad."

We drank together. Later, he asked me, "You have girl, Rainbow? You have baby?"

I shook my head. No girl, no baby.

He shook his head. "Too bad. Two babies for me," he told me. "One boy, one girl. Boy go fight. Dead now. Girl okay though. She number one daughter. Take good care of me."

"You don't have wife?"

"One wife. Bomb get her, then boy go fight."

"American bomb, right?"

"Number ten bomb."

I nodded. "Too bad. Maybe things get better."

"Maybe." He was shaking his head, though. "I don't think things get better for me. Maybe they get better for my baby."

He looked around, noticing how late it was getting. "I go lock up now," he said. "You drink. Miss Winnie take good care of you, bring you more bottle." He paused, then offered his hand. "Good luck, you."

I shook with him. "Good luck, Bob. You take care of your baby."

"I try," he told me. "Always I try."

Winnie had pulled on some kind of shift. She came and sat beside me. I offered her some of the cognac, but she shook her head. "No drink," she said firmly. "Bad shit. You go sleep now?"

I nodded and picked up the bottle. She led me down a hallway behind the bar to a small, windowless room with a cot, a table, and a wall full of pictures cut from movie magazines. "This good room," she told me. "Number one. My room. No take GIs here. You sleep here?"

I smiled at her and set the bottle on her table.

"My father say you okay GI," she said. "You want me?"

"Yes."

She nodded matter-of-factly. "Good. Tonight we fuckee-suckee. Tomorrow you give me present. Maybe I don't call you no fucking queer."

She stepped out of her dress and started working on my pants. When she finished, we lay down and danced the old dance. She was strong. She held me tightly and ground her teeth at the end, and I was completely drained when we finished. She slept with her back to me on the narrow cot. The room was hot. No air moved, and we stuck together with our sweat. I didn't sleep until late, very late, and I woke up early. She made us a breakfast of rice and an egg with a little hot sauce. I gave her all the piasters I had left and caught a cab back to my quarters.

Given the time and place, it hadn't been such a bad twenty-first birthday. Remembering it had made me thirsty, though. I called the bartender over and asked if he stocked Martell's. He did, and I bought a snifter, for whatever the memory was worth.

April showed up as I was finishing it. She had showered and put on a

96

summer dress in some fabric that looked like silk. Pale yellow, with a pair of sandals that matched.

I gave her a low whistle and she grinned happily at me.

She marched up to the bar and ordered a beer in a loud voice. The bartender asked what she wanted, and she looked at me. "Bring her a Bohemia," I told him.

"What's Bohemia?" she asked me.

"Mexican beer."

He brought over a bottle, a frosted mug, and half a lime and set them in front of her. She didn't reach for them, but just stared at him. "Well?" she demanded.

He looked confused. "Well, what?"

"Aren't you going to check my ID?"

I laughed. He sighed.

"Okay. May I see your ID, miss?"

She dug the driver's license and passport out of her purse and handed them over. He looked at them carefully, checked the pictures against her face, and handed them back. "Thanks," he said, and walked away shaking his head.

April leaned over to me. "They must serve just anyone in here," she said. She wanted me to share her outrage. "The first time I've ever been legal, and he didn't ask for my ID!"

I watched in the mirror as she sampled her beer. Her first sip was hesitant; her second was enthusiastic. Looking at her, I was tempted to play her game. I had lived with her for four days, talked to her, even slept with her if you count sleeping. She had brought some heavy questions to my door. Who killed Toker? Who set the second explosive device in Toker's house, and why? Who was rooting around in Johnny Walker's business in Phoenix? What did Toker mean when he said that Squall Line was broken? Who had been waiting in our motel room that last night in Phoenix? And on, and on.

But the question that interested me the most, the one question I had no handle on at all, was why Toker had brought April home. He had despised the Vietnamese. As far as I knew, he had known Miss Phoung only peripherally. And yet her daughter had grown up in his house. He had been as good a father as he could to her, apparently. Why? There are always reasons for killing people. The reasons for caring for them could be more elusive.

April had finished half of her beer. I reached over, took the lime, squeezed it over her mug, dropped the rind in.

She looked dubious, but tried it and smacked her lips.

I grinned at her. "Let's go eat."

We carried our drinks into the restaurant and ordered the surf and turf special. It wasn't bad. After we'd eaten, I asked April when she was born.

"November 25, 1969," she recited.

"No, I mean your real birthdate," I said.

She looked at me suspiciously. "Why do you want to know?"

"Just tell me, damn it!"

But she saw an advantage and decided to take it. She looked at me impassively. "Truth or Consequences."

I sighed and said, "Let's go then." I was going to have to play, eventually, and might as well get it over with. April looked triumphant. I wondered what she had planned for me.

I ordered a snifter of Martell's and another Bohemia for April and paid the bill. We carried the drinks back to the room and sat on the balcony overlooking the city.

It was early evening, pleasantly cool after the day's heat. The city lights fell away from our location on the side of the mountain, down toward the black strip that marked the Rio Grande. On the other side, the lights were few and farther between. Juarez. It would be easy to get lost there.

The balcony was as wide as the room, but only about five feet deep. April leaned back in her chair and propped her feet on the wrought iron railing that fenced us away from a three-story drop to the parking lot. Her dress slid up to midthigh. There was no moon, but there was enough light from the room behind us for me to see her face. She looked excited.

"Me first," she said.

"I've already started," I told her, "but I think you better tell me the rules."

"Simple. We take turns asking questions. We can answer or not, but if we answer we have to tell the truth. If we don't answer, we have to take the consequences."

"Isn't this a little silly?"

She laughed. "Your first question. No, it's not silly. You swear to either tell the truth or take the consequences. So there's no reason to lie. And if you take the consequences, that tells me something too. My question." She looked at me. "What is Squall Line?"

"That's outside the game. I told you I'd tell you about it if the time came that I had to. Not otherwise."

"Then I'll rephrase it. Why does Squall Line have to be outside the game?"

"Squall Line was the code name of a government operation. A top secret operation. Knowing about it could get you in trouble. I wish I didn't know about it. My question. When and where were you born? I want the exact date and place."

"I don't know the place. A house outside Ho Chi Minh City, I think. It was on April third, 1971. Why?"

"That's your question. Because it means you were conceived in early July of 'seventy. I wanted to know when so I would know who was in-country."

"Who was?"

I shook my head. "That will be your next question. How did Toker find you?"

"I don't know. We were living in a kind of shed in the camp in Hong Kong. One evening a policeman and an immigration officer came. It was about dark, and we were eating. We had rice, I remember, and a little bit of fish, and I didn't get any of the fish because I was not part of the family, and also maybe because I was only a girl.

"When they came in, I was scared, and I went to the place where we

slept and tried to hide. They talked to Mr. Nguyen for a little while and then he yelled for me. He looked very angry. I didn't come right away because I was afraid, but the other kids pushed me out so that he wouldn't be mad at them. And also because they didn't like me because I wasn't a real Vietnamese and I was a burden on their family. Then Mr. Nguyen grabbed my arm and handed me to the policeman. He looked like he hated me.

"But the policeman didn't look mad at me, so I stopped crying after we left. They took me to an office. It was the first time I'd been inside the camp offices. A man came in, an American with a funny beard, and asked me some questions, and then they took me to a nice place. They gave me food. Fish and a sweet bun. I stayed with the American for a day, and I was in a different part of the camp for almost a week. Then Mr. Bow came and told me he was going to adopt me and take me to America where I could be an American too. I asked if he was a cowboy, and he looked surprised, but he said that he wasn't.''

She took a deep breath. "Now, who was there when I was conceived?''

Answering my question had been hard for her. I tried to put my hand on her shoulder, just to touch her, but she shrugged me away. She didn't want sympathy. She wanted an answer. "Who?'' she demanded.

"As best I can remember, we all were,'' I said. "Roy. He was a captain by then. Captain William Rodgers. He was getting short. And there was Sissy. Master Sergeant Juan Cisneros. He was the first man Roy took into our operation. He had been out of the country, in Manila, and had just rotated back in-country. He was killed later. Johnny Walker was Staff Sergeant John Coleman. He was about to ship out. He had just recruited Toker to take his place, to wind down the operation and close the books. Toker you know about.''

"And you.'' She looked at me accusingly.

"Yes. And me.''

"So any one of you could be my father?''

"I don't think so. I couldn't, for sure. I never made love with . . . with your mother. It couldn't have been Walker. You aren't dark enough. That leaves Roy, Sissy, and Toker. But Toker had only been around for a

100

couple of weeks. He didn't know Miss Phoung very well. He didn't know any of us very well yet, for that matter. I mean, as men. Of course, we were all in it together.''

"In the operation?''

"That, too. I meant in the war.''

"And this Sissy man?''

"That was Juan Cisneros. We called him Sissy. He was the first man Roy brought in. He was also the one who met your mother and introduced her to Roy. He was killed in 'seventy.''

"Killed how?''

"In Squall Line.'' I cleared my throat. "It's my turn. How did Toker treat you?''

"He was good to me.''

"I mean, did he treat you like a daughter? Or like a woman?''

She stared at me. I was a little embarrassed and didn't meet her eyes. "You want to know about sex? Did he ever try to have sex with me?''

"Yes. It's just that I don't understand his motives.'' I felt awkward talking about it and cleared my throat. "I told you that he didn't like the Vietnamese much when we were over there. So I guess my question is, what was his motive? Sex? Did he act like he felt guilty about the war? Was he using you to make up for something? Or did he treat you like you were really his daughter?''

She thought about it. "I always felt he treated me like a daughter,'' she said slowly. "He wasn't a very warm, touching kind of man. I thought about it sometimes when I was alone, after I got older, and I decided that if he had a real daughter, he wouldn't have treated her any differently. But of course he cut me out of his will. He wouldn't have done that to a real daughter. And then I found out that he had never really adopted me. I guess I can't answer your question. I don't know what his motive was.''

We sat in silence, thinking about Toker. Then April shook herself. "My turn,'' she said. "What was my mother like?''

That was hard to answer. Painful. I knew I wasn't going to like this game. "She was a pretty woman,'' I said. "She was about your age at that time. Shorter, though. Maybe five foot three. Slim. Long black hair, like yours. Her eyes were darker, and her cheekbones were very high. She had more slant to her eyes. Her hands and feet were long and narrow. She liked to wear Ao Dai's.''

"I don't mean that. Was she a prostitute?''

That came out of left field, but I could see where she might have gotten the idea. "No. Of course not. She was just a woman who made the best of a difficult situation. Her father was some kind of government official, but he died. Her mother died shortly before Sissy met her. I never knew she had a sister. They must have been pretty poor. Then Sissy fell in love with her. I guess it was love. Anyway, he talked her into living with him. He set her up in the house off Tu Do Street. That was back in 'sixty-eight, I think. Over a year before I met her. Roy was doing a tour in the Southern Command, Panama, at the time. Sissy and Walker were running the operation by themselves. All that happened before I came on the scene, so I can't tell you exactly how it was, but she wasn't a prostitute. She just had some hard decisions to make, and she made the best ones she could.''

"But how did she wind up with Roy?''

"Sissy finished a tour in March of 'sixty-nine and arranged a short tour in the Philippines. We had business there. After he left, Miss Phoung stayed on. It was her house. At least I think Sissy put it in her name before he left. The rest of the group, Roy and Walker at that time, kept meeting there. It had become a sort of headquarters. I don't know exactly how it happened, but Roy was living there with her when I was brought in. That was in May. And now it's my turn. Tell me about life with your aunt.''

She was slow to answer, and she spoke dreamily. "The first I remember, we were living in an apartment. It was near the fish market, I think. I remember how bad it smelled. I grew up there, in a little room on the third floor. We were together all the time. No one would play with me because I was half American. When I was old enough, I helped her. She had a shop, a little booth, really, on the street. She used to sell things. Cigarettes, batteries, newspapers, things like that. She taught me. I didn't go to school much because of the things the teachers said about me. But I learned to read and write and use the abacus. I could make change very well, and I was proud that she let me do it. I loved her a lot. It was very hard to leave her, to get on the boat. I cried for days.''

"Did she have money?" I asked.

"Yes. I never thought about where it came from, but I can see now that there was more than she got from her shop."

"Did she ever get letters from America?"

"Of course not! That would have been dangerous, especially with me there. She might have been killed. People disappeared all the time."

April turned to me and wiped her eyes. "My turn. Tell me about the first and last times you saw my mother."

I stared into the night, toward the darkness that was Juarez. "The first time was in June of 'sixty-nine. I'd just been transferred to the MPs. Roy took me to the house. I knew that I was going to have to start paying for the transfer, and I was nervous and excited. Roy introduced me to your mother, but I didn't pay much attention to her at the time. She left us alone, and he told me about the operation, about what I would do if I came in with him, about the others and where they were. Anyway, I just remember that Miss Phoung was wearing an Ao Dai and that she was pretty.

"The last time was in January of 'seventy-one. Roy had resigned his commission and taken a job in-country, with Air America, he said. But he was being very mysterious. I rarely saw him. Toker and I were running the operation by ourselves, winding it down while the people we dealt with slowly finished their tours and rotated stateside. One day I went by the house and Miss Phoung was there with Max and some workers. The place was almost empty. She had a few boxes left that they were loading on a truck. She wouldn't say where she was going. She just said goodbye and left. She was wearing an Ao Dai that time too, a white one."

"White is a special color in Vietnam," April said quietly. "Did you know that?"

"Yes. It's the color of mourning."

"Do you know who she was mourning?"

"No. She wore white almost all the time toward the end. Sissy was dead. Roy was gone. She was pregnant. Maybe she was mourning herself."

"You said this Max Corvin was with her, the last time you saw her. Why? Did she like him? Could he be my father instead of Roy?"

"No! Absolutely not! She hated him. He was . . . well, she blamed him for Sissy's death, I think. I don't know why he was there."

"But it was his men who were loading her things on the truck?"

"Yes." I didn't want to think about that.

"So she could have gone off with him?"

"I can't believe that."

"But she could have? Was she afraid? Did she act like he was forcing her to do something? To go with him?"

"No. It was more the other way around. He acted like he didn't want to be there. He glared at me."

"Did you talk to him?"

"I didn't say a word, April. I had nothing to say to the man. He used to be dangerous to us, but we'd pulled his teeth." I rubbed my face. It was getting late. "Last question," I said. "Just before Toker was killed, you wrote in your diary that you wanted to find your real father. Did you ever try?"

"No. I didn't know how. And Dad had told me not to. I had to respect his wishes."

"Did his attitude toward you change?"

"He seemed a little worried about something. I didn't think it was me, though."

I stood and stretched. "That's it," I said. "Bedtime."

"Not yet." She faced me. "I get my last question. When you said goodbye to my mother, did you kiss her?"

I blushed. Fortunately, it was too dark on the balcony for her to see. "No answer," I said. "The game is over."

"Not yet. Answer me or take the consequences."

There must have been some power in the game, because I was reluctant to lie to her. "The consequences, then."

She walked over and stood in front of me, staring up into my eyes. "Kiss me."

I tried for her cheek, but she wasn't having any of that. She turned her head and met my lips fully. She put her arms around me and pulled me tightly to her. Her breasts were soft against me, her mouth opened, and I folded my arms around her. Her back and her buttocks were soft under the thin dress. We stood like that for a long time, and I felt myself stiffening against her. I pulled away.

"The consequence was a kiss," I said. "A kiss is all you get. And stay in your own bed tonight."

"Sure," she said.

She was lying, of course. I stripped down to my shorts and crawled into bed. She headed for the bathroom. When she slipped in beside me, she was naked again. The lights were off. My back was to her. She propped herself up on her elbow and leaned over my ear. I felt her nipple rubbing against my shoulder blade. "One last time," she whispered. "Truth or Consequences."

"No."

She slipped her arm around me, put her hand on my chest, and then ran it down my belly. She wrapped it around my testicles and squeezed. "Yes," she said. "Truth or Consequences. One last time."

She had me. "What's the question?"

"My mother. You loved her, didn't you?"

I didn't answer, and she squeezed me again.

"Yes," I said tightly. "I loved her. In a way."

"But you aren't my father?"

"No."

"You never had sex with her?"

"No."

"But you wanted to?"

"Yes."

"Did she know you loved her?"

"Maybe. I didn't tell her, but she might have known."

"Why didn't you tell her?"

"I couldn't. I never had a chance with her and I knew it."

April squeezed her hand again, but it was gentler, more of a caress. "And that's the reason you don't touch me. Because you loved my mother."

"I touch you," I told her. "Just this afternoon, I grabbed your toe."

"That's no big thing."

"Maybe not to you. It's a good toe."

"Then it's because of me. You like Oriental girls, and I'm half American."

I rolled over onto her. She spread her legs to accommodate me and hooked her heels behind my knees. My secret was pressing into her belly. "Does it feel like I don't like you?" I asked.

"No," she said softly, and kissed me.

I returned the kiss with a passion I could barely control. "Then stop being silly," I whispered. I rolled back off her and said, "Now go to sleep."

A long time passed in the dark before our breathing calmed. Just before I drifted off, I heard her laugh quietly to herself. It sounded like the tinkling of silver bells.

It was early when I woke. I showered and dressed before shaking April. I told her I'd meet her in the restaurant and left. She smiled at me, but said nothing about last night, and when she came into the restaurant she was all business.

After breakfast, we drove down to the county records office. I made a list of all the properties I could remember Roy owning and all the names and corporations he'd been using. Nearly twenty years had passed, though, so it was a fairly short list. A woman named Felicia showed us how the land titles were filed, and we began working our way through the list.

The idea was to find the transfers of title. One of the properties was the Paseo Del Norte Office Complex. I had helped Roy buy it in 1972, using a middleman named Teletex Investments. At that time the price had been six hundred thousand, with a hundred down and an assumable note for five hundred. It was immediately traded to a New Mexico corporation named Quintana Holding Company. In 1973, Quintana traded it to Grimmuth Investments for a ranch near Tierra Amarilla.

Grimmuth operated the property until 1981, when it was sold to Pascuale Enterprises. In 1988, Pascuale sold to Prism Corporation, and three months ago Prism had sold to De Angelus Holding Company. The chain ended with De Angelus. They had paid $2.4 million and assumed what was left of the note. So, in nineteen years, Roy had turned a $100,000 down payment into over $1.75 million. He had gotten a decent income while he was waiting, and he probably still hadn't paid a dime in taxes. All more or less legally. That was Roy.

We followed the same routine for the other four properties I could remember. A couple of the names involved were familiar to me, but they were all suspect. Roy could be anyone he wanted, just by signing a couple of pieces of paper. I knew that better than anyone.

The work was tedious and slow. It was early afternoon by the time we finished. We broke for lunch, then returned to the hotel and dug out the phone book. Eight of the names we'd found were still listed.

I copied out their addresses and we went out to do some drive-bys. Most of the names were easy to eliminate. They were legitimate, going businesses. Large offices, receptionists, secretaries, managers. Not Roy's style at all. Only Prism Corporation looked promising. Its office was a post office box in the downtown area.

I drove to a pay phone and called the appropriate branch of the post office and asked to speak to the postmaster. I identified myself as an attorney, James Madison. You can get away with anything, given the present state of education. I could probably have been George Washington if I'd wanted.

When he answered, I told him I was trying to settle the estate of John Arbuthnot, who had owned stock in Prism. I needed to contact them about a stock repurchase, but the post office box was the only address I had and my letter had been returned. I asked if they were still using that box.

The postmaster excused himself and returned in a few minutes. The box had been closed, he told me. There was no forwarding address. I asked what name had been on the card when the box was rented. He sounded annoyed, but excused himself again. When he returned, he told me the card had been signed by the vice-president of Prism, Mr. Walter Johnson.

There were several Walter Johnsons listed. I called each number in turn and asked for Mr. Rodgers. There was no response at any of them, but at one the woman who answered spoke only Spanish. She said there was no Señor Rodgers there. Bingo.

By that time, it was late in the afternoon. We were both tired, and we called it a day. We headed back to the hotel and had dinner. April watched television for an hour or so, then she crawled into bed. We went to sleep without conversation.

The next morning I called the Texas State Corporation Commission with a list of all the corporations we hadn't eliminated the day before. Only one of the fourteen suspects on the list was currently in the telephone book, Prism Corporation. The others were either no longer in business or no longer looking for business.

The clerk at the corporation commission was only willing to look up three names for each call. Policy, she said. She seemed to feel that a polite citizen would make her job easier by asking his question through the mail. That would have given her four to six weeks to get the information I wanted instead of the three hours, five phone calls, and half a roll of Tums my curiosity wound up costing me.

Every corporation doing business has to have a registered agent for service of notices. In case somebody wants to sue, they know who to deliver the papers to. I got the name, address, and telephone number of the registered agent for each of those fourteen corporations. The agents all had different names and addresses, but eight of them had the same telephone number, the one answered by the Spanish-speaking lady who said Señor Rodgers *no vive aqui*. The problem was finding a way to get past her.

The direct approach is always nice, when it doesn't get you killed. I thought it might be a good idea at least to scout it out, so I ran April through a fast-food hamburger joint that made me wait ten minutes for service. It wasn't fast and it was only food in the FDA's rather loose definition of the term.

April ordered a cheeseburger, large fries, and a Coke. She dug into them while I picked at my burger, Tums, and coffee. As soon as she finished her fries, she started talking. She seemed to think the job was all but done. I told her to slow down a bit. Enthusiasm is a fine thing if you can sit back and watch, preferably with a drink in your hand, but it can be painful if you're expected to share it. "What's wrong?" she asked. "We've almost got him, haven't we?"

"What would you do next?" I asked.

"Call the number again. Make that woman put him on, or at least give him a message!"

I shook my head. "If he's involved, that'll just tell him we're in town, maybe let him set us up. And say he isn't. Roy is a lot spookier than Walker ever was. If he gets a third call on that line, he may just close it down. Hell, he may have closed it when he got the second call asking for Mr. Rodgers."

"What do you want to do, then?"

"Let's see if he has a back door. Let's try to find his phone. If that doesn't work, there'll be plenty of time to call again."

After we finished lunch, I hit the phone again. The fourth call netted a business in the neighborhood that had a reverse directory and didn't mind letting a fellow businessman take a peek at it. We drove over and I checked out the number. I wasn't surprised to find it was unlisted.

The next step was the telephone company. I called the business office, gave the operator Roy's number, and told her I was interested in getting information on some of their extended services. She was happy to oblige me.

"What services in particular, sir?"

"Well, you have call waiting, call forwarding, automatic messaging, and I've been thinking some about getting WATS service. Are those available in my area?"

"Of course. They're available to all our customers. Which one do you want?"

I asked her for details on them, then asked about prices. She talked for a while and I listened politely, then told her that it sounded like I already had the call waiting. I wasn't sure. My bills were higher than I thought they should be, and I hadn't been getting them regularly. She called up the records for the number and told me that I had only the basic service. I asked her to verify my billing address. She gave me a post office box number and I confirmed that it was correct.

"But why am I getting so much static on the line?" I asked her. "Really, I'm not sure that something like WATS would work when I can't hear people calling from across town as it is."

She was concerned and offered to have a service man check my line. "Of course," she told me, "if it turns out that the problem is your telephone equipment and not our line, we'll have to charge for the trip."

"That's fine. I don't care what it costs, as long as I can talk to people without all that damned hissing. Does your serviceman have the right address?"

"Of course he does."

"Verify it for me, will you?"

She repeated the service address. I told her that was the wrong address. She insisted it was right. I asked her what telephone number we were talking about. She read it back to me. I got mad at her. "Damn it," I said, "that isn't the number I gave you. I'm not even in that area!"

She apologized and asked for the right telephone number. I told her to forget it and hung up.

The billing address wouldn't be of much immediate use unless I wanted to stake it out and wait for a pickup. The service address could be checked out immediately, but I needed proper equipment.

We went over to the newspaper office and asked to see some back issues. I found what I wanted in the classified section of Sunday's paper. Three garage sales that included hunting rifles. I called the first number and asked the man who answered if they had been sold. He had one left. I asked about its condition and the price. When he told me, I thought that was a little steep and asked if he had anything else he wanted to get rid of. He didn't, but I struck gold on the next number. An hour later, I had an old Browning automatic and a box and a half of cartridges, and I felt more comfortable. Roy had been a friend a long time ago, but I wasn't sure he still was. And even friends can behave unpredictably when they have uninvited guests.

April was my next problem. I didn't want her along when I invaded Roy's turf. I took her to a coffee shop downtown and explained the next step.

"It will be like Los Angeles," I said. "You drop me off in front of the building. Twenty minutes later, you drive by again. I know you want to see him. If it's safe, I'll be standing by the entrance. You park and I'll take you up. If there's a problem, I'll be standing at the corner. Slow down for me. If I'm not at either of those places, come back in ten minutes. If I'm still not around, go back to the motel, pack, and get back to Albuquerque. Check into the Hilton downtown. If I don't show by noon, the day after tomorrow, go to my lawyer. You met him. He'll have some things to tell you. Listen to him. Then get out of town. Hide."

She listened seriously and nodded, and we took off. The phone we were interested in was on the third floor of an old office building in a slum near the International Bridge. The building was in the middle of a block of brick-faced offices and stores that dated from early in the century. The store next to it sold used clothes, *ropa usada.* April pulled the car up in front of it and stopped. I got out. So did she.

"What the hell are you doing?"

She ignored me. She headed for the entrance. I cut her off, grabbed her arm. "Get back in the car," I hissed. "You agreed to let me go in alone."

"No, I didn't. I just nodded that I understood you wanted to go in alone."

She twisted out of my hands and pushed through the door. I caught up with her on the stairs. "Please don't do this," I said.

"I'm going to see my father."

We stood there for a few minutes, breathing heavily, glaring at each other. Any kind of commotion would have attracted attention. There was no choice, so I gave in. "Okay," I said. "You can come. But you stay back. You follow me. If there's any trouble, you run. Do you agree?"

She nodded.

I shook her. "Nodding doesn't cut it anymore, sweetheart. Tell me you'll do what I said. If you don't, I'll carry you out of here!"

"I'll do it," she promised.

I stared at her angrily, then released her, and we continued our climb.

The third floor was not well lit. Dirty windows at either end of the hall showed an old linoleum floor that hadn't been swept recently. Four doors opened off the hall. Room 303 was on the left, halfway down. There was no sound on the floor. Faint voices filtered up the stairwell from the floor below. The paint on the door to 303 was peeling. I stood just to one side, listening and thinking. To knock or not to knock, that was the question.

After about ten minutes, April, behind me, began to move impatiently. I motioned sharply to her to be still. A little later, a telephone in the room rang once. There was no indication it had been answered, but it didn't ring again.

I began to get an idea of what lay inside and puckered my lips. Roy was about as cagey as they come. I reached for the knob and twisted it gently. Locked. It was an old lock, almost meaningless, but putting a new lock on a door in that neighborhood would practically beg for a break-in. I pulled my pocketknife and pushed it into the crack by the latch, levering the blade outward until I felt the tip bite into the tongue of the lock. The only sound was the muffled traffic outside and the hiss of my breath. April didn't seem to be breathing.

I stood in front of the door, exposed to anyone who wanted to put a round through it, and lifted on the knob and pulled it to the side at the same time I twisted the knife. I felt the tongue slide back and the door shifted slightly. I stepped quickly to the side and pulled the Browning, then pushed on the door with my knife hand. It swung open a few inches. There was no reaction.

I went through it fast and low, and dropped into a crouch, pushing the

112

door against the wall with my back and waving the pistol vaguely around the room. The door went all the way to the wall behind me. I looked around. I was alone. I stepped to the door and waved April in, then closed and locked it behind her. We stood side by side, looking around.

The room held only an old metal desk. No chair, no filing cabinets, no wastepaper basket. There was a telephone and a small machine the size of a VCR on the desk. There were three telephone lines leading into the machine. Two led to jacks on the wall. The third was connected to the telephone.

April looked at the setup without understanding. "What is it?" she whispered.

There was no need to whisper, but something made me do it anyway. "A call forwarder," I answered. "People call this number, and it automatically forwards the call somewhere else. Anywhere in the world. They don't know the call is being forwarded. Even the telephone company doesn't know."

She sagged. "He isn't here, then."

"I told you he was cagey."

"So what do we do now?"

"You search the desk. I'll look at the equipment."

She pulled out one drawer after another. There was nothing but dust in any of them. I looked at the machine. Without the instructions, I had to wing it, but one of the buttons was a three-way switch. The panel under it read PROGRAM—ANSWER—TEST. After trying to think of an alternative without success, I decided what the hell and flicked the switch to the test position. A number appeared on the digital display just above the switch. It was not the kind of number I wanted to see. It was a Juarez number. The telephone rang. I jumped and April let out a small scream. I flicked the switch back to the ANSWER position. The phone rang again, the machine blinked, and then nothing happened.

"Let's get out of here," I said.

April nodded vigorously.

We returned to the car and drove back to the coffee shop to use the pay phone. April was fighting an adrenaline high from the excitement of entering Roy's office, and at the same time she was disappointed that it had gotten us no closer to her father. She ordered coffee and sat at the counter, talking nonstop. I grabbed the yellow pages and ignored her as much as I could.

The likeliest man for the job I needed done was named Archuleta. He had a small listing under DETECTIVE AGENCIES. The office was about five blocks away. If he did business in this neighborhood, I figured he had to be hungry. I called to make sure he was in, then walked back to the counter and told April we were going.

Disappointment must have won the battle with excitement for domination of April's mood. She waited in the car while I went in. Archuleta's office building was almost identical to Roy's. It had the same dingy exterior, the same unswept floors, even the same worn gray vinyl flooring. The only real difference was the number of stairs. His office was on the second floor. The door had a frosted glass panel with B. ARCHULETA, INVESTIGATIONS stenciled on it. I had a feeling I'd seen the place before, only the name had been Spade. It wasn't a good feeling.

B. Archuleta was on the phone, speaking in the low, suggestive tone usually reserved for new lovers. He looked up and murmured, "Gotta go. See you later." He stood and offered his hand. "You the fellow who just called? Mr. John Smith?"

I nodded, shook, and said his name politely. He was a couple of inches shorter than I was and had maybe twenty pounds on me. He looked like he'd been in pretty good shape ten years ago. Now he looked soft. He smelled good, though. On the whole, my impression was very favorable. I wouldn't trust him with a nickel till payday, and the sun would die before he'd make a moral judgment. I cut the amount I was going to offer him in half.

He motioned to a chair. "Call me Ben," he said. "You have a very common name, Mr. Smith. Or should I call you John?"

"Call me anonymous." I laid a fifty on his desk.

"You're a nonamus." He said. He didn't reach for the bill, but it was on his mind. "So, what's your problem?"

114

"A man owes me money. I want to know where he is."

"He got a name?"

"A telephone number."

"You don't look like the kind of man who'd pay me to look up a number. So there's a catch, right?"

"It's a Juarez number. You have contacts over there?"

"Contacts is my stock in trade, compadre. And in exchange for this lonely little general on my desk, you expect what? An address?"

"I want a street address, directions, and a description of the layout. That's all." I smiled at him. "General Grant will get some company if you do the job. Maybe a Ben, Ben?" I could be just as cute as he could.

He pretended to think about the offer. He was wondering how much more I'd stand, how much I was hurting. "Make it two Franklins," he said, "and you got a deal."

"Double or nothing," I offered, "if you perform before ten in the morning."

"No problem, my friend." He reached for the bill. "Where do I collect?"

"I call at ten. Make me happy and I'll make you happy."

He shook his head. "Come by. Show me what I want to see and I'll tell you what you want to hear."

I nodded and left him fingering the bill. April was standing in the shade of the building when I got out there. She wiped her forehead when she saw me coming and met me at the car. It was like an oven inside.

"What was he like?" she asked.

"Cool. He was real cool." I described the man to her.

"You think he'll get the address?"

"He'll buy it. Probably for ten or twenty bucks."

"Then why pay him so much?"

"So he'll feel smarter than me."

She shook her head, then asked, "What's next?"

"A cold beer and a dip in the pool."

The car's air conditioner didn't make much headway against the West Texas sun. By the time we reached the hotel, April was more interested in cooling off than in chasing the cowboy.

There aren't many ways to kill time in a motel. The most popular was out, at least as far as I was concerned, and I didn't feel like sitting around a bar. That left the third.

We changed to our swimming suits and spent an hour or so in the hotel pool. April splashed me and I chased her around for a while. She laughed when I caught her, then splashed me again. The exercise reminded me that I had missed jogging for the last week. This was better than jogging, and I gave some thought to putting in a pool. It wouldn't have been the same without her, though, and I decided that, on the whole, running was probably better for me.

After dinner, she asked me what Roy was like. Before answering, I thought back to the first time I met him. I'd been sitting in the sand, drinking beer and watching the surf roll in across the South China Sea. The waves were good at China Beach. They had thousands of miles to build up steam. Some of the troops taking their in-country R&R had checked out boards from the Special Services hut and I was watching them try to catch waves. When I'd first come to China Beach, the scene had seemed unreal. Farm boys learning to surf under that blazing Asian sun, with barbed wire in the distance, M16s stacked on the beach, lifeguards with heavy machine guns, and artillery pounding away somewhere inland. But by the time I was ready to leave, it had seemed normal. The way the world was.

"It's backwards, isn't it?"

I had looked up and seen Roy standing over me. He was of average height, built like a grenade. Very stocky. Not fat. Muscular, explosive. He wore his light brown hair cropped close to his head and had the beginnings of a short Van Dyke beard, which he rubbed constantly. He had very pale skin, and the sun had worked on him. He looked like he would blister if he stayed out any longer.

"What do you mean?"

116

"The sun should set over the water. Here, it rises over the water and sets over the land. It isn't natural."

"California, right?"

"I spent some time," he said. "Mind if I sit?"

"Pull up a beer."

"Brought my own, thanks." He dropped down beside me, pushed the cooler in my direction, and said, "Feel free."

"Thanks." His were cold. I popped one and went back to studying the surfers' techniques. Most of them didn't have a technique. They just waited for the next wave and then paddled like hell. If they caught it, they rode it all the way in. If they could stand, they tried to balance on one foot. If they fell, they fell. Half of them couldn't swim. They didn't care. The water was safer than the land.

We watched them for hours, saying little, pushing the cooler back and forth. The sun dropped behind the palms and evening in Vietnam blessed the beach with a cool breeze, a purple interlude of peace while the Americans chowed down and Charlie boiled his rice. Then darkness fell and the firing intensified.

Eventually we got to talking about who we were and what we were doing there. I told him about my last fire fight, the iron I'd taken in my back as I crawled toward Sam with the dead medic's bag between my teeth, my stint in the hospital, the return trip I was due to take the next day.

"You're young for a sergeant," Roy commented.

"Rank comes fast in the boonies. When you're good at your job," I told him.

"And you're good?"

I stared over the sea. "Yeah. I'm good."

"You like it?"

I shrugged. "Maybe too much."

"Combat, you mean?"

"That's part of it."

Roy had been interviewing me for a job, though I didn't know it until the next morning, when he showed up at the enlisted men's quarters with his proposition.

I tried to give April a taste of those first impressions. Perhaps she understood, but I doubted it. I was describing a brief time-out from the war more than I was describing Roy. But they felt like the same thing.

"He was an officer?" April asked when I fell silent.

"He was still a lieutenant at that time."

"But he sat with you?"

"Roy didn't give a shit about rank. He had his own program over there, and the Army's distinction between enlisted and officers didn't have anything to do with it."

"He was shorter than you?"

"A couple of inches. He was built like a tank. And fast. He had very fast hands. He said he was a boxer when he was younger. Golden Gloves, I think."

"Do I look like him?" she wanted to know.

I looked her over. "No. Not at all."

That was all we said about him then. Later, she crawled into my bed and lay beside me without touching. It was companionable, like she just wanted to hear me better. She asked about Roy again, but the question was about her mother as much as about him.

"Did he love her?" she asked.

It would have been nice to say yes, he had loved her deeply, but I couldn't lie. "I don't know."

"Did he kiss her?"

"I never saw him kiss her. He touched her sometimes."

"How? Like this?" She touched me.

"No. Not intimately. He would put a hand on her back if they were close. I saw him hold her arm a couple times. Like that."

"Then he didn't love her." She said it with finality, as though the failure were proven.

"I don't know what happened when they were alone."

118

"He couldn't have been in love with her. When I'm in love, I want to touch all the time."

"There's a difference between loving and being in love. And you aren't Roy. You can't know what he felt or didn't feel."

"I know what I mean by love," she said. "He couldn't have been in love. What about my mother? Did she ever touch him? Did she try to kiss him?"

"No." I don't know why I added, "but there was a war on." It seemed to make sense when I said it.

April nodded, then turned on her side and butted her back against me. The light was off. We lay in the dark for a while, and then she asked, "What about you?"

"What about me?"

"Did you ever touch her?"

"She wasn't mine to touch," I said simply.

"How sad for her."

Just before I went to sleep, she asked, "What is the one thing you remember most about her?"

"Her laugh. When I made her laugh, she put her hand over her mouth and laughed sideways at me. And her laugh was like bells, like little silver bells."

"That's pretty," she said, "but no one laughs like bells."

I woke about three in the morning, not quite sure where I was or who I was with. Or how old I was. It was slow coming back to me. I lay cupped around April. Her bottom was pressed against my lap and my face nestled against the nape of her neck.

When I breathed, her hair came partway into my nose and mouth. It smelled sweet. My arms were around her, and she held my left hand clutched to her right breast. The nipple was full in my palm. I licked her neck, tasted her as I had wanted to taste her mother. She sighed. I told myself to go back to sleep. It took a long time, but I didn't mind. By the time sleep came, I wasn't sure who I was holding.

When I woke in the morning, she was gone. I showered and dressed, then went down to the restaurant. She wasn't there. I found her in the pool, doing laps. She blew water at me. "I thought you were going to sleep forever," she said.

"I felt like it. What's with the mermaid trip?"

"Exercise. I don't want to get fat."

"You're too skinny. Come on out of there. I'll buy you breakfast."

I'd finished a plate of huevos rancheros by the time she appeared. She ordered an omelette and I told her about the way I wanted to approach Roy.

"We need to get him over to this side of the river," I said. "Juarez is too dangerous. I don't want to go over there unless I have to. Or unless I know, absolutely know, that he isn't involved in Toker's death."

"How can you know? I mean absolutely."

"That's the problem. He's our only suspect, but this sort of thing, bombs, killings, just isn't his style. If Roy shorted those accounts, I don't think anyone would get upset at this late date. I wouldn't. I'm healthy. We all got healthy. So why the killing? But we have to know."

"Then what do we do?"

"First, find out from Archuleta where he is. Then we'll call the number, see if we can't lure him out of hiding. At least, we can ask some questions. If he is guilty, he may give himself away. If he isn't, he may have an idea who is."

April finished her omelette while she thought about that. "How can you get him over here?" she asked.

"There's only one person I ever saw him afraid of. We'll use his name."

It was after nine-thirty when we took off. April drove. She parked in front of Archuleta's building just at ten. I left her in the car again and walked in alone. The foyer was silent and hot. I walked up one flight and knocked on Archuleta's door. There was no answer. I had a bad feeling about that. I pushed on the door, and it swung open. Archuleta was waiting for me at his desk. His eyes were wide and staring. His tongue was pointing at me. His face was black. He didn't smell as good as he had yesterday.

The room was sweltering, but I was freezing. I ran to the window, tore

120

it open, and looked out. The car was at the curb below me. I grabbed the telephone from Archuleta's desk, tore the cord from the wall, and dropped the telephone out the window. April opened the car door and stepped out, looking up. I waved her away frantically. She stood for a moment, undecided, then stepped back in the car and pulled away from the curb.

I closed the window and turned back to the room. I was shivering. It had been a while since I'd been responsible for a man's death, and I wasn't as used to it as I once was. I stood still, breathed as deeply as I could, and tried to think.

There was a tissue box on his desk. I grabbed a handful and wiped off the window where I'd touched it. I also wiped off a spot on the desk that I wasn't sure I hadn't touched. I went back to the door and wiped the outer knob, just in case. Then I closed the door and turned around. If April remembered the old drill, I had about sixteen minutes before she returned.

The stink in the room came from Archuleta's pants. The black color in his face came from a guitar string wrapped around his neck. The flesh had swollen so that only the ends of the wire and the two dowels they were tied to were visible. They hung down behind him like pull strings on a talking doll.

I didn't have to search the body. Someone already had. Wallet, keys, change, an address book were scattered in and around the mess on the floor under his chair. I opened the address book. There was no Juarez address in it. There was an address and telephone number in a feminine hand, after the name "Rosalinda Garcia." I checked his wallet. "Garcia" wasn't the name on his driver's license. I tore the page from the book and searched the rest of the office as quickly as I could. If he had had an address for me, it was gone. I closed the door behind me when I left, wiped the knob once more just for the hell of it, stuffed the tissues in my pocket, and walked downstairs as calmly as I could.

April cruised slowly down the street just as I stepped from the building. I picked up the broken phone from the sidewalk and hopped in the car. She sped away. "Well?" she asked.

"Hit a store," I said. "I want a cigarette."

"No, you don't," she told me. "You haven't had one of those damned things for three days, and you don't want one now. Just tell me."

That surprised me. I didn't think it had been that long. But she was wrong; I wanted one bad.

"He was dead," I said. "Garroted. Strangled with a wire."

She nodded slowly, taking her time about adjusting to it. "Was there an address for Roy?"

She trusted me to check. I liked that. "No. Nothing. But maybe a chance." I told her about the address book and Rosalinda Garcia. We stopped at the first phone we passed and April made the call. I wanted to make it, but she argued that the woman would open up more for her than for a man, and she was right. When she returned to the car, she told me that the woman was both nervous and suspicious. Her husband was out of town and she was afraid of being found out. April didn't tell her that Archuleta was dead, but she got her to agree to see us.

The address belonged to a small ranch-style house on the east side. We went to the door together. Rosalinda met us in a house dress and led us to the den. She was a short, slender Spanish woman in her early thirties, very attractive and clearly upset. We sat on a couch opposite her. She licked her lips and spoke to April.

"You said you got my name from Ben?" she asked.

April held up the page from the address book. "From his book," she said. "Your friend is dead. He was killed."

The woman turned pale. "Dead?"

"Yes. Murdered."

"Who did it?" She looked at me. She was more frightened than ever.

"We don't know. Mr. Smith found him this morning." April nodded at me when she said the name.

"Was he shot? How did you find me? Will the police come?"

I took over. "He was garroted. Choked to death by a wire around his neck. I found your name in his address book. And the police won't come unless I send them the page from his book with your name on it."

122

"They mustn't come! My husband——" She covered her mouth and looked back at April, as though afraid she had given something away.

"He knows about your husband," April told her.

"But you promised."

"I lied. I had to."

"My husband will kill me," she told me.

I took the page from April and waved it. "This is the only connection between you and Archuleta," I said. "Tell me what he learned and you can have it."

"Learned about what?" Her eyes were glued to the paper.

"He was going to get an address for me. In Mexico."

The woman was shaking her head. "I don't know," she said.

"Ben was here last night," I guessed.

She nodded.

"You made love. In your husband's bed."

She blushed and looked away from me.

"Did he spend the night?"

She nodded again.

"So he had already been across the river. What did he tell you?"

"He was scared. He said he didn't know what he had got into. He said he was going to get more money."

"That's not good enough," I told her. "I need an address."

"But he didn't have one. He just had another name. I can't tell you an address if he didn't get one! Please, you have to give me the paper!"

"What was the name?"

"Las Colonias del Sur. That's all he said."

"Do you know who he talked to?"

"Yes. A friend of his at the telephone company there. Juan Ortega. I've met him."

I stood up and motioned April to follow me. Rosalinda trailed along behind us. I stopped at the door and told her, "Call Ortega. Get the address of this Colonias place from him. I'll call you later. If you get it, I'll mail you the paper. If you don't, the police will get the paper."

She put her hand on my arm. "Please," she said, "you don't know my husband. He'll kill me. I'll do anything, but I have to have the paper. Anything. You understand?"

"Do what I asked you." I walked to the car.

April started to follow, but the woman grabbed her arm. I couldn't hear what she said, but I could see the desperation on her face. April listened silently, then walked over and climbed into the passenger seat. "Give me it," she said.

"You're going to give it to her?"

"Yes." The woman was standing in her doorway, her hands hanging at her sides. She looked hopeless. I handed the paper to April.

"Try to get her to find that address," I said.

The woman hugged her. She was crying.

We drove in silence for a while. Then April said, "That was cruel."

"I didn't get her involved with Archuleta. I didn't kill him. But I need that address."

"Maybe she'll get it."

"Maybe." I didn't have much hope. Of course, I still knew where Rosalinda lived and I could go back if necessary. Alone.

We returned to the hotel. I felt as though death were dogging my heels, and I still didn't know where it was coming from. It might be Roy. But suppose I eliminated Roy somehow and it kept on coming? He had been an ally once, a long time ago. He might be again. I had to see him, and there were only two approaches left. One was in Juarez, and I wasn't going to go there if I could help it. That left the telephone. It was eleven-thirty.

I picked up the receiver and dialed the Juarez number directly. *"Señor Rodgers, por favor."*

"No esta aqui."

"One hour. *Una hora,*" I told her. "Tell him that Max Corvin has his daughter. She will die if he doesn't answer when I call back. One hour." I hung up.

April sat staring at me. "What was that about?" she asked.

124

"Max was the only man who ever frightened Roy," I told her. "Maybe he'll answer the god-damned phone for him."

"Why did you mention me?"

"If he knows about you, he might want to protect you. And if he doesn't, he might be curious. We'll find out when I call back."

"You talked about killing me."

"Somebody already tried once, with that booby trap," I told her. "We've got to find out who."

"But what made you think of this Max?"

"Toker said Squall Line was broken. Max created Squall Line. That's all I could think of. If it isn't Roy doing all this, it has to be connected with Squall Line."

"What was Squall Line?"

"Later."

We waited. It was quiet in the room. There was a knock on the door at noon. The maid wanted to make the bed and clean up. I told her to come back in an hour, and we waited some more.

At twelve-thirty, just as I was reaching for the phone, it rang. The sound scared the hell out of me. April flinched.

I picked up the handset and said, "Yes?"

"What the hell do you think you're doing, Porter?"

It was like Roy to get the jump on me. "Looking up old friends," I told him. "How are you doing, Roy?"

"Can it. What's this bullshit about a daughter?"

"Toker's daughter. Your daughter. Miss Phoung's daughter."

The line was silent. Eventually he said softly, "I know nothing of this. Tell me."

"Miss Phoung was pregnant when you left. Her daughter was born April 3, 1971. She was raised by her aunt and put on a boat for Hong Kong in 1981. Toker found her there and brought her to the states. He told her he had adopted her, but he never completed the paperwork. And he cut her out of his will completely."

"His will? He's dead?"

"He was blown away eight days ago. Somebody planted a Claymore in his office. There was another trap set for the girl, a grenade. Someone has been after Johnny Walker in Phoenix. My house was searched. And this morning a man was killed here in El Paso, a detective I paid to get your address."

He took a minute to digest that. "What's going on, Rainbow?" he asked.

"You tell me."

"I'll tell you one thing. The kid isn't mine. I'd tell you if she were, and I'm telling you she isn't. As for the rest, I don't know. My first hint of anything wrong was the calls. I've never used the Rodgers name on this line. Was that you?"

"Yes." I didn't like the way this conversation was going. If Roy wasn't involved, who was doing the killing? "I have to talk to you. Toker left a message."

"What was it?"

I told him. He repeated part of it, but not the part I expected. "The accounts were off? He said the accounts were off?"

"That's what he said. Are you responsible for any of this?"

"I didn't juggle the books, Rainbow." His voice was dry. "But I'll give you something to think about, old buddy. I know where you are. And you're still there." He hung up. I stared at the receiver for a moment before replacing it.

"What?" April asked.

"Pack," I told her.

"Are we going to Juarez?"

"Not if I can help it."

LUZON

E WERE AT THE AIRPORT IN AN HOUR. THE FIRST flight south was to Mexico City. I bought two tickets under the Carter and Stephenson names. Using those names made me nervous. Roy had found us when we used them, and he would be able to follow that trail. If he was the one stalking us, we would have to hope he lacked the resources to follow us outside the country. But we really had no choice. They were the names on our passports, and we didn't have time to pick up new identities. All I could do was check out the other passengers and hope I could spot a tail later. It seemed pointless, given the last-minute purchase, but I looked them over anyway. They all seemed innocent enough. Families and businessmen.

Customs took about forty minutes in Mexico City, and then I found a taxi and told the driver to find us a hotel with a pool, somewhere out of the smog, no gringos if he could manage it. He got enthusiastic when I showed him a twenty. We wound up at a little place just outside the city proper, very nice, no gringos, guaranteed. The lobby was tiled, open to the pool and cabana area, with hanging plants and bright colors. Very clean. No Mariachi music. I argued with the desk clerk long enough to establish that I wouldn't pay gringo prices and then checked in. A boy with a quick smile and a ready hand carried our luggage to the room. April and I wandered out to the pool bar and took a table. She ordered two Bohemias and I began to relax for the first time since Archuleta stuck his tongue out at me.

As advertised, we seemed to be the only gringos in the place. The speakers were spreading a Brazilian rhythm, but softly. Judging by the crowd around us, the clientele was mostly Mexican businessmen with their secretaries, doing business by the bar and poolside, and tourists from South America. There was also a smattering of Europeans—Spanish and French, mostly, and one young Swedish couple. Honeymooners, perhaps.

April sipped at her beer and looked around curiously. The bright colors, the palms in large clay pots, the brilliant red and yellow flowers seemed to please her. She smiled at me and sat back. Some of the stiffness that had been in her back and neck since Roy preempted my call seemed to flow away and her eyes softened.

"This is nice," she said.

"Yes. Nice."

"It's like none of the other stuff ever happened. Like my dad . . . Toker, I mean . . . is still alive. . . ."

"It happened. All of it. And it's still happening."

"But why?"

I shook my head. "If we knew that, we'd know who was doing it. And if we knew who, I could stop him."

"Roy . . . ?"

"What reason? Even if he's your father, why should he care if you found him? Why would he kill Toker? And why was your house searched?" I closed my eyes and listened to the murmuring of the different languages in the background as I spoke.

128

"Something must have been taken from your house. Unless the killer was looking for the message that Pearson gave me. Roy might have cared about that message. But how could he have known it existed? Toker wasn't questioned or tortured. The killer just wanted him dead. That must have been the most important thing. His death. Shut him up about something. And then, later, the killer must have realized there was something worth going back to the house for. So he went back, and found it or didn't find it, and decided to take you out too, if he could. But Roy? It isn't like him. He had a violent streak. Okay. I once saw him beat a man to death, a Vietnamese who pulled a knife when we caught him in one of the warehouses. But he did it with his fists, when he was angry. He would use whatever weapon was at hand if he had to kill someone. His hands or a gun or a knife. But if Roy had time to think, he'd work it out so his enemies were helpless. He'd break them, or get them transferred out of the way, or get something on them.

"He was cold and devious and never made a move unless he had three good reasons. You only saw one of the reasons at first, figured out another later, and never knew about the third. He'd be violent in a violent situation, but he'd arrange things so they never had a chance to get violent if he could. And if he was your father, he had twenty years to arrange things to his liking."

April shuddered. "I don't know what my mother saw in him."

"He was a good man to have on your side. Especially in a place like Saigon. Don't forget, fifty thousand men never came home from that war. We did. And we came home rich, thanks to Roy. I think your mother must have had something to thank him for, too."

"But he must be hiding something! Why wouldn't he talk to us? To me? Why did he just hang up?"

"Of course he's hiding something," I told her. "Roy hides everything. The question is whether he's hiding two murders."

She stared at her glass, spinning it on the table in the puddle of water that had condensed on it and rolled down the sides. "How can we find out?" she asked.

"There's only one way now," I said. "We have to go to Manila."

"The Philippines?" She swallowed and looked at me gravely. "Does that mean it's time?"

I nodded. "I'll tell you about it tonight. Let's take the rest of the afternoon off. For a change, nobody's trying to kill us. Let's enjoy it."

We found our room on the second floor, overlooking the pool area, changed to swimsuits, and returned to the pool. The bikini I had thought was skimpy in El Paso seemed modest in Mexico City. Many of the touristas were wearing little more than ribbons. They looked at home in the sun, surrounded by flowers, and except for her pale skin, April was at home among them. She went straight to the deep end of the pool and jumped in. I followed her and began swimming laps. The lack of exercise was getting to me. I worked hard for an hour, then climbed out and rewarded myself with another beer. There was a lot to look at. I devoted myself to the study of comparative anatomy and let the immediate problem go its own way.

April was in a good mood when she finished swimming and sunbathing later that afternoon. I decided it was time to talk about her future. "Holly," I said.

She looked startled. "What?"

"Do you like the name?"

"It's okay. Why?"

"It's yours from now on. You can't be April anymore, you know that."

"I know." She sounded subdued.

"April was in the country illegally. At least, she couldn't prove she was legal. No birth certificate. No adoption papers filed. The cops will figure that out eventually. They'll pass the word to immigration."

"I know."

"And you don't have a prayer of breaking Toker's will."

She didn't say anything. "What do you want to do with the rest of your life?" I asked.

"Finish school." She thought awhile. "Get a job, I suppose. Find a life. Can I stay in America if I'm Holly?"

130

"I don't see why not. The ID will pass. But what would you like to do if you could do anything?"

Another long pause. Then, "My aunt used to talk about her grandfather. Her mother's father. He was French. The French ruled Vietnam for a long time, longer than the Americans were there. She spoke French, too. I didn't tell you that. Anyway, I picked French for my foreign language in high school. I'd kind of like to go to France someday. If I ever have enough money."

I took a deep breath. "You know I don't have a wife," I said.

She jerked around toward me and sat up straight. "So?" She was watching me intently. I realized I hadn't started well.

"I don't have any children, either," I added.

"So?"

"And I have plenty of money. More than enough for two people. So, if you want, and if everything turns out right, you could go to France. Maybe study there. If you're interested. Are you?"

"Yes!" She was grinning. "Yes yes yes!"

I smiled at her. "Good. That's settled then."

"When could we leave?"

She wasn't understanding me. "I suppose I could take you, get you set up," I said. "And I could visit. . . ."

"But you wouldn't stay with me? I don't know if I'd want to go if you didn't come."

"Of course you would. There are plenty of men in France. Frenchmen. Your own age."

She turned away from me and watched the people on the patio. "Look around," she said. "What do you see?"

"Men. Women. People."

"How many of the men are your age? How many of the women they're with are my age? Or younger?"

Her point was obvious. And when I looked at her, my own body told me it wasn't unthinkable, had already been thought of on one level or another. "We'll talk about it later," I told her.

"Talk about it now!"

"Later. It's time to get ready for dinner." I stood and walked away. I was almost dressed when she came into the room. She took her time getting ready. As she walked around the room, she seemed to be posing, showing off her body, trying to provoke a response. I waited patiently and smiled a lot.

It was almost seven by the time we found the restaurant, still a little early for dinner in Mexico. We ordered prawns sautéed in butter and garlic, with rice, tomatoes, and peppers. It was the best I'd eaten in a week. I decided to come back if circumstances permitted.

We made a leisurely meal of it. April avoided talking about France. Instead, she chatted about UCLA and the men she'd known there. Her point seemed to be that they'd all been older than her. And the older, the better. I listened politely.

After dinner we sat on the veranda. I ordered a snifter of Martell's, and April had one with me. The moon was full and the air was full of the scent of flowers. There were lamps hanging from the trees, and a quartet playing Latin music. The other guests danced and laughed quietly. April coaxed me into dancing with her, and I joined the other middle-aged men holding younger women. She felt good in my arms and we moved well together. I forgot, for a couple of hours, that she was fresh from her teens, the daughter of an old friend. I forgot so thoroughly that I kissed her once, but only on the cheek.

Later, after I had made my customary suggestion that she stay in her own bed and she had made her customary promise to do so before slipping in beside me, she tried to repeat the kiss.

"Not now," I told her. "Now we talk about Squall Line."

That was about the only thing that could have stopped her. She sat up and faced me with her legs crossed and her hands on her knees. She wasn't trying to excite me. She was completely focused. "Tell me," she said.

So I told her.

We had been paying Corvin off regularly. Ten thousand a month for sixteen months. And each month we had set an equal amount aside for the

132

final bite we were sure was coming. But the money hadn't been necessary. When Corvin made his final demand, he wanted services, not cash.

He showed up at the house one evening when we were all there, Johnny Walker, Roy, and I. That was in February of 'seventy. Sissy was out of the country, arranging some things in Manila. He wasn't due back until the next month. We had finished dinner and were talking about the operation when someone began pounding on the door.

The sound galvanized us. We were always tense when we worked on the books, just because of what was going on. Roy pulled his automatic, chambered a round, and held it under the table. I moved out of sight and found my own weapon, a bayonet, in case the situation could be handled quietly. Walker grabbed the ledger and dropped it behind him, then kept his hands above the table, trying to look harmless. Miss Phoung answered the door. When she returned, Corvin was following. He looked as he always did, like a snake trying to smile.

When he saw him, Walker cursed. I came into the room behind Corvin and let him see me and the bayonet. He didn't look either surprised or alarmed. Roy just stared at him.

"You fellows nervous about something?" Corvin asked.

"You're going to get yourself killed someday, Max," Roy told him quietly.

"I've got insurance," Corvin said.

"Wouldn't do you any good," I said.

Corvin smiled thinly and pulled up a chair. He looked like an accountant that night. Thinning hair cut close to the skull, pale blue eyes, civilian clothes that looked out of place, an emotionless expression. "You know, you boys never seem happy to see me," he said.

"Why are we seeing you?" Roy asked. "You've already had your payday this month."

"Well, I was thinking about our little situation here," he answered, "and I thought that you boys might like to see the last of me." He smiled innocently.

We all looked at each other, wondering if this was it. "Leave us," Roy told Miss Phoung. She disappeared and he turned back to Corvin. "What were you thinking, exactly?"

"So you're interested?"

Roy nodded. "If the price is right. And if you can make some guarantees."

"Like what?"

"Like no more bites later. Like no hassles from the agency."

"That's a can do."

"How? And how much?"

"No cash. You might even make a bit on the deal, if you're smart. And the guarantee is good. We need a service. Some deliveries. They have to be done very quietly. You arrange them for us and we'll leave you alone. We'll have to. It's a service we won't want talked about later."

It sounded almost too good to be true, but Roy thought about it. "So we do this thing for you and then you stay off our case so we won't talk?"

Corvin nodded, watching him carefully.

"Must be some service." Walker offered.

"Three deliveries. Off shore." Corvin told him.

"Where?"

"Luzon."

"The Philippines!" I hadn't meant to speak. I was surprised. "You've got planes and ships going through there all the time."

Corvin glanced at me, but spoke to Roy. "This is a black operation," he said. "Very quiet."

"Delivering what?"

"Arms."

"Shit!" That from Johnny Walker.

"Why?" Roy asked.

He shook his head at us. "None of your concern. You interested? Three deliveries? And then you've never seen me?"

Roy looked from Walker to me. Our opinions were obvious. "We'll listen to it," he said.

134

Corvin took a pull from the bottle on the table and replaced it. "The shipments will be M16s, ammo, mortars, heavy machine guns, mines, maybe some other stuff. Heavy. You'll need to charter a boat. Not Vietnamese. Can do?"

"Panamanian?" Roy asked.

"Fine. We don't care, as long as it isn't Asian."

"Who's going to pay for it?"

I expected him to say we were. He surprised me again. "The agency. Three hundred per trip. We provide the merchandise. You pick it up here. Make the deliveries in person. None of the crew gets ashore for the delivery. And this deal doesn't leave the room. Only the three of you are involved. Agreed?"

Roy nodded. He looked at Walker and me. We nodded in turn, and then he told us the rest of it.

I took a deep breath at that point. April had been listening to the story, fascinated. "What was the rest of it?" she asked.

"There were to be three deliveries," I said. "One in April, one in July, and the last one in December. The cover was a cargo of farm tools. They were provided at cost. We were to deliver the weapons at night, on the northeast corner of the island, below the Sierra Madre Mountains, and then steam around to Manila and off-load the farm equipment. If we could make a buck on it, the profit was ours. On top of the three hundred for the shipment. The deal was pretty straightforward, at least the way Corvin told it that night."

"But I don't understand. Marcos was the president of the Philippines, wasn't he? Wasn't he our friend? Why couldn't this Max just ship the weapons straight to him?"

"Because they weren't going to Marcos," I explained. "They were going to the Huks."

"Who were the Huks?"

"A band of revolutionaries. Communists. They were trying to depose Marcos and throw the U.S. out of the islands. We had a couple of bases there. Clark Air Base and a naval station at Subic Bay."

"But why would our government give weapons to people who wanted to throw us off the island?"

"That took us a while to figure out. But it was really obvious. At that time, the boys in Washington were making a big deal about how the war was an international effort. They wanted troops from as many countries as possible sent over. Like in Korea. Just as tokens, you understand? They wouldn't do much fighting, but we could point to them as proof that the war wasn't just the American government fighting a bunch of poor villagers."

"But how would the guns help?"

"Marcos was reluctant to play along. It was a pressure play. When the Huks started acting up, our government could say to Marcos, do us this favor. Send over a couple thousand troops. Make a few speeches about how the Viet Cong are a threat to the free world, to all of Asia. We have some B52s at Clark. Let us fly some missions out of your country, and we'll help you with this little problem in your backyard. We'll find out where the Huks are getting their weapons and put a stop to it."

"And it worked?" She sounded incredulous.

"Marcos sent the troops," I said. "The bombers flew. Of course, it didn't help us win the war."

"So you did it."

"We didn't have any choice."

"What was it like?"

"The first delivery was a piece of cake."

I remembered how it had been. The delivery was timed for a new moon. It was dark, almost black that night. Roy had leased a tramp steamer named the *Celestina*. She was old and dirty, as only a ship can get. She stood a mile off the beach. The only sound was the lapping of the waves against the hull. The shore was invisible except as a line of total darkness, silhouetted against the southern stars.

The captain put two boats in the water and loaded them. They were almost swamped. Walker and I took one boat in, and Roy handled the other by himself. We steered for a small light that blinked three times in quick succession every sixty seconds.

We took both boats straight in and beached them next to a finger of sand that stuck out into the sea. A man named Freddy met us with a small crew. Guerrillas, I suppose. We didn't talk much that time.

They piled the cargo on the beach, then helped push us back into the water. Freddy tossed the payoff to Roy, and we headed back out. The whole thing took about two hours. Except for making myself climb down into the boat, the hardest part was finding the *Celestina* again in the dark. The captain must have heard our engines. He flashed a light, and we were right under the hull. We picked up the boats, made the trip around to Manila, unloaded the tractors, took on a little cargo, and headed back to Saigon.

"What cargo?" April asked.

"Roy was never one to miss an opportunity," I told her. "As soon as he realized we would have an empty hold and a free pass through customs, he got in touch with Sissy in Manila and arranged a return cargo. Liquor, medicine, perfume, birth control pills, anything that was in short supply or expensive in Saigon."

"But you weren't supposed to do that."

"No. We weren't. But we did."

"And Sissy wasn't supposed to know. But you told him."

"That's right."

"Wasn't that dangerous?"

"What could they do? Send us to 'Nam?"

She shook her head slowly. "And it worked out all right?"

"Like a charm. We made the three hundred for the delivery and another couple of hundred off the white cargo. The tractors paid the lease on the *Celestina* and her crew. The return trip was pure gravy."

"And you did that three times."

"No. Only twice. The second delivery, everything turned to shit. That was at the end of July. Sissy was back in-country. Toker had just been recruited. Walker was breaking him in, so Sissy took Walker's place.

"The approach was smooth. Just the same as the first time. We hit the beach and found Freddy waiting for us. We started unloading. Just about the time we finished, everything fell apart. We started taking fire from the tree line.

"Sissy went down right away. We didn't have any place to run. I grabbed my M16 and made it to the trees. Roy and Freddy hit the sand and started returning fire. I wouldn't have made it without their cover. But once I was off the beach, it was like I was back in 'Nam, before I hooked up with Roy. I located two of the attackers from their muzzle flashes. One I took out right away. The other took longer."

I didn't tell her that I'd had to close with him, use the knife. I didn't want to describe it to her.

"Anyway, the others realized what was happening. They had someone in their midst, and they couldn't tell who. They started shooting in all directions, trying to hit me. They were firing at each other as often as not. It was easier for me. Everyone was the enemy. I just fired now and then and let them work on each other. After what seemed like hours of that, the ones still alive began pulling back.

Roy, Freddy, and the surviving guerrillas were in the trees by that time. We chased them a bit, just to keep up the pressure, and then we fell back to the beach to regroup. Roy told me to take one of the boats and get back to the *Celestina*. I didn't want to leave him there, but he said he wanted to take care of Sissy. He would meet me in Manila. I did what he wanted. But I almost didn't find the ship. The firing had spooked the captain. He was about ready to get under way when I reached him."

"That was scary," April said.

"I haven't told you the scary part," I said.

"Tell it."

"The guys that attacked us. When we started firing back, they were yelling at each other in English. American English."

She thought about that. "What did it mean?" she whispered.

"Somebody double-crossed us."

"Max?"

"Probably. He denied it when we got back to Saigon. Roy met me in Manila like he promised but he wasn't on the *Celestina* when we sailed. He

138

flew into Saigon a couple of days later. He was pissed. I've never seen anyone so mad. He wouldn't even let me go with him when he faced Corvin. He called him at the embassy and told him to get his ass down to the docks or Roy was going to blow the whole operation to the press. Then he left me and met Corvin.''

''What happened?''

''He told us that Corvin denied the whole thing. There was some snafu up the line. The delivery was supposed to go according to schedule. Roy called him a liar and made him pay the three hundred we'd lost. We put Sissy on the flight manifest of a chopper that got downed on its way north, and he was written off as a KIA. The body wasn't recovered, of course. The last delivery was canceled. And that was the end of it.

''We all agreed to shut down the operation as quickly as we could. Walker was supposed to re-up, but instead he mustered out the same month. Roy finished his tour in November and resigned his commission in-country. He hung around for a month or so, though I didn't see much of him. Toker and I took care of the books and wound things down slowly. I finished my last tour and was mustered out through Oakland in March of 'seventy-one. Toker came home in time for Thanksgiving that year. By then, Roy and I were working the cash shuttle, closing accounts and making the final payoffs. That took until 'seventy-four. You know the rest of it.''

I felt drained. I looked at April to see what she thought. She was staring off into space, looking at something I couldn't see. ''July was a busy month,'' she said.

It took me a minute to get it. ''Yes.''

''That was the month I was conceived, too.''

''Yes.''

She stretched out on the bed, on her stomach. With her breasts hidden and her bottom pointed at the sky, she looked like a forlorn child. I patted her back.

''You could have been killed,'' she said.

''That was probably the idea.''

''What about Max? Could he have been my father?''

The idea chilled me. "No. He was never alone with your mother. At least not that early."

"That you know of."

"That I know of," I agreed. "But why would Miss Phoung have slept with him? She hated him. She was with Sissy. And later Roy."

"She didn't love Roy, and Sissy was killed."

"She still hated Max. She blamed him for Sissy."

"What sort of man was Sissy?"

"Full of life. He was a drinker and a lover. He once told me that he'd fuck a snake if he could teach it to French-kiss."

"I see." Her face was in the pillow and her voice was muffled. Her shoulders began to tremble.

"What's wrong?"

"Three fathers," she said. "Three! And I hate all of them! Roy. Sissy. Toker. One is in hiding. The other two are dead. One of them was a sex freak. The other cheated me. And you. You hate me."

"I don't hate you, April."

"You don't want me, either. You want to send me off to France. To get rid of me."

"You know that's not true."

"Then what is true?"

"This." I kissed her back, between her shoulder blades.

She rolled over. "Do that again."

I did.

"Again. More to the right." She pushed a breast at me.

"No."

"Why not?"

"Because it wouldn't be good for you." Or for me.

"Why?"

"When Toker sent you to me, he sent a message. He said to tell me that I owe him. Remember?"

"That wasn't the message."

"What?" I was lost.

140

"He said to tell you that you owe me. Not him. Me."

I shook my head, not sure what to make of that. "All the more reason," I said finally. "Let's go to sleep. We've got things to do tomorrow."

I turned off the lights and lay down with her. After a time, she spoke in the darkness beside me. "I'm not a child," she said. "I'm a woman. And it isn't a father I need, if that's what you're thinking. I've had too many of those."

Her breathing was slow and heavy beside me. I could smell her perfume, her body. My shoulder and hip were hot from her nearness. Not taking her then was the hardest thing I'd ever done in my life. "What do you need?"

"A man."

"I'm not the right one."

"What makes you think it's your decision?"

"Why haven't you asked what I need?" I tried to take her hand. She pulled it back and rolled away from me. She said something that was muffled by her pillow. It sounded like ". . . fuck you."

We breakfasted early and caught a taxi downtown. Suddenly, things were going our way. Our first stop was the Philippine Embassy for visas. Once I was sure we'd have them, we went to the airport. I bought two one-ways to Manila. The first available flight left the next morning. Mexico City to Los Angeles to Honolulu to Manila.

It wasn't yet noon and the chores I'd reserved the whole day for were done. That doesn't happen often. It had never happened to me in Mexico before. To celebrate, I bought April a fairly decent lunch and took her through the National Museum, then let her shop up and down a street market. She spent two hours buying a pair of sandals and a T-shirt with a picture of Montezuma saying YOU'LL GET YOURS.

She enjoyed the day and I enjoyed watching her enjoy it. We returned to the hotel and took a short siesta, then went down and watched the Swedish couple samba until we were hungry again. April stuck with the prawns. I sampled the beefsteak Tampiquena, and decided that I was definitely coming back. We turned in early. When April slipped into bed naked again, I pointed out that she had a perfectly good T-shirt now, and that she had said all she ever wore to bed were T-shirts. She told me she could never sleep in a shirt with a picture of Montezuma on it. There was nothing I could say to that because I didn't understand it.

The taxi picked us up at seven. We made it to the airport by eight-thirty and were in the air by ten. Our connection to Honolulu took us west over the Pacific late in the afternoon. As we chased the sun into the night, I watched the last light glittering off the swells seven miles below like flecks of white fire. April dozed beside me, and I thought about flying back into Asia. She was moving toward a home of sorts, though a lost home. There was a lost home for me, too, out there somewhere. But not in the home-is-where-the-heart-is sense. Well, maybe, if the heart were trapped in a bad dream.

The layover in Hono was short. If I'd had any sense, or patience, I'd have scheduled an overnight layover. But I was moving back into the mystery and wanted it solved quickly.

I slept only fitfully during the twenty-six hours between Mexico City and Manila. My mind went into high gear every time I closed my eyes. I kept hearing the slap of the round Sissy took as it cut into him and seeing the flecks of white fire in the darkness as I ran for the trees. And feeling the ripping of tendons as I pulled my knife through the neck of the second man in the jungle, the one whose interrupted prayer, "Sweet Jesus . . . ," had gurgled away into the night.

The hotel in Manila was different in only one essential point from the one in El Paso. The rooms were the same size. The beds were as soft; the service was perhaps a little better; the furnishings were a little older. But in Manila, we got a ceiling fan. I'd forgotten how good those were to sleep under. As soon as we were in the room, I called for two bottles of San Miguel beer on ice and two large omelettes and pointed April toward the shower. She signed for the order while I was taking my turn under the tepid water. The eggs tasted good, but different. The beer was as I'd remembered it. In the tropics, there is nothing better than San Miguel. I finished my beer and part of April's. She ate her omelette and part of mine. Then we fell into bed.

It was well after midnight before I woke again. I dressed quietly and went downstairs. The bar was still open. As I hoped, it was almost empty. The bartender came over and took my order for a coffee, then hung around when I pushed a twenty at him. He was a thin man in his sixties. The name embroidered on his white lace shirt identified him as Pete.

The place was small and dimly lit. There was no one else at the bar. Only two tables were still occupied, one by a Japanese businessman with his mistress and one by two American tourists, man and wife from the way they acted. They hadn't been on the plane. Neither of the groups showed any interest in me. The waitress stood at her station at the far end of the bar, smoking a cigarette and resting her feet one at a time. She looked bored. The juke box was playing last year's American hits.

Pete kept his eye on the twenty. "What can I do for you, sir?" He probably thought the American tourist was lonely, maybe looking for a little female companionship to take the edge off the rest of the night.

I told him I hadn't been in the Philippines for twenty years, that it looked like things had changed a lot.

"Oh, yes, sir. Many changes. New hotels. New business. Many more Japanese here now." He glanced at the Japanese couple at the table. "I haven't seen so many since the war. But of course, they are different now. They use money instead of bullets."

"And the politics, too," I said.

"Oh, the politics," he said. "Yes. Very different. Marcos is gone. Now we have a woman. Very different." He made a face that was hard to interpret, like a cross between a grimace and a wink.

"But things are better now?"

"Yes, much better now," he said. "Once I was a poor student. I studied architecture at the university. Now, you see, I have a job. I am much better off. Much better."

I pushed the bill toward him and asked for more coffee, then laid another twenty on the bar. He refilled my cup, glanced down, and said, "So much money for coffee. It must be cheaper in the states, yes?"

"Coffee like this is not available there," I told him. "The last time I was here, there was trouble in the mountains."

"There is always trouble in the mountains, sir."

"Then it was the Huks."

"The Huks." He shrugged. "Now it is the NPA, the New People's Army. Always there is someone in the mountains."

"But are they new people?" I asked. "Or the same people with a new name?"

"Twenty years." He looked straight into my face. "People grow old. They die. Some die without growing old. It is hard to say. You are a tourist, sir?"

"A visitor," I told him. "A man who wishes to visit with an old friend. A man he met twenty years ago. In the mountains."

"The mountains are a dangerous place, sir. A man might be advised to stay away from the mountains. Even a welcome visitor might be advised to stay away from the mountains." His face was impassive.

"Even if the old friend would wish to see him? Even if the old friend owed a debt he might wish to repay?"

"Even so, sir. Not all in the mountains are friends. And it is my experience that old debts are often forgotten." He moved the twenty from the bar to his pocket.

"I appreciate your advice," I told him. "You are very gracious to a visitor. Perhaps you could do me a small favor? Help me find someone to do a service for me?"

"Perhaps." He glanced at the waitress. "You wish a companion? One who can show you the delights of Manila?"

"In a way. I wish to see more of your beautiful islands. I want to find a driver who can show me what there is to see. Here in the city, and perhaps elsewhere. A driver who would know how to avoid the dangers you spoke of."

"Such a man might be hard to find."

I put another twenty on the bar. "There is a saying in America: A good man is hard to find, but once found, he is priceless."

The bill disappeared. "You are not in America, sir. Here, there is a price for everything. But you are obviously a generous person, and generosity is

144

frequently repaid. Perhaps you will find what you seek in the morning. About ten o'clock, it is usually possible to find a taxi in front of the hotel."

I thanked him and held up my cup. "Is it permitted to take the cup to my room?"

"Here in the P.I., what is not specifically permitted is forbidden." He allowed himself a small smile. "But that is permitted. Enjoy your stay, sir."

He and the waitress both watched as I walked out. April was awake when I got back to the room. She was sitting in one of the chairs with her arms crossed over her breasts. "Where have you been?" she exploded. "I've been up for an hour! I was worried sick!"

"I haven't been gone an hour."

"Don't change the damned subject! Where have you been!"

"I went out for coffee." I waved the cup at her.

"It doesn't take an hour to get coffee!"

There was no point in repeating that I hadn't been gone an hour. "I arranged for a driver for the morning." I described my conversation with Pete, my impression of the political situation here. That mollified her a little, but she was still angry.

"You promised you wouldn't go off on your own," she told me. "You should have gotten me up. I could have helped."

"How? He wouldn't have opened up with you there. Some things have to be done alone," I told her. "You'll get your chance to help. Remember, I let you talk to the woman in El Paso first. Because it was better that way. When it is better for me to do the talking, I will. We can each do our part, but I'm going to be the one to decide!"

"We'll see about that," she said grimly. "Aren't you going to drink your coffee?"

"I'm going back to bed."

"Then give it to me."

I handed her the cup and turned in, feeling persecuted. I lay awake until she calmed down and crawled in beside me. It took her long enough. After she turned off the light, she dug an elbow into my side and said, "Next time, wake me." Then I could fall asleep. The punishment was over.

There was only one taxi on the street at ten the next morning. It was an old Chevy, heavily dented. The driver had about a thousand medallions, statues, religious pictures, even Barbie dolls glued to the dash. The upholstery was worn and torn. It might have been beige at one time. The most valuable part of the car was the stereo. That worked too well.

The driver hopped out when he saw us leave the hotel and look around. "You want a driver, sah? See all Manila? All Island? Maybe see mountains?"

He was in his late twenties or early thirties, with a thin face and bushy eyebrows. He combed his hair straight back, where it fell to the collar of the lacy white shirt favored by all the men on the street who weren't obvious laborers. His smile was open and attentive, but he held himself as though he had spent many hours at attention, or on a parade field.

April started to answer. I overrode her.

"You bet, guy! You got a name?"

"You call me Pete, sah! Number one driver. I can take you anywhere you want, you understand?"

"That's great, Pete! My girlfriend here wants to go shopping. You know a good store?"

That threw him. "Shopping?" He looked at her dubiously, as though not sure he had the right couple. "Shopping can do! What do you want to shop for, sah?"

"Pearls, Pete," I told him. "The pearl of the Orient, right? Maybe a nice emerald ring for the little lady. And maybe some furniture too. You know about monkey wood?"

April was looking at me as though I'd gone crazy. Maybe I had. But I was spooked.

"Monkey wood? You mean monkeypod? Like for bowls?"

"Sure! Bowls too. We want to shop for everything."

"You don't want to see mountains?"

"We've got mountains back home," I told him. "Anyway, I hear the mountains are dangerous here. Snakes or something. You take us shopping, okay?"

"Shopping. Right on, sah." He drove, shaking his head.

146

We spent the day going from place to place. April was impatient at first, but after an hour or two she got into the act, demanding to be taken to one store after another. I insisted on buying one particularly nice emerald dinner ring for her, mostly just to stay in character, and after that she caught the bug. By the time Pete dropped us back at the hotel late that afternoon, the backseat of the Chevy held a number of packages, mostly laces and silks.

Only after we had carried them up and dumped them on the bed did she question me. "What was wrong with him?"

"Maybe nothing. He looked wrong. I'm jumpy. We'll wait and see. But if anything comes up, remember who you are. Holly Carter. I'm a dirty old man from Los Angeles with more money than sense, treating my girlfriend to a trip around the Orient. Right?"

"Just tell the truth, huh?"

"Right."

We cleaned up and went down for dinner about eight. There wasn't a table immediately, so we went to the lounge for a drink. Pete Number One was behind the bar again, listening to a Filipino in dress slacks and another of those fancy shirts. He didn't say anything when he saw us. I waved to him and smiled like I'd just found a long lost friend. "Hey, Pete," I called, "thanks for the driver! He did a number one job!"

I sat April at one of the booths and ordered two San Miguels from the waitress. As soon as she left, the man who had been talking to Pete came over. He pulled out a chair and sat without asking.

"Mr. Stephenson?"

"You got that exactly right, friend!" I gave him a hearty handshake. "And who might you be?"

"My name is Yabut. Colonel Yabut." His black eyes stared into mine. He spoke without smiling. "You gave my driver quite a runaround today."

"Your driver? You mean that nice fella was working for you? You own a taxi company or something? You've got some damned nice employees. That Pete was real patient with us, and he knows some of the best shops in town."

"I do not own a taxi company, Mr. Stephenson. You should think of me as a policeman."

"What? We just went shopping, you know. Did we break any laws?"

"You asked about the Huks and the NPA last night. These people are very dangerous. They are killers, Mr. Stephenson. Bank robbers. Gangsters. They run whorehouses and extortion rackets. They take the money of your soldiers and airmen and use it against our government. And you talked about contacting them. Naturally, we are very interested."

"Last night? I was just talking about finding Freddy, for God's sake! I don't even know if that was his right name. I just met him the once, when I was stationed out at Clark. But he did me a big favor and I wanted to look him up."

"You want to find a man name Freddy," he repeated. "Tell me about him. Also about this favor he did you."

"Like I said, I don't even know if that was his name. He was a rice farmer. He must be almost seventy years old now. Anyway, I'd taken a jeep out for a ride. Wasn't supposed to, of course, but I had some time off and I figured, what the hell, I'd never see the Philippines again, so I went for a joy ride out toward the mountains where they grow the rice, and the damned jeep broke down. Well, I was stuck! I didn't know crap about fixing cars, and if I didn't get that jeep back to base that night, I was up for a court-martial. You see my problem? And then Freddy came walking down the road with his daughter, and he offered to fix the damned thing for me. So you can see why I remember him. He saved my tail that day."

"You want to look up a man who fixed a jeep for you twenty years ago? That hardly seems likely, Mr. Stephenson."

"Well, there was a little more to it than that," I told him. I acted embarrassed and glanced at April. "This all happened way before you were born, honey. You got to remember that."

I turned back to Yabut and leaned forward, speaking earnestly. "You see, Colonel, while Freddy was working on the jeep, there was nothing for me and the girl to do, and it was hot on the road, so we went off to a little stream for a drink. And one thing led to another, and . . . well, anyway, I guess we had a little affair. And I felt bad about that ever since, after the way Freddy helped me and all. So that's the real reason I wanted to look him up. Because I felt bad about what I did back then.''

He looked at me in silence. Finally he said, ''You are playing me for a fool. A man doesn't come halfway around the world to see a woman he made love to twenty years ago.''

''Well, I didn't,'' I said. ''We were here anyway, and I got to remembering, and I snuck down and kind of sounded out the situation. That's all.''

''You were going to see her!'' April accused me. ''You were going to see another woman. On our trip! You promised me you'd stop the women if I came with you, and already you're at it again! On our first night!''

It was hard to keep my admiration from showing when I looked at her. ''Darn it, Holly, I never went to see anyone! It was just the remembering, that's all.'' I put my hand over hers and tried to look soulful. ''You know I love you, honey. Them other women were just mistakes, that's all.''

Yabut decided to interrupt us. ''Let me see your passports,'' he demanded.

We handed them over and he studied them carefully. When he passed them back, he asked, ''Do you work for the American government in any way, Mr. Stephenson?''

I saw where he was going and decided to muddy the waters a little bit. ''I have worked for them in the past.''

''But not now?''

''I'm a taxpayer, colonel. I work for them the first five months of the year. After that I get to work for myself.''

''You're being deliberately vague,'' he said. ''You might be interested in knowing that I have been in contact with a man from your embassy about you. A man in a position to know the American interests here. He has assured me that you are not acting for your government. That you are on your own. You do not have their protection. And that means you are vulnerable. You should be very careful what you do here.''

''The American government has interests, and then it has interests. Don't trust what you hear from a clerk.''

"The man I spoke to is hardly a clerk. I have dealt with him for many, many years," he paused and watched me thoughtfully. "But I am all too aware that your government sometimes plays more than one game at a time."

I smiled at him innocently. "Well, all that's neither here nor there. I'm just on vacation with my . . . my girlfriend. And I sure don't need any more trouble than you've already got me into."

"Pig!" April said.

"Then stay out of the mountains, Mr. Stephenson." Yabut stood up. "We will be keeping an eye on you. For your own protection, of course." He left us.

April watched him leave, then turned to me. "A farmer's daughter?" She laughed. "Your jeep broke down on the road, and this farmer came along and offered to fix it if you'd just take his daughter into the bushes for a drink of water?"

"Can it," I told her. "The bar has ears. Let's go eat."

Yabut's appearance had cast a pall over the evening, at least for me. It had also given me some things to think about. The NPA and maybe some of the old Huks were still active in the mountains, of course. But they were going to be harder to find with official attention directed my way. And then there was the mysterious man from the embassy Yabut had been in contact with. Our passports would stand a superficial scrutiny, but I didn't want them looked at too carefully. If anything had been set in motion by Yabut's questions, our time was limited. We had to get back to the states and lose these identities quickly. On the other hand, I'd left Yabut with some doubt about my true status, and possibly some suspicion of the man from the embassy. And he had given me an idea for making contact, if I could get April to go along with it.

Our internal clocks were set to some time zone in the middle of the ocean. We turned in soon after dinner. By nine in the morning, I had rented a jeepney and checked us out of the hotel. I didn't say goodbye to Pete.

We drove around Manila for a while, taking in some of the sights and doing a bit of shopping for the sake of the eye Yabut had promised to keep

150

on us, and then drove to Angeles City, out near Clark Air Base. By early evening, we were checked into a hotel called the Presidente. We spent another few hours driving around, familiarizing ourselves with the area. The hotel was within walking distance of the strip.

I recognized it immediately. The buildings were two or three stories, hotels and apartments above, bars, massage parlors, and strip joints on the ground level. A lot of traffic on the street: young Americans wearing short hair and civilian clothes. The bars had names like the Green Light, the Yellow Pearl, the Half Moon House. Their neon signs featured girls dancing in bikinis. Glass-covered pictures framed the doorways. I didn't have to look at the pictures to know what they advertised.

April looked at me curiously when I took a second tour through the area, then watched the girls standing in the doorways. They were inevitably young, pretty, and very friendly. Their clothing tended to be party dresses and high heels.

"Nice neighborhood," she said dryly.

"Just looking."

"Do you have a reason?"

"Yes." I drove us back to the hotel and found the restaurant. After dinner, we went to our room. I told April that I was going out and that I'd be late. She followed me to the door, as I had expected.

I turned on her. "Look, you can't come tonight."

"Where are you going?"

"When Yabut was talking to us yesterday, he said the Huks run the whorehouses in town. I'm going to look them over. You'd be out of place."

"Why?"

"Why?" I shook my head. "Why would a man take a girl along to a whorehouse?" I asked her.

"Maybe I'm kinky?" She said. "Do you think I'm crazy? I'm not going to let you out alone in a place like that. You might be tempted to do more than ask questions."

"I wouldn't be half so tempted if you'd wear a nightgown like a decent woman."

"Who said I was a decent woman? Besides, I want to see."

"See what, for Christ's sake?"

"See that you don't get in any trouble, for one thing."

"I won't get in any trouble."

"You might not call it trouble." She put her back to the door and glared at me. "If you go, I go."

I tried one last tack. "With you along, I'm going to have more trouble explaining what I'm doing there. You won't be helping. You'll be making it harder."

"You never had a hard time explaining anything in your life," she said. "If anyone asks, tell them you're looking for a farmer's daughter. And as for the other, I'm used to making things harder for you. I'm going."

There was no way out. "Okay," I said. "Let's go. But keep your mouth shut."

"Great!" She was delighted. "I'll be ready in a minute." She spent half an hour on her face and applied way too much makeup. I finally had to remind her that she was supposed to be a shopper, not merchandise.

My intention was to spend the evening drinking and looking over the action. I wanted to get an idea how much money was flowing through the shops, and maybe a hint of which ones were run by the Huks. The owners of record would be middlemen, of course, but it might be possible, with enough pressure, to learn what I needed to know. How to contact Freddy, if he was still alive.

Our first stop was a place called the Bird of Paradise. It turned out to be a straightforward strip joint. April watched the girls on stage grind their way down to tassels and G-string, then toss those into the audience and parade back and forth. She seemed more interested in the audience than in the girls. Of course, they had nothing she needed to pay to see. I watched the action at the bar and promoted a conversation with the girl behind it that went no-where.

She was interested in selling me drinks, of course, but became very stupid when I asked who the owner was. A few minutes later, an older woman came up to me, told me she was the manager, and asked if she could help me. I told her I was an American journalist and I wanted to do a feature on the local night life. She didn't buy it for a minute, but I got the feeling that she owned the place. I took April out of there as soon as the next girl finished her set.

The second place was called Seven Delights. It was a big step down from the Bird. The girls danced there too, but without a stage. They danced on a table in the center of the room, and they started where the others had ended. Naked. Not nude. Nude is too classy a word. These girls were bare-ass naked.

I tried a different approach. Instead of talking to the employees, I bought a drink for a sergeant named Jim, who looked like he had spent more than one tour in the Orient and was too old for his rank. He was a leathery, brown-haired man about my age. He let me buy the drink, but his mind and his eyes were on April.

"Who's the lady with you?" he asked.

"The lady with me." I emphasized *me*. April was listening and pretending to ignore us. I felt her foot on my leg under the table.

"So what's the score?" he asked.

"Looking around. Checking things out."

"Looking for anything in particular?"

"A little information, if you've got any."

He looked wary. "What about?"

"Not you. Not the base. The action." I nodded vaguely toward the bar, the girls. "You been around? You know what's what?"

"Got a crib in the neighborhood. Yeah, I know what's happening. What you wanna know?"

"The ownership around here. I've got a little free capital, and I was thinking it's a shame to see all this green going to waste. I was thinking maybe I could pick up a piece of the action."

"Buy in, you mean?"

"If necessary."

"So let's see some of that free capital you've got."

I laid a fifty on the table and he put it away. "So, ask already," he said.

"I hear rumors about who owns some of these joints. I hear the Huks."

"That's mostly the other side of the street. There's a place called the Back Door that's theirs for sure, but most of the joints on that side are owned. If you're straight about looking for an in, you stay away from them." He gave me a measuring look. "Course, that's if you're being straight."

"How sure is this?" I asked.

"It's sure. The girls talk to each other, and my shack job is one of the girls." He nodded at the one on the table. I looked her over. She was pretty. Dark eyes, light brown skin, hair piled high, a butterfly painted on her left cheek in fluorescent pink. She was bending over at the moment, watching us expressionlessly from between her legs while she did a series of slow grinds.

"Nice," I told him.

"You wanna trade? For the night?"

April kicked my leg. "I'm satisfied," I told him.

He shrugged. "Whatever you're up to, be careful. This place is rough. And the piece you're with is some powerful bait. I'd hate to see a fellow American get in trouble so far from home."

"Hate it enough to help?"

"Not a chance, buddy. I live here."

"Fair enough." I put another bill on the table. "Don't remember me," I told him.

"Who?" he asked.

Outside, April grabbed my arm. "Trade?" she said.

"You kicked me," I told her. "I had to guess what you meant."

"I should have kicked you harder. And higher."

We walked across the street and down a block to the Back Door Club. The place was a step sideways from the Seven Delights. The lighting was just as dim, and the smell was the same. Female sex and cheap whiskey. But the girls didn't dance. They smothered you. Three of them converged on me as I entered, then hesitated when April followed me in.

Two of the girls were Filipinos. The other wasn't. I got an idea. I wrapped my free arm around the third girl and steered her toward a booth in the back. She was wearing a white vinyl skirt with a fringe, matching cowboy

154

boots, and a vest. She wore nothing under the vest. She looked about sixteen. April followed closely.

"You buy me drink, GI?" the girl whispered. "You GI?" Her eyes were
on April. She looked puzzled.

"Sure. I'll buy," I told her. We sat. One of the other girls came over
and took our order. Two beers and a glass of what I pretended to believe was
champagne for the girl. Thirty dollars. I handed it over. She tossed down the
champagne.

"Don't push it," I told her. "No more champagne." She started to
stand. I grabbed her arm and held it. "Ten minutes," I said.

"You hurting me, GI," she said.

"No I'm not. You talk a minute. Then maybe I'll buy another drink."

She sat back down and the muscle man at the door relaxed. "What you
want to talk about?"

I nudged April. "El Paso," I told her. She nodded slowly, staring at the
girl. April said hello in Vietnamese. The girl jerked as though she'd been
slapped. She focused on April and started chattering. I grabbed my beer and
headed for the bar. "Hey!" I called. "Bring me some goddamn champagne.
What's the matter with you guys?"

The girl behind the bar sold me a bottle. She wanted a hundred, but I
told her I wasn't that stupid and gave her a fifty. She took it with a smile that
said I was. I carried the bottle back to the table. The girls were talking too
fast for me to follow.

I leaned over them and put a hand on each of their backs. "You know
what to ask," I whispered to April.

"I need time," she said.

"Right." I headed back to the bar, slid onto a stool, and nodded toward
the girl with April. "How much?" I asked the barmaid.

She looked at an older man sitting at the end of the bar.

"You like her?" he asked. "Very pretty!"

I moved down next to him. "She'll do," I said. "My friend likes her."

"She likes girls?"

"She likes to watch."

"Me too," he said. "You want a room?"

"You got bugs?"

He shook his head vigorously. "No bugs. Nice clean room. One hundred dollars. You take all the time you want."

"Not here," I said. "My hotel. All night. How much?"

"She can't go out. You stay here. All night, five hundred dollars. Where you stay?"

"The Presidente," I told him. "Five hundred dollars is too much. One hundred."

"Five hundred. All night."

"I want to rent her, not buy her. Five hundred is too much. I pay two hundred."

"She not for sale. That cost you five thousand, anyway. Four hundred, all night."

I shook my head at him. "Two hundred."

"Why go to the Presidente? It is very nice here, very clean. Three hundred here, all night."

"I don't want you to watch," I told him. "Three hundred at the Presidente. But I don't pay the girl any tip. You pay her."

He looked at me, then decided he'd gotten all he was going to get. I was probably paying three times her going rate anyway.

"Three hundred," he agreed. "But you treat her nice. Big tip."

I pushed the money toward him. He handed it to the girl behind the bar and stood. Both April and the girl watched him carefully as he approached. She looked frightened. He spoke to her in rapid Filipino for a few minutes, and she went into the back room.

"She come in one minute," he told me. "You treat her nice. She good girl. Fuck like rabbit."

April stood beside me. She looked frightened too. He paid no attention to her. "You send her back okay," he warned me. "I don't want to look for her. You understand?"

"I understand."

The girl joined us at the door. She had changed into street clothes, perhaps to pass inspection at the Presidente. We walked back to the hotel in silence. The girl seemed very nervous. April took the key from me and led her upstairs. I started to follow, but she shook her head at me.

I found a bellboy and gave him a ten and an order for some food and beer. I told him to take it to the room. Then I went into the lounge to wait.

The bartender and I stared at each other for three hours before April showed up. She looked drawn and pale. She picked up my drink and downed it in one swallow, then sat opposite me.

"They sold her," she said. "Her name was Josephine. Her family was Catholic and gave her a French name. After the war, the VC took her father away. He never came back. Her mother sold everything and got them on a boat. They went south. They tried to get to Thailand, but some pirates got them. They killed her mother. They kept Josephine for a long time, maybe a year. They raped her and used her. She was a slave! Then they sold her. The men who run the bar bought her. She was just fourteen. She's been there for two years. Two years."

I nodded and listened while she talked it out.

"She was a boat person, just like me," she said. "Just like me."

"No. You were lucky. She wasn't."

"That's the only difference. I was lucky. She was a nice girl, a nice little girl. But I was lucky." She was crying.

I let her cry for a while, then asked, "What did she say?"

"I just told you."

"Not what I want to know."

April grabbed my arm, high up, just under my armpit. She dug her nails into me as hard as she could. "You are a bastard, you know that?"

I nodded. I knew it.

"I have to help her."

"How?"

"Get her out of that place."

"How?"

"I don't know. But I have to. You have to help me."

"Let go of my arm."

She'd forgotten she had it. When she let go, I rubbed it. She had more strength than I'd imagined. "Maybe we can try," I told her. "But she isn't the only one. You know that. There are lots of them." I hesitated. "Did you ask her what she wants? If you helped her, what would she want?"

"No. I didn't ask."

I handed her my wallet. "Go ask," I told her.

It took half an hour. When she came back down, she threw the wallet at me. "You're a son of a bitch," she said. "I really hate you."

"Okay."

"How did you know?"

"It's just the world. Things can't be undone."

"I feel worse than before."

"I know how you feel."

We sat together in silence. The bartender came over a couple of times, but I gave him money and he went away. Eventually, April told me what she had learned.

The money man was a lawyer with an office in Manila. His name was Paul Roxas. I called the next morning and got an appointment for noon. We killed some time walking from one shop to another. Pete number two followed us, but after a couple of hours he started to wait outside when we entered a building. We had a hasty lunch in a restaurant on the ground floor of a downtown office building, then slipped upstairs. The lawyer's office was on the fifth floor. When the receptionist showed us in, he stood and shook hands.

Roxas was a short man in his early thirties, just enough overweight to be called pudgy, not enough to be called fat. His slightly protruding eyes were very quick, darting from me to April with a cautious curiosity.

He led us to a group of chairs arranged around a low table in one corner of the office and offered tea or coffee. When we declined, he dismissed the girl and sat opposite us.

"I have very few American clients," he began. "But my specialty is

158

commercial law, and I'm always interested in new business. Perhaps you are looking for an investment in our country?''

"My problem is a little more delicate than that," I told him. I pulled out my wallet and laid five hundred-dollar bills on the table between us.

He glanced at the money, then back at me. "You are perhaps being a little premature, Mr. Stephenson. Before I can agree to help you, I must know the nature of your delicate problem.''

"In America," I said, "payment of a retainer will establish a lawyer-client relationship. This guarantees the confidentiality of anything we discuss. Is that true here?''

"Within limits, it is. Of course, here the government has ways of compelling evidence that are sometimes, shall we say, to one side of the law. So it would depend on what you wish to discuss.''

"Then I'd like you to consider this a retainer. I want to buy your discreet attention to my problem.''

"You are being very mysterious. But I suppose it will do no harm to listen. And I can guarantee that your words will stay here, in this office.''

"I don't want them to stay here," I told him. "I just want them to go in only one direction. Not to the police. To the mountains.''

"To the mountains . . ." he murmured. His eyes bore into mine. "A very dangerous direction. Why have you come to me? What makes you think I would, or could, send a message in that direction?''

"My reasons are unimportant . . ." I began.

He interrupted me. "They are not unimportant to me!''

"Hear me out, Mr. Roxas. You have not been compromised in any way, and I will not ask you to compromise yourself. I don't expect that you can help me directly. I hope that if you hear my story, I may be contacted by a man I have to speak with. If I am not, well, you have your retainer and I have your assurance that our conversation will not be repeated where it might be dangerous for me. And if I am contacted, if I speak successfully with this man, I am prepared to pay a far more substantial fee. Without, of course, drawing any connection between this consultation and any subsequent meeting.''

He spoke carefully. "Obviously, I cannot accept a fee for putting you in contact with anyone who might be engaged in an illegal activity, Mr. Stephenson, but there are many worthy causes here in the Philippines. Perhaps I might suggest one that deserves your support."

"I would welcome the guidance of my attorney on such a matter, and of course I am eager to help the Philippine people in any way possible. If my simple needs are met."

"Just how simple are your needs?"

"The conversation I've described would be worth five thousand dollars American, regardless of what I learned. If I spoke to the correct man."

He nodded slowly. "A most valuable conversation," he said. He picked up the money. "Very well, I can listen to your problem. Perhaps something will come of it. You understand, of course, that I cannot involve myself in any illegal activity, and that if you describe such an activity I must advise you to contact the police. Contacting them would be your responsibility."

"Of course."

"Then tell me about your problem."

"It is a twenty-year-old problem. In July of 1970, some men made a delivery of certain goods to a small group on a beach on the northwest corner of this island. The leader of that group was a man named Freddy. That is the only name I have for him. The delivery was interrupted by other interested parties. There was a dispute. Several men lost their lives. The questions I must have answered arose out of that event. They do not relate to the present, at least in your country. The man I must speak to is Freddy. If he is no longer alive, a conversation with any of the others present might be helpful to me. But it would be significantly less valuable."

Roxas seemed to stop breathing as I spoke. When I finished, he stared at me for a long time, then stood and walked to his desk. He wiped his face with his hands. "You are wrong about one thing, Mr. Stephenson. The event you describe had repercussions in my country. Repercussions that extend into the present."

I waited for him to go on. Eventually he added, "Of course, this Freddy

160

was probably associated with a group called the Huks. It is an outlawed organization, and so I can only advise you that your inquiries should be directed to the local police department. Perhaps they can help you. I cannot."

I nodded and stood. "I understand," I told him. "But there is one other matter to be considered." I told him about our meeting with Colonel Yabut and Pete Number Two.

He listened gravely. "You say this Pete followed you here?"

"Only as far as the restaurant downstairs. He is probably waiting outside. We have been doing a lot of shopping. And of course we have much more to do."

He nodded. "That is a good plan. There are many fine things to buy in our country, many beautiful things. You might consider a short trip to the town of Baguio. There are gold mines there. Much beautiful jewelry in the local shops. Much to see." He forced a smile. "The Hotel Magsaysay is very convenient. Many tourists like yourselves stay there."

"We will consider it," I told him.

"Please do," he said. He showed us to the door. "And do not forget. The matter you've described belongs to the police. Not to a simple lawyer such as myself."

Pete Number Two looked relieved when he saw us leave the building. He followed us rather more closely for the rest of the afternoon. We didn't talk about the meeting with Roxas until that night. Then April told me she thought he was a slimeball. A fat little pimp.

"Maybe," I told her. "But sometimes it's wrong just to look at what people do. Sometimes you have to look at the reasons for their actions."

"What do you mean?"

"Look at you. You've been sneaking into my bed ever since Phoenix. If I didn't know better, I might think you had a thing for older men."

"Is that what you think?"

"No. I think you have lost too much in your life. You lost your mother when she was killed. Then you lost your aunt when she put you on the boat. You lost your country at the same time. Then you lost a father when Toker was killed. You lost him again when you found out he had never bothered to adopt you. I think you're trying to find someone you won't lose.''

We were sitting at a table in our room, having some coffee before turning in for the night. The window was open and the warm tropical air wafted through it. April played with the emerald ring I had bought her in Manila as she listened to me. "Let me guess," she said. "You were a psych major. Right?"

"Wrong." I smiled. "Actually, I studied mathematics."

"Have I ever told you that you're full of shit?"

"Once or twice."

"Some things bear repeating."

"You tell me, then. Why are you doing it?"

She hesitated. "Why do you have to ask? All this analysis, it's just crap, Rainbow. I want you. You want me. Why do you have to look deeper? Under the surface? That stuff doesn't matter. It isn't real!"

"It matters, April," I said. "It's the only thing that's real. What do you want, some guy who can't see past your skin? A man who wants you for your slanted eyes? Because you've got a nice body? Or because he knew your mother?" I shook my head. "You only look at the surface, that's all you'll get. The surface. That changes, and you've lost everything. And the surface always changes. Always."

"But your way, you turn this thing I feel into some kind of a test," she said. "It's like an audition. I'm telling myself sure, he wants me. But am I really good enough for him? What about my motives? Are they pure enough? That's where the crap comes in."

"You're asking the wrong questions." I was getting impatient. "You should be asking if we're right for each other. What are you offering? A couple of nights in the sack? I chase away the boogeyman who killed Daddy and get to fuck you, kind of like a reward? Is that what you want? Or do you want to be around for a while? A place in my life, is that what you want? If so, we've got to know there is a place for you. Shit, you haven't even asked

162

yourself what I really am. Me! An old soldier still stuck back in the boonies, still fighting some goddamned war everybody else wrote off as a loss about the time you were born!" I had her full attention. I nodded toward the bed. "If all you want is someone to stuff your twat for a week or so, strip down and we can get right to it. If you want more, you have to put something on the table besides your ass. You understand?"

She had nothing to say to that, but later, when the lights were off and we were lying side by side, she said, "You're still wrong, you know. Maybe right in a way, but wrong, too. It's all the thinking about it. Sometimes you have to take care of the needs first and let the analysis sort itself out later. There's nothing wrong with wanting to find someone to love and taking a chance. You have to take the chance."

"I know it, April," I said. I found her hand and held it in the dark. "But there are chances and there are chances. You have to look at what you stand to lose as well as what you stand to gain. And you have to know how much damage you can do, how much you can hurt the other person." We fell asleep like that. Only our hands touching. The next morning, Pete Number Two followed us to Baguio.

Roxas was right. There were some pieces worth looking at in Baguio. We spent the next day visiting small shops and sightseeing. No one made contact, but I had the uneasy feeling there were more eyes than Pete's following us. We ate and retired early.

The following day, I bought April a small gold monkey on a chain. She didn't like it as much as I did, but she liked the idea that I had found it and bought it for her. She liked that enough to wear it to bed. She pressed the monkey into my chest and asked me if I really thought she was trying to find something she couldn't lose, if I thought that was the only reason she slept with me.

"You tell me," I said.

"Suppose you're right. Do I have a chance?"

"No. You lose everything. We all do. Your only chance is to find something that lasts for a while. And I'm too old to last as long as you'd need me."

"You don't know how long I might need you," she said. "You don't even know why I need you."

"Then tell me."

"You're the mathematician. Figure it out for yourself," she challenged me.

I held her close and thought about it without getting anywhere. Her breasts, her belly pressed against me, her breath warm on my neck, the way she wrapped her legs about mine, all were too distracting.

"Tell me what you need," she said.

"What do you mean?"

"Every night, we lie together like this." She ground her pelvis against mine. "You're so hard, like a rock. It must be driving you crazy. But every night you hold me and you don't ever do anything about it. You just hold me. There must be a reason. What is it? You don't think I'm a virgin, do you?"

"No."

"Then what is the reason? You know you could have me just by moving a little bit. But you won't do it. Why? Is it because you knew my mother? Or because you've got me all mixed up with that stupid war?"

"Figure it out for yourself," I told her.

The next day was more sightseeing.

The following morning, I was about to give up. April persuaded me to give Roxas one more day. We spent it driving along the coast, stopping in a couple villages and talking to the people. They were cautious but friendly. That night we had dinner and sat outside for a while, tossing around motives for Toker's killing. We didn't get anywhere.

A quiet knock woke me after midnight. I pulled on a pair of pants and answered the door. A boy, about fifteen, slipped into the room. "You come," he said.

At last.

He waited while we dressed, then led us down the hall. The lights had been dimmed and there was no sound from any of the rooms we passed. We

164

followed him past the elevator to the stairwell and down to the street level, then out through the kitchen.

An old van was waiting around the corner from the lobby entrance. I stopped when I saw it, but the boy grabbed my arm and pulled me along. "You come," he said. "Hurry."

"You should wait here," I told April.

"You wish," she said, and hurried ahead.

The side door of the van slid open. There were two men inside, sitting well back. Each had an AK47 pointed at April. "You get in, please," the boy said. He flashed a quick smile at me. "In back, please."

April crawled in first. I followed her. The men kept the weapons trained on us, but they said nothing. The boy walked around to the front and climbed behind the wheel. The van jerked forward. April fell against me and I rolled off balance. One of the two men, the shorter one, jabbed the barrel of his weapon into my neck. I cursed and regained my balance, then sat on the metal floor with my back against the wall. April was beside me, between me and the back doors.

The bigger man turned a flashlight on us. There were some dirty rags on the floor, but the van was otherwise empty. I noticed that the back doors where chained together. The man who had jabbed me pushed his weapon carefully toward the front of the van. The other sat on it while he wired our wrists together. He didn't twist the wire too tight; it was just tight enough that I couldn't move without cutting off circulation. When that was done, he carefully retrieved his rifle.

The only way out was past the men. They watched us carefully. Their weapons were not on safety. The van rocked back and forth. April and I leaned against each other for balance.

I didn't like the situation at all. The thing I didn't like most about it was that we hadn't been blindfolded. Either we weren't coming back or we were going to have to pass some sort of test before we did.

April didn't say anything, but she was breathing heavily and sweating.

An hour passed. We got cooler and then began to warm up again. I thought we had climbed over some mountains, perhaps a low range, and then dropped back to a lower altitude. I gestured toward the shorter man's weapon. "AK47. Good."

He glanced down at it, then back at me. He nodded. "Good." His friend said nothing.

The Philippines are warm, tropical islands. Very humid. It was stifling in the van. I could smell the two men.

April whimpered softly and I became aware of how she was sitting. I cleared my throat so I wouldn't startle anyone. "Stop," I said.

They lifted their weapons threateningly. The boy called back, "You be quiet, please."

I said, "Stop the van."

He pulled the van to a crawl. "What's the matter," he said.

"You stop."

"Why stop?"

"Piss," I told him. "Piss stop."

He stopped, jumped out, ran around the van, and opened the side door. "Okay," he said. "You be fast, okay?"

The two guards got out first and held the flashlight as April and I crawled out behind them. My legs wouldn't work right. I had to help April. I noticed that her wrists were bleeding from the wire. I tried to help her pull down her pants. She shook her head. "They're watching," she said.

"They're going to watch, April," I told her. "It can't be helped. They're grown men. They've probably seen a woman take a leak before. Just do what you have to."

She bit her lips, then turned away from them, and squatted. I took care of business too. I thought I heard an engine, very faint, a long way behind us. I started talking to April, telling her that we were going to be all right. She was shaking when I helped her straighten up and get back in the van.

When we were moving again, I took her wrists and held them where the guards could see the blood. They glanced at each other. The short one put away his weapon and loosened the wire. April tried to smile at them and said thank you.

166

Another hour passed before the driver slowed the van to a crawl and turned off the road. We bumped along a path for a few miles, then stopped. We all got out of the van and stood for a few minutes while the cramps in our legs passed. Then the boy started walking into the trees. A faint path led downhill.

The trees around us were mostly palms. I thought I could hear the surf a long way off. The moon was up, somewhere above the trees, but very little light penetrated to the path.

If my sense of direction was right, we had come almost due north up the central valley of the island. If I had really heard the ocean, we were somewhere near the point on the northwestern coast of Luzon where I had been ambushed the last time I'd visited the island. I didn't know if that was a good thing or not. It hadn't been such a good thing the last time. But tonight it might indicate we were about to meet someone else who had good cause to remember the place.

The driver signaled a stop. April was breathing heavily. She had had no experience in her life walking in the dark with armed men. Fear makes exercise easier for some and harder for others. It made it harder for her. She was barely keeping up.

We stood in silence while April caught her breath. The absence of noise suddenly caught my attention. No bird calls. No insects. I sensed that there were more than three men around us.

The boy spoke. "You go, Mr. Stephenson. Miss Holly wait here. We take care of her."

April gave a low cry. "No!"

I raised my arms and dropped the loop they made around her. "I have to go, Holly." I told her. "You have to wait."

"But you promised. Please don't leave me."

"I'll come back," I promised her. I kissed her.

Someone jabbed me with the muzzle of a rifle. I had to let her go. As we walked down the path, I could hear her sobbing. The sound carried a long way before I couldn't hear it.

We marched in silence. Shadows joined our procession. Soon there were at least five men around me. Two preceded me and three brought up the rear. The path was heavily overgrown. Every few minutes a palm frond slapped my face.

Suddenly it was lighter. We stepped out onto a beach. It was not as deep as I remembered it, only about thirty feet from the tree line to the surf. The sand was white in the moonlight. I stopped and looked around. I remembered the long spit that pushed into the sea to the west of me. This was almost exactly the spot where we'd beached the boats twenty years earlier. The attackers had fired from up in the forest where April was now hidden.

One of the three men behind me shoved my back. I growled, spun, and dug an elbow into his solar plexus. He fell back on the sand, gasping. The others stepped away from us and raised their weapons.

A man had been waiting on the beach. He said, loudly, "Wait!" and walked up to me. He stood in front of me, staring at my face for a long time. I returned the look. He was a short man, thin, with a narrow face, lightly pockmarked.

"Hello, Freddy," I said.

"I thought it might be you," he said. "None of the others would have had the balls."

"They were just busy tonight," I told him.

He stepped back and barked an order in Filipino. The man I had elbowed twisted the wire from around my wrists. I waited, rubbing the circulation back into my hands. Freddy squatted on the sand. I sat beside him.

"You remember this place?" he asked.

"Very well," I told him. "Why are we here? It is a long way from the hotel."

"It was a favor for the lawyer." He lit a cigarette. "His brother was one of the men who died here that night. He thought that if you were not the man you claimed to be, this would be a fitting place for you to die."

I reached into his pocket and took a cigarette. I figured I wouldn't have to tell April about it. "But I am the man," I said.

"You are the man," he nodded. "And you have come a long way to ask questions. Why didn't you ask the others, the Americans."

168

"I couldn't believe them."

He grunted and we smoked for a time.

"What are the questions?"

"First, what happened to the payment on the last delivery?"

He looked surprised. "It was paid. The man called Roy took it away in the boat with him."

It was my turn for surprise. "But he didn't get in the boat. I left him here on the beach, with you and the one who died."

"The one who died?" he asked.

"His name was Sissy. He took one of the first bullets when the shooting started."

"What are you talking about, my friend?" The moon was harsh on his face. "There was no shooting on the last delivery. It went smoothly. It was a couple of miles west of here."

"What?" I was completely confused. "The last delivery, here, on this beach, when the men were killed?"

"That was in July. The last delivery was in December. Payment was made in full. Two hundred and fifty thousand dollars. To Roy." He looked at me for a long time. "I think maybe it is good that you came."

"How was it set up?" I asked softly.

"Not the same as the others. It was arranged before, at the same time as the others, but Roy changed the place before he left to meet you. After the fighting."

"I didn't know about this. Was this the time he stayed behind to bury Sissy?"

He was shaking his head. "No American was buried here, except for the ones who died in the woods. The ones who shot each other, and the one you killed with your knife. On our side, only the lawyer's brother and another man, a friend, died here."

I didn't know what to say. Nothing I had believed for the last twenty years was true. "Only the two died?" I felt stupid.

"Only the two."

"And the American who was shot? Sissy?"

"He took his bullet in the leg, here." He touched my leg on the outside, high up, just below my hip. "It was broken, but he was not bleeding heavily. The one called Roy carried him away to Manila. I have seen many such wounds. He would not have died if he could get to a doctor."

I nodded. I had seen such wounds too. They were not usually fatal.

"One other thing," I said. "Sissy was carrying a small sack, about so big," I held my hands up. "Did you see this sack?"

He shook his head.

I had a decision to make. I asked him, "About the girl with me, Holly . . ."

"She is well. My men are keeping her where we buried the CIA Americans."

"They were CIA? You are sure?"

"CIA or Army Intelligence. Who knows. I know only that they were dead."

That made it easier. "We had to stop on the way up here," I told him. "I heard a truck behind us."

That galvanized him. "A truck?"

Some of the others had at least a little English. They stood and ran back to the tree line. Freddy and I ran with them. We dropped to the sand just inside the shadows.

"You are sure?" he asked.

I nodded. "I don't know if we were being followed. But I heard it. Didn't Roxas tell you about the policeman who was following us?"

"That is why we met like this, my friend."

"I don't like it," I told him.

"This is an unlucky beach."

"I have to get to Holly," I said.

He called the others over and spoke to them. "We will try to lead them away," he said. "The girl is with my son and the two guards. They are straight up the path, maybe six hundred yards."

"I'll find them." I turned to the circle of men and shook hands all

170

around. I said, "Good Luck," to each man. I could wish them good luck without wishing them victory.

There was a short burst of automatic weapons fire up the mountain followed by a pause and then a longer burst.

"My son . . ." Freddy said.

"I need a weapon," I said.

He gestured and one of the men unslung his M16 and tossed it to me. It felt good in my hands. Freddy handed me a knife. "I think you used to be good with this," he said. "If you see my son . . ."

I nodded and crawled into the forest.

The firing had been well ahead of me. If the shooters were coming down in a skirmish line, I had at least five hundred yards before I could expect to see them. I charged up the path for about three hundred yards, then took cover and waited, listening.

The silence was complete for a few minutes. Then I heard men walking, whispering to each other as they moved downhill. At least they weren't speaking English this time.

It was very dark, but I saw their shadows as they passed me. There was a burst of firing and several rounds cut through the palms overhead. I fired a short burst into the backs of the group that had just passed and then hit the dirt and rolled away.

One of them screamed. The others began shooting wildly. Below them, Freddy's men started firing. I crawled left, along the slope, trying to get out of the line of fire. After five minutes of that, I stood and began making my way uphill again.

The shooting, sporadic now, was to my right and downhill. A couple of rounds snapped into the trees near me. I was scared silly, and at the same time, I could feel my face twisting into the old rictus, half terror and half delight. I kept moving uphill. After I'd climbed another two hundred yards, I dropped to my hands and knees and started moving to my right and up. The firing continued, but it seemed to be moving away from me. I came to a clearing. There were two darker shapes lying in the faint moonlight.

I made my way around the edge of the clearing, straining my ears, but I could hear nothing near me. The shapes resolved themselves. The shorter guard, the one who liked to jab me. And the boy, the driver.

There was nothing I could do. I continued up the hill, parallel to the path and about six yards from it. After ten minutes, I heard a faint crying. April. With a small group of men, no more than three. I made my way slowly toward them.

She was moving awkwardly in the dark, stumbling often, and making a lot of noise. I took a chance and ran ahead of them. I sounded like a herd of water buffalo, at least in my own ears, but they were preoccupied.

I took a position a yard to the left of the path, under a large fern. My eyes were fairly well adjusted to the dark. I could see them approach from fifteen yards away. The lead man had a flashlight pointed at the ground in front of him. I smiled, checked my safety, and waited.

Pete Number Two was walking point. The girl was two yards behind him, closely followed by two men. They carried their weapons at port arms and walked clumsily. The shadows from the flashlight were confusing them. When April was even with me, I took out both the men following her with one long burst and then screamed, "Holly!" I jumped against her, knocking her off her feet and off the path. I rolled once and came up in firing position.

Pete Number Two dropped the light and spun around. He was trying to pull his rifle into firing position, but he was way too inexperienced and way too slow and probably couldn't see a damned thing. I blew him away with a burst of three rounds into the center of his chest and then rolled into a crouch above April.

I waited, listening carefully and trying not to breathe. She was crying softly. I was grinning from ear to ear and my breath came in harsh sobs. I put my hand over her mouth and held it there until she was quiet. I heard some shouting from down the hill, then the sounds of another firefight. We probably had a few minutes. I set the safety and slung the M16 over my shoulder, then I scooped April up and carried her about thirty yards farther off the path, where I lay her gently on the ground.

She still had the goddamn wire on her wrists. I pulled it off and threw it away, then held her close to me. My hands ran up and down her back, over her ass and her legs and her shoulders, feeling for wetness, for bones that didn't move right, waiting for a scream. Her heart was like a drum against my chest. Her cheeks were wet, and then I realized my cheeks were wetting hers. "Holly," I said. "God damn it, Holly."

She put her arms around me and said, "Ruh, Ruh, Ruh. . . ."

We were on our knees facing each other, clinging to each other. She started saying it again. "Ruh, Ruh, Ruh. . . ."

I had to stop her. I couldn't stand the sound. I put my mouth over hers and kissed her hard. She began to claw at my back, but she was trying to pull me into her, and her body began to relax against mine. "Rainbow," she said.

"God damn it, Holly." I ground my hips against her.

She bit my neck and dropped her arms and fumbled at my pants. I lost control completely. I kicked my pants down and pulled at hers.

I tore into her like a lost man, and she met my desperation like she thought she could save me, matching me thrust for thrust. We ground away at each other for an eternity, and in the end, she did save me. We saved each other. She cried out and I groaned into her ear and collapsed on top of her. We clung together like that and listened to the shooting. We moved slowly against each other, inside each other and surrounding each other, and savored the sweetness of the moment until it dwindled and was gone. I stirred and lifted my weight off her, kissed her ear, and began to pull out of her. She stopped me, hugged me tightly with her arms, and pulled me back into her with her legs.

"That wasn't me," she breathed in my ear. "That was Holly. You couldn't have done that with me."

I nodded without agreeing. It was Holly with me in the forest. But April was there too. Even Phoung had been there. But I could never tell her that.

We separated, stood, and retrieved our clothes. I found April's face with my hand and brought her close to me. I asked if she was strong enough to be alone for a while. She asked why.

"I have a favor to do," I told her, "for an old friend."

"And I can't come?"

"You wouldn't want to."

"Should I wait here?"

"No." I led her back to the path above the bodies. I left the M16 with her and told her to shoot anyone who didn't smell like me. She said that would be easy.

I went back to the bodies and carried Pete's ears back to the clearing and left them with Freddy's son. I figured Freddy would feel a little better about it, and Pete didn't need them anymore. Then I went back to April and led her up the path. We stopped just off the road.

There were two guards by the van, staring nervously into the jungle. They were completely exposed in the moonlight. They were easy. I took a firing position and aimed. Behind me, April dug her nails into the muscle between my shoulder and my neck. She whispered, "No. No." I ignored her and squeezed the trigger. Two short bursts and they were both down.

We took the long way back, along the coast. I left the weapon in the sea before dawn. The sun had been up an hour by the time we reached Baguio. I hated returning to the hotel, but the passports were there. Our only hope was that Yabut wasn't aware anyone had escaped his trap.

We spent an anxious ten minutes packing, then took the jeepney into Manila and turned it in at the airport. There were no flights available, but a thousand dollars a seat persuaded a Chinese couple from Taiwan to postpone their departure a day. The last thing I did in Manila was post a check to Paul Roxas.

WASHINGTON, D.C.

WE WERE IN AND OUT OF TAIWAN AND IN AND out of Tokyo before the sun set. We flew from Tokyo to Vancouver and cleared Canadian customs there, then rented a car and drove into the states. Customs was not a problem. They didn't even open our bags. Perhaps they would have if we had had to show passports, but the agent just asked our citizenship and waved us through. The right accent will take you anywhere.

We drove down to Seattle, turned in the car at the airport, and took a cab to the Hilton, where we registered as John and Stephanie Nickles. It was almost nine in the morning of the same day we fled the Philippines, but twenty-four hours later. We had spent most of the time in the air, unable to talk about the only thing on our minds. And we had been too tired to talk when we got in the car. We just drove until we were ready to collapse, then found a bed and collapsed.

Seattle is a good place for the spirit, and we both needed a rest. We slept until early the next morning and woke up ravenous. April grabbed the bathroom first and I ordered breakfast from room service. Eggs Benedict, lots of coffee. It arrived while I was dressing. We sat on the bed and ate without speaking. Some conversations are hard to start. I didn't begin this one well. I said, "Holly . . ."

"April."

"What?"

"April. My name is April. You called me Holly."

"Sorry." I felt silly. "I'm still tired, I guess."

"It doesn't matter. I'll answer to anything. You can call me Phoung if you like."

"I don't like. I know who you are."

"Forget it." She spoke listlessly. "Was it worth it?"

"What do you mean?" I thought she was talking about what happened between us, and I didn't see how she could ask if it had been worth it.

"The killing. Was it worth it?"

"They had you. I had to get you back."

"What about the men at the van? They didn't have a chance."

I shrugged. "They were in the wrong place at the wrong time. They had seen the van. I couldn't tolerate a trail back to us, so they had to die. We might have met Yabut again. We were lucky we didn't."

"So it's just luck? We're alive and they're dead and it's just luck?"

"Luck and brains. They were stupid. They shouldn't have been in the open like that. The moon was out. I could see them and they couldn't see me."

"Maybe they were afraid of the dark?"

"You can't be afraid of the dark, April. Things in it can hurt you. You have to go into the dark if you want to be safe."

"Are we safe now?"

"Safer, anyway."

She sighed, lay back on the bed, and looked at the ceiling. "I have a question," she said slowly. Her tone disturbed me. I sat beside her and

176

waited quietly. She spoke hesitantly, "Why did Roy hire you? I mean, he already had Sissy. And Johnny Walker. There were thousands of men over there. So why you?"

She had finally gotten around to it. "He needed me, or someone like me."

"For what?"

"He was a businessman. He bought and sold things. He made contracts with people. Of course, when there was a dispute over a contract, he couldn't go to court. So there had to be another way. Usually, it was just a matter of negotiation. A little more cash, a change in currency, push back a delivery schedule, maybe an introduction to a man in another line of business. . . . Everybody was out to make money. Very few people were out to make trouble. But for those few who were, he had to have a credible threat. That was me. I was the credible threat."

She looked me over skeptically. "I've seen bigger men."

"Sure. Everybody has." I smiled at her.

"So?"

"I had a quality Roy liked, April. I can control myself, even when I'm out of control."

"Like in combat, you mean?"

"Then, yes."

She was watching me carefully. "And in the jungle," she asked, "when you made love to me?"

"Then too."

"But if you didn't lose control, if you wanted that to happen, or let it happen, what was your problem before? Why wouldn't you make love to me before?"

"I couldn't. You're Phoung's daughter."

She looked away from me. "I thought you might be afraid that I was your daughter, too."

"I knew you weren't, April. But I wished that you were."

"That changed in the jungle?"

"It changed. It wasn't the jungle though. It was you."

She sighed. "Some good came of it then."

I was surprised. "A lot of good came of it. I talked to Freddy. Not for long, but long enough. Some things are beginning to make sense."

She seemed to welcome the change of subject. "What did he say?"

"There was a shortage in the accounts. Two shortages, depending on how you count them. When Sissy took Walker's place on the *Celestina* for the July delivery, he was carrying everything we had accumulated for Max's payoff. It was going to one of the accounts in Manila. It was in the form of stones. Rubies, emeralds, sapphires, and other stones. We assumed it was lost during the firefight, or that the Huks took it from Sissy's body. But he didn't die. He was shot, but he lived."

That got her attention. "He's alive!"

"He was," I said, "but there's more. Apparently the third delivery was made after all. The one scheduled for December. I think that's why Roy stayed in-country after he resigned his commission. The son of a bitch stuck around long enough to make the final delivery. And he pocketed the payoff."

"This changes things," she said slowly.

"Yes."

"If Roy kept the money from the last delivery, wouldn't he be afraid you might find out and want some of it?"

"He might have decided the final delivery was outside the operation. None of our concern. After all, he did it on his own. We weren't involved. Besides, that happened twenty years ago. Why should it come up now? I wouldn't have cared, and I don't think Walker or Toker would have either. We were happy with what we had. Anyway, it was Toker who was killed, not Roy. And Toker never saw any of the money."

"Somebody searched my house."

"But not for that. If Roy got his hands on it, it was gone for good."

"The other, then? The jewels?"

"Toker didn't have them, either. And there's still the time factor. What happened to start all this shit?" I didn't know what to make of it. I had a couple of pieces of the puzzle at last, but they didn't seem to fit anywhere.

"So what do we do now?"

178

"We talk to them. All of them. Roy and Sissy and Max."

"Why Max?"

"Because I'm curious about him. He set up the operation. He was around all the time. He was the sort of man who would have used a Claymore to kill Toker. Roy wasn't. Sissy wasn't. But Max would have liked the idea. And he ran a number of operations for the agency while he was in-country. He would have known about booby traps."

"So you're suspicious of him?"

"That's right. I don't understand where he fits in, and I'm suspicious."

"What about Roy and Sissy?"

"Same thing. I'm suspicious. They each wound up with a big piece of change off the books. Why? And what happened to it?"

"Roy is in Mexico," she said slowly. "Where's Sissy?"

"I don't even know if he's still alive. But we have to start somewhere, and his hometown is the logical place."

"Where was he from?"

"New Mexico. Santa Fe, I think."

"So we go there next?"

"Not yet. We don't know if he's still alive. Roy could have taken him out on the road to Manila. And even if he is around somewhere, we aren't sure that he wound up with the bag. Max is the next step. He had the technique for the killing, but he didn't have a motive. Let's see if we can find a motive."

"And if Max didn't have a motive?"

"Then we're down to Roy and Sissy."

"You don't want it to be either of them, do you?"

"No. Do you?"

"One of them was my father," she said. "No. I want it to be Max."

"Then let's go get him."

We packed and checked out. I ordered a cab and had him stop by the closest photographic studio. We had our pictures taken, then headed out to the airport. There was a flight to Washington, D.C., leaving in three hours. I bought tickets under the Nickles names and then led April to a restaurant, or what passes for a restaurant in an airport, and ordered a couple of sandwiches. While we waited, I asked her if she wanted to pick her new name.

"Holly Porter," she said. I told her that Porter was a bad idea. If we were being traced, it would ring too many bells.

"You choose then," she said. "But don't change Holly. I want to keep that."

"Why?"

"Because of the mountains. And you called me Holly this morning."

I settled on Holly Anderson for her and Roger Bacon for myself and placed a call to my man in Albuquerque with the particulars, then mailed the photos to him. He was to mail the new documents to us in care of General Delivery, Washington, D.C.

We arrived late and it was hard to find a hotel. We finally wound up at an all-suites place over the river in Virginia. It had a kitchenette, sitting room, bath, and two bedrooms. I wasn't sure that I liked it. I'd gotten used to having April by my side.

I needn't have worried. She completely ignored the second bedroom. She slipped in with me and laid her head on my chest and put her hand on me.

"April," I said.

"Holly."

"That only worked once, April."

"It can work again. It's already working."

"April, we need to talk about what happened in Luzon."

"When you rescued me."

"After I rescued you."

"Oh. Do I want to hear this?"

"No."

"Then don't say anything."

"You're forcing me."

She took her hand away. "It's about me?"

"No."

"Vietnam, then. My mother?"

"No. Why I took Roy's deal. Why I didn't want to go back into the field."

She propped herself up on an elbow, leaning over me, and looked down in my face. She was beautiful. "Then tell me."

"Do you remember how I was, when I took you in the forest?"

"You were excited."

"Yes." I hesitated. "Very excited," I said. "Before I took you. Before."

"I don't understand."

"Think about it."

She thought. Her eyes slowly widened. Then she rolled off me and went to the other bedroom. I lay awake a long time thinking of all the reasons I shouldn't have told her. But she was acting like a woman in love. She deserved to know what she loved.

The next morning I was up early. April's bed was empty. I lay down in it for a few minutes, feeling sorry for myself. Then I cursed and went out for breakfast. I spent the day on the phone.

Roy created the Saigon operation and the four of us ran it, but there were others involved. We were a sort of board of directors. Our payroll was large. American and Vietnamese civilians and military personnel ranking from private all the way up to one lieutenant colonel ate from our table. Some of them ate well. All of them owed me, and most wanted to forget it. So I had leverage.

It took only three calls to get a lead on a man who was still in the service, a man who had been a sergeant in the military police at Long Binh. He was a senior master sergeant now, stationed at the Pentagon. But he was hard to reach. I finally got him at home just before suppertime. April still hadn't showed.

Sergeant Foster wasn't exactly happy to hear my voice. "What do you want, Porter?" he demanded.

"A name."

"Whose?"

"Someone from the old days. Someone in the intelligence community now. Someone who remembers what he owes me."

"Everyone owed you, you son of a bitch."

"You, too, Foster. Don't forget that."

"I can't."

"Then give me a name. I need someone from Military Intelligence, or maybe Air America."

"The agency?" He sounded worried. "What the hell kind of game are you playing?"

"Twenty questions," I told him. "But don't worry. I'm not playing with you. I need to know about a man who was over there around then. Maybe records would work. But someone in operations would be better. The only thing is, he has to talk. I have to be able to make him talk."

He was silent a long time. I waited him out. When he spoke, the name he gave was perfect. "Pauley," he said. "Sam Pauley. The captain. He's a colonel now. About ready to retire. He should do."

"What's his assignment?"

"Military Intelligence. He's in charge of the records section."

He gave me a work number. It wouldn't be good until the morning. I said goodbye and he hung up without a word. He didn't tell me not to call him again. He knew I would if I had to, and he couldn't do a damned thing about it.

Pauley wasn't in the book. I had to wait for the morning to reach him. I sat and waited for April to return. She finally came in around ten. She was drunk.

She glanced at me when she entered, then went into her room. I waited. When she came out, she was wearing the Montezuma T-shirt. She had the monkey pendant in her hand. She threw it at me. It hit my chest and fell on the floor. I let it lie.

"What did you do today?" I asked.

"Walked around. Took a cab to the Smithsonian. Had a couple of drinks." She spoke carefully, as though she were afraid of slurring.

"And?"

"And I spent some time thinking," she said. "About us."

"What did you decide?"

"Decided not to decide. You decide. If you want me you can have me."

"I want you, April."

"Then take me." She held her arms out. I picked her up and carried her into her room, laid her on the bed.

"You trying to confuse me?" she asked.

"I'm trying not to hurt you, April."

"Hurt me. Don't care." Her eyes were closing. "Don't care," she repeated.

I pulled the blankets over her. I found the monkey and put it on her bedside table, then put out the light and sat with her until she fell asleep. I went to find some supper.

There was a place called the Bamboo House down the street. Chinese food with a dimly lit lounge. I picked up a menu and sat at the bar, trying to decide what I wanted. Mongolian chicken or April. The bartender was a Chinese girl in her late twenties. She poured me a Johnny Walker and left me alone with the menu. I stared at it for a while, then set it aside and ordered another Black Label. When I finished the drink, I ordered another. I started to feel good, so I went home and put myself to bed. I didn't much feel like feeling good.

April was in a quiet mood the next morning. I took her to a House of Pancakes where we both drank a lot of coffee and pushed some eggs around our plates.

"About last night . . ." April began.

"Forget it."

"No. I was drunk. But I meant what I said. You decide."

"I didn't think you'd remember that."

"I thought about how to say it all afternoon."

"It'd be a lousy deal for you."

"Either way?" she asked.

"I don't know. The problem is who you are. Or what I am."

"I know what you are."

"Maybe not."

She put her hand over mine. "All afternoon," she said, "I thought about you. You know what I kept remembering? That you decided not to go back to the field."

"There wasn't any choice," I told her. "You know, when I went over there, I was a believer. I had principles."

"I figured that out."

"How?" I stared into my cup.

"You have to be a believer before you can stop believing." She dug the pendant from her purse and put it on the table between us. "Take it," she said. "If you want to give it to me again, I'll wear it. If you don't, I'll understand."

I picked the damned thing up and put it in my pocket.

Sam Pauley was in his office when I called at nine. He wasn't any happier to hear my voice than Foster had been. I told him what I wanted and where I wanted him to bring it.

He met us in the lounge at the Bamboo House at noon. The years had been hard on him. He was pushing sixty and looked five years older than that when he walked over to our table. He dropped the folder in front of me and glared at April.

"Why aren't you alone?" he demanded.

"Sit down, Colonel," I told him. "And don't worry. I'm not going to introduce you."

"I should have busted you twenty years ago!"

"You were too greedy. Where did your money go? Nice little split-level in Virginia? Don't get moral with me."

"Just get it over with!"

I picked up the folder and leafed through it. "This is all you have on Squall Line?" I asked.

"That's it. I should have guessed your bunch was involved."

"What makes you think we were involved?"

"You had a finger in everything that turned a dollar in Saigon," he told me. "And the fact that you asked about it now. But I'm warning you, if anything shows up in the papers about it, I'll have your ass! Dead!"

"I'm not in the army anymore," I told him mildly. "If you want my ass,

184

you're going to have to bid for it like everyone else. And frankly, you don't have what it takes. You're mine, Colonel. As long as you want to enjoy your comfy little retirement, you're going to dance when I pull your string. Remember that."

"Don't be too sure. I can arrange one last little operation. I could have you taken out anytime I want."

"I'm a hunter too, Colonel. Better be sure what kind of animal I am before you load your gun."

The bluster left him and he eyed me carefully. "Okay. Tell me."

"Some crap has come up from the old days," I said. "People are dying. Maybe it's connected with this"—I touched the folder—"and maybe it isn't. You reviewed the file before you brought it. Why don't I just ask some questions? If the answers are right, you can walk out of here with your cherry intact."

He had no choice and he knew it. "Shoot," he said.

"Who arranged Squall Line?"

"It was an agency operation."

"Who authorized it?"

"The director, I suppose. I just have our files on it, not theirs. We were only peripherally involved."

"That means you provided the cargo?"

"Yes."

"Who was liaison?"

"A man named Max Corvin. He was nominally with Air America in the old days."

"How did it work?"

"It was Corvin's baby. He set up Manila and handled the Saigon end, as well as arranging for the transport. I suppose that's where you guys came in."

"We aren't anywhere in the file?"

When he shook his head, I told him not to add any footnotes. He looked at me like I was crazy. I asked him about the payoffs.

"The Manila funds were paid through a blind out of Hong Kong," he said. "Three hundred thousand per load. Corvin got another three hundred a shipment to pay for the transport."

And there it was. Corvin skimmed three hundred thousand off each delivery.

"You're sure of those figures?" I asked.

He nodded.

"But wasn't that . . . exceptional?" I couldn't find the word.

Pauley exploded. "It was outrageous! Corvin operated on his own most of the time. He was a loose cannon! Money was pumped into the operation on his say-so. Some genius near the top came up with the idea. The originator was at the very highest level. You understand what that means. And you remember what things were like then. The light at the end of the tunnel was just around the corner, and the shit kept on raining down. We were reporting two hundred KIAs a week and shipping home five hundred boxes. It was an international police action and nobody supported us. Those turkeys in Washington would have sold their mothers to get some international support. Well, Corvin had a way to line Marcos up, and they bought it. The hell of it was that it worked, and so what if it cost a couple of million. They were spending that much every hour over there."

"What's Corvin up to now?"

Pauley shrugged. "No idea. He isn't official anymore. A couple of years ago he was doing private contracting. He still has some ears. And when a job comes along that can't be considered for political reasons, he's available. He's used, not liked."

"Who would get excited if he disappeared?"

"It's like that?"

I didn't answer. It was a stupid question.

He thought about it. "It would depend on how it happened," he said. "Some people might get nervous. But if there were no repercussions, nothing surfacing later, I think a lot of our people might be happy. That might even please some of the other agencies."

"Happy, or grateful?"

He looked surprised. "Are you in that line of work?"

186

"I want to know how big a pain in the ass Corvin is."

"I might be willing to put you on to him. If you could guarantee no repercussions."

"You couldn't get that guarantee from God Almighty," I told him. "One last question. How did Squall Line end? Who blew the whistle?"

"No one. It ran to completion."

"All three deliveries were made?" I asked. I wanted to see how far out Corvin had strayed.

"Only two were scheduled," he told me. "That's all that were ever planned. Two deliveries. You understand the symbolism of the name? A squall line is a storm front. The sea is calm, then the wind comes up, you take a pounding from the waves, the squall line passes over you, and there is calm again. It was never our intention to unseat Marcos. We just wanted to shake him up a bit."

"What happened on the second delivery? Why the ambush?"

"That was a screw-up. The Manila office was kept in the dark about the whole operation, but they noticed an increase in activity in the mountains. Two banks were hit, and a bus was ambushed. Civilians were killed. Women and children. Several police stations were raided. The captured weapons were traceable by their serial numbers. They were originally consigned to Vietnam. So when Marcos's police asked for help, the local boys stepped in. Their idea was to help a friendly government, that's all. They acted on their own. They didn't know they were stepping on any toes."

"They knew where the landing would take place," I said. "They knew all about it. There must have been a tipoff."

"I suppose so," he admitted. "Our file doesn't show the source."

"I think I know it."

"Corvin?"

I nodded.

"Well, it would have been in keeping with policy at that point in time. After all, they were Communists."

"We weren't."

"Yeah. Well, you shouldn't have been there."

I didn't remind him who put us there. "I want Corvin," I told him. "Find out where he is. I'll call tomorrow morning. Give me that and I'll say goodbye."

"Make it a permanent goodbye and you've got a deal, Rainbow."

"Fat chance." I pushed the folder back to him.

After Pauley left, we ate. April kept the conversation to the problem of Max. I liked the topic, too. It was safer than the other thing on our minds.

We still didn't have a clear-cut motive for Toker's death, but there were a couple of interesting possibilities. First, of course, was the money. Assume Roy had picked up the usual three hundred for the second delivery, and the other cargo had paid off the *Celestina* and her crew. Assume it was intact, hadn't been invested or otherwise grown. I couldn't remember the exact amount of the accumulated payoff we set aside for Corvin, but it was in the neighborhood of two hundred thousand in green, converted into stones at favorable rates. Say a bit over four hundred thousand in uncut emeralds, rubies, sapphires, maybe some other shit. Assume it had also remained intact. Figure in two decades of inflation on the jewels. There was something like a million and a half floating around in this deal. Plenty of reason for a killing or two.

April liked the money angle. I didn't. Nobody involved was poor. Roy had an accountant's dislike of waste. He would have picked up the money if it were just lying around, but it looked like a fair chunk of it, maybe all, was already in his pocket way back in 'seventy-one. In any case, he wouldn't have killed Toker for it. I'd helped him give more than that away, partly to Toker, while we were closing the accounts. So, if not for money, why had Toker died?

Max had some advantages as a suspect, even beyond the fact that I would enjoy killing him. He had a taste for money and he had the skimming to hide. Of course, he had known about part of the loot, at least, for a long time without going after it. And if he was trying to hide the skimming, who from?

Corvin's buddies in the agency didn't know about it, but who would tell them? Toker? He may have found out about the skimming, but how? And

188

would he care? I didn't give a damn. Why should he? And wouldn't he have mentioned it in his letter if he had known?

The other loose ends didn't throw much light. The detective in El Paso, Archuleta. It looked like he had been a target of opportunity. Whoever had followed April and me had decided to intercept whatever Archuleta learned in Juarez. The rancho at Las Colonias del Sur. Roy's hideout. Or maybe Roy had had the detective wasted to keep his secret. Both of those alternatives had merit, but there was no way to decide between them yet.

The biggest puzzle of all was the one I had been staring at since the afternoon April arrived on my doorstep. Why had Toker brought her home? And I hadn't a clue on that one.

After lunch, we checked the post office. The package from Albuquerque was waiting for us, and we officially became Holly Anderson and Roger Bacon. To celebrate, I took us to dinner and a play. They filled the evening, and I didn't have to think about the pendant until bedtime. It spilled out onto the bedside table when I emptied my pockets. I left it there, but it was on my mind and I couldn't sleep. Finally, I put the thing around my own neck and then I was able to drop off. April spent the night in her room. I hoped she slept better than I did.

When Pauley answered his phone at nine-thirty the next morning, he was in a better mood. He sounded as if he was smiling. That made me nervous. "You get it?" I asked.

"Naturally. He's incorporated as M.C. Consultants. The listed address is in Georgetown. But I doubt it'll do you any good."

"Why?"

"Well . . . look, Porter, I couldn't just ignore what you said. The old days are over, you understand? I had to talk to some people about you—your offer, I mean—"

I cut him off. "What did you do, Sam?"

My tone must have disturbed him. It should have. He began to apologize, to explain himself. "Nothing that would hurt you. I wouldn't do that, Rainbow. You know that. It's just that I can't forget my oath. I'm an officer, for Christ's sake! The past is past and can't be changed, but—"

"Shut up!"

"What? You can't talk to me like that!"

"Yes I can, Sam, because the past is never past. I can talk to you any way I want and you'll damned well listen. Or else. Now tell me what you did."

"I told some people that Squall Line was making some waves again, that I'd had a confidential inquiry about Corvin. I didn't mention your name. I just wanted to know, very hypothetically, you understand, how people would react if the operation resurfaced."

"And?"

"Nobody would be happy, that's the essence of it, Rainbow. I let my people think Corvin was making the waves. You'll be very interested in what they said. It ties in with your offer."

"That's the second time you mentioned an offer. I didn't make an offer, Pauley. Get that out of your head."

He paused, then tried another tack. "Well, maybe you should think about making an offer. My people would be grateful to see the last of Corvin, given the right circumstances and guarantees. Very grateful."

The man was trying my patience. "Get this through your head, Colonel: I made no offer to you. If you've led anyone to believe that you could get me to clean up your messes, you made a mistake. I got off the government payroll twenty years ago and I'm not signing up again."

"Did I say this could be very lucrative?"

"You said it. The pay and the work were shitty in 'Nam and this deal sounds worse. You boys are big enough to wipe your own asses. Don't try to hire me for the job. I mean that."

He was silent for a moment, then said, "You're putting me in an awkward position, Rainbow. I made certain representations, in good faith, based on what you said to me yesterday. If you try to back out now, I can't be responsible for what might happen."

"Cut the crap, Pauley." I laughed at him. "If your butt is hanging out on this one, it's your problem. Cover it yourself. But remember, any shit comes my way and I'll kick butt. Yours."

I hung up on him and told April about the conversation while we drove

190

out to Georgetown. M.C. Consultants was located in a rent-a-room office complex a mile or two from the Mall. I walked around it first and saw no sign of activity. Then April went in posing as a temporary secretary and talked to the receptionist in the lobby. She told her she'd been called by M.C. Consultants for a project and asked when someone would open the office. The receptionist was helpful and apologetic. She said that no one had opened the office in over two weeks, that Mr. Corvin's desk was covered with unanswered mail. She didn't give the impression that she thought much of April's new employer.

It looked like Corvin was out hunting. So were we, but we needed a new target. I had to book first class to get tickets on the afternoon flight to Albuquerque.

TIERRA AMARILLA

THE NIGHT APPROACH TO ALBUQUERQUE FROM THE east is beautiful. The Sandia Mountains lie right on the edge of town. As you fly in, you see scattered lights from houses built in the mountains, then nothing as you pass over the national forest, and then the city lights explode beneath you. The plane passes over the entire city and then banks into a U-turn over the mesa. You lose most of your altitude over the west bank of the Rio Grande River, and then, after you cross the river for the second time, the land below climbs quickly up to meet you at the same time you drop toward it. You are on the ground before you expect it.

Except for the grand concourse, the airport could be anywhere. It is only after you step outside that you realize you're in the desert. The air is thin and dry. Albuquerque International is about a mile high. When the humidity shoots up to thirty percent, the natives wipe their foreheads and complain about how muggy it is.

After the Philippines, Seattle, and Washington, it felt like heaven, or as close as I expect to come to heaven. We picked up our bags and caught a shuttle to the car. I gave it the same attention I had the last time we flew in. There were no surprises under the hood this time either.

We had dinner in Albuquerque and then headed home. Placitas is quiet in the early evening. There was very little traffic on the main drag and none on the road to the house. At the driveway, I stopped and told April to take the wheel and follow me the rest of the way in. I walked up the drive with my eyes open for surprises.

There had been traffic since we left. I couldn't tell how recently, but I thought it was in the last couple of days.

The house was waiting silently when we reached the clearing. I motioned April to stop behind me and studied it. The red Jaguar was parked by the front door. The door was closed and the windows all looked okay from this distance. Same with the garage.

April came up beside me. "What are you waiting for?"

"Confidence."

She studied it briefly. "It looks fine to me."

"It isn't. Stay here until I call you." I slipped into the woods and worked my way around the clearing to make sure no one was waiting to do to me what I'd done to the two soldiers by the van on Luzon. The woods were clear. I walked around both the house and the garage. The house hadn't been approached, as far as I could tell, since the Filipinos, Mexicans, or whatever they had been, that Jenny told me about. But someone had been at the garage. The side door showed signs of forced entry. I unlocked it and stepped cautiously inside, then gave my eyes a chance to adjust to the gloom.

If we had returned an hour later, when it was dark, or if I hadn't been so spooked, we would have died. Even so, it took me a while to see what had been done.

A line ran from a small stone cemented to the floor about where the front bumper would be. It ran straight up, through an eye-hook screwed into one of the joists, and then over to a small, curved black package that pointed down toward where the windshield of the car would stop. Another Claymore. You drive in. The bumper hits the line and triggers the mine. It explodes and sends a shower of shrapnel through the windshield. Finis.

I backed out of the garage and locked it, then headed for the house. It wasn't likely that two devices had been set, but I didn't take any chances. I checked each room, the refrigerator, the furnace, the crawl space, everything. It took over an hour. When I was done, I checked the Jaguar. Everything but the garage was clear. I waved April in. She was angry at the wait until I told her what was in the garage.

"How are they finding us?" she asked.

"I don't know. Maybe they followed you here the first time. Maybe they followed us back from Los Angeles. Corvin has resources from his agency contacts. He could either use them or rent talent. Or do the job himself."

"And if it's Roy?"

"Roy probably has a good idea where I live from the old days. He knows Walker is in Phoenix. He didn't know we were going to the Philippines, but he might have figured that out. The only thing is, I can't see him putting together the attack on Luzon. Not on such short notice."

"And Sissy?"

"Sissy is a question mark. Maybe we'll learn something tomorrow."

We spent the night there. April was nervous. She asked if she could sleep with me. I told her sure. She came to bed wearing Montezuma and stayed on her own side until we fell asleep. When we woke, we were together in the middle of the bed, but that was just an accident.

It was light enough in the morning to tackle the garage. I carried a ladder out and disarmed the bomb, then carried it up the mountain and disposed of it. The explosion reflected my mood.

April had done the laundry while I took care of that business. When I returned we were repacked and ready to go. I looked at what she had done and added a few things. An AR15, the civilian version of the M16, but modified for full automatic fire, and a .45 automatic. She said nothing when I bagged them and carried them out to the car. We stopped at a pay phone in

Bernalillo and made reservations at the La Fonda in Santa Fe, then drove on up.

The room wasn't ready when we arrived, just under an hour later, so we drove out to the high school and looked through old yearbooks until I found Sissy's picture with the class of 'fifty-nine. Juan Cisneros.

He had lettered in track. He hadn't participated in any clubs or other sports. His ambition had been to drive a corvette and make a million. Like eight out of ten of the boys on the page, he'd worn his hair in a DA. His friends had voted him most likely to marry a movie star. His expression in the senior picture was friendly, but there was a dissatisfied quality to it. That had intensified in the ten years before I met him in Saigon.

I copied out the names of the other members of the track team and we left. The La Fonda was ready for us when we returned. Perhaps because of its age, the rooms there are smaller, more like the rooms in a private house. Everything in them feels antique. They have no balconies. There is no swimming pool. The adobe walls in the older parts of the building are plastered and a foot and a half thick. You get the feeling that your great-grandfather might have slept in the same bed. On the same mattress.

Three of the boys on the track team with Juan Cisneros were listed in the phone book. I gave each of them the same story. We were in 'Nam together in 'sixty-nine. He told me to look him up if I ever got to Santa Fe. Did they know where he was?

They all told me, as gently as possible and with much hesitation, about his death on his last tour. Something about a helicopter. In one case he was a gunner, but the other two said he was just catching a ride. They all agreed that his death had been heroic. They all told me I should be proud of what he had done, his courage in signing up for all those tours. They had been civilians, of course.

I told them all that I was sorry to hear he hadn't made it back. I said I wanted to talk to his parents, to tell them how he had been in Vietnam.

They understood that, and they all thought his parents would appreciate hearing from me. But they had moved. No one knew where they were living now.

I got his address when he had been in high school. They all gave the same address. I asked when they had seen him last. None had seen him after Christmas of 'sixty-six, when he was home on leave before his first tour.

One of them asked if I had talked to Jack Tafoya.

"Tafoya? No. Who is he?"

"Jack was Juan's best friend in school," he said. "He has his own insurance company now. If anyone knows where the family went, it'll be Jack."

I thanked him and hung up, then found Tafoya's name in the phone book. I made an appointment with him for later that afternoon.

April and I had a leisurely lunch at the restaurant downstairs before walking over to the Gallisteo Street office. Tafoya was about three inches shorter than me, with ten more years on him, and graying temples to prove it. He waved us to a couple of chairs and asked what he could do for us. I gave him the same speech I'd given the others, except that I now knew Cisneros hadn't made it back.

He developed a sorrowful look when I mentioned Sissy's name. "The best friend I'll ever have," he said. "We did everything together. Chased the girls, got drunk the first time, everything. I even met my wife through him." He shook his head sadly. "It about killed me when I heard he was dead. I was drunk for a week, man!" He tried to laugh, but it didn't work.

"How did you hear?"

"His mom called me. She was crying. An officer drove up from Albuquerque just to tell her. She appreciated that. It was nice of the Army to send an officer up. He stayed with her until her neighbor, Mrs. Martinez, came over, and then she called Tony. Juan's dad. And then she called me. She knew how much I loved him."

"When did you see him last?"

"Christmas. Just before his first tour. He never came home after that. All those tours, and he never thought about himself. He was a real patriot."

"Who was Mrs. Martinez?"

"She lived across the street. They grew up together, I think. They were like sisters. That's why his mom called her when the officer told her to call someone.''

"Maybe she knows where they moved?''

He shook his head. "No. I asked her when I went over and found the house empty. She said they just packed up and moved out. That was about two months after Juan was killed.''

"I'd really like to talk to them,'' I said. "Can you think of anyone else who might know where they went?''

"No way. If there was anybody, I would have found them. He was close, you know? It really hurt when the family moved out like that. They should have left word. It wasn't right.''

"No, it wasn't,'' I agreed. I motioned to April and we got up to leave. I thanked him for talking to me. He dismissed it and shook my hand. His eyes were moist and he was reaching for a handkerchief as we walked out.

On the way back to the hotel, April asked what I thought.

"Two months,'' I said, "is about enough time to recover from a leg wound and make it back to the states.''

"But you don't think he knew?''

"Tafoya? No. Maybe they were best friends in school, but Cisneros seems to have dropped everybody after he got involved with Roy.''

"Why?''

"Maybe he was ashamed. Or maybe he just grew apart from them. Maybe the war came between them. How the hell should I know?''

She was quiet for a few steps, then suddenly reached over and patted my chest, pressing the monkey under my shirt.

"What's that about?''

"Just checking,'' she said. "You still have it.''

"If I don't have it, you will.''

We took a car out to the old address. It was a poor neighborhood but not a bad one. We knocked at the house across the street. It took a long time for the door to open. Mrs. Martinez was a short, bent woman with a head of thick hair just beginning to gray. She looked to be in her early seventies. I introduced myself and began the same story I'd told the others. She started shaking her head before I finished.

"*No comprendo. Yo no hablo Ingles,*" she said.

I started over in halting Spanish.

She shook her head again. "I already told the other man. I don't know nothing about them," she said.

"You speak English?"

"I don't speak nothing. I already told the other man." She closed the door in our faces.

Back in the car, I sat staring out the windshield.

"She knows where they are," April said.

I nodded.

"Can we make her talk?"

"I don't want to. She's an old woman."

"Then it's a dead end?" April asked.

"Maybe I'll think of something tonight. But we aren't the only ones looking for him. Somebody else thinks he's alive."

We had dinner at a restaurant I liked on Rodeo and returned to the hotel early. April tried to talk about how we would find Sissy, but I kept losing my train of thought. Eventually, she gave up and went to bed. I joined her after midnight. The next morning I woke with an idea, a long shot.

After breakfast, we drove out to the cemetery. The headstone said Juan Cisneros, December 25, 1941–July 17, 1971, Staff Sergeant, USA. I hadn't known he was born on Christmas Day. The grave was not kept up. Of course not. It was empty.

The next stop was the parish. I talked to the priest. His predecessor, Father Steibner, had been there in 'seventy-one. He was living at a retirement home in Pennsylvania. I got the name of the place and put in a long distance call from the hotel.

Steibner remembered the Cisneros family well. He had officiated at the memorial services for Juan. When I asked about Sissy's parents, he said that they had not told him where they were going. They hadn't even said goodbye. He still seemed hurt by the memory of that old snub. But he did

198

remember one thing. Mrs. Cisneros had come from a little town up north. Tierra Amarilla. So had her friend, Mrs. Martinez.

I was smiling when I hung up.

"What is it?"

"The family was from Tierra Amarilla," I told her.

"I've heard that name! Where?"

"In El Paso. While we were tracing those properties, trying to find Roy. One of the companies had holdings up north. In Rio Arriba County. And the county seat is a small town called—"

"Tierra Amarilla!"

I smiled. "Feel like a drive?"

"Yes!"

We checked out and bought a couple of hamburgers for the trip. We took Highway 84 out of town and then followed it north, through Tesuque and then down into the Rio Grande valley to Española. The highway falls steadily from an altitude of seven thousand feet at Santa Fe down to the Rio Grande crossing at Española, then rises as it traces the east side of the Rio Chama to Abiquiu. It crosses the river there, and bears west, toward the Continental Divide.

Northern New Mexico is dry, but it is not a desert. This high, the land is rolling hills between mountain ranges. It is covered with scrub oak, juniper, piñon, and small pine trees, separated by grasses. Cattle range freely over the land. The people are mostly of Spanish, Anglo, and Indian descent, and many of the families have been in place for hundreds of years. Thousands, for the Indians.

At Abiquiu Reservoir, Highway 84 turns more northerly and parallels the continental divide, thirty to fifty miles east of it. It cuts through a corner of Carson National Forest and then edges into a vaguely triangular chunk of private land bounded by the national forest on the east and the Jicarilla Apache Reservation on the west. The altitude there climbs steadily, averaging between seven and eight thousand feet, but it frequently pokes above ten. The canyon walls that constrain this part of the highway are frequently barren. Yellow and red cliffs break through the hills on either side of the road.

Between them, however, the canyon floor is covered with taller trees: poplar, oak, and cottonwoods. The soil is rich, and enough water reaches it to nourish the gardens and pastures of the people who live there.

Tierra Amarilla means "Yellow Earth." The village lies more or less in the center of the triangle. It was settled in the early eighteen hundreds. Today, the population of the whole county is just a little over thirty thousand. It might be possible to find two citizens who didn't know each other, but it would be a sure bet that they would know at least one person in common. And if their families had been around awhile, it was probable that they would be related.

We took a cabin at a small lodge that catered to the fishermen who came for the nearby Heron and El Vado reservoirs, or the Chama River and the small streams that feed it. The room was small and primitive. A bed and dresser filled it. There was no television, and I had a feeling that few of the guests spent much time in it. We followed suit. It was only three-thirty, so we asked directions to the courthouse.

The woman who brought us the land records we asked for was in her early fifties. She was friendly and eager to help until she heard the name we were looking for: the Quintana Holding Company. Then she told us that there was no such land holder in the county. I told her to bring the books over anyway. She did it reluctantly, then left the room.

We found the parcel immediately. Four thousand acres. I wrote down the section numbers of the land, and we continued the trace. Quintana Holding had sold out in 1979 to the Lower Chama Investment Company. Two years later, the parcel had been sold to a man named Felix Romero.

We had just found that transaction when the woman returned with a deputy sheriff. He was a brown bear of a man with a broad face and a thick black mustache.

"Can I help you folks?" he asked.

"We're doing just fine," I told him. "The lady is taking good care of us."

He hooked his thumbs into his pistol belt and stepped closer to me. "She says you're being rude, causing trouble."

200

The woman wouldn't meet our eyes.

"I'm sorry she got that impression. We didn't mean to cause any trouble."

"Maybe you better leave now."

"We aren't finished here."

He shifted his pistol belt self-consciously. "What are you doing?"

I decided there wasn't much point in hiding anything. It would be hard to make inquiries without attracting attention in any case. "I'm looking for the family of a friend of mine. Some people named Cisneros. They had a son named Juan."

"Never heard of them," he said. "Come on. It's closing time anyway."

"The sign says the office closes at five," I pointed out. "It isn't four-thirty yet."

"It's an old sign," he said. "They're closing now."

I put down the book. "Okay. We'll come back tomorrow. What time do you open?" I asked the woman.

She looked at the deputy.

"Closed tomorrow," he said.

"A holiday?"

"Think of it that way. What do you want with the Cisneros family?"

"I knew their son. In Vietnam. I just wanted to talk to them about him."

"I'll ask around," he said. "If there is a family named Cisneros around here, I'll ask if they want to talk to you. They say no, you're out of here. Understand me?"

"I understand," I told him.

"Then go. Now." He followed us out and stood watching as we drove away.

I found a gas station and filled the tank. I asked the attendant where I could get a USGS map of the county.

"Fishing?" he asked. "A fishing map would be better. I've got some inside. Shows all the trout streams and lakes. You want one?"

I told him no, I was thinking about doing some hiking. He told me to try the park office out at Vado Lake.

It was a twenty-minute drive. The office was closed when we got there. The deputy sheriff's car picked us up on the way back and followed us to the motel. I turned into the parking lot and he pulled in behind me. His lights began flashing. I got out and met him between the cars.

"I'm beginning to feel unwelcome," I said.

"Let's see your license and registration."

I shrugged and walked back to April's side of the car. I leaned in and opened the glove compartment and fished around until I found the registration. When I came out, he had his pistol pointed at me.

"Keep your hands where I can see them!" he barked.

"You can see them now, Sheriff." Two fishermen were standing in the door of the next cabin, watching us. "Everyone can see them."

He looked around. "You shouldn't go into a glove compartment like that without telling me. I don't know what you got in there."

"My registration," I held it out to him. I kept my hands in sight and well away from my sides. "That's where everyone keeps their car registration. You asked for it."

He ignored me. "And your driver's license."

"It's in my wallet. You want me to get it out?"

"Don't be a smart-ass."

I took my wallet out carefully and held it toward him.

"Take the license out, please."

I did so carefully. I almost gave him the new license, the one in the name of Roger Bacon. But I caught myself in time and passed over the Porter license. He carried it and my registration back to his patrol car and got on the radio. A few minutes later, he holstered the pistol and brought the papers back to me.

"Sorry about that, Mr. Porter. I had a report of a stolen car. The description was sort of like yours."

"Report from the state police?" I asked.

He looked at me carefully. "No. It was a verbal report. The state police don't have it."

I didn't believe him. "Be sure you pass it on."

"If I confirm it. No point in passing on a mistake."

"No point in shooting a man over a mistake either," I said.

"Yeah. That would be sort of regrettable. You planning on being around long?"

"Depends on how long it takes to find my friend."

"I asked around. Nobody of that name in town."

I looked at his name tag. It said CISNEROS.

"Different branch of the family," he said. "Don't bother people, Mr. Porter. We're very serious about disturbing the peace around here." He nodded to me and returned to his car.

April was shaking when I opened her door. I didn't feel exactly calm myself. She put her arms around me and hugged me. That helped some. I hugged her back. I could feel the monkey sharp between us.

We ate at a restaurant on the highway to Chama and sacked out early. The food was terrible but filling. The mattress was lumpy, but the company was good. The next morning I drove to the Sheriff's office and left April in the car with the keys and instructions to find the state police if I didn't return in half an hour.

The sheriff was a short thin man named Peña. He didn't smile when I introduced myself and offered my hand, but he shook.

"What can I do for you, Mr. Porter?" he asked.

He didn't offer me a chair. I took one anyway. "I think your deputy has a problem with me. I'd like to get it straightened out before someone gets hurt."

"What makes you think that?"

I described what had happened at the motel the day before. "I haven't broken any laws," I added, "and I'm not here to make trouble for anyone. I just want to find an old friend."

"I checked around. Your friend is buried in Santa Fe. His family moved away from here over forty years ago. There is nothing here for you, Mr. Porter. I think you would be smart to look somewhere else."

"The grave is empty. You know it and I know it. And I have reason to think the family moved back. I want to talk to them."

He looked at me expressionlessly. "Suppose they did," he said. "You have no right to bother them. If they don't want to talk to you, it is my business, the business of my whole department, to protect their right to privacy. And we will do that."

"Have you spoken to them? Did they say they don't want to talk to me?"

He smiled at me. "I can hardly talk to people who don't exist, can I?"

"If they don't exist, I'm hardly bothering anyone by looking for them, am I?"

"Don't nitpick, Porter. You're bothering people. You're bothering me right now. Stop it. Leave town."

"I'll leave when my business is done," I said. "In the meantime, if I have another run-in with your department, I'll file a complaint with the state police. If you want to cover your ass, you'd better play by the book from now on. That means protecting law-abiding citizens like me. Your deputy frightened my friend badly last night. Don't let that happen again."

He glanced pointedly at his watch. "My ass is very well covered, Mr. Porter," he said quietly. "If you want to avoid trouble, you should begin by avoiding trouble. And I'm afraid there is only trouble here in Tierra Amarilla for you. Goodbye."

He stared at me until I left.

When I described the conversation to April, she acted as though I should be outraged.

"They're just trying to protect their own," I told her.

"But we aren't threatening anyone!"

"You don't know that. If Sissy was involved in those killings, I'm a threat to him. A serious threat. And he knows it."

"So you think he was involved?"

"I think he's alive, somewhere in Rio Arriba County."

204

We drove up to Chama and found a survey map of the county. I studied it long enough to locate the land that had been owned by Quintana Holding Company and sold to Felix Romero.

Since we were having trouble finding the front door, I planned to hike around to the back. We did a little shopping. Jeans, hiking boots, wool shirts, and heavy jackets for each of us. A small backpack and a canteen. After lunch in Chama, we drove back to Tierra Amarilla. The deputy picked us up on the way and followed us to the motel. He parked out front for forty minutes, but didn't come to the door. Eventually, he drove away.

We spent the afternoon in our cabin, going over the map and discussing the plans for the night. I'd wanted to leave April behind, but she wouldn't hear of it. She maintained that her presence might provide a hold of some sort over Sissy. I had to agree that she could be right. If he turned out to be her father. And if he wasn't doing the killing. Anyway, if there was an effective way to leave her behind, I hadn't found it.

The property wouldn't be hard to find. There was a turnoff near a place called Nutrias. The map showed it as a primitive road. I hoped it wasn't too primitive for the car.

We left at dusk. I had hoped to be unobserved, but a patrol car was waiting across the street. It escorted us when we pulled out of the parking lot. When we turned south on 84 and started out of town, it fell back and paced us from a distance.

Nutrias was no more than a small collection of homes with a small store. I drove past it. The patrol car pulled off there and we drove on, alone in the night.

April turned in her seat and stared back into the dark as the headlights diminished behind us. "He stopped," she said. "Why did he stop?"

"It's an old tradition in the west. We've just been escorted out of town."

"We're a long way out of town."

"That was the turnoff to Sissy's place. He followed us long enough to make sure we didn't take the turn."

Ten minutes later, I pulled over and turned out the lights. We climbed into the backseat and changed into the jeans and boots. I got the weapons from the trunk, checked the clips, and put them on the front seat. Then we turned around and headed back toward Nutrias.

It was almost nine. There were lights in several of the houses scattered around the turnoff. There was no sign of the patrol car.

I cut the headlights and made the turn slowly, trying to minimize our engine noise. We moved up the dirt road at fifteen miles an hour. The terrain was rugged and climbed steadily. We were soon surrounded by tall pines that nearly met overhead and blocked what light the moon gave. I had to turn the lights back on. I rolled the windows down and tried to listen for other vehicles, but the sound of our own passage prevented that.

The road hadn't been graded in years, though it showed signs of regular use. In several places it was no more than two ruts winding between the boles of the surrounding trees. The car bucked when the tires climbed out of the ruts and then fell back in. A couple of times I heard or felt earth scrape on the undercarriage when the mound between the ruts rose too high.

April found the second turnoff. I would never have seen it. It was hardly even a pathway. The ruts split and a faint trail cut into the trees on the right. She said, "There!," and pointed. I had to back up to make the turn.

A hundred yards up, the trail widened abruptly. It was graded again. I stopped and turned off the lights and engine. The silence was overwhelming. We sat in the dark for a few minutes, listening. An owl hooted in the distance, and a faint breeze rustled the needles of the pines.

I turned on the interior light and rechecked the clips in the pistol and the AR15. I chambered a round in each and set the safeties, then turned off the light and waited for night vision to come. The wait did no good. There wasn't enough light penetrating the trees to see a damned thing. If the map was right, the Romero property was about a mile ahead. I intended to take the next opportunity to turn the vehicle around and then finish the trip on foot.

As I reached for the ignition, I heard an engine, very faint, somewhere behind us. I froze and glanced at April. She had heard it too.

"Are they following us?" she whispered.

There was no way to tell. Chances were good that we were being followed. There was nothing else out here. I started the car and drove ahead as quickly as I safely could.

Within a quarter mile, I could see headlights flickering between the trees behind us. There must have been a watcher in one of the houses. But the headlights were higher than they would have been on a patrol car. More like a pickup. I didn't know if that was good or not.

I told April to hide the M16 under the front seat. There was no point letting Sissy know I'd come armed.

Our tail caught up with us a couple of hundred yards later. He approached to within fifty feet and then followed. I slowed down. There was no longer any hope of surprise, and I saw no point in taking chances. I handed the pistol to April and asked her to put it in the glove compartment.

A few minutes later I had to stop. A second pickup, facing us, with its headlights on, blocked the road ahead. There was no way around it. The trees were too close.

April was shaking. "What do we do now?" she asked.

"We wait." I turned off the lights and the engine.

The truck behind us stopped twenty yards back. The engine was turned off, but the headlights stayed on us. I heard a door open and slam shut, and someone scurried into the trees to the left. I kept my hands on the steering wheel and waited. The only sound was April's ragged breathing.

A shot sounded ahead and to the left. I was too blinded by the headlights in my eyes to see any flash. I waited.

"Get out of there, you son of a bitch!" The voice sounded young.

"Slowly," I told April. "We don't want to startle anyone."

We climbed out very cautiously and held our hands above our heads.

An older man spoke behind us. "Walk forward and stand in front of your car."

We did as he ordered.

He called out again, "Watch them, Juan! If they try anything, you shoot! Okay?"

"I'll shoot, Tio." It was the young voice. It sounded nervous.

Behind us, I heard the door of my car open and the bumper settled against my legs. A minute later, I heard, "Sons of bitches have guns in here!"

The one in front of us came closer until he was silhouetted by the headlights. "You want me to shoot them?" he called.

"No!" I said.

"Not yet," the older one answered. I hoped it wasn't just because he'd realized he was in the line of fire. The bumper shifted behind my knees as the one in the car crawled out.

He walked around to the side and I could begin to make him out. A man, maybe in his mid-fifties. But he carried himself as though he were in good condition. He spent a minute thinking.

"Lay down, both of you," he ordered.

We lay in the dirt.

"I'm going to search them," he told the young man. "You shoot if they try anything!"

"I don't want to shoot the girl," the younger one said.

"Don't shoot her," I said.

"You shut up!" A boot caught the side of my head, but it wasn't a strong blow. I winced. "You shoot the one that moves first. Even if it's the girl."

His hands patted me down carefully. Then he moved over to April. I heard her gasp once but she didn't move. He walked back out of the line of fire. "They don't have no more guns on them," he told the other. "You stand up now," he said to us. "What do you want here?"

I stood slowly and helped April to her feet. She was still trembling. I murmured a question at her and she nodded. She was all right.

"I want to see Sissy," I called to them. "Juan Cisneros. I'm a friend of his."

"You're gonna have to see him," the old one said. "He'll decide if you're a friend." He stepped up by the boy and whispered to him. Then they both backed away and he told us to start walking.

We passed the second pickup and then walked slowly down the center of

208

the road. It was hard to see at first, but the trees began to thin out and soon there was more light.

We walked in silence with our hands up at chest level. We could hear footsteps behind us and the owl, now very faint, far behind us. After half a mile or so, there was a light ahead. We walked into a wide clearing. Several bright lights were set on poles around the clearing. A garage, a barn, and several corrals were scattered around it. They all glowed with the silvery sheen of very old wood. The house was directly ahead, a sprawling one-story adobe. We headed for the front door.

"Stop there!"

We stopped. The young man ran around us and opened the door. There was an older woman behind it, peering out at us.

"Are you all right, Juanito?" she asked.

He nodded and told her to move back.

"Take them to the den," she said. "He's waiting."

The boy stood to one side and gestured with his rifle. It was an old .30-30. We entered. There was a modern kitchen to the left. The woman stood just inside and stared at us as we walked past her. She was wearing a house dress. I heard her whisper when she saw April clearly. "A girl!"

We walked past a living room on the right and down a hall. The den was a large room, fifteen feet by about thirty. The walls were paneled in dark pine. A man sat on a long horse-hide sofa at the far end with a revolver held loosely in his left hand. He was almost fifty years old now. His hair was still thick, but there was some silver in it. His face showed a quiet strength I had never seen in Saigon. When we entered, he picked up a cane, stood with difficulty, and limped toward us. He stopped ten feet away and looked us over with unfriendly eyes.

"You don't look dead," I told him.

He nodded and said, "Rainbow."

The older man came in and stood to one side. He carried the M16 and the .45 in his left hand. The other hand held a 30.06 hunting rifle. Sissy glanced at them, then back to me.

"You bring weapons to see an old friend?" he asked.

"I brought more than that. I brought your daughter."

His eyes widened. "My daughter?" He looked at April. Behind us, the woman gasped. *"Madre de Dios!"*

April said, "Hello."

"You want to talk?" I asked.

He nodded. "Maybe we better." He turned and limped slowly back to the sofa and sat. He called to the boy, "Bring chairs, *hijo.*"

The other man put my weapons in the corner and kept his rifle on us while the chairs were brought and arranged. Sissy waved in his direction. "My brother, Tony," he told me. "Did they have any other guns?" he asked Tony.

"No. Just these."

"Then I think you can put your rifle away."

We sat. The woman came and stood beside Sissy. "What does he mean, your daughter?"

"Be quiet, Anna," he told her. "I don't know what he means. I don't have a daughter."

"Miss Phoung's daughter, then," I said.

"You aren't my father?" April asked in a small voice.

He studied her, glanced at his wife, then shook his head. "No. Roy told me she was going to have a baby. But it wasn't mine."

"Then whose?" I asked.

He laughed softly. "Who can say? Maybe yours."

I was getting angry. "You know better than that!"

"I don't know a damned thing. I was taken out before the end, remember?"

"You were around when she was started."

"When?"

"July. Just before we went to Luzon."

"Roy told me it was later than that," he said slowly.

"He lied."

Sissy turned to April. "Why are you here?" he asked. "Why aren't you home?"

She started crying.

I was watching Sissy carefully. He seemed confused. "It was you," I said. "You knew she was in California."

He looked down at the gun in his hand. "Okay," he said. "Sure, I knew it. When I found out that Phoung was dead, I decided her kid should get a cut. I went to Toker. He was the only one who could take care of a kid. I told him about it and he agreed to try to find her. Five, six years later, I almost forgot about it, and I heard from him again. He'd found a girl in Hong Kong. He said she was Phoung's baby. I told him to bring her back, and he did. There was no way I could see her. But I made sure she was taken care of."

"You didn't tell me this," the woman said. "You should have told me."

"I couldn't, Anna," he said. "You never understood about what happened in 'Nam. I told you I had a girl over there. You didn't talk to me for two weeks."

"A little baby is different."

"She isn't mine," he said. "I did it for Phoung. For her memory."

"That's worse, Juan," she said. "It means you loved her."

"It was a long time ago, and she was dead before I met you."

"Still," she said. She gave April a look I couldn't interpret. "Are you sure this isn't your daughter?"

"Yes."

"How?"

"You know. She couldn't have been."

"I see." She looked troubled.

April had stopped crying. She sat there studying Sissy. "Who?" she demanded. "Who was he then?"

"I don't know. Roy said he thought it was that son of a bitch Corvin."

"Max Corvin?" She sounded forlorn.

Sissy looked surprised. "You know about Max?"

"There are some things you have to know," I said.

"Then tell me. Start with that." He waved at the weapons in the corner.

"You first. What's with the guards? And the revolver?"

He tightened his grip on the pistol and looked belligerent.

"We used to trust each other, compadre," I said softly. "Remember?"

He continued staring at me, but his expression changed. "I remember," he said. "But it's been a long time. I've been in hiding for a long time."

"Tell me about it."

"When I got this"—he slapped his hip—"after you left us on the beach, Roy and I spent the night in the jungle. After that Filipino guy, Freddy, left, we talked about what happened. It looked like we were set up. And it looked like Corvin did it."

I nodded. "It had to be him."

"So we decided there was only one way to protect our group. I had to die. Pretend to die. But Roy would let Corvin know I wasn't dead. And if he made another move against the group, I'd blow the whistle on him. I was the safety man.

"They got me to Manila, to a doctor friendly to the guerrillas. He took out the bullet and fixed me up as well as he could. I spent six weeks in his house. Then Roy came back. He had a passport I could use one time. I made it back to Santa Fe and called my father. We had a family council. They brought me back here. I've been here ever since."

"Why didn't he tell the rest of us?"

"You know Roy. There was no reason to tell you. He never did anything without a reason. Besides, you couldn't talk about what you didn't know. As long as I was alive, you were safe from Corvin."

"And in return for providing us with this service, you were to get . . . what?"

"The payoff money. And one of Roy's two shares."

I thought that sounded generous for Roy. But of course he had the third delivery up his sleeve. He hadn't shorted himself. He had come out ahead. That was Roy.

"Was it worth it?"

"I visited my own grave, man!" He grinned at me. "Not many men can say that!" But then he sobered. "Of course, there was a price."

212

"You had to hide for the rest of your life."

"Yes. . . ." He closed his eyes for a moment. "But it wasn't so bad. Roy came through for me. I got all this." He waved his hand around, vaguely including the house and the four thousand acres it sat on. "And there was Anna. My son, Juanito, over there. And my brother, my family. They helped."

He looked at me directly. "It wasn't such a bad bargain, my friend. When I die, my family will have something. Something that will last for generations. How many men can say that? It was worth a leg, I think."

"And a life in hiding?"

"I don't have to hide all the time. The people in the village accept me as Mr. Romero. The ones who know, who have known my family for generations, they look out for me. There was only one danger."

"Corvin."

"Yes. I don't think he ever stopped looking for me. If he could find me, he could go after the rest of you, one at a time. And then he would be safe. But he didn't come for a long time. Sometimes, in the early years, I would go into the village, to the church or to a *baile,* a dance, you know? That was how I saw my Anna the first time." He patted the hand she lay on his shoulder. "I was pretty safe for a long time."

"What happened?"

"I don't know. Last week I got two telephone calls. People were looking for me in Santa Fe. So I pulled in, holed up."

"That was me," I told him. "Me and someone else."

"Max?"

"It seems likely."

"What is all this about? Why is this happening?"

"People are dying."

"Like who?"

"Toker was first."

"He's dead? Who killed him?"

"Not me. Not April. Did you?" I heard his son shift angrily behind me.

"Easy, Juan," Sissy told him. "It is a question that he had to ask." He turned to me. "I haven't been out of New Mexico since I came home," he said. "Even when I met Roy, I only went as far as Albuquerque. I had to be careful."

"Why didn't Roy come here?"

"He only knew about Santa Fe. He didn't know where I ended up. We figured it would be better that way, back there in the jungle on Luzon. After that, he never asked and I never brought it up. When he needed to see me, he sent a post card to my cousin, Steve, in Santa Fe."

"When did you learn about Miss Phoung?" I asked.

"Maybe 'seventy-five? Just about the time of the fall of Saigon. We signed off on some property, and we were just sitting around, bullshitting about the old days. We were in a funny mood. Real . . . well . . . I can't describe it. You know?"

I nodded. I'd been in a funny mood, too, the month of the fall of Saigon. I'd read every paper and magazine I could find and put my fist through a couple of walls, and then I hadn't read a damned thing for maybe six months.

Sissy continued, "Anyway, I asked Roy how Phoung ended up. He'd always promised me he'd take care of her, you know? And then he said she was dead. Shot. He didn't know who. Maybe the VC, he said. I asked him about it, and he let it drop that there was a baby. Man, I almost killed him! He promised me he'd take care of her. Promised me! All those years I thought she was doing good, married or something, and then he says she was shot. And she left a little baby. I almost killed him."

"'Seventy-five. That's a long time to go without asking." I shouldn't have said that. I had never asked either.

"I know." He spun the cylinder of his revolver idly. "But there was Anna. And little Juan. And it was so far away. I guess I didn't know how close it still was, until the fall."

April cleared her throat. She was sitting stiffly, her eyes glued to Sissy. "You did care about my mother," she said.

He looked at her and smiled weakly. "I loved her," he said softly. "I would have gone back to Saigon for her. I might have married her. If I

214

hadn't been killed on Luzon. Yes, I loved her. But I'm not your father. I'm
sorry.''

I couldn't tell if the apology was to April or his wife, who was gazing
across the room at nothing in particular. The son, perhaps.

"How did Roy say she died?" I asked.

"The war. Somebody shot her." He pulled himself together. "Anna, I
want you to bring the whiskey bottle for my friend and me. Please. Juanito,
Tonio, put away the weapons. These are my friends. Juan, you will go get
the truck and Rainbow's car and bring them to the yard. And Tony, if you
could return to your watch, I would be very grateful."

He had developed authority over the years. They all moved, Anna wiping
her eyes and young Juan dragging his feet. "Pull your chair closer, Rainbow,
and tell me the story of Toker's death. It seems our problem is now bigger
than just hiding from Max Corvin."

I did as he asked and began the tale with April's appearance on my
doorstep. He listened carefully as I spoke and did not interrupt me with
questions. Midway through the story, his wife returned with a bottle, two
glasses, and a Coke. She stood quietly, out of Sissy's sight, and listened as I
finished describing the ambush on Luzon and what I'd learned about Corvin.
Then she set the drinks on the table and went to stand behind her husband.

Sissy poured two bourbon and Cokes. I made a face at him and took a hit
directly from the bottle. April took the second mixed drink, tasted it, and
pushed it away from her.

"You haven't changed," I told him. "Good taste in women, terrible
taste in booze."

"I've changed," he said. "The leg changed me. Anna changed me. Little
Juan changed me. Twenty years on the ranch changed me. Don't say I
haven't changed, Rainbow. Back in the old days, I couldn't keep it in my
pants. You remember."

"I remember. That's why I don't know how you can be so sure. About
April."

He shot a glance at his wife that I didn't understand. She had her hand
back on his shoulder. "Believe him," she said.

I didn't think it would do any good to pursue it. I decided to see if he could answer the big question. "Tell me about Toker, then. Why did you go to him?"

"I couldn't go to Roy. After he lied to me about taking care of Phoung? And who else was there? Johnny Walker had a new wife. And there'd be too many other problems there because of the color thing. You? Roy told me about you. He said you were . . ." He stopped.

"What did he say?"

"He said you were outside the perimeter. Out in the jungle somewhere. Not crazy, exactly, but not normal. I'm sorry, Rainbow. That's what he said. So it had to be Toker. I arranged to meet him. He took a ski trip and we connected at Angel Fire. I told him about Phoung and he agreed to try to find the child. Take care of her."

"Why not you?"

"I was dead. How does a dead man sign the papers to adopt a kid? Besides, there was Anna. And she wasn't really mine. I got Toker to take her in, and I gave him the whole payoff for her."

"You what?"

"Sure. The whole bag. All those pretty little rocks. What did I want with them? I had my fair share. I couldn't take any trips around the world, you know."

That explained one of the things that had bothered me. Toker's house had been searched for the gems. But it still didn't explain why the search took place after Toker was killed. "It wasn't in Toker's house, Sissy. And it wasn't in his will. He cut April out completely."

"Son of a bitch!" He stared at me angrily. "You think the bastard got it?"

"Looks like it," I said. "Why don't you give me a name. Who do you think the bastard is?"

"Corvin knows bombs," he said thoughtfully. "And he has contacts in the Philippines. Your neighbor told you those guys looked like Filipinos."

"The detective in El Paso?"

"Maybe Roy is holed up like me. Maybe Corvin wanted to get to him one jump ahead of you."

"Corvin getting the jump on Roy," I said. "Now, there's a concept."

"He did once. He got the jump on all of us."

"Twice," I said.

Sissy rubbed his leg. "Yeah. Twice."

We looked at each other in silence. "We're agreed, then?" I asked.

"Yeah. We've got to take him out. But where?"

"Here."

"Why here?"

"You've got the privacy."

He looked around the room. His wife sat, frozen. She didn't seem to see any of us. His son fingered his rifle nervously. "What about Roy?" Sissy asked.

"I'll go to Juarez. Talk to him. He has to be brought in. You know that. Besides, there are still some questions. He may have the answers."

"What questions?"

"What started all this crap?" I said. "The status quo held for twenty years. What happened to it?"

"We might never know."

"But we have to ask. I'll leave in the morning. Can you put us up for the night?"

Anna rose and headed for the door. This was something she could do. "Of course. You come with me."

I stood up. April didn't move. "I have some questions," she said. "About my mother. Please?"

Sissy nodded. "You help with the bags," he told his son. "I will talk to the girl for a few minutes."

I shrugged and followed the woman. The boy tagged along behind. When we reached the hall, Anna told him to go on to bed. "There will be things to do tomorrow," she told him. "Tonight, you need your sleep."

"But I want to help."

"Tomorrow." She said firmly. "The rest of this is not for you."

He wanted to protest, but he obeyed her. She led me out to the car to get our bags. When we were back in the house, she turned to me. "We have only one guest room."

"That's okay."

She nodded. "I thought it might be." She led me to the bedroom. It was comfortable, homey. Her furniture was in the heavy wooden style of northern New Mexico. A hand-carved crucifix stood on the dark dresser, next to a porcelain Madonna. I dropped the bags. Anna sat on the bed and patted the mattress beside her. "Sit," she said. "There are things I have to say to you."

I sat.

She hesitated, looking for words. "You don't understand why the girl can't be Juan's daughter."

I nodded.

"It is difficult for him to talk about. It would hurt his pride. But I think you need to know." She looked off into space. "You see, when I met Juan, I was pregnant."

"The boy? Juanito?"

"Yes. It was a mistake. I was foolish, and I found I was going to have a baby. The boy wouldn't marry me. The situation was very bad. But my sister knew Juan. They went to high school together in Santa Fe. She knew he was alone and didn't have much opportunity to . . . to meet girls. So my mother talked to his mother, and they arranged for us to meet at a church dance. He liked me, and I liked him. It was a solution for both of us. So we married. He gave my baby his name. He treats him just as a son."

I nodded. She transferred her gaze to my eyes. After a moment she continued.

"He is a good man," she said earnestly. "I came to love him very deeply. The other, the boy's father, was nothing compared to Juan. And he came to love me, too." Again, she hesitated. "We are Catholics," she said. "You know that birth control is forbidden. For some, it is just a matter of going to confession every week, but not for us. We wanted to have children

218

between us. So we never used the pill or anything. For eighteen years, we have never used anything. And nothing. No babies.''

"So you think it has to be Juan," I said.

"I already had a baby, so it has to be him. That is why he is sure that he cannot be the girl's father.''

"Okay," I said. "But there is still another question. Why did he go to Toker? Why did he give Toker the jewels, if it wasn't because April was his daughter?''

"It is really just as he said. Because of that woman in Saigon. April's mother. I always sensed that there had been someone else. That is why I became so jealous the time he tried to tell me about her. Of course, I didn't know she was dead, then. But he didn't know she was dead, either. She was between us in my mind, perhaps long after she was out of his mind. I think he felt that, and so he couldn't tell me what he did with the jewels.''

"You knew about them?''

"I saw them once or twice, back in the seventies. They were very impressive. Very beautiful. But I didn't want anything to do with them. They were part of the other world, the other woman. I wouldn't let him sell the stones. We didn't need the money. And I wouldn't have wanted it even if we did.''

I believed her. The man she described didn't sound like the one I had known in Saigon, but as he said, he had changed. And maybe I hadn't known him as well as I thought back then. Maybe I hadn't understood Miss Phoung, either. When Sissy returned from his tour in the Philippines, she had gone back to him. It is possible she had never left him in her heart. Her relationship with Roy had puzzled me even then. But there was April. If she wasn't Sissy's, Miss Phoung had had a choice to make that I hadn't been aware of.

"One other thing," Anna said. "About this Max.''

"What about him?''

"He has kept my husband here on our land for a long time. Like a prisoner. I can see that Juan must deal with him. Just to be free. But this is my home too. And if there is any other way . . . any other place . . . ?''

"You don't want it to be here." I said.

"I'm afraid it would spoil my home."

"I understand."

Anna had said all she had to say. "I'm going to bed," she told me. "Perhaps you should too. Let Sissy talk to the girl. It will be good for him."

I agreed and turned in after she left. April didn't join me for a long time. When she came, she was very quiet. I rested my hand on her hip and we lay together like that until we slept.

In the morning, very early, I left her sleeping and went outside. The boy was up, saddling a horse. I joined him and he cut out a mare for me. We rode through the chill morning air. The shadow of the ridge behind the house fell over a mile to the west, toward the Chama River, across the valley. The sky was pure turquoise and the air was clean, scented with sage and pine. Far to the northwest I could make out a piece of Heron Lake and, above it, the thin dark line of Tecolote Mesa.

Young Juan rode in silence, breaking away now and then to head some cattle down toward their pasture. I left him alone and enjoyed the morning. As I rode, I saw that April's aunt had told the truth, assuming Phoung said that Sissy was her baby's father. He had been a cowboy after all. At least his family had come from cattle country.

About eight o'clock, we turned our horses back toward the house. Anna was making breakfast. Chorizo and scrambled eggs. We ate and Sissy led me outside. We walked over by the corral and watched the horses while we talked ways and means. Then I went in and packed my bags. April came in and began packing hers.

"I want you to stay here," I told her.

She shook her head firmly. "That isn't our deal. Besides, now we know who is doing the killing. Roy isn't the danger. It's Corvin." She continued packing.

I tried again. "We don't know where Corvin is."

"He's trying to find Sissy. If you're worried about me, I'll be safer with you than here."

220

"I'm just one man," I told her. "Sissy has an army of family and friends here."

"I'll feel safer with you," she said.

The real reason, of course, was that she now thought Roy was her father and wanted to see him. Without using force, there was no way I could keep her here. Of course, force was available. But she had a right, and it was her life.

LAS COLONIAS

WE DROVE DOWN TO EL PASO BECAUSE I WANTED to keep the items in the trunk close to hand. The drive took nine hours, counting a stop for lunch at the Palace, just off the plaza in Santa Fe. It's one of my favorite restaurants, and I wanted to eat there, just in case.

April had said very little as we drove. She was working on some problem of her own. Halfway through lunch, she let me know what was on her mind. "Why do we have to do it this way?" she asked. "Why can't we call the police or something?"

"Get the government involved?" I asked. "They don't want to be involved. The Philippine operation is still too sensitive. You heard Pauley in Washington. He practically begged me to get rid of Corvin for him. They don't want Corvin involved in the legal system. They want him silenced, but they sure as hell don't want him in jail, talking to lawyers, maybe even to the press.''

"But killing him is wrong. Don't you think it's wrong?''

I shrugged. "He has to be stopped. Otherwise, he's going to come after Sissy, after Roy, Walker, me, you. He has his own plans for the future, April. We aren't in them.''

"But if he were in prison . . . ?''

"For how long? Forget about the damage a trial would cause us. Forget that you'd probably be sent back to Hong Kong, what the publicity could do to Sissy and his wife, Walker's family, Roy, and me. It might not even be possible to convict Corvin, but suppose that it is. He'll do a couple years, maybe a little more, and then the system will kick him out just to free up a cell. And the shit will start all over again. He's not the sort of man to let things slide. He'll come after us. And when he does, I'll be planning the same sort of operation, but without you.'' I shook my head. "That isn't any kind of a solution. This has to be done the hard way. It has to be done now.''

"Are you sure you aren't just thinking of yourself? Trying to stay out of jail?''

"What could I be sent to jail for?'' I was surprised.

"For the operation. For what you did in Saigon.''

"Not a chance, April. I have enough money to buy some really good lawyers. And where is the evidence against me? You think a prosecutor could subpoena anybody in Ho Chi Minh City? Hell, there isn't even a court that would have jurisdiction over that! The only way the government could act against me now is by claiming I owe taxes, and I don't. I paid taxes on every dime I have, and I can prove it. No, the only one who could move against me, the only one who would even want to try, is Max Corvin. And I'm going to see that he never moves against anyone again. I'm going to send that boy to hell.''

She was quiet for a few minutes, then asked, "Do you believe in that? Hell?''

"Do you?''

"My aunt raised me Catholic. Lots of Vietnamese are Catholic. So I guess I believe. I used to, anyway."

"I used to believe, too," I admitted. "Now, I don't know. I'm sure there isn't a heaven, but there might be a hell. I'll find out, eventually. It'll give me a chance to see my old friends."

April ignored my little joke. "I still don't think it's right," she said quietly.

"It doesn't have to be right, April. It just has to be a little righter than the alternative."

"And you decide?"

"If I want to come out of this alive, I have to decide." I smiled. "Corvin would probably make the wrong choice. From my point of view."

She apparently saw that my purpose was fixed. She dropped the subject. We got on the road and had supper in Las Cruces. It's a pleasant little town, but if I have to die in Las Cruces, I'll forgo the last meal.

A room was available at the Executive Suites in El Paso. After we carried our bags up, I dialed the Juarez number. The old woman came on and told me, *"Señor Rodgers no esta aqui."*

"Tell him to call me." I gave her the number.

The phone woke me at midnight. Roy's tone was sharp, impatient. "What is it now, Rainbow?"

"I've been to Luzon," I told him.

"So?"

"I met Freddy. He told me about the last delivery. You shorted us."

He didn't say anything for a long time. Then he asked, "So? Do you care?"

"He also told me about Sissy."

There was another long wait. Eventually I ended it. "I found him," I said. "He's in a place called Tierra Amarilla. We spent the night there."

"We who?"

"April and I."

"I see." He didn't sound very interested.

224

"Look, we've got to talk."

"What about?"

"About Corvin, damn it! He has to be the one who killed Toker. He's the only one it could have been."

"That's obvious. I just don't know why."

"Well, maybe it doesn't matter why, Roy. You know what we have to do."

"As long as Sissy stays in Tierra Amarilla, that isn't necessary."

"You know it is. Things are falling apart."

He sighed. "Okay," he said. "We'll talk about it."

"Where?"

"You remember where we met? The last time I saw you?"

"Yes."

"There. I'll meet you at ten tomorrow morning. Gringo time."

"We'll be there."

"You. Come alone."

"April's coming. She wants to meet you."

He hung up.

She had gotten up when he called and was sitting at the table. I told her we would meet him in the morning. She nodded. I turned off the light and lay down. She didn't come back to bed.

"What?" I asked the dark.

"Sissy told me about my mother. We talked for a long time last night."

"What did he say?"

"He said she knew how you felt about her."

I stared at the ceiling I couldn't see. I blinked several times. I was grateful for the dark. "I see. And he knew?"

"Yes." Her voice was soft, barely a whisper. "He knew. But only later."

"He was out of the country when I tied up with Roy," I said. "He'd been gone for months. He didn't come back until later. In March of 'seventy. I could see there was something wrong between Miss Phoung and Roy, but I didn't know what it was. I just hung around as much as I could. But then Sissy came back and Roy moved out and he moved in. . . . You say she knew how I felt?"

"Yes. She told him."

"I didn't think I ever had a chance with her," I said.

"He thought you did. He said that was one of the reasons he could leave. Because he knew you would be there."

"No."

"He said he thought you were my father. When he had Toker find me. That was another reason he went to Toker instead of you. He thought you knew and didn't do anything."

"I didn't know, April. If I had known, I would have done something. I would even have gone back."

She moved in the dark. I heard the whisper of her legs and then the bed sank under her weight. Her hand was on my chest.

"I believe you, Rainbow."

I put my hand over hers.

"Tell me what happened," she said. "Tell me about the last days, after Sissy didn't come back and when she was pregnant. Because if Sissy thought you had a chance, then you did. He knew her. Very well. He still thought you were my father, even last night. He didn't believe you weren't until I told him that we were sleeping together, that we were lovers on Luzon."

She was right. That did put a different light on it. But it took April to see it. I was too close.

"The *Celestina* arrived in midmorning on July twenty-seventh," I told her. "As soon as we docked, I headed for Tu Do Street. Miss Phoung had to be told and I had to do it, but I was afraid. I didn't know how she'd take it.

"She was sitting on the terrace, drinking her morning coffee in the sun. There were pots full of red and yellow flowers all over the place, plants she groomed and watered every day. And when I told her that Sissy was dead, she started breaking them. I tried to hold her, to comfort her. But she called me a name and told me to get the hell away from her. She hit me and scratched my face. I let go of her and she went back to breaking the pots and

226

cursing. She cursed Max and me and Roy and Johnny Walker. Mostly Max. Then she went into her room and lay on the bed and cried. I sat with her for hours. Just sat beside her, waiting for her to stop, in case she needed me for anything. When she cried herself out, I told her I would help her. I guess I told her I loved her. It was the wrong thing to say. Or the wrong time. I was stupid. But I couldn't think of anything else to say to her. She told me to get out of her sight, to go away and never come back.''

April squeezed my hand. "Did you?"

"I left then. But I went back the next day. I had to know that she was all right.''

"Was she?"

"She acted as if it had never happened. She treated me just the same as she always had. There was no difference. But she wouldn't talk about Sissy, and she wouldn't let me do anything for her. She said she didn't need anything from me.''

"Where was Roy when this happened.''

"He stayed in Manila when the *Celestina* sailed. I suppose he was making arrangements for the final delivery, the one he made in December. Anyway, he didn't get back until two days after we docked. He flew in. I didn't see him until the next day, at the house. He'd spent the night there, but he was packing his things. Miss Phoung acted very cold to him. And he was about as mad as I've ever seen a man. At Max, though. Not at her. He took off to see Max, and I didn't see him again for a couple of days.''

"Did he ever move back in with my mother?"

"No. Well, yes. He moved in and out a couple of times. Mostly, she stayed in the house alone. We kept meeting there for a few months, but things were different. Walker rotated out and was discharged, and it was only Roy and Toker and me. Toker hadn't ever spent a lot of time at the house. It didn't mean anything to him. Miss Phoung didn't tell us to stay away, but she wasn't ever happy to see us. Then Roy took his separation in-country, and I just didn't go by very often. I told you about the last time I saw her.''

"The time Max was there?"

"Yes."

"How was that? How did she treat him?"

"She ignored him. And he acted angry. Like he didn't want to be there."

"What did you think?"

"About Max? I still wanted to kill him. But he had something on me and I had something on him. It was a standoff."

"I mean about why he was there."

"I assumed she was using him. It was his men moving her out. I thought she had figured a way to get a knife into him and was twisting it a little."

"I see." We waited in the dark for a while. Then she asked, "About that last time. You were alone with her, weren't you?"

"Yes. For a little while."

"And you didn't know she was pregnant?"

"No. I couldn't tell."

"And you kissed her?"

"I tried to. She told me to go."

"And you went." She sighed and kissed my hand, then slipped down onto the bed beside me. My hand was wet from her face. We held each other until sleep came, with no thought of sex.

The next morning, we walked over the Juarez bridge. The American Bar was down the street on the left, just a few blocks from the border. It is called a bar, but it's mostly a restaurant. There was still a suspicion I hadn't resolved. I stopped outside the bar and told April to look at Roy carefully.

"If you recognize him, don't say anything. Order a Bohemia beer. If you don't recognize him, order a Carta Blanca."

She looked puzzled, but nodded.

Roy was waiting at a table in the back. He didn't stand when we came in. He looked at April curiously. I introduced them and we sat down.

"Rainbow." he said. "April."

"Long time, Roy."

He hadn't changed much in the last seventeen years. He was a little heavier and there was a touch of gray in his close-cropped brown hair. He'd picked up a new mannerism. He rubbed his chin almost constantly. I assumed he was nervous.

April looked at him intently during the introduction. When the waiter came over, she ordered a Carta Blanca. I had a Dos Equis. Roy was drinking gin and tonics.

He spoke to her first. "So you're Phoung's girl?"

She nodded and cut directly to the chase. "Are you my father?"

"No." He didn't act like he cared one way or the other.

"But you lived with my mother?"

"For a while," he said, "back in 'sixty-nine. She went back to Sissy when he got back from Manila."

"Why?"

Roy cleared his throat. "He was the only one for her, I guess. She didn't think he'd come back. But when he did, she kicked me out and stuck to him."

"Didn't he care? That she had lived with you?"

"Sissy understood how things were. You can't understand. You weren't there."

She shot me a quick, questioning glance.

"That's the way things were," I said.

"Even love?"

"Yes. Life was more important than love."

"This is all history," Roy said. "Let's talk about Corvin."

I agreed. The history was getting to me. "He killed Toker," I said. "It had to be him." I listed the reasons. Roy paid close attention. "The only thing I don't understand is why it started up again now."

"Maybe Corvin had no choice," Roy suggested. "If April was going to hunt up her daddy, a lot of things were bound to come out. Including Corvin's little game in the Philippines."

"So you think he got rid of Toker to cover himself?"

Roy grimaced. "I think it would be very convenient for Corvin if we all died. As long as he couldn't find Sissy and we didn't stir things up, we were all safe. But April threatened to stir the pot. So Corvin took Toker out and tried for her, and he probably hoped the rest of us wouldn't find out, or that we'd see he had no choice and ignore the situation. Our understanding had held for twenty years. I think he was hoping for another twenty. That would be as good as forever."

"But how could he know about April?"

"There's only one way. The phone in El Paso."

"You think he has a tap on it?"

Roy shrugged. "How else?"

"That means Toker called you when April told him she wanted to find her father."

He rubbed his chin. "He called me," he admitted. "That was the first I'd heard about her. That she was in the states and living with Toker."

"Why call you? Why not call Sissy? He was the one who got Toker to find her."

"What could Sissy do?" Roy asked levelly. "He was locked away in the mountains somewhere. He couldn't do a damned thing."

"What did he want you to do?"

"Call you," he told me.

"I see."

April was confused. "What did he think Rainbow could do?"

"Rainbow has talents," Roy spoke as though I weren't present. "That's why I recruited him. He can deal with problems. They don't bother him like the rest of us."

"Easy, now," I said.

He looked at me coldly. "You object? You deny it?"

"They bother me," I told him.

"But you still deal with them. Toker knew that. That's why he called me. He didn't know how to reach you. He thought I would."

"But that doesn't make any sense!" April said.

I looked at her and shook my head.

"What?" Roy said. "What doesn't make sense?"

230

She ignored my warning. "Why would he call you when he knew where Rainbow lived? He told me how to reach him!"

"It wasn't the call that was important," Roy told her. "It was pressure he wanted from me. Our boy here doesn't work for free. But maybe you found that out for yourself?"

She looked at me. An expression of distaste grew on her face. "So . . . ," she said.

"Cut the crap, Roy," I told him. "Corvin is the problem. Not me."

"Okay. Let's talk about Corvin."

"He has to be taken out."

"So take him."

"It won't work that way," I said. "Only one thing is guaranteed to draw him out. The chance to solve all his problems at once. If we don't give him a shot, he's going to stay in hiding and we're going to spend the rest of our lives looking under the bed every night."

"You and Walker more than me," he said. "Sissy most of all."

"He's close to finding Sissy. And once Sissy goes, the rest of us are all fair game. Even you."

He thought about it. "Okay. How?"

I described the plan Sissy and I had come up with. "The only problem will be contacting him," I said.

"There's a better place," he told me. "Las Colonias. My ranch. Sixty miles south of here. No federales, no nothing for miles. All the action will be contained. Anything left over can be disposed of right there." He spent a few minutes telling me about the place.

I liked it. And it would also solve Anna's problem. "How do we get him there?" I asked.

"Call me at the El Paso number. Tell me that you're going to bring Sissy down. If Max has it tapped, he'll show up. And if he shows up, we'll know he is the one."

"We already know it." But I agreed.

"Are you sure you can get Sissy?"

"He's tired of hiding," I said. "He'll come."

"Who else? Johnny?"

I shook my head. "Walker won't play. He's got a wife and a kid on the way."

"It would be better if we could get him there."

"It's a no can do."

Roy worked on his drink while he looked it over, examining all sides of it the way he always did. Finally, he nodded. "How many guns do we need?"

"We've got three," I said. "You, me, and Sissy. Max has only two that I know of, the guys that staked out my place. But we'd better figure that he'll pick up at least three more, and maybe twice that. He's going to want odds."

"I've got a couple of men I can trust. And Max is going to figure he has an edge. Surprise. If we set it up right, he won't have a chance."

"What about ordnance?"

"I've got plenty."

"And the time?"

"You can't get Sissy down before noon tomorrow. It'll take a couple of hours to get to my place. We'll have to get set up there. We'd better plan on the next morning for Corvin. But he might show up anytime after sundown."

"Then we'd better get moving." I stood. "Come on, April."

Roy put his hand on her arm. "I need her with me," he said.

She looked surprised. "Why?" she asked.

"There's a lot to do at the ranch," he said. "All Rainbow has to do is make a couple of calls and show up tomorrow afternoon. You can help me set things up while he's doing that."

I leaned over the table and spoke to April while staring at Roy. "He's covering himself," I told her. "He doesn't want your help. He just wants to be sure I won't leave him there to face Corvin alone. He figures I'll have to show up if you're with him."

She looked at him. "Is that right?"

He nodded, watching me.

232

"Then I'll go with him."

"I don't like it," I told Roy. "I don't like it at all."

"Just show up. She'll be fine."

"You know the score. She better be smiling when I get there."

"For God's sake, Rainbow, she's Phoung's daughter!"

"I remember. See that you do." I hugged her before I left. She was stiff in my arms and pushed me away before I was ready to let go.

It took half an hour to walk back to the border and collect the car. I drove to the hotel and called Tierra Amarilla. Sissy listened without comment as I described the change in plans.

"We've got no choice," I told him. "It's Roy's game now, and he's right. Las Colonias is better. You don't want to crap in your own backyard. Think about how Anna would feel, living at the ranch after that."

"My family is here," he said. "We'd have all the people we need."

"You'd have to bury him on your own land. You really want him there?"

"No."

"Then let's do it Roy's way."

He agreed, reluctantly, and said he would be in town by noon tomorrow.

"Are you coming alone?"

"Don't be crazy."

"Who are you bringing?"

"I don't know yet."

After we hung up, I went down to the car and carried up the weapons. I spent the afternoon cleaning them and repacking the clips, just for something to do. I ate in the hotel. After dinner, I called the El Paso number and asked for Señor Rodgers.

"No esta aqui," the woman told me. I told her to put him on or else. Five minutes later, Roy picked up. We spoke loudly for Corvin's benefit.

"Who is this?" he asked.

"It's Rainbow," I told him. "Look, we've got to talk."

"We talked this morning. There's nothing more to say."

"Bullshit. I'm bringing Sissy and April over the border tomorrow night.

You either see us or things are going to get unpleasant. Very unpleasant. You understand me?" He got belligerent and then caved in. He gave me directions to Las Colonias, just in case Max hadn't gotten them from the dead detective. When the charade was finished, I hung up and went to bed sweating. The hand had been dealt. I hoped I could figure out which cards were up which sleeve before the game started.

There was no telling if the call to Roy had been necessary. At least not yet. Tomorrow night would answer that question, among others.

Sissy showed up at eleven the next morning. When he knocked at my door, his son, Juanito, and the brown bear of a deputy who had hassled us in Tierra Amarilla were standing behind him, along with another man, about thirty. The boy looked both excited and frightened. The others were grim. I let them in.

Sissy introduced us. The deputy's first name was Andrew. The other man was Steve, the cousin from Santa Fe Roy used as a contact. He had been in the infantry, stationed in Korea, but had never seen action. Still, he looked like he could do what had to be done. I wasn't sure of the boy. I gave Sissy a questioning glance.

"He has a right to be here," he told me. "This is a family matter."

"And his mother?"

"She isn't happy," he said simply.

"You remember Freddy, from Luzon?" I asked.

He nodded. I told him about the last time I had seen Freddy's son, lying in the clearing in the forest. He didn't look happy. "This is not cowboys and Indians," I said. "Men are going to die. I don't want your son on my conscience."

"It will be as God wills," he said.

I shrugged.

The war conference lasted about an hour. I described the layout at Las Colonias as Roy had described it to me. "It's about twenty miles off the main highway south. The dirt road is graveled past the turnoff. From that point, it's about five miles to the ranch. The road runs straight most of the

234

way, then does a dogleg to the east and enters the canyon. The ranch house itself is about half a mile up the canyon. According to Roy, the walls of the canyon are pretty steep at the entrance and turn into cliffs thirty or forty feet high before you get to the house and buildings. We'll have to make our stand in the rocks below the cliffs.''

"Wait for Corvin to come to us?" Sissy asked.

"Right. And then close with him.''

"How do we draw him in?'' the deputy wanted to know.

"You don't,'' I told him. "I want you and Steve and the boy to watch at the turnoff. Pick up food and water on the way out of town. When you reach the turn, get out of sight and wait for Corvin. He may come tonight, or he may come tomorrow morning. Try to get some rest, but keep one man on watch all the time. After Corvin comes in, you close the road behind him. Then wait ten minutes, no more, and follow Corvin as far as the dogleg. Come the rest of the way on foot. Come slowly and cautiously.''

I pointed to the deputy. "You will be in charge,'' I told him. "Spread out. Move quickly, but not too quickly. I think they'll take about half an hour at the entrance to the canyon to make plans. Then they'll start in. They'll probably be moving slowly, hoping for surprise. Be sure you don't overrun them. If possible, disable their vehicles, then come in slowly. Stay to the sides of the canyon. You don't want to be in the line of fire.''

He nodded. "What do we do if there's shooting?''

"This isn't a police action,'' I told him. "There isn't any if about it. We aren't here to arrest Corvin. This is going to be an ambush. The shooting will happen. I'm going to make it happen.''

His face showed that he didn't like it, but he said nothing.

"When you hear the firing, you move forward. Take a defensible position. Don't close with Corvin right away. He'll try to withdraw at first. He should be exposed at that point, because he'll be trying to cover his front. That's when you open fire.''

"We shoot them in the back?''

Juanito looked sick. "I won't shoot anybody in the back!''

"This wasn't a game," I told him. "This is real life and real death. What matters is that I don't have to tell your mother that she's lost a son. Or a husband."

I turned to Sissy. He was just beginning to realize what he had gotten the boy into. It was a family matter, he had said. He hadn't remembered that funerals were family matters, too. "What kind of weapons did you bring?" I asked him.

He cleared his throat. "Rifles and pistols," he said.

"Hunting rifles?"

All three of them nodded.

"I was afraid of that." I picked up the AR15 from the bed and tossed it to Steve. "You remember how to use that?"

His training took over. He checked the weapon expertly, then nodded.

"Corvin's crew will have automatic weapons," I told them. "When you take your position, your job will be to turn them back to us. I want heavy fire. Try to sound like there are more than three of you. They won't expect anyone behind them, so they'll be confused. Keep them confused. I expect about six of them. Try to take out as many as you can, but pin them down. We'll move on them from the front when you start firing. We'll have them surrounded. It should be a turkey shoot." I didn't believe that for a moment, but it didn't hurt them to hear it.

I looked each of them over in turn. They looked like they needed a pep talk. "One thing to remember," I said. "This has been going on for twenty years, but it's going to stop now, one way or the other. Corvin will put an end to it, or we will. I want to drive back across the border with you. All of you. I want to buy you a drink in Tierra Amarilla someday. You're good men. If you do as I told you, that day will come."

We packed the weapons and headed for the door. I pulled the deputy to one side. "Keep Juanito out of it if you can, Andy," I told him. He nodded.

We split up in the parking lot. They had driven down in a Chevy pickup. Andy, Steve, and the boy took the truck. Sissy and I took my car and led the way.

There was no problem at the border. There rarely is, going south. It

236

took half an hour to navigate through Juarez and find the highway. The drive
south was through the same sort of country you see in southern New Mexico. Dry. High, barren mountains that look as though they haven't seen
shade in centuries. The heat rose off the blacktop in waves and formed a
little mirage on the pavement way ahead of us that looked like a puddle of
water, a puddle that you could never reach, no matter how fast you drove or
how thirsty you were.

I'd bought a pack of cigarettes the night before to keep me company at
the motel. Sissy and I worked on them while the mountains crept slowly
northward around us. He had smoked in Saigon, but he hadn't lit up while
we were in Tierra Amarilla. I supposed that Anna would have one more
thing to thank me for. An hour passed while we followed the blacktop south.

We found the graveled turnoff without any trouble. We'd lost sight of
the pickup somewhere along the way. I drove quickly, kicking up a cloud of
dust that rose twenty feet behind me and drifted away to the south in the
slight, hot wind. You couldn't call it a breeze. The word sounds too cool.

Sissy rode in silence. He was sweating heavily, despite the hot air blow-
ing through the open window beside him.

"When we get there," I told him, "don't say anything about the others."

He looked surprised. "Why the hell not?"

"Just because."

The road to Las Colonias was on the right. It had been graded recently,
but not well. Dust from the grading lay in the old ruts like fine powder and
kept pulling my wheels to one side. I hadn't expected this. Our passage was
too well marked. I slowed and looked behind us. There was no dust on the
road as far back as I could see. I hoped the deputy would realize what was
happening and slow down to avoid advertising himself. I hoped he hadn't
missed the turn.

It was almost three when we arrived. Las Colonias wasn't a true ranch.
The land around there would take at least a hundred acres to support a steer,
and it'd be a damned tough steak you cut off it. But there was a corral with
five horses watering at the trough attached to an old stable. The house,

backed up to the cliffs on the left side of the canyon, facing the corral and stable. It was a large hacienda with a mission tile roof and walls plastered white. Behind it, a rough trail cut up through the red sandstone of the canyon wall toward the top of the mesa. There must have been water close to the surface. A stand of cottonwoods towered over the house. I could not see a windmill, and only a telephone line led to the house. No power lines. That puzzled me at first, but when I shut off the engine I heard the low drone of a generator coming from somewhere up the canyon.

As soon as the dust settled around us, I crawled out of the car. "April!" I called.

She came running from the front door and flung herself at me. I caught her and held her tightly. When I asked if she was okay, she nodded into my neck. Roy came up behind her, followed by three men carrying machine pistols. He had a pistol of some sort in a brown leather holster strapped to his belt.

"You didn't really have to worry, Rainbow," he told me. "She's just fine."

"I trusted you, Roy. As much as I trust anyone."

He laughed at me.

Sissy limped around the car. "Hello, Roy," he said.

Roy lost his smile. "You're looking good, Sissy."

"I'm still alive, compadre." There wasn't much friendliness in his voice.

"Well, let's try to keep it that way." Roy turned to me. "How long do you think we have?"

"I don't think they'll get here before sunset. Probably make their approach at night. They'll have about half a moon, starting after midnight. I think they'll come in late, maybe an hour before dawn, take some time to scout the place, and then hit us just before sunrise. That's the way I'd do it. But Max may be playing by a different rule book. We have to be prepared for action anytime after sunset. That's when he expects us to arrive. He isn't going to start shooting until he's got all his fish in one barrel."

Roy made a face. "Your imagery sucks, Porter."

238

"Tough. Show me what we've got to work with. Start with the ordnance." I tossed my keys to Sissy and told him to bring in our contribution. April stayed with him to help.

Roy led the way into the ranch house. It was an old adobe one-story, with walls two feet thick. There were only a few windows facing the outside. The main door was of heavy wood, hand-carved and stained a dark, almost black, mahogany. It opened onto a central courtyard that had been paved with native stone and decorated with trees and plants set in large clay pots. The rooms were built in a U-shape with doors and windows that opened off the courtyard. We followed Roy to the right and through an open door into a large den, about forty feet by fifteen, that seemed to take up that whole leg of the building. It was reasonably well lit by two large windows that opened onto the courtyard. The walls were white plaster, broken only by furniture in the heavy Spanish colonial style. It was a good room, comfortable.

The weapons were piled on a table in the center of the room. Four M16s, an AK47, an Uzi, two service automatics, clips for all of them. He also had a small stack of grenades, both concussion and fragmentation. I picked up one of the grenades and hefted it, feeling the old familiar weight. Roy was watching me carefully. I winked at him. "It's been a while," I said.

He just looked at me.

Sissy and April came in, moving slowly, with the .45 I'd brought and two 30.06s. Roy looked at them in silence, then said, "This is what you brought? Not what I expected, Rainbow."

"The rifles are Sissy's," I told him. "I had confidence in you."

He nodded, but looked puzzled. April was standing behind him. "Would anyone like a drink," she asked. "It must have been a hot drive."

Sissy asked for water. I said I was fine and went about checking the weapons. "I'm going to have a beer," she told us. "I think I'll have a Bohemia."

I glanced over at her. She was staring directly at me.

"All I've got is Carta," Roy said. "I told you last night."

"I really feel like a Bohemia," she insisted.

"No beer," I said. "No drinking until this is over." I went back to the job at hand, but my mind wasn't on it. The last few pieces of the puzzle were bouncing around in my head, almost eager to fall into place.

Roy stood near me by the table, radiating tension. I finished with the weapons, selected one of the 16s for myself, and stuck my .45 in my belt. I turned to him.

"We have to get something out in the open," I told him. "Sissy said you promised to keep an eye on Miss Phoung when he came home. She was killed. He's pissed. So the question is, can you two work together? If the answer is no, he's got to leave now, before we start this. I have to know where all the bullets are going."

He looked at Sissy. "I've got no problem," he said.

Sissy was antagonistic. "I've got a problem," he said. "You promised to take care of her."

"I couldn't do it. She blamed me for your death. She wouldn't have anything to do with me. With any of us."

"He's telling the truth," I offered.

Sissy didn't look away from him. Roy put his hand casually on his holster. "There was nothing I could do," he said. "I tried, but she just . . . faded away. She kicked me out. I did all I could. Gave her title to the house. Money. But she didn't want any of us around."

"You could have told her I made it."

He shook his head. "We agreed about that, Cisneros. Nobody was to know. Only Corvin."

"You really couldn't do anything?"

"Not a thing. Believe me, I tried. But she slowly cut us all off. She was even hanging around with Corvin."

"You're a fucking liar!" But he was no longer certain.

"We all tried, Sissy," I said. "I saw her with Corvin myself. Nothing could be done."

He sighed and shook his head. "Something should have been done. Something."

"What happened, happened." Roy said. "We've got to put it behind us."

Sissy nodded slowly and I took my hand off the butt of the .45 in my belt. "So you're okay?" I asked.

"For now. Let's get this over with. I want to see the last of this son of a bitch."

I distributed the weapons. April got one of the pistols. I told her I'd give her a lesson later and took Roy outside to look over the terrain.

He started to tell me how we should play the coming battle. I cut him off. "I'll tell you how it's going to go," I said, "after I've seen the land."

He bristled. It was his land and his troops I was using.

"You remember why you hired me?" I asked. "You think you're better at what has to be done than I am?"

It took a moment, but he calmed down. "No."

"Then let me get on with it."

His men were standing under one of the trees, smoking. We walked over and Roy introduced us. Jorge, Nestor, and José. Hughie, Dewey, and Louie, I thought. They were all in their late thirties, lean and tough. They handled their weapons with casual familiarity.

We walked around the property, scouting positions. The canyon was about eighty meters wide at that point. The middle forty meters, where the house and stable had been built, were flat. On either side, the ground sloped up to the yellow cliffs. Jumbled rockfalls lay at the foot of the cliffs. They would provide good cover. I gestured toward the path I'd seen behind the house.

"What's up there?"

Roy was terse. "Landing strip."

"Let's look it over." I told Hughie, Dewey, and Louie to put together food, water, and blankets. Three packs. They looked to Roy for confirmation. He nodded at them. I started for the path. He hurried along behind me.

"What's the idea?"

"We'll have to spend the night in the rocks. We don't know when Corvin will get here." I took the path at an easy lope. It was almost like jogging up my mountain back home. Roy was breathing heavily and sweating when we reached the top.

The land above the canyon was flat, broken only by clumped sagebrush and mesquite. The landing strip paralleled the edge of the canyon, set back maybe fifty meters. It was only about ten meters wide. Good enough for small planes. There was a fuel tank near the top of the path, hidden under some camouflage netting. I walked the length of the strip looking for signs of another road, or anything that might force a change in my plans. Nothing. Roy walked along beside me, sweating heavily. I noticed that the flap on his holster was open.

"Get much traffic, Roy?" I asked when we were done.

"Enough." He looked wary.

"You can button your flap," I told him.

"Oh?" He kept his hand well away from the holster. Smart of him.

"What are you running?"

"Commodities."

"Like the old days?"

"No. Newer stuff."

I nodded. "Your operation?"

"I just trans-ship the stuff, Rainbow. You got a problem with that?"

"Your business is your business," I told him. "Any money in it?"

"Enough." He was tense, sweating too much. "Interested?"

I shook my head casually. "Not my field," I said. "Take it easy, buddy. I don't give a shit what you do. I'm here to kill a man. Then I'm gone." I turned and walked away from him. My ears hurt, I was listening so hard. All I heard were his footsteps on the packed earth behind me. He caught up with me halfway down. I noticed he had closed his holster.

"How do you want to play it?" he asked.

"Later. After supper. We'll talk." I meant that I'd talk. He'd listen.

When we got back to the hacienda, I put Roy, Sissy, and April on

242

kitchen duty and inspected the packs his men had prepared. To them, food seemed to mean beef jerky, but other than that, the packs were okay. They had included enough water. I took the men with me and went for another tour.

There were a number of good positions. I picked three rock falls that were easily defensible and offered good fields of fire. Two were under the cliffs on the western side of the canyon. They were already in shadow and were cooling quickly, as things do in the desert. The one farthest north was behind and above the house. The second was a couple hundred meters closer to the mouth of the canyon. The third was across the canyon from the first two positions. Together, they marked the points of a triangle. If Corvin and his mob reached the center of the triangle, they'd be trapped.

I put one of Roy's men at each position with a shovel and showed them where to dig. I wanted shallow trenches, each big enough for a man to rest in. Then I went down to the valley floor and verified that the positions would be invisible. I left them to work and walked up the canyon. I hadn't found what I wanted yet.

The canyon narrowed rapidly. By the time I'd gone two hundred meters, the walls had closed in on me. The cliffs were no more than twenty meters apart and I was walking in cool shade between two smooth rock faces. The floor was sandy. There was some brush and a few lichens growing on an occasional rock, but otherwise the way was barren. Five minutes later, the canyon narrowed to a crack, no more than five meters across. There were still some tracks in the sand, so I kept going. The canyon opened up suddenly and I had what I was looking for.

I was in a large room of stone, open to the late afternoon sky. The far side of the room was blocked by an enormous slab of stone that had fallen from the eastern face. It was smooth, but climbable. I made my way to the top and looked around.

A dune buggy sat under a camouflage tarp next to a clump of sage. I pulled the tarp back. The keys were in the ignition. I removed the distributor cap and hid it under some brush where I could find it easily if I needed it,

then headed back. I'd known Roy would have a back door, but this was my party and I didn't want anyone leaving before the last dance was over. Also, it was good to know which way he'd run if things got tight.

On the way back, I stopped at the corral, opened the gate, and shooed the horses out. They milled around in front of the stable. I grabbed a set of reins and whipped them until they took off down the canyon. Then I moved the two vehicles parked in front of the house as far up the canyon as I could and disabled them both. The Mexicans watched me and looked at each other, but they said nothing.

Dinner was ready when I returned. Steaks and beans. Roy watched me furtively as we ate. He was probably wondering where I'd been. Hughie, Dewey, and Louie sat together under the trees. The rest of us ate on the patio. April sat beside Sissy. They watched me too. Everyone was getting nervous as the hour approached.

After dinner, I waved them all over and told the assembly how I wanted things to happen.

"They're going to come up the road," I said. "They won't be on it. They'll stick near the brush on either side. They'll move up in small groups, depending on how many there are and on their discipline. I figure there will be two groups, with three or four men in each. One will take cover while the other moves up. They're going to be hard to see. You'll probably hear them long before you see them, so keep your eyes and ears open. When they see the house, they're going to stop and wait. They won't move right away."

Roy interrupted me. "Why did you turn my horses loose?"

"I didn't want to shoot them," I said.

He just looked at me.

"If Corvin reaches the house or stable, he's going to know he's in a trap. I didn't want to leave him any way out. Not even a desperation run on a horse. We'd probably get him, but we might not. And we'd have to shoot the horse anyway, just to stop it. You can round the horses up tomorrow. They'll survive a night in the desert."

I waited until he nodded.

"Here's the setup. We're going to take three positions. Sissy and April will be on the west side of the canyon, just behind the house. They are the least mobile, and they're going to block the back of the canyon. They'll provide general fire and take any targets that present themselves. In addition, their job will be to stop anyone trying to reach the hacienda or the corral and block the path that leads up to the airstrip. We don't want a siege if we can avoid one, and we don't want anyone escaping up to the mesa. It'd be too hard to chase them down up there.

"Roy, you'll be on the same side of the canyon, two hundred meters closer to the mouth, with one of your men. You will be responsible for blocking their escape back down the canyon. The other two will be opposite you, but a little closer to the house and slightly above it. Between the two of you, the road and the canyon from the house and stable will be covered."

"What about you?" Roy asked.

"I'm going to float. My first position, while Corvin makes his approach, will be in the rocks a hundred meters down the canyon. As soon as they pass me, I'll drop closer to the road. When they are even with Roy, I'll open fire. That will confuse them. It should also push them forward into the trap and turn them around to return my fire. At that point, they'll be exposed to the positions on either side of the canyon. The survivors will take defensive positions in the rocks and brush near the road. They'll be boxed in. If they move up the canyon, April and Sissy will force them back. If they move back, I'll tie them down and you and your men can work on them. Once they've taken cover, we fire for effect until no targets present themselves. At that point, Roy, his men, and I will have to close with them."

"It sounds to me like you're more worried about them getting up the canyon than back down it," Roy said.

"I walked up to the end. It's closed by a rock slide, but a man might be able to climb it if he had to. I didn't have time to try, but there's no point in taking a chance. Anyway, if we do this right, Roy and the other group will both be above and slightly down-canyon from Corvin. He'll come in with maybe eight men. We should be able to take out four of them in the first few minutes. After that, the rest will be pinned in the rocks and brush along the road. And no matter which side they hide on, someone will be behind them.''

''We're just going to shoot them. Not even give them a chance.'' April looked sick.

''When a man wants to kill you, you don't give him a chance,'' I told her. ''Don't forget that Corvin killed Toker. He tried to kill you. He killed Archuleta. And he was behind the attack on Luzon.''

She swallowed like she was trying not to throw up. The three cowboys watched her without interest. I told Roy to pick the man he wanted with him and led the way outside. I showed April and Sissy their position. He picked up two M16s and a pistol and April shouldered the pack of food. I told him to show her how the weapons worked when they reached their position. I told her to try not to kill Sissy when the shooting started.

They began making their way slowly toward the rocks. She led with the knapsack and he limped along behind. I went back to Roy and asked him where the water valve for the house was. We turned it off, just in case anyone made it that far, and kicked over the horse trough. I told Roy to turn off the generator and get into position. He grabbed one of the remaining packs and took off. I prepared a light backpack for myself and then looked over the two men I'd been left with.

Hughie and Louie. If I remembered right, their names were Jorge and Nestor. I tossed the remaining pack to Jorge and led them up to the last position. The sun had almost set. Only the rim of rock above me was still lit. A thin sliver of gold that rapidly turned red. The sky overhead began to purple as they settled in.

Their position was about nine feet wide and four deep, just a little roomier than a coffin. Our backs were to the cliff. Rocks lay in a jumble on the other three sides. There were four decent gaps in them. One on the left faced down the canyon. The gap on the right offered a view of the house, stable, and a clear field of fire that included the path up to the airstrip. The remaining two faced the opposite wall of the canyon. Across the way, I could make out the spine of a large slide. Roy and his man, José, were somewhere just below it.

I heard the scratch of a match behind me. "No smoking," I said. Hughie looked at me belligerently and stubbed out his cigarette on the cliff behind him. I met his look until he dropped his eyes.

"No cigarettes until this is over," I told them.

"I was below the rocks. Nobody could see me."

"They could smell you. Feel the wind?"

He felt it. "Shit, man!"

"Turn around and try to keep your eyes open." They both nodded. I crawled through the gap on the right and moved up the canyon. The rocks along the base of the cliffs were pretty much continuous. They offered plenty of cover if I kept my ass down. I wasn't worried about company yet, so I went to check the other positions. I kept near the cliff until I was opposite the path behind the house, then crossed the canyon and cut up toward Sissy and April. I could hear them talking softly long before I reached them. He was telling her about life in Tierra Amarilla. They jumped when I stood up beside them.

"You didn't hear me coming," I said.

Sissy just looked out over the canyon. April started to apologize. I lay down beside her and told her to shut up. I made her show me how to change clips and release the safety on the M16 she was carrying. She had paid attention when Sissy gave her the lesson.

I put my hand on her shoulder. Her muscles felt like wood. "Try to relax," I told her. "Wait until Sissy starts shooting. Try to fire only one or two bullets at a time. Don't use all your ammunition at once, but don't be afraid to waste a little if you have a good target. You understand?"

She squeaked, "Yes."

"You're going to be fine, April. Just fine." I tousled her hair and turned to Sissy. I laid a fragmentation grenade in the dirt by his leg. "Don't let them get too close, compadre. It would not be a good thing to be captured."

His hand closed around the steel ball and his eyes flicked understanding. The three of us spent a few minutes listening to the wind. Then I got back to business.

"Where did you see him?" I asked April softly. She looked confused until I prompted her. "The Bohemia, remember?"

"Oh! I'm not positive, but I think he was the man in Hong Kong. It was a long time ago, and the man had a beard. Funny-shaped." She drew a Van Dyke on her chin. "Like this."

Sissy was listening. "What is she talking about?"

"She's describing the man who located her for Toker."

"You think it was Roy?" He sounded incredulous.

She said, "I'm not positive," but she nodded.

"What does that mean?"

"It means we're going to have another talk with Roy after this is over. In the meantime, cover your asses. Expect trouble from any direction. And spend more time listening and less time talking."

It was getting very dark. I backed out of their position and into the rocks. The last of the light had faded and the stars were spread across the sky like a blanket of fireflies. The cliffs had a faint silver sheen, but there were shadows everywhere, and the floor of the canyon was as well shaded from the distant stars as it had been from the closest. My eyes were as adjusted to the light as they were going to get, and I could barely see my own hands. There was no way I could see to walk, so I crawled, feeling my way among the rocks along the western face of the canyon. It was very slow-going, but it was quiet. I paused every ten feet to listen and look.

On the far side of the canyon I saw an orange flicker. The light from a match. A bird cried far down the canyon, near the mouth. An occasional blackness fluttered overhead, a silhouette against the stars. Bats feeding. Something rustled in the brush along the road. I was alarmed at first, but after five minutes of heavy sweating I decided it was some sort of fauna. Mice, snakes feeding, something like that.

Forty minutes of groping and crawling, waiting and listening, brought me to Roy's position. I approached from behind and eased into the space next to him. Neither he nor the Mexican looked around, but they both tensed up.

248

"Can't you be any quieter?" Roy hissed. "We heard you coming fifty feet away."

He was lying, of course. His idea of psychology. "Just out for a stroll before bed," I whispered.

"What's happening?"

"Nothing. I just made the rounds. I'm moving down to my position now. Thought I'd tuck you boys in first."

"You're a real sweetheart, Rainbow. Do I get a good night kiss?"

"It isn't dark enough for that."

"We thought we heard something down by the road."

"Just critters," I told him. "Don't get spooked."

"Right. Exactly where are you going to be?"

"About a hundred and fifty meters down, this side."

"And you want to fire the first shot."

"You got it. Wait for me."

"What if they take you out early?"

"I'll try to make a little noise while they're killing me. After that, you're on your own."

"Right."

"I'm serious about that, Roy. You wait for me. Open fire early and you'll blow the whole deal."

"We'll wait."

I slapped his back and slipped into the night. It took almost an hour to work my way along the base of the cliff to the rock fall I'd chosen for myself. It was high enough to provide a decent view across the valley once the moon had risen, but the cover wasn't ideal. Still, I didn't plan on being there when the action started. Down near the road, about forty meters away, there was an outcropping of rock. As soon as Corvin had passed me, I'd take a position behind it and start the action from there. I estimated that moon rise was just over an hour away. I opened my pack and stuffed the grenades in my pockets, then chewed on a stick of jerky for a while and washed it down with water from my canteen.

I settled back and listened to the rustling of the night feeders in the sagebrush and mesquite on the valley floor. Way up the canyon, somewhere behind Sissy and April, an owl hooted a couple of times. Maybe it could see to hunt. I sure as hell couldn't. Next time, I decided, I'd get a starlight scope. Being blind was hard on the nerves.

After an hour or so, the water began working on me. Or maybe it was just anticipation, the old familiar excitement that had driven me to accept Roy's offer. I lay still and breathed deeply until the erection passed, then rolled to one side and took a leak. The moon began to rise.

At first it was only a brightening of the sky as a very thin layer of stratus cloud diffused the light. Then the top of the cliff behind me began to glow with a silvery light that slowly crept down the face toward my hiding place. The night was very still. Too still. The leaves on the cottonwoods up by the house began to dance in the growing light, and the sage looked frosted. I heard the muted padding of runners on sand off to my left, way down the canyon.

I hunkered down with only my eyes above the rock line. It took a long time to see them. They came about as I had expected, but there were three groups of shadows, not two. The first two groups took turns moving. One would run forward ten to twenty meters and take cover in the brush. The second then moved forward past them and took cover. When they stopped, the third group moved up to the position the first group had left. It always stayed behind the others.

It was impossible to make out individuals until they were almost even with me. I took a count as they passed. There were four men in each of the first two groups, three in the last. Corvin and his two Filipinos, I assumed. It was more company than I'd expected. My adrenaline high was building.

I left the knapsack where it lay and eased my way down from the rocks. Once I reached the foot of the slope, I could no longer make out any of them. I began moving from one clump of brush to another, toward the outcropping. When I reached it, I paused and listened. I couldn't hear anything coming up the canyon behind me. I wondered where the family was, if this was supposed to be a family affair. But there was nothing to be done. They were either around or they weren't.

I thought briefly of Anna, waiting back in Tierra Amarilla. It would be hard to face her again if something had happened to Juanito. I rose to my knees and peered over the top of my rocks. There was a flurry of movement up ahead, almost even with Roy's position. I released the safety on my weapon. It was about time to start the dance. I began looking for the third group, the one I figured Corvin for. My first target. I'd just located them and begun to sight on them when two things happened, one right after the other.

I caught a flare of light out of the corner of my eye, like a match lit and instantly extinguished, and then either Hughie or Louie fired a short burst, maybe ten rounds. The Uzi made a gentle burping sound. The muzzle flash was clear. The rounds ricocheted off the rocks directly in front of me. I rolled back behind them and cursed. Things were going to get complicated, but it was good to know how things stood.

I peered around the edge of my rocks. None of Corvin's people was visible any longer. I had to assume that the burst was meant to mark my position and maybe get me to firing. But Corvin couldn't know I was behind him, and he had sure as hell seen a target up ahead. I did nothing, just waited. There was some muffled conversation up ahead, then someone fired a burst up toward the east face of the canyon, toward the source of the first burst. Hughie and Louie returned fire. This time they seemed to be aiming at Corvin's group. I took the opportunity to roll away into the brush. I began making my way slowly forward. The last place I'd seen Corvin was about eighty meters ahead and across the road.

Roy joined the firefight. He also seemed to be shooting down into Corvin's positions. I heard a scream from that direction.

There was a shallow gully in the brush, about a meter deep. I rolled into it, rose to a crouch, and ran up it, maybe fifty meters. I figured I was about forty meters from the last place I'd seen Corvin. I began a low crawl toward the road. The firing was getting heavier. Rounds were pouring down almost continuously from both sides of the valley. They seemed to be aimed for a general area thirty or forty meters ahead of me. Two of Corvin's groups were returning fire from either side of the road. Corvin gave no hint of his location, but I had last seen him across the road, perhaps twenty meters up from my present position.

I had to risk a look. I crawled as close to a clump of mesquite as I could and rose to a half-stand, just high enough to see over it. Corvin wasn't visible, but there was a small crop of rock between his last position and the beginning of the slope up to the cliff. I assumed he would have tried to reach it. I pulled the pin on a frag and threw it as hard as I could in that direction. Then, just for luck, I lobbed another in the general direction of the nearest group of his men, the one on my side of the road, and hit the dirt.

The grenades went off with two cracking whumps that echoed up and down the canyon. All the firing stopped. I heard some cursing and a low, moaning kind of wail from the nearer group, nothing from the rocks I thought Corvin might have made for. The cursing was a gringo. The wailing had no nationality.

I crawled up along the road a few meters and hid by a pile of prickly pear. Roy and the Mexicans began pouring fire down again. They were spraying the whole area, as though they weren't sure of their targets. There was return fire from two locations on the other side of the road. On my side, nothing. I waited, listening. After a few minutes, I heard some rocks clattering back in the direction of the ravine I had just left. I moved back in that direction and waited. The firefight seemed to be concentrating on the other side of the road.

The sounds of moving men came closer, and then I saw them. Three shadows, moving slowly. The one in the center seemed to be wounded. I dropped them all with a wide, sweeping burst, then ran forward and flopped down in their middle. They were all out of action. One was still breathing, but his chest was bubbling badly.

He must have felt me near. He said, "Medic? Medic?"

252

He must have known there wasn't a medic in miles. I suppose it was more a prayer than a request. Or maybe just a reflex.

I chucked their weapons out of reach, picked up a couple of clips I could use, then dashed back to my cactus. There was another lull in the fighting. Corvin's crowd trying for a better position, I thought, and the others waiting for targets. I worked my way ten meters back down the canyon. I expected them to try to withdraw.

The moon was now fully above the cliffs, and it seemed as bright as the midday sun had been. There was no sound from any of the animals I'd heard before. I waited for developments. They weren't long in coming, but the quarter was unexpected. There was a clatter of stones falling from high up on the western face. Roy was on the move. A short burst came from the rocks at the foot of the eastern face, down-canyon from me. Corvin was retreating, and he had gotten past me while I dealt with the party in the ravine. But then a new group began firing. An M16 and two hunting rifles farther down than Corvin.

Everybody stopped when those shots were fired. I smiled to myself, dashed across the road, and rolled into a shadow. My back exploded with fire. I convulsed and rolled back out beside the road. More goddamn cactus. There wasn't time to do anything about it. I rolled over again in the dirt, trying to break off the spines, then crawled for cover.

A hunting rifle cracked about twenty feet away. I said, "Andy?" as loud as I dared. There was silence, followed by a rustling, and he appeared beside me.

"Porter? You hurt?"

"Yes. No."

"You act hurt."

"I tried to hide under a cactus. Where are the others?"

He waved down the canyon. "Back there. Maybe a hundred feet."

"Get back to them. Move them into the rocks down the canyon. Corvin's trying to move that way. Lay down enough fire to stop him, but keep your heads down. Keep Juan out of it if you can."

He grunted and disappeared into the brush. I began crawling painfully toward the rocks Corvin's men had fired from last. When I was about forty meters from them, I found a low ridge and waited. My back and right hip were burning. I tried to ignore them.

I heard a man running somewhere up-canyon, off to my left. I figured it for Roy or his partner. There were two bursts of automatic fire way up the canyon. April and Sissy. I hoped they were shooting at shadows.

There was some movement up the cliff toward the right. Two shadows. Hughie and Louie joining the fun. I sighted on them, but before I could pull my trigger, they were cut down by a burst from below. They folded and fell soundlessly. The rest of us poured fire into the rocks. Ricochets were sparking fire from the cliff face and zinging back overhead. I stood and lobbed a grenade into the rocks above their position. It detonated and shards of rock whistled through the air overhead. A silence followed.

I saw a black shadow wave back and forth against the moonlit stone. "Hold fire," I yelled.

There was another burst from my right. "Goddamn it, Roy, hold your fire!" His weapon fell silent.

"You can't let the bastards off, Rainbow!"

"My call, Roy! Hold your fire!"

A pause. A gringo yelled from the rocks. "How about a truce?"

"Nothing doing!" I called. "Stand and come down slowly! No weapons!"

There was some conversation up above, but they didn't have much to talk about. There was only one choice for them. Die now or maybe die later. How much later wasn't up to them, and they knew it. Three shadows detached themselves from the rock and began a reluctant descent.

"How many are you?" I called.

"Three."

"How many dead?"

"Two."

"Corvin with you?"

"No."

I cursed, remembering the firing from above the ranch house. I stood and called Andy over. The others stood, slowly. Roy was forty paces to my right. His weapon to his shoulder. I shouted, "Don't do it, Roy!"

He fired anyway. Two of the three dropped in time. The third was blown backward. I had my weapon on Roy.

"Goddamn it!"

"You getting soft, Rainbow?" he called. "Come on, we've got to finish them. You know that!"

"We've got other business," I told him.

There was another burst of fire above the house. I yelled at the deputy to take over and began running toward the road. After a two-second hesitation, Roy followed. He was behind me, but I didn't care at that point. Anyway, I figured I had moved down to number two on his list.

The firing continued, intermittent, ahead of us. I seemed to be flying over the ground and yet everything was in slow motion. I hit the road and pounded up it. There was another burst of fire. A short group of three rounds. I figured that was Corvin or his remaining Filipino.

I hit the open area between the house and the corral. Roy was about thirty feet behind me. I cut to the right of the stable and waved him to the left. The brush whipped me as I ran for the rocks. A short burst came toward me from halfway up the slope. I couldn't return fire for fear of hitting April or Sissy. There was a flash and a loud *ka-whump* from the rocks. I hit the dirt, rolled once, and went up the slope at full speed, screaming.

Roy was firing behind and to the left of me. A splinter of shattered rock cut into my calf and then I was with Sissy and April. She came at me with tears all over her face, yelling something I couldn't understand. Sissy stood six feet away. He had propped himself against a large boulder and was aiming downslope. I became aware of a howling. *Aaah! Aaah! Aaah!* I hugged April into me and turned to look down.

Corvin was spread out against the sand twenty feet below us. His right leg lay beside him, connected only by a strip of skin. His right hand was somewhere else. The bones of his forearm were white and black in the moonlight and pointed up at Roy, who was pointing down at him with something black that barked twice. Corvin's head exploded and what was left of his arm dropped into the black mud.

I let go of April and aimed my M16 at Roy's chest. He grinned up at us. "We got him," he called. "It's over!"

"Not yet, Roy," I said.

His smile faded. "What do you mean?"

"Drop it, Roy."

He lowered the barrel, but kept his finger on the trigger. "What's going on?" he asked. "He killed Toker. I had to kill him. You know that!"

"This wasn't about Toker," I said.

"Huh?" Beside me, Sissy had lowered his weapon. He looked at me without comprehension.

Roy forced a laugh. "Sure it was," he said. "Corvin was trying to hide his skimming on the Luzon deal. You said so yourself."

"But how did he know April had started looking for her father, Roy? If he was close enough to tap your phone, he could have just taken you out. How would we have known? So he wasn't your enemy. He was a puppet. You pulled a string and he planted the Claymore that killed Toker. You pulled it again and the detective died. Only you could have known I'd go to Luzon, but Corvin showed up there, calling in some markers from the old days. He was the so-called embassy man the Filipino cop talked to."

"But I didn't know about April!"

"Sure you did. Toker promised Sissy he'd find Phoung's kid, but he didn't know how. Hell, he sold cars for a living! He had to turn to you for help. You were the man who found her in Hong Kong, Roy. She finally recognized you." April stirred uneasily in the shadows beside me.

"I wondered why you kept rubbing your face when we met in Juarez," I continued. "I figured you were nervous, but it was just a habit. You'd shaved off a beard, and your hand remembered it. You had to shave, because the last time April saw you, ten years ago in Hong Kong, you had a beard."

Roy stared up at me. "You've lost it, Porter."

"Then tell me how Corvin knew, damn it! How did he know about

256

Johnny Walker in Phoenix or about my place in Placitas? How did he know April wanted to find her father?''

Roy's head didn't move, but I could see his eyes sliding from side to side even in the moonlight. "You're lost in the boonies, Rainbow," he said softly. His face was a ghostly white against the dark rock behind him. "Corvin had contacts! Maybe we'll never know how he learned about you, about April, but think about it, old buddy! Corvin was tied into Toker, into that shit in the Philippines, probably into the detective. Corvin!"

He spoke quickly, earnestly. "I covered your asses for years. I took care of you, you and Sissy and Toker and Johnny, every damned one of you, and I never took a nickel! Not a nickel!

"You've got Corvin for everything without involving me. Shit, I even did the dirty work for you!" He waved the barrel of his weapon at the mess by his feet. "Why are you trying to lay this crap at my door? Why turn against an old friend?"

"Because of the second booby trap," I said softly. "The grenade was shoddy workmanship, not Corvin's style. But it fits you, Roy. Toker's house was searched after the cops left. That was you. You never liked leaving anything on the table, so you went after the jewels. Corvin didn't know about them, but you did. Toker told you. He trusted you. And once he was dead, they were fair game. You went after them and you took the opportunity to tie off the last loose end. If that grenade had taken April out, all the bodies would have been buried. But Toker had already told her about me. That was your bad luck." I was acutely aware of the white knuckles on April's rifle as she stood by my side, breathing heavily.

"Rainbow . . . ?" Roy swallowed. I was surprised he had any spit left. There was a kind of hesitation in his voice. Not like fear, exactly. More like a gambler who is about to push his last chip onto the come line. "This is where it all falls apart. I didn't have any reason to kill Toker, and Corvin did. He had the skimming to hide. But what did I have to gain? The jewels? They're peanuts to me. Hell, I gave them away in the first place, remember?''

But I was tired of listening to him squirm. Tired.

"Cut the crap, Roy! It wasn't Squall Line and it wasn't the jewels. It was Phoung. She's dead, and you killed her, you bastard! Somehow, you found out she was hanging around with Max Corvin. She knew about the third delivery, and you were afraid she was going to sell you out to him, so you killed her."

Beside me, Sissy groaned. Roy shook his head hopelessly and dropped his weapon. He raised his hands and started climbing slowly toward us. "No," he said. "No. You don't understand. Max couldn't do anything to me. It was Phoung . . ."

He was gasping for breath, trying to talk and climb at the same time. "I tried to keep my promise to Sissy! I tried to get close to her again, and I told her too much. The third delivery. Corvin's skimming. But she wanted to punish us. For Sissy, you see? For his death. She blamed us. All of us."

He scrambled over what was left of Corvin, talking desperately. He looked like a ghost in the moonlight, but he was no ghost yet. I could smell him, and the rocks clattered away down the slope when he stumbled in his haste.

"She was going to go to army intelligence. She would have ruined everything for us. For you guys too. Don't you see? I did it for all—"

I had begun to squeeze the trigger when an explosion on either side of me hit my ears like hammer blows. Roy was thrown backward and downslope and came to rest on top of Corvin. The echo of the shots rang up and down the canyon and died away. Roy twitched once with some sort of spasm that looked like he was trying to sit up, but he was dead.

April dropped her weapon and fell against me, sobbing. Sissy lowered his and slid slowly down to sit on the rocks and stare at us, his bad leg stretched stiffly out in front of him. We looked into each other's eyes for long minutes, until April got herself under control and pulled away. Then we went down to the house. I started the generator and put April to bed on a couch. I left Sissy sitting there beside her with a bottle of American whiskey. I found a shovel and went out to get the cleanup started.

Andy and Juanito had their two captives stripped and spread on the ground when I reached them. Steve challenged me from the dark as I approached. I was in such a mood that I just barked at him. Fortunately, he recognized me.

We set Juanito to digging a hole. Steve and I took the captives and made them carry the dead back to where he was digging. Fortunately, there were no wounded. I had managed all the crises I could stomach for one day and was happy not to have to decide what to do with wounded prisoners. When we had all the meat accounted for, I told Juanito to give the shovel to the prisoners. They took turns with it, digging slowly, interrupted by fits of shaking. I let them shake. When they tried to talk, I fired a round over their heads. I didn't much feel like conversation.

The sun was well up by the time they finished. The captives dumped all the bodies but one into the pit. I stopped them as they reached for Roy and rolled him in myself. I didn't know why I wanted to do it. For old times' sake, maybe. I had no words for him.

The prisoners filled in the hole and then I gave them a chance to talk. They were just mercenaries, hired for the job. Nothing I had to worry about. I sent Steve to the house for paper and pens. When he returned, I dictated a couple of confessions. They wrote as I spoke. By the time I was through, they were happy to sign. They had a chance to live. As long as I never heard of them again.

We tied them up and stashed them in the bed of Sissy's truck. I sent his family out to make a final, daylight sweep of the area. I told them not to bother picking up the brass. There was too much of it. But it was important that there be no unexplained bodies lying around. All the weapons would have to be accounted for and destroyed. I told them to drain the fuel tank by the landing strip and refill the horse trough, but to let the animals run. I figured that eventually someone would steal them, and that was about as good a shot as they were going to get. Then I went in and woke April. I had a favor I needed done.

She had tweezers in her purse and was delighted to help. I stripped down, very painfully, and lay on my stomach on the floor while she dug the needles out of my hide. I think I dozed off toward the end. That's hard to do. Try it sometime.

Sissy woke me early in the afternoon. He wanted to send his son home, to let Anna know he was alive. I told him to let the boy and the others go. After they left, he and April and I went over the ranch as carefully as we could. Roy had kept an office in the bedroom wing. His records were complete enough that I could identify most of his assets. Unfortunately, it would be impossible to convert the majority of them. They would have to be abandoned. I kept the records on those I thought could be salvaged and burned the rest. I supposed that the Mexican government would wind up with everything the lawyers and bureaucrats didn't steal.

We did find a safe. It took me two hours to open it. There was nothing inside but cash and two kilos of cocaine. Two hundred forty thousand and change in green, just over a hundred thousand in Pesos. I pocketed that. I'm no fonder of leaving money on the table than Roy was.

We scattered the cocaine in the sand outside the house.

There was no sign of the principal object of our search, the bag that Sissy had given Toker ten years before. Eventually, we gave up and drove to Juarez. I handed the two mercenaries ten dollars apiece for their trouble. We dropped them off in front of a bar a couple of blocks south of the bridge and drove back to the land of opportunity.

PLACITAS

APRIL HAD GOT THE MOST SLEEP AFTER THE SHOOTING stopped, so she was elected to drive the first shift. She took us as far as Truth or Consequences before she pulled over and shook me awake. I made it to Santa Fe before I rousted Sissy. He took us on to Tierra Amarilla. I was awakened by Anna's cries of joy. She hugged Sissy and babbled in Spanish for five minutes before she thought of us. I didn't mind. Watching her fuss over him felt good.

Juanito stood awkwardly to the side. He looked proud of his father, and at the same time like he thought somebody should be fussing over him, too. I stretched myself awake and went over and thanked him and shook his hand and told him he'd done a good job, that I'd think of him next time I needed a shooter. He smiled nervously and told me he'd rather I didn't.

Anna hurried over as soon as she saw me with her son. Her smile looked forced, but it was there. Sometimes they aren't. "I don't know how to thank you for taking care of my men, Mr. Porter," she said. "Juanito has told me about . . . about what you did. I am very grateful to have them back alive."

I smiled at her. "My pleasure," I said.

She wasn't happy meeting my eyes. "Nevertheless, I'm very grateful. If there's ever anything I can do . . ."

I decided to take her off the hook. "Chorizo and eggs and the use of the guest room are all the thanks I need. And call me Rainbow, please."

"Of course." She turned away quickly. "Of course. I should have thought . . ." She headed for the kitchen. Sissy followed her. April followed him. I followed her. Juanito followed me. We were a parade.

The chairs in the kitchen were padded, but I sat down gingerly. The long drive up had worked a couple more spines loose. April noticed and borrowed some rubbing alcohol from Anna, then grabbed her purse and pulled me back to the guest room. I wasn't tired enough to sleep through that session. She finished with me about the time Juanito knocked on the door to announce supper.

There were the eggs with chorizo I'd requested, but Anna had also fried up some venison steak and potatoes with onions and green chiles. I took a second helping while Sissy and April told their story again. In a way, they had had the worst of it that night. They had sat in the dark and listened to the shooting, the grenades, the bullets ricocheting around the canyon, and fought their imaginations. That's the toughest fight there is.

When they got to the end, their description became very confused. It took a little while to straighten out what had happened. I was standing between them when Roy died. Each of them had fired and heard a shot from my direction, and each of them thought I was the other one shooting. They each assumed that they had missed and that I was the one who got him. I thought about it for a few minutes while they told their stories, and in the end I let them believe what they obviously wanted. There was no good to come from telling them that I hadn't finished squeezing my trigger. Either one of them would have a harder time handling the guilt than I would. And what the hell. In this particular affair, I was practically an innocent.

262

Anna had more difficulty understanding why it had all happened than she did with what had happened. We talked that out for an hour or more and eventually decided there were some things we would never know. The biggest question mark of all, at least for Anna, was Miss Phoung.

I thought I understood. "She did it because Sissy came back to her after that short tour in Manila," I said. "When he left, she just assumed Roy was going to inherit her. But when Sissy came back she realized he loved her. That was when she let herself love him. The sex didn't matter. It was just sex. But love was something hard to find in Saigon, something rare. And for Miss Phoung, it was precious. When she lost Sissy, she asked herself who had taken him, who was responsible. And she had two easy answers."

"Max and Roy," Sissy said.

I nodded. "Corvin had set up the operation and forced it on us. Roy sent Sissy on the last delivery instead of Johnny Walker. He needed Walker in Saigon to show the new guy, Toker, how the supply end of the operation worked. If it hadn't been for Corvin and Roy, Sissy would have been alive. So Miss Phoung decided to get even with them, to hit them where they'd hurt the most. She went after their money. Corvin paid up because he didn't have a choice. As long as Sissy was in the background, ready to blow the whistle on his part of the Luzon deal, the skimming and the double cross, he had to pay. He probably thought that Roy was behind it."

"What double cross?" Juanito interrupted.

Sissy answered that. "We were ambushed when we were making the second delivery. By one of the American security agencies. Corvin betrayed us to them, told them where and when we would be landing."

"Why did he do that?"

"It was his idea of a final payoff," I explained. "We had agreed not to tell anyone about the operation, so Corvin assumed we would all be on the beach at Luzon. He arranged for someone to hit us while we were making the delivery. The idea was that we would all die and some of the Huks would get killed. Marcos would be grateful. A bunch of Filipino soldiers would go to 'Nam. The Communist threat to the Philippines would be broken, at least until we needed them again. And best of all, Max would keep the full payment for the arms delivery. In fact, Max would get another bonus. Everyone who knew about his extortion game would be killed at the same time. It was really a sweet deal. You've got to admire him, in a way."

Anna shuddered. "He was a despicable man," she said. "He can't be admired. But it sounds like that woman, that Phoung, thought Roy was just the same as Corvin."

"She might have thought he was," I told her. "She knew Roy better than any of the rest of us, at least as a woman knows a man. But Roy was a different matter. There was nobody to keep him in line the way Sissy kept Max in line. Roy paid for a while. I don't know why. Sentiment maybe. Maybe he was trying to honor the promise he'd made Sissy, to look after Miss Phoung. But something happened. For some reason or other, his feelings changed. He lost his temper when they met, and he killed her. Maybe he took back the money. Maybe it went to her sister. Maybe the money bought April's passage to Hong Kong."

April had a strange expression on her face. Something like pity. "You don't know what changed him? You haven't figured it out?"

I felt a chill. "You have? Tell me!"

She looked away. "It doesn't matter anymore," she said.

"Tell me!" I took her arm in my hand and squeezed.

"You're hurting me!"

"Tell me!"

She stared into my eyes with a peculiar mixture of hostility and sorrow. "You said Corvin was with my mother when you saw her the last time," she said.

I let go of her arm. "What of it?"

"Did you ever tell Roy about that?"

"I may have mentioned it." I didn't like this. At all.

"When?"

"I was discharged in July 1971. I saw him a couple of months later. Maybe September."

She didn't have to say anything else, but she did. "My mother was killed at the end of September 1971."

264

They all stared at me. I stood up and walked away from them and leaned over the sink. My stomach hurt. And there were some more barbs in my back. I held my eyes wide open until I could blink without shaming myself.

"You couldn't have known," April said behind me.

"It was Roy who did it," Sissy said. "It wasn't your fault, my friend."

"No. But that explains it." I turned back and faced them. "He decided that she was working with Max. Just as Max thought she was working with Roy."

Sissy nodded slowly. "Poor Phoung," he said.

"Yes. She never had a chance." I rubbed my face. "It's getting late, and I want to go home first thing. I'm going to sleep, now. Unless anyone else has an insight to share . . . ?"

Nobody said anything. I left them.

Sleep did not come easily that evening. I spent hours staring at Sissy's white ceiling and seeing Phoung standing in the golden sunlight on her deserted veranda that last day in Saigon, the skirt of her ao dai drifting with the breeze, white, the color of mourning for a man who hadn't died. I had asked her where she was going. She waved her hand vaguely in the direction of the countryside and said, "Home." Now I thought, as I remembered the conversation, that her expression had been sad or wistful, but it hadn't seemed so at the time. When she spoke then, I had thought she was angry, angry at me, or perhaps just at the war and what it had done.

"You don't have to," I had said. "You can stay here. With me. You know that."

"I can't stay," she said. "You don't understand."

"Tell me."

"I can't."

"Then let me tell you something. Something I've wanted to tell you for a long time."

She had laughed then, whether from nervousness or tension, I couldn't tell. She put her hand over her mouth and ducked her head and laughed and it sounded, as it always did, like the chiming of silver bells. I had thought she was laughing at me. I know better now, but then I thought she was laughing at me and so I left. I did kiss her goodbye. It was like kissing a porcelain figurine.

I relived that last hour a dozen times before April came in and lay down with me and I put my arms around her and pulled her tightly against me and slept.

It was still dark when I woke. My watch said five-thirty. I dressed and went outside and sat on the fence at the corral. The sun rose over the ridge behind me. The shadows that pooled in the valley slowly retreated back to the east, toward me. Juanito came out and saddled a horse and took off. He looked at me often, perhaps wondering if he should offer to cut out a mare for me, but I ignored him and he finally left without saying anything.

Later, Sissy limped over and climbed on the fence beside me. "How are you feeling, Rainbow?" he asked.

"I'm all right."

"It's hard, no?"

"It is what it is," I told him.

"Yeah."

We sat for a long time without speaking, and then I opened the only subject that still was closed. "Your bullet," I said. "Back there on Luzon. Where did you take it?"

He didn't look at me. He just slapped his thigh.

"But it was a little higher than that, wasn't it?"

"Yeah. Just a little."

I looked over at him. He sat on the rail like he'd been there a thousand years. There was a pack of cigarettes in his shirt pocket. I pulled it out, took one, lit it, and handed the pack to him. He lit one for himself and went back to watching the horizon. We smoked together until Anna came out and called us to breakfast.

April was up and had packed our things. We ate quickly and said our goodbyes and I carried the stuff to the car. I shook hands with Sissy and with Anna when she offered her hand. She did not offer to shake hands with April. When April went to say goodbye to Sissy, he surprised her with a long

266

and powerful hug. "You take care of yourself, you hear me?" he told her. Anna watched them expressionlessly, then went into the house.

We made good time on the trip back, but a stop in Bernalillo for hamburgers and groceries took forty-five minutes, and it was after two when we pulled into Placitas. It felt good to come home without any fear of an explosive surprise. We put the food away and wandered around the house a bit. I tried to talk to April, but she had been in a strange mood ever since Tierra Amarilla. Maybe since Las Colonias.

In truth, we had been so tired after the firefight in the canyon that she hadn't really had a chance to show what mood she was in, and I probably wouldn't have noticed if she had. I was kind of numb myself, though that stemmed more from what April had made me see than from the action down south. In any case, we didn't find much to say to each other. Eventually, I decided to take my afternoon run. April thought an afternoon nap made more sense, so I told her she knew where the bed was and pulled on a pair of shorts and my jogging shoes.

After so long, the run was like meeting an old enemy. Less than half a mile up the road, I realized that I had done fairly well without exercise for the last few weeks. There was really no point in resuming the torture. I kept running. A little later, I decided that it made no sense to just jump into the routine. Far better to ease into it gradually. Stop now, walk back. Walking's good exercise. Add a couple of hundred yards tomorrow. Or the day after. I ran on. Sometimes you have to use your head, and sometimes you have to ignore the damned thing.

By the time I reached the overlook I had pretty much gotten my liter and an half of gray matter reconciled to the pain. Actually, it wasn't reconciled. It had decided to go somewhere else, think about things, let the stupid muscles have their way if they were going to be so stubborn. What it decided to think about was money. Specifically, how much to charge Johnny Walker for avoiding the nastiness at Las Colonias.

There were a couple of points. Corvin had brought eleven men in with him and two had survived. That meant nine dead. Count Roy and you've got

ten, an easy number to work with, if I charged him by the head. A thousand bucks a pop would make it ten grand. Of course, a thousand was either too little or way too much. What's a life worth? In a situation like we'd had down there, the best valuation was the cost of taking it. Cost of the ammo plus a couple of grenades would be maybe thirty dollars a head. Of course I hadn't had to pay for the grenades or most of the ammo, so I would be overcharging him at that rate, even if I factored in my time at, say, minimum wage.

On the other hand, I really hadn't done the job for him alone. I had an interest in it myself, and Sissy as well. Even Toker, though he was dead, should bear part of the obligation. I couldn't include April because this came out of the old operation. She was more of a bystander. So whatever the final number was, I could only charge Walker a fourth of it. As near as I could figure it, the bill would be in the neighborhood of a hundred and twenty dollars, plus tax. It didn't seem worth the time it would take to explain it to the IRS.

I killed another five minutes with fruitless speculation and my body began to get impatient to be on the move again. I listened to it. After all, I already knew what the bill would be. My standard rate. One dollar and all found. As usual, I'd found enough to make the venture worthwhile. More than I'd hoped for, and less.

There were two sharp reports far behind me. Instinctively, I threw myself into the dirt beside the road, rolled behind a small tree, and came up listening, ready to run. I heard the growl of a laboring engine down the canyon. It backfired again and then I recognized it. I dusted the pine needles off and got back on the road. A few minutes later, Jenny Murphy pulled her old Dodge van up beside me.

"Hi! You're back! How was your vacation?"

I smiled at her. "Just fine, Miss Murphy. How're things around here?"

"Hey, if you only talk to me in the village, you can call me Miss Murphy. If you can bring your groceries over when you go on vacation, you know me well enough to call me Jenny."

Her tone was mock-severe. Apparently I had escalated our relationship without meaning to. I hoped it wouldn't spread to the rest of the neighbors on the road. There were four of them. I didn't think I could stand that many friends. "You're right, Jenny," I said. "And you feel free to ask any time you need a favor, too."

"Think nothing of it," she said. "I'll replace your stuff soon as I get a chance."

"Don't bother. I just didn't want it to spoil."

She told me not to be silly and to enjoy my run and drove on. I pounded my way back to the house and found April in the kitchen. She had dressed in an ivory blouse with dark slacks and sandals, and she was trying to put together a supper. It was hopeless, of course. She's a modern woman and I won't have a microwave in my kitchen.

On the off chance that she might be interested, I gave her a glass of wine and let her sit at the kitchen table and watch while I threw together a quick meal. Medallions of beef with my version of a hunter's sauce, mixed wild and white rice, some baby carrots for color. It took forty minutes because of the wild rice. Long enough to put a couple glasses of wine in the cook.

After dinner we sat on the deck and watched the sun drop down into Arizona. April seemed mildly depressed. I asked her what was wrong. She swirled the wine in her glass and stared at it before answering.

"Nothing, really. I feel kind of let down. I hoped I would find out who my father was. I suppose I should be glad that nobody's trying to kill me anymore."

I thought about that while the sky turned purple and the shadows deepened under the pines near the house. "Why do you want to know, April? Why is it important to you?"

"I don't know. It just is. I have so little history. My country's gone. My mother's dead. Both of the men who might have been my father are dead. Roy killed Corvin"—she hesitated before continuing—"and you killed Roy. I've been disinherited. They say that life goes on, that you've got to keep moving. I guess I felt that if I could just know that one thing, my father's name, I would have a place to start from. It's hard to keep moving when you don't know where or what you are."

"What about Toker?"

"I don't know how to feel about him. I thought I knew, but that was before I found out how he felt about . . . Vietnamese people, and before I found he'd disinherited me."

"He was what he was," I told her. "You should let your feelings be formed by the way he treated you, the things he did for you while you lived with him."

"Then I still don't know how to feel."

I thought about that for a few minutes. "Tell me something. Suppose your father were here, on this deck. What would you say to him?"

She didn't answer. I looked over and found her staring at me with a pale face. "No!" I said quickly. "I don't mean it like that! I mean, just suppose he were sitting beside you. What would you say?"

"I'd ask him why he never came for me, never tried to find me. I'd ask what his life was like. I'd ask how he could abandon a little girl without even caring what happened to her."

"And if he answered all those questions, what would you want from him? Money? Recognition?"

"It would be nice if he recognized me. But if he couldn't, I suppose I would live with that. Mostly I just want to know."

"I think you already do know, April. But let me help you out a bit. When Sissy was shot, the bullet went in a little higher than he let on."

"Sissy? It was Sissy?"

I nodded in the dark. "It had to be him. Phoung might have used sex against Max or Roy if she needed to, but not while she thought Sissy was alive. She loved him. He said so. Roy said so. I say so. It could only be Sissy. And look at what he's done. He didn't know you existed. When he learned, he found Toker and got him to find you and take care of you. He gave him the money he'd saved all those years."

"Then he knows?"

"Sure, he knows. Do you remember how he hugged you when we left?"

"Yes!" She sounded happy for a moment, then remembered something. "Anna knows too."

270

"I think so. But she doesn't want to. And Sissy is afraid that his marriage will be over if she finds out."

"But that's silly! I happened long before he met her. How can he think that?"

"We don't know what kind of marriage he has, April. If he thinks that recognizing you would destroy it, maybe it would."

She said nothing for a long time, then shivered and hugged the thin silk blouse she was wearing closely to her. She came over and sat beside me. I put my arm around her and she nestled into my side. "Feeling better?" I asked.

"Yes. You?"

"Yes."

She put a hand on my chest and kissed my neck. I ignored that. "It's your turn," she said.

"What do you mean?"

"If my mother were here, sitting where I am now, what would you say to her?" She waited patiently while I thought about it.

"I guess I'd apologize," I said at last.

"What for?"

"You know what for."

She shook her head. "That's not good enough. I'm Phoung, and I'm sitting here beside you. Talk to me."

It was hard. The words tried to choke me. They wouldn't come out.

"Go on. Talk to me."

"I'm sorry," I said. "For not being able to do more. For telling Roy I saw you with Corvin. For not telling you how I felt about you."

"How did you feel?" Her hand played lower, down my belly.

"I loved you, Phoung," I said. "I loved you, and I let you go. I couldn't save you. I'm sorry."

She began to work on my belt. I took her hand away. There was nothing in there she could use.

"I knew how you felt," she said. "I knew it all along. But there was nothing I could do either. There was always someone else. You know that."

"It didn't matter. I really didn't want anything from you."

"Not even this?" She took my hand and put it on her breast. It lay in my hand like the soft weight of a little bird, and her nipple kissed my palm.

"There's always that," I said. "There was always the wanting, Phoung."

She lifted her lips to my ear and whispered, "I forgive you, you know. I never blamed you for what happened."

I squeezed my hand gently and she put hers back between my legs. This time there was something for her to find. I turned my head and kissed her lips and her tongue found mine. She made a little noise and I put my hand under her blouse, lifted her brassiere up over the breast, and cupped her bare skin.

"Wait," she said.

She pushed me back and straddled me, then lifted off her top and tossed her bra away. She tore open my shirt and lay back down on me, so that her nipples rested on mine. The golden monkey hanging from my neck dug into my chest just over my heart. I tried to move it out of the way, but she took my hand and placed it on her hip. I hugged her and let my hand slip under her slacks, between her panties and her skin, and cup her cheek and pull her against me. She ground against me and then murmured impatiently and pulled away. I caught at her, but she stood and pulled her pants and panties off and started fumbling at my belt. I helped her, kicked off my pants, and tore off the rest of my shirt, my shoes and socks. Then she bent over me and caught me in her hand and lifted me up and crawled on top of me again and guided me where I had dreamed of being for so many years.

I slid easily into her and she shuddered and lay still for a long moment, feeling me within her, and I closed my eyes and felt her hot moistness enclose me. She kissed my cheek and whispered. "What's my name?"

"Phoung," I gasped.

"No!" She said. "Phoung would never do this with you!" She rocked herself up and down my length. "What's my name?"

"Holly."

"There is no Holly. You made her up. She only existed for a little while, for those few minutes you needed her in the Philippines. What's my name?"

I gave up and began moving in and out of her. "April," I said. "April."

Then we began moving together. She rolled over and pulled me on top of her. "Again," she said. "Say it again!"

I said it again and again, and we made the world over new, just for the night, just for the hour. Then we held each other until it was time to sleep, and we walked inside hand in hand. She started to cuddle up against me in the dark of the bedroom, but I reached for her and said her name again.

She rolled toward me and held me and kissed my chest, but she held me away instead of holding me to her. She had a question. "About what happened at Las Colonias," she said.

"What about it?"

"Was it the same for you? I mean the same as it was in Luzon? Did you . . . were you . . . excited?"

"It will always be the same," I told her.

"Then I have another question," she said. "When Roy offered you the job, the chance to leave the jungle, why did you take it? If you liked the killing?"

"I didn't say I liked it. I said it turned me on. Not the killing, but the risk. Putting everything on the line."

"But why leave it?"

I thought about it for a while. "I guess it's because I don't believe in heaven," I answered slowly. "If I kill a man, I can't tell myself I'm sending him to his reward. I'm just stopping him. I have to make up my own moral principles. One of them is not to do more harm to others than I have to. But first I take care of myself, my family, and my friends. In no particular order of importance."

"I didn't know you had a family."

"There's you. Sissy. Johnny Walker. That's about it, now. A week ago I would have included Roy."

She held me for a long time, and then she nodded and opened herself to me.

I woke early in the morning, well before dawn. April lay beside me, breathing gently. I stared up into the darkness for a long, long time, thinking about what had happened. And then I thought about the one question that had never been answered. The question of her legacy.

Where had the payoff money gone? Sissy swore he had given it to Toker. It wasn't in Toker's house after his death. Roy claimed never to have seen it after Luzon, and though I'd turned the Rancho de Las Colonias upside down, it was not to be found there. I stared into the dark, listened to April breathe, and waited for the sun to come up. When it did, an answer, one possible answer, came with it.

I climbed quietly from the bed and pulled on a pair of jeans. I went out to the garage and grabbed my toolbox. Then I began dismantling the red Jaguar. I was still at it two hours later when I noticed April sitting on the front steps, stark naked as usual, watching. I ignored her.

Half an hour later, I found it. Toker had removed the dashboard and formed a pocket in the wiring between the radio and the instrument package. Then he had covered the heavy canvas bag with a piece of formed plastic and screwed it into the fire wall. It would never have been found. I'd never have found it if I hadn't been sure that Toker wouldn't steal from April. He might not have adopted her, but he had felt something for her. He had recognized the obligation.

It was not a bad hiding place if you assumed that Toker hadn't expected to die. He owned the Jaguar dealership in town. No other mechanic would ever work on the car, not while his shop was available. He could get to the jewels anytime he wanted just by telling April the car needed to be serviced. Even if there had been an accident, he could have gotten hold of the car without any trouble. And yet the stones were at a safe distance from him. Accessible, but safe.

I carried the bag into the house. April followed me. I emptied it carefully on the kitchen table. A mountain of blue and red and yellow and green. None of the stones was smaller than a quarter carat, and none was larger than three carats. That was the way Roy liked to buy. Easier to dispose of, he said.

I scooped up a double handful. They were cool in my hands. April reached over and scooped up a double handful for herself. There was a large pile left on the table. She let them trickle through her fingers back into the pile on the table. I poured my handful over her hands and she wriggled her fingers under the shower of jewels.

"Beautiful," she said.

"They're all yours," I told her. "Sissy gave them to you. Toker saved them for you. Both your fathers."

"Maybe I don't want them," she said, but she said it experimentally, as though to test her own reaction to the words.

"Don't be silly," I said. "They're yours. You do have a history, you know, and these are part of it."

She nodded slowly and lifted one handful after another. She held her legs together and poured them into her lap, a glittering mound that seemed to spill out of the blackness of her hair, a treasure born of a treasure. Beautiful, I thought.

Just at that moment, Jenny Murphy pushed the door open with a grocery sack in her arms and said, in rapid succession:

"Knock, knock!

"Oooh!

"Jesus, Mary, and Joseph!"

Then she paused, looked at us, and asked, "Can I play?"

I broke out laughing. "Ask April," I said. "They're hers."

April answered solemnly. "You can touch," she said, "but you can't keep."

Jenny blushed. "You all don't mind me," she turned and set the bag on the counter. "I was just returning some of those groceries you left with me when you took off." She hesitated, then added, "The door was open, you know, and folks around here, well . . . ."

"I know," I said. I emptied my hands. "And we thank you. April, why don't you get some clothes on?"

It took her several minutes to separate herself from the treasure. She managed to look nonchalant as she walked from the room.

Jenny apologized again and began a hasty retreat. I insisted she stick around for breakfast. She agreed without too much resistance and went to sit at the table, staring down at the jewels. Curiosity must have been killing her, but she held it.

I started some eggs and toast. April came back in wearing a T-shirt and went directly to the table. The two women started sorting the stones by color.

"What are you going to do with them?" Jenny asked.

"I'm going to Paris, I think. If I can talk him into coming with me."

I fingered the golden monkey on my chest. "Maybe you'd better take the groceries back with you," I told Jenny, "at least for a while."